BRIEL HUNT

HUNT AMONG THE KILLERS OF MEN

DAVID J. SCHOW

A GABRIEL HUNT NOVEL

HUNT
AMONG THE
KILLERS
OF MEN

TITAN BOOKS

Hunt Among the Killers of Men
Print edition ISBN: 9781781169964
E-book edition ISBN: 9781781169971

Published by Titan Books
A division of Titan Publishing Group Ltd
144 Southwark Street, London SE1 0UP

First edition: July 2014
1 2 3 4 5 6 7 8 9 10

A CIP catalogue record for this title is available from the British Library.

Printed and bound in the United States.

www.huntforadventure.com

Did you enjoy this book?
We love to hear from our readers. Please email us at readerfeedback@
titanemail.com or write to us at Reader Feedback at the above address.

To receive advance information, news, competitions, and exclusive
offers online, please sign up for the Titan newsletter on our website
www.titanbooks.com

A GABRIEL HUNT NOVEL

HUNT
AMONG THE
KILLERS
OF MEN

Prologue

THE SIGN WAS IN ELEVEN LANGUAGES INCLUDING
Arabic, German, Dutch, English, Russian, and both
Mandarin and Cantonese variants for the locals. The
English interpretation read:

> THE CHINESE COOPERATIVE CONFEDERATION
> WELCOMES ITS HONORED GUESTS
> (PRIVATE RECEPTION)

In any language the message was clear: *Keep Out*.

If this polite suggestion was vague, the men keeping
watch over all ingress and egress were heavy with
implied threat. They were all uniformed members
of the People's Armed Police Force, carrying the
authority of the Central Military Committee. Dressed
in tightly belted army greens, they bore both sidearms
and automatic weapons; in comportment they looked
the same as the officer directing the hectic traffic mere

blocks away, not far from the world-famous bronze statue of Mao Tse-Tung pointing boldly toward the future. The statue still stood outside the Peace Hotel on the Bund, though Mao's historical significance had lately been overshadowed by the political and economic reforms of his successors.

At night the Bund is brilliant with golden light, presently competing with an ever-increasing array of garish neon advertisements in all languages. The most unusual building found on the Bund sits in Pudong Park in Lujiazui. It is called "the Pearl"—short for the Oriental Pearl TV Tower. It looks like a recently landed spaceship from another planet. A massive tripod base supports three nine-meter-wide columns of stainless steel that encase a variety of metallic spheres and globes. The topmost globe, at an elevation of nearly 1,500 feet, is called the "space module." From the large lower sphere, one can see all the way to the Yangtze River. The design aesthetic was to create "twin dragons playing with pearls," derived from the presence of the Yangpu Bridge to the northeast and the Nanpu Bridge to the southwest.

The Pearl is home to commerce, recreation, and history. The Shanghai Municipal History Museum is housed in its pedestal. The topmost sphere features a revolving restaurant. In between are shops, more restaurants, hotel facilities and the transmission headquarters for nearly two dozen television channels and FM radio stations. The Pearl is so dominant on the Bund that it can be seen from twenty miles inland; lit up at nighttime, it is a truly eerie, otherworldly sight.

Zhongshan Road was seething with traffic—everything from skate-sized diesel automobiles to pedicabs and bicycles (thousands of bicycles)—binding and blending with pedestrians (thousands more). Every twenty minutes the Sin Shan Ferry brought more people, more vehicles. A roiling, complex sea of humanity.

At night the abundance of artificial light from the Bund, and from the Pearl, makes the Huangpu River appear almost black.

Qingzhao Wai Chiu, whose given name meant "clear illumination and understanding," understood appearances and how to manipulate them. Klaxons sounded for the docking ferry, and she debarked, pulling her little wheeled suitcase behind her.

There was a beggar trying to negotiate the upward slope of the ferry ramp. It was a legless old woman, hauling herself along on a wheeled platform by means of wooden blocks, totally alone on the concrete ramp until the steel mesh gates withdrew and the complement of ferry passengers surged toward her in an unbroken wave. She kept her eyes down, as is common for beggars. Inevitably her cup was jostled and a few meager coins pinwheeled down the ramp or disappeared beneath the shoes of the incoming.

The disparity between the old wretch and Qingzhao could not have been more striking. Qingzhao was tall for a Chinese woman—five foot nine, rendered even taller by expensive spike heels so new the soles were barely scuffed. Unlike many women, she knew how to walk in those heels. Her stride itself could be a weapon, a statement. Her full, lush fall of ebony-black hair concealed many scars. Her gaze could be as steely dark as espresso but it was shielded now behind tinted glasses. She walked with a purpose.

She tucked a one hundred-yuan note into the beggar's cup, noticing the depth of the ragged woman's platform. It was designed to conceal her lower legs. She was a fake. She looked skyward and off-center at the sound of paper rustling in the cup and Qingzhao saw her milky, cataracted eyes. She probably was not really blind, either. No matter. Qingzhao was faking, too.

The beggar was swallowed by the crowd as Qingzhao made her way toward the rocketship, the TV tower—the Pearl.

The policemen flanking the sign ate her up head-to-toe with expressions just shy of leering. She knew what they were thinking: *An entertainer, probably a prostitute.* That was what she needed them to think.

First hurdle cleared.

In the Tower lobby there was more security on behalf of the reception for the CCC—double guards and a walk-through booth twice the size of an airport scanner. Qingzhong knew this was a recently emplaced piece of Japanese technology that could present a body scan in X-ray schematic.

The scan of her trolley case revealed that it contained, among other things, a flamboyant, metallic wig—the sort of thing a dancer might wear. Or a stripper.

The guards made her open the case anyway, mostly so they could sneak peeks down her cleavage. Her silk blouse and leather jacket had been strategically chosen and just as strategically deployed. These baboons would never see the big X of scar tissue beneath her left breast, or care.

Qingzhao was waved toward a lift with brushed aluminum doors. The car shot up nearly a thousand feet in fifteen seconds; she felt her ears pop.

Second hurdle cleared.

The Chinese Cooperative Confederation was the brainchild of a financier who had changed his name to Kuan-Ku Tak Cheung, although Qingzhao knew the man was Russian by birth. It represented a new sociopolitical horizon for twenty-first century China, which irritated all the traditionalists and old Party members but represented an enticing commercial future for China's so-called "new generation." As far as the old school was concerned, giving Cheung a political foothold would be akin to the Mafia fielding a presidential candidate in the United States. But it did not really matter as long as the correct palms were silvered. And Cheung, ever the tactician, was perpetually developing inroads to curry the favor of his harshest opponents.

Of course, politics had nothing to do with the reasons Qingzhao had come to kill Cheung, whose real name was Anatoly Dragunov.

THE NOISE LEVEL WAS PAINFULLY HIGH IN THE MIDDLE of the Moire Club, overlooking the Huangpu fro m the midsection of the Pearl.

On a revolving chromium stage, expressionless dancers in white bodystockings and face-paint moved like robots, tracking the gyrations of naked men and women being projected onto them from hidden lenses.

At least five hundred guests and noteworthies were portioned into pie-wedge areas sectioned by hanging panes of soundproof karaoke glass. In the midst of chaos, silence could be had. The glass was also bulletproof, grade six, arranged to accommodate any sized group and isolate them in plain sight. Each alcove of glass was a different projected color. The support wires could also transmit billing information from any of the glass-topped scanner tables.

The servers were all *Takarazuka*—female Japanese

exotics dressed as tuxedoed men, supervised by a matron dolled up in an elaborate fringed gown and a mile-high pile of spangled hair, himself a transplant from a Dallas, Texas drag show where he had specialized in Liza Minnelli.

At the mâitre d' station there was another body scanner. Even an amateur could have picked out guest from bodyguard. The watchdogs were too confident, too arrogant, too chest-puffy. They had seen too much Western television and been inspired by too many Western films.

Ivory was disappointed by this crew, but it was not his place to say so. His job was not only to watch the crowd, but to watch the watchers. He was a dark-haired, sharp-eyed son of Heilongjiang Province—although those records had been erased long ago. His current name was Longwei Sze Xie—nickname, "Ivory," source unknown—and he looked like he was in charge of everything.

An immaculate, six-foot blonde Caucasian woman had just raised the hackles of the mâitre d' at the scanner. She was packing a sleek .380 in a spine retention holster just below the elaborate calligraphy of the tattoo on the small of her back. Vistas of exposed flesh, yards of leg, a good weight of ample bosom, and yet she could still artfully hide a firearm inside the slippery, veiled thing she was almost wearing.

Ivory quickly interceded: "She's one of Cheung's." Meaning: *Her gun is permitted.* Just like the similar gun concealed amidst the charms of her opposite number, an equally statuesque African goddess named Shukuma—Cheung's other arm doily for the evening.

Kuan-Ku Tak Cheung, a.k.a. Anatoly Dragunov, was holding forth from a VIP area near the center of the swirling carnival. Ivory put the man to be in his mid-fifties; barrel chest, huge hands, a face like unfinished sculpture. From his vantage Ivory could see that Shukuma had Cheung's back at all times. Good. Either she or the blonde, Vulcheva, would signal if Ivory needed to be called into play.

Down in the VIP pit, Cheung placed a denominational bill on the glass table before each of his honored guests, four in focus: Japanese yen for Mr. Igarishi, a new euro for Mr. Beschorner, modern rubles for Mr. Oktyabrina, and good old U.S. of A. dollars for Mr. Reynaldo.

Mr. Igarishi said, "We are equally honored." He spoke with a Kyoto inflection.

Cheung said, "I respect the charm of a gesture." Turning to Beschorner, he added, "True wealth is invisible, ja?" in Frankfurt German. To Mr. Oktyabrina he added, "Ones and zeros are what we are really after," and completed the sentence in English for the benefit of Mr. Reynaldo: "...so we cannot deny the purity." He had just delivered an unbroken speech in four languages. He was showing off. They were all multilingual. But it helped to choose a negotiative tongue that could not be readily comprehended by, say, the average waiter.

"Paper currency is almost extinct," he told his familiars. "What you see is the last gasp of that outmoded idiom, and I guarantee it will pass muster anywhere in the world. Paper currency will erect our economical siege machine. In the aftermath of what we do, digital currency will make us all wealthy beyond the belief of ordinary human beings."

"*If* you can deliver China as promised," said Beschorner.

"I anticipate all phases complete within the next two years," said Cheung.

Ivory monitored all this via earbud. New dancers, tricked out in painfully complex PVC fetishwear, had taken the circular chrome stage.

Then somebody opened fire on Cheung, Ivory's boss, and people started diving for cover. Except for Ivory, still standing, eyes unfazed, gun already drawn.

QINGZHAO QUICKLY APPROACHED THE BACKSTAGE corral as the white-bodystockinged dancers hustled off. She smiled as her "fellow performers" passed. Half of them returned her expression, no doubt thinking: *What was her name again? I'm sure I've met her.* The men got deferential avoidance of eye contact, otherwise they might spend too much time later trying to place her face.

The hosed and goggled PVC outfits had been wheeled to the prep floor on a giant mobile rack whose casters creaked with the weight of the gear. All the evening's entertainments had been either calculatedly androgynous or garishly sexual, and Qingzhao could advantage either opportunity as it arose. The next troupe went on in another ten minutes.

The only privacy backstage was found in the staff toilets. Performers had a splendid nonchalance about nudity, which meant that Qingzhao could use her breasts, ass, and million-watt smile as further distractions from the fact that she was not supposed to be there at all. She stripped off her wrap skirt, her jacket, her blouse, while striding purposefully toward her destination. On the way, she lifted one of the PVC costumes from the rack.

In the loo she cracked open her little wheeled suitcase. The wig inside matched the gear for the PVC dancers.

After opening the case handle, popping the hidden seam on the heavy-duty hinges, and unclicking a concealed hatch on the wig mount, Qingzhao assembled the components for her pistol—a big AutoMag IV frame jazzed up to resemble the prop space guns that were also part of the forthcoming presentation. A steel tube disgorged a full magazine's worth of specialty ammunition. They were heavy-caliber loads with black and yellow hazard striping on the cartridge casings.

Miraculously, the assembled gun actually fit the holster that was part of the stage costume—an unanticipated plus, there.

The white facial pancake and black lipstick and liner she rapidly applied made her indistinguishable from the others, male or female. This, she had counted on.

Feeling like an ingénue in a chorus line, she filed onstage with the rest, having no idea whatsoever about marks, timing, position, or the number to which they were supposedly herky-jerking around. It did not matter. She needed five seconds, tops, before she was blown.

Outside the Pearl, a dirigible bloated with neon circled the convex windows.

In a single liquid move, Qingzhao pivoted, crouched, sighted, and fired.

The bullet rocketed across the room and hit the plexi about a foot away from Kuan-Ku Tak Cheung's head. The tempered material spiderwebbed but did not shatter. The round left a broad, opaque splatter like a paintball round.

Which began to effervesce. Acid.

Immediately, Ivory and the two female bodyguards Shukuma and Vulcheva triangulated to shield Cheung, guns out. The highly paid bodyguards of Cheung's international guests lacked such reaction time. They were still unholstering their weaponry and trying to acquire a target. By the time they found their senses, Qingzhao had fired twice more.

The compromised plexi disintegrated and the unfortunate Mr. Igarishi took a round in the head that nearly vaporized his skull.

Ivory brought up his pistol in a leading arc and returned auto-rapidfire through the breached glass single-handedly—something not many men could do with a sense of control. The OTs-33 "Pernach" in his grasp stuttered, instantly reducing its double-stack 27-round mag by half in the first burst. "Pernach" meant "multivaned mace" in Russian, and a jagged line of Parabellum rounds chased Qingzhao's wake as she dived off the stage.

Ivory did not pause in astonishment as Qingzhao hit the circular lip of the stage, shooting back while in mid-fall. He already knew how capable she was.

Vulcheva's shooting arm violently parted company with her body, the spray causing everyone to duck. The hanging plexi all around the club was jigging now with bullet hits as other enforcers tried to determine what threat, from where, and filled the night with panic fire.

Ivory broadsided Cheung and caught two hits in the chest. He did not go down. It took him less than a tenth of a second to register the acid and he quickly stripped his jacket, which was lined with whisper-thin body armor of Japanese manufacture. Spotlights exploded above him.

Ivory and Shukuma bulldogged Cheung into the body scanner at the mâitre d' station. Ivory hit the device's panic button, which dropped chainmail-style rollups to enclose his boss. Cheung's skeleton showed on the screen in blue, but no bullet could harm him there. The less-lucky mâitre d' was slumped across the dais, having interrupted the travel of several conventional rounds fired by other bodyguards.

Ivory only had eyes for Qingzhao, who was now boxed in near the panoramic windows with no place to run. The blimp cruised past behind her, flashing advertising in polyglot: *CortCom. Vivitrac. Eat Nirasawa-Mega-Output Beverage!*

Qingzhao brought an entire framework of glass panels down on Ivory's head. Then she put the rest of her clip into the big curved window, which disassembled itself and succumbed to gravity.

Ivory had her dead in his sights as she jumped. He spent the rest of his clip trying to wing her on the way out.

He ran to the window, icy night air scything inward. From this high up, the light of the Bund made it impossible to see the river. No parachute, no falling body, just blackness.

Qingzhao, Ivory knew, would have counted on that.

1

"I GIVE UP."

Gabriel Hunt was widely known for solving mysteries and rising to challenges. This time, however, frustration had bested him.

"I give up. You do it."

He relinquished the Rubik's Cube, placing it onto the table (itself a Chinese antique gifted by a beneficiary of a Hunt Foundation grant) next to a more obscure and even more difficult puzzle called the Alexander Star.

"It's a toy, Gabriel. Children do it."

"So give it to a child then," Gabriel said.

Michael picked the cube up, began idly turning its sides. Instead of colors, each square was labeled with a piece of the Hunt Foundation logo against a different metallic background—silver, copper, bronze, gold— and the toy itself was made of stainless steel rather than plastic. "You give up on things too quickly," he said. In his hands, the facets slowly reorganized themselves.

"Name one thing I've given up on," Gabriel said. "Just one. Other than this toy."

"The Dufresne report."

"I brought back the mask. Dufresne should be happy."

"He wants a report."

"Here's your report: I brought back the mask, close quotes, signed, Gabriel Hunt. What else does he want to know?"

Michael shook his head. "He has a board of trustees he has to answer to. It's not enough to hand him a carton and say, here, here's your mask. That's not the way things are done in the foundation world. You should know that."

Why was it that every time Michael opened his mouth, he sounded like he was the older brother rather than the younger? Gabriel was his senior by six years and change.

Michael set down the Rubik's Cube, its sides neatly arranged, entropy defeated once again.

"Never mind," he said, heaving a familiar sigh. "I'll write it."

"Make it good," Gabriel said. "Tell them I had to sneak past a tribe of cannibals to get it."

"In the south of France?"

"Gourmet cannibals."

"I'd appreciate it, Gabriel, if you could show a modicum of seriousness about these things."

"I know you would, Michael. It's what I love about you. You use words like 'modicum' with a straight face."

They were a study in contrast, Gabriel and his brother.

Both were still in tuxedos—how often had *that* fate befallen them?—the evening's entertainment having consisted of the Hunt Foundation's annual Martin J. Beresford Memorial Awards dinner two floors below. But where Michael wore his bespoke tailored suit with quiet dignity, Gabriel had untied the bowtie and cummerbund of his rented number and undone the shirt studs halfway down his chest. Michael was scholarly, almost tweedy, bespectacled; the pallor of his skin reflected a life spent largely indoors, these days behind a computer screen much of the time, or else talking on the telephone to similarly pale men halfway around the globe. Gabriel was darker—hair as black as shoe crème, skin browned by the sun of many lands. He was chiseled, the muscles of his long arms ropy. The last time he'd found himself behind a computer he'd been using the thing as a shield. You can't beat a nice solid IBM laptop for stopping a bullet.

The aegis of the Hunt Foundation had made both brothers moderately famous in their respective ways, and to an extent they depended on one another for their success. Gabriel's discoveries in the field and unearthments of historical significance would not have been possible without the Foundation's financial support. Michael, in turn, acknowledged grudgingly that much of the Foundation's prestige derived from the attention Gabriel's higher-profile successes had brought in—the kind of risk-taking that is indefensibly reckless until it yields something suitable for publication.

"Your presentation went over well," Michael said in a conciliatory tone.

"It had pictures. Everyone likes pictures."

"Oh, you're in one of your *moods*," Michael said.

"Four hours of speeches from guys in penguin suits

will put anyone in a mood. Anyone but you."

"Maybe so." Michael sorted through some of the neatly arranged papers on the table, pulled a sheet and turned it to face Gabriel. "Before you go." He uncapped a fountain pen and held it out. "You still have to co-sign the endowment for the Indonesian group." All significant expenditures of the Hunt Foundation needed to bear the signatures of both brothers, though Michael handled all other aspects of the organization's administration on his own.

"The Molucca figures," said Gabriel. "Right." He reached out for the pen, and at that moment both brothers heard the sound of footsteps outside the office door. The knob turned, the door swung toward them, and a member of the Foundation staff stuck his head inside. "Mr. Hunt?"

"Yes?" Michael said. "What is it, Roger?"

But Roger said, "Not you, sir," and turned to Gabriel.

"Me?"

"There's a woman, sir, asking for you. Quite... informally dressed. She insists on speaking with you. I let her know you were occupied with Foundation business, but she insisted she has something of utmost importance to discuss with you... in private, sir."

"Do you know who this is, Gabriel?" Michael asked. "Some old paramour of yours?"

"Probably," Gabriel said. "Though how any of them would know to look for me here I don't know."

"Possibly your last name on the plaque by the door," Michael said, "next to the word 'Foundation,' had something to do with it."

"Where is she?" Gabriel asked Roger.

"In the club room, sir." Roger's expression was

unreadably neutral. He was very good at his job.

Gabriel bent over the Indonesian papers, signed them swiftly in triplicate, re-capped the pen, and followed Roger to the door. "Don't wait up for me," he told Michael.

"Oh, I know better than that," Michael said.

AS ROGER LED HIM DOWN A GENTLY CURVING AND lushly carpeted flight of stairs, Gabriel ran through in his head the women who could possibly have tracked him down here. Annabelle? Rebecca? No; they were both still in Europe and lacked visas to travel to the U.S. Joyce Wingard? Fiona Rush? Unlikely in the former case, strictly impossible in the latter. Then who? He could have continued guessing indefinitely without ever thinking of the woman who turned from the window at the far end of the room to face him after he entered the club room and shut the door behind him.

"Hello, Gabriel."

"Lucy?"

He saw her bristle at the name.

Lucy Hunt had been born Lucifer Artemis Hunt, thanks to parents whose knowledge of classical antiquity and Biblical scholarship exceeded their ability to anticipate the taunting a girl might be forced to endure from her peers if they named her Lucifer. They'd meant well, naming all three of their children after archangels from the Bible, but Gabriel and Michael had gotten the long end of that particular stick and Lucy the short. When she'd run away from home at age seventeen, her name hadn't been the cause, or at least not the sole cause—but all the same, she'd taken to calling herself Cifer. She'd also severed all ties to the family, the Foundation, and her prior life. Gabriel had seen her a grand total of two times in the past nine years, neither of them here in the building where they'd grown up; and he knew Michael hadn't seen her even once. He'd exchanged e-mail with the mysterious "Cifer" from time to time, but had no idea who it really was, because at Lucy's request Gabriel had never told him.

"What are you doing here?" Gabriel asked.

She came forward. She was wearing scuffed, mud-spattered sneakers and well-worn leather pants; a battered denim jacket with a black t-shirt underneath; and a canvas rucksack over one shoulder. She had obviously just thundered in out of the rain. Her wet hair was dyed brick red and chopped short and she had a large Celtic tattoo Gabriel didn't remember decorating one side of her neck. She'd filled out a bit since Gabriel had seen her last, put on some weight that she'd badly needed; she was in her mid-twenties now and quite pretty, and cleaned up she'd be a killer. But that was about as likely to happen, Gabriel knew, as a televangelist refusing a tithe.

She stopped beside him. "I can only stay a short time, Gabriel. I'm not even supposed to be in the country. I'm supposed to be under house arrest in Arezzo." She lifted one leg of her pants to reveal a bit of high-tech apparatus clamped around her ankle; a red LED on it flashed silently every few seconds. "I hacked it so it says I'm still there. But they do visual sweeps every three days, which only gives me till tomorrow night to get back."

"Jewelry-wise, you might want to go with something a bit more spidery," Gabriel said. "So I repeat, what are you doing here?"

"When I heard about Mitch, I had to come. She needs help. Which means I need *your* help." She took note of Gabriel's monkey suit, nodded toward it. "Hey. Wedding or funeral?" she said.

"Funeral would have been more fun," said Gabriel.

"Why I got the hell out," she muttered. "So, what about it? Talk?"

"Sure, what the heck? We can get Michael down here, make it a real family reunion. There's got to be some ice cream in a freezer around here someplace. Marshmallows. We can put on our pjs and talk all night."

"Serious," she said, shucking water like a cat. She took him by the wrist, tugged him toward the door.

"What's wrong with talking here? It's wet out there." But she kept tugging. "Fine." Gabriel grabbed an umbrella from an elephant-foot stand, buttoned up his shirt with his other hand. "After you," he said.

"I'VE GOT THIS FRIEND, MITCH," LUCY BEGAN. "SHORT for Michelle."

She had steered Gabriel to a caffeine dive in the Village where the espresso ran extra-strong and the lights were kept mercifully low. On the way out of the townhouse, Gabriel had abandoned his suit jacket for a nicely broken-in A2, US Army Air Corps vintage circa 1942, with the emblem of the Eighth Air Force and the Flying Eight-Balls on one shoulder. He was still wearing the white piquet tuxedo shirt under it, though.

"Mitch is air force—or she was, before they threw her to the wolves for a helicopter crash, a training flight accident. They needed a scapegoat and wouldn't nail the pilot because of rank. Plus they hate the idea of a woman in the program, needless to say."

"Is this going to be another feminist soapbox thing?" said Gabriel. "Or does it get interesting?"

"Just shut up and listen and I'll get to it."

"Okay." Gabriel took another sip. The coffee here really was very good; the kind of drink that made you want to sit and contemplate deeper mysteries.

"So: Mitch gets defrocked. She comes back to New York to stay with her sister, Valerie, who works in the records department of a company called Zongchang Limited. But the day Mitch arrives, Valerie goes to a meeting with Zongchang's foreign corporate heads at a hotel. The police find her heels-up in a dumpster at 1 A.M. the next day with the stale Caesar salad. Her throat's been cut, and she's been shot through the heart."

"Both?"

"Yeah—and that's not even the interesting part. Do the cops go hunting for someone who might have done it? No—they nail Mitch for it. For the murder of her own sister. No way in hell, but that's what they've decided. She tweeted it on the way to jail. I snuck myself onto the next flight over."

"Tweeted?"

"Think of it as way you can update a blog from your cell phone—" She saw Gabriel's blank stare. "Never mind. Point is, she told me what was happening. They're only calling her a 'material witness' for now, but it's obvious they think she did it. The only good part of the whole thing is that, over the prosecutor's objections, the judge has set bail. Which by the way means I need some bail money."

"If what you want's money," Gabriel said, "Michael's got the checkbook."

"I can't ask him. Can you picture that, first time I see him in a decade, it's *Hey, Michael, can you get my friend out of jail? And by the by, I'm sort of under arrest myself...*" Lucy shook her head. "Anyway the money's not all I want. Listen. The high muckety-mucks in this company have something to do with 'ethnographic Chinese antiquities.'"

"I think I remember reading something about that," Gabriel said, "the head of Zongchang being a collector. Ching, or Chung, something like that."

"Yeah, well, Mitch is pretty sure Ching-or-Chung whacked her sister because she found out something she wasn't supposed to. But now the men who did it have high-tailed it back to China—to the CCC. You know what that is?"

Gabriel pinched the bridge of his nose. The CCC. He knew this political movement-cum-Mafia only by ruthless reputation, since he had somehow managed to avoid a hands-on run-in with them. "The Chinese Cooperative Confederation. It's a lot like Russia after the Soviet Union fell apart. Like Morocco during World War Two."

"Bastards who play for keeps, was how Mitch put it," said Lucy. "They're outside international law. No extradition—"

"No diplomatic inquiry," said Gabriel, nodding.

"Once someone's tucked away in there, there's no getting them out."

"And you want to get someone out?"

"Mitch does. And unless they keep her locked up for the rest of her life, she's going to go after him herself. Neither of which is a great alternative. I mean, Mitch can take care of herself, but I wouldn't want to see her go up against an organization like this."

"Unlike me, for instance," Gabriel said.

Lucy nodded, and the look of utter confidence in

her eyes shot right through Gabriel's defenses. It was like when she was eight years old and he was twenty, freshly back from a year in North Africa, and she'd listened to his exaggerated tales of his exploits with rapt attention each night after Michael had headed off to bed. She'd believed he could do anything. He'd believed it for a while himself.

"And who is this woman?" asked Gabriel. "Why is it so important to you to help her?"

Lucy paused before answering. "She's a friend," Lucy said. "I've known her a long time. She got me through some very bad stuff. I owe her a lot."

"All right," Gabriel said. He mulled over the possibilities. "The CCC," he said. "Well, moving around inside China's easier than it used to be, though you'd still want cover for something like this. One possibility, Michael was telling me about a lecture series he's setting up at a bunch of Chinese universities. He's supposed to give the lectures himself—but who'd really complain if I showed up with him?"

Lucy allowed herself the ghost of a smile. "Or instead of him. You'd really wake up some of those rooms."

"No doubt," Gabriel said. "So, tell me straight: what exactly is it you want me to do?"

"First thing is help me get Mitch out of jail," said Lucy. "And then convince her that she doesn't need to fly to China to kill this guy."

"Because I'll do it for her? I'm not some sort of assassin, Lucy."

"You'll think of something," Lucy said. "You always do."

2

MICHELLE "MITCH" QUANTRILL WAS A PIECE OF WORK
indeed. Twenty-nine years old, tall and square-
cut, sturdy and practical, strong, attractive but not
glamorous, zero makeup. Blonde hair, cut indifferently.
Eyes of milky green.

For Gabriel, it was worth the bail money just to
meet her. And to see her and Lucy together provided
some interstitial links.

"*Not* what you think," chided Lucy, but Gabriel had
a feeling it was exactly what he thought.

"You're Lucy's brother?" said Mitch. Her handshake
grip was strong and to the point.

"One of them," Gabriel said.

"Well, I appreciate your getting me out of there. I
was beginning to lose my mind."

They caught a cab outside the precinct house and
told the cabbie to take them to Valerie's apartment, a
building near 45th and Eighth.

DAVID J. SCHOW

"Have you ever heard of Kangxi Shih-k'ai?" said Mitch, who was in the back seat with Gabriel. Lucy was turned around in the passenger seat up front, watching them through the plexiglass divider.

"Sure. The warlord of warlords," Gabriel said. "Around the turn of the century—the last century—he mantled himself the Favorite Son of China. He's said to have personally killed twenty thousand enemies. He died in, what, 1901 or 1902, something like that? Assassinated by his own bodyguards, as I recall."

"Right. Well, Valerie told me that working at Zongchang she'd uncovered some kind of dirt on a guy named Cheung—the guy in charge of the CCC, the one they're saying will be the new Mao? She said she'd found proof he wasn't Chinese at all—he's really a Russian trying to pose himself as a Chinese. Specifically, as a blood descendant of Kangxi Shih-k'ai, who was known to have over two hundred children."

"Cheung is the guy who collects the statues," said Lucy.

"What statues?" said Gabriel.

"The terra-cotta warriors. Life size."

"You mean the famous ones?" said Gabriel. "Those are all in government hands. They have been since they first started digging them up in the 1970s."

Gabriel dredged up what he knew about China's First Emperor and his statue-making predilection.

In 246 B.C., the then 13-year-old Emperor Qin had tasked over 700,000 workers with building his mausoleum. The project, including the terra-cotta army of over 8,000 figures, took nearly forty years to complete. When a group of farmers digging for a well in Shaanxi Province uncovered the first terra-cotta head in 1974, they had no idea they had uncovered the archeological find of the twentieth century. It dwarfed even Howard Carter's 1922 uncovering of Tutankhamen's tomb—yes, Qin's tomb was larger, the size of two entire cities, complete with a pearl-inlaid ceiling to simulate night-time stars. Besides the figures of soldiers, generals (the tallest figures, averaging six feet in height), acrobats, strongmen and musicians, there were 130 chariots drawn by 520 terra-cotta horses, not to mention another 150 additional horses for the cavalry. The "four divine animals"— dragon, phoenix, tortoise and a sort of giraffe-like chimera called a *qilin*—were represented, as well as the unicorn, or *xiezhi*. Diggers found the remains of artisans and craftsmen (in addition to all of Qin's barren concubines), suggesting that they were sealed inside the complex to prevent them from divulging their knowledge of the tombs... or of the 30-meter-high adjacent building discovered nearby in 2007 by Chinese archeologists. The side building remained unexplored to this day.

"Cheung has offered a flat ten million dollars to anybody who can find the terra-cotta warrior of Kangxi Shih-k'ai," said Mitch.

"But that makes no sense," said Gabriel. "Kangxi Shih-k'ai lived at the end of the 19th Century—the terra-cotta warriors are two thousand years older."

"Kangxi Shih-k'ai apparently had his *own* terra-cotta army made," Mitch said. "That's what Valerie told me. And it has never been found."

"Hold on," Gabriel said. "You're saying he built an entire second terra-cotta army and buried it somewhere in modern China and nobody has ever heard about it except your sister?"

"No, Mr. Hunt," Mitch said. "Except my sister and

this guy Cheung. And he's looking for it."

"Did she say what he wants with it?"

"The main resistance Cheung is getting to the rise of the CCC is from old-school Chinese traditionalists. If he can prove he's somehow related to Kangxi Shih-k'ai, that resistance evaporates."

"And how would the statue prove anything?"

"Because it contains Kangxi Shih-k'ai's skeleton," she said. "Sheathed in lead and gold. Or at least his skull—Valerie wasn't clear which. But *something*. Something Cheung could use to perpetrate a bit of DNA flummery, I guess, or maybe that wouldn't even be necessary. It's such a powerful cultural icon, just possessing it would give him enormous credibility."

"Your sister told you this?"

"Yeah," said Mitch. "Right before she went to a meeting with Cheung and wound up dead."

The cab drew up to the curb beside Valerie's building. Gabriel gave the driver a twenty and followed Mitch out the door.

They plodded through the typically New York experience of the walk-up: twelve steps, turn; twelve steps more. Mitch had a fistful of keys out, but it was Lucy who reached the apartment door first. She paused, then raised one hand in a silencing gesture.

"Hang on," she whispered. "It's already open."

UPON SIGHTING THE FORCED DOOR AND THE VISUAL evidence of damage to the jamb and molding from a professional jimmy—someone had come prepared enough to outfox the overkill of multiple locks in Manhattan—each of the three people in the stairwell reacted differently.

Lucy, experienced in urban rat-traps, flattened against the wall so as to provide herself with maximum cover should an assault issue from the doorway.

Mitch's hand automatically flew down to draw a gun she did not possess. It was a flicker, a notion instantly replaced by the reset of her body into a defensive combat stance, one forearm up to shield, the other to strike, sharp key-points extending between her knuckles.

Gabriel had already moved past both of them to be first through into possible hazard. "Hold it," he whispered. "I don't hear anything inside."

They were at his back (in a classic triangle defense pattern, he noticed; good for them) as he toed the door open. His perimeter senses were keyed up full. His shoulders relaxed.

"Whatever happened here, I think they've already come and gone."

Mitch sagged as though she knew what they would find. The one-bedroom was in a state of disarray that suggested a thorough yet not particularly malicious burglary—drawers dumped, knickknacks scattered. Mitch's eyes went straight to the desk where it looked Valerie had had her computer setup.

"They took her hard drives," Mitch said numbly. She dropped the keys in the newly empty space on her sister's desk.

Gabriel scanned the room. "Two men, I'll bet. One for lookout, one for the turnover." He ran a finger over the surface of the computer table. "Powder," he noted. "They came in wearing latex gloves." He turned to Mitch. "I don't suppose she told you what kind of evidence she had?"

"There wasn't any time," said Mitch. "She picked me

up at Newark when I came in. We had lunch at some fancy joint, one of those places where they have a whole separate menu for water. We couldn't talk too openly there, with all the waiters listening. She was going to tell me later—but first she had this meeting. I thought it was weird that it was so late at night, but she said these guys had come in internationally, were still on Shanghai time. It was a 'face' thing. And the meeting was important to her—she was going to confront them with what she'd found, tell them she couldn't be involved in any sort of cover-up; she wasn't telling them what to do, just backing out gracefully herself. You see how well that worked. I was sitting around here like a patsy when the cops showed up, and meanwhile the Zongchang boys were private-jetting it back to the CCC."

"So," Gabriel said, "the first, best hope for the new, modern China, the dedicated wannabe chief big grand kahuna of the CCC, this guy who is Russian pretending to be Chinese, the guy hunting for a one-of-a-kind statue of a dead Chinese warlord, comes to New York and, confronted with evidence that he's not what he says he is, kills the woman who found it and ransacks her apartment?" Gabriel was looking around the apartment—the leftovers of Valerie's life—with a renewed intensity in his gaze.

"Yeah," said Mitch. "Or it was done on his orders."

Gabriel turned to Lucy. "Okay, *now* I'm interested." He picked up the ring of keys. "Your sister gave you these?"

Mitch nodded. "In case I needed to go out before she got back."

The bundle contained four door keys, a main entry key, a foyer key, a mailbox key, a trash-door key, and a riot of dead weight in the form of a pewter Empire State Building, a rabbit's foot (dyed pink), a big rubber sandal with the name VAL embossed on it... and something else.

"What's this?" said Gabriel, peering closer.

It was a silver charm in the form of a little hardcover book about a half-inch tall. The cover was engraved with the legend DRINK ME.

Gabriel pried the seam with a thumbnail and the tiny book popped open like a locket to reveal its cargo.

"Aha," he said, looking at the narrow black sliver inside. It was plastic and had tiny metal contacts at one end. "It's a... thing."

"Give me that," Lucy said. Gabriel plucked it out of the book and handed it over. He could navigate the tunnels of the Paris sewer system in the dark and tell you where an obsidian blade was made by the strike pattern on the stone edge; modern technology, though, was not his bailiwick.

Fortunately, it was his sister's. "Memory stick," she said, turning the sliver over. "Four gigs. The kind you plug into a cellphone."

"Like this one?" Mitch held up a unit she'd unplugged from a charger dock that lay overturned on the floor. It looked like the kind of biz-crazy portable device that did everything except unzip your duds and make you see the face of God.

"We have a winner," Lucy said, popping a hatch on the back of the thing and sliding the stick inside.

Mitch, meanwhile, was staring into one of the desk drawers, riffling its contents. "Her passport's still here. Some credit cards. ID." A tear leaked from one eye, dropped and spattered across the back of her hand.

"Let me see that," said Gabriel while Lucy worked on the phone. "I'd like to see her face."

The family resemblance was undeniable.

"This is some bizarre stuff," said Lucy, scrolling through data on the phone's tiny screen. "Mostly spreadsheets, it looks like. Amounts of money, invoices, bills of lading."

"She must have known something was going to happen to her," said Mitch, straining to keep the tremor in her voice from showing. Gabriel could tell she was the sort who wanted to be in control, in charge of her messier emotions, and who would beat herself up for any public display she thought looked weak. "To leave all this stuff behind."

"We need to print this out," Lucy said. "You can't read it properly on a screen this size."

"I'm sure Michael's got a set-up we can use, back at the townhouse," Gabriel said. And to Mitch he said, "You want to come with us? I'm not sure it's good for you to stay here alone." He put a hand on Mitch's shoulder, but she shook it off.

"I'm fine," she said roughly, sounding anything but.

"I'll stay," Lucy said. "I don't have to be on a plane till tomorrow morning—"

"I'm *okay*," Mitch said. "You don't have to get yourself in trouble on my account." She turned to Gabriel. "And you don't have to take care of me, either. I'm not a fragile flower. I'm a soldier, goddamn it. Or I used to be. I'm not going to sit around moaning or feeling frightened—I'm going to find the men who did this and make them sorry they did."

"Maybe," Gabriel said. "Or maybe they'll make you sorry you did. I don't think you know the kind of power you're talking about taking on."

"Listen, stud, if you're scared and want to drop out, that's fine," Mitch said. "You posted bail. That's plenty."

"If you want to go up against the CCC and you want

to live to tell about it," Gabriel said patiently, "you'll listen to me and you'll do it very, *very* carefully."

"He can be a pain," Lucy said, "but he does know what he's talking about, Mitch."

Mitch threw up her hands. "All right. You've got something to say, I'll listen. But I'm not waiting long."

"Fair enough," Gabriel said. And to Lucy: "I'll be back as quick as I can. Couple hours at most. You guys can stick around here that long, right?" Lucy looked anxiously over at Mitch, who was pacing impatiently. She nodded.

"All right. Call me if anything happens."

Gabriel left them to pick up the pieces at the apartment while he headed back to Sutton Place with the cellphone and the memory stick.

Michael would be able to print the document, and from there, well… they'd see what they would see. He shared Mitch's preference for action and distaste for waiting around, but jumping into a conflict with the CCC wasn't something you did lightly.

Or at least it wasn't something *he* would do lightly.

It wasn't two hours later that Valerie's cellphone, now sitting in a docking station attached to one of Michael's computers, started vibrating, and when Gabriel opened it and brought it to his ear, he heard Lucy's voice shouting at him. "Gabriel? That you?"

"Yes."

"She's gone," Lucy said. "I went to take a shower, and when I got out…"

"No Mitch," Gabriel said.

"She left a note," Lucy said. "Just one line."

"And what's that?"

"'Enough's enough,'" Lucy read. "'I'm going to get those bastards.'"

3

"FOR GOD'S SAKE, GABRIEL, YOU DON'T KNOW anything about the Han Dynasty," Michael grumbled. "The *Later* Han Dynasty? The Three Kingdoms and the Period of Disunion? You'll never get away with it."

"For one or two lectures? I think I can. And then you can take over from me after that, finish the tour yourself."

"What, are you going to speak to Mandarin students in Cantonese?"

"I'll speak English. They'll chalk it up to American arrogance and move on. They're used to it."

"You... you don't even have a *degree!*" Michael protested, flustered. If you started counting up Michael's assorted doctorates on your fingers, you'd be compelled before long to remove your shoes.

"We're not talking about a debate, Michael. I don't need to hold my own. You'll give me your slides and I'll work off them. Not like I can't regurgitate names and dates with the best of them."

Michael switched gears: "You don't even know if this Cheung had anything to do with that woman's death."

"Well, according to *you*, these documents show he's guilty of plenty else." He waved the sheaf of print-outs in Michael's face. "Arms trafficking, drug smuggling, racketeering, not to mention a murder or five."

Michael flushed crimson. "Gabriel… it's a different country. Different laws. We'd be intruding where we're not invited."

"My specialty," said Gabriel, with slightly more pride than he needed to drive his point home. "One day of travel in, one day out. In between, a couple of days of poking around the edges of things. See what spills forth. Michael—it's what the Foundation does *best*, don't kid yourself. You clear the paperwork and I kick down the doors."

"You really think," Michael said, "there's a second terra-cotta army out there no one's ever seen, waiting to be discovered."

"I do," Gabriel said. "And even if there isn't, there's a young woman out there who's going to get herself arrested and executed for trying to kill somebody who, as you point out, we don't even know has done anything—not to her, at least."

"This is the girlfriend of your… what was she again, one of your nurses in the hospital in Khartoum?"

Gabriel had made up a story, at Lucy's request; she didn't want Michael to know she was in New York. So Gabriel had, but he unfortunately no longer remembered what it was he'd said. "Something like that. Look, Michael, it won't cost much—"

"It's not about the money, Gabriel. It's the principle of the thing."

"I agree. And as a matter of principle, I don't like to

let innocent people get themselves killed when I can prevent it."

"I suppose," Michael said in a resigned tone, "you'll be taking the jet."

"Yes," said Gabriel. "For two reasons. One: I can't go as you on a commercial flight—they'll check my passport."

"What's the other reason?"

"Because I don't want to run *this* through baggage check."

Gabriel hoisted up his work-belt, worn around the world in one situation or another. It was tooled steer-hide with faded intaglio, furry at some of the rivets, an old friend and constant companion that had seen him through more than one tough scrape. Lashed to the belt was a big holster. Sheathed inside was an even bigger sidearm, itself a pricey antique, Gabriel's own restored single-action Colt Peacemaker—a first-generation Cavalry model circa 1880 with the 7 1/2-inch barrel, chambered for the .45 "Long Colt" cartridge. The original heavily distressed ivory grips had been replaced, by Gabriel himself, with burnished mahogany.

Nearly two centuries ago, Samuel Colt had been the man who did not understand the meaning of the word "impossible" when naysayers told him the idea of a repeating handgun could never be realized. While he did not actually invent the revolver, he won his first patent in the early 1800s and was instrumental in introducing the use of interchangeable, mass-produced parts.

Whenever people said "impossible," or that a thing *should not* be done or *could not* be done, Gabriel always thought of old Sam Colt.

Michael was staring at his older brother with an odd tilt of head, like an explorer mantis or a curious

puppy. "Okay," he began carefully. "What part *aren't*
you telling me? What are you leaving out?"

"There is one thing," Gabriel said.

"I knew it."

"The name of the man behind the second terra-cotta
army," said Gabriel, not without a dramatic flourish. "It's
Kangxi Shih-k'ai, Michael. The Favored Son of China.
The last real-man warlord before the modern world
stomped them down. The Vlad the Impaler of Chinese
history—the history that the Cultural Committee never
talks about during stuff like the Olympics. We're not
talking about an ordinary monarch, Michael. We're
talking about one of the most frightening figures of his
time, or any time. You remember what he called his
champions while he was alive?"

"The Killers of Men," Michael murmured.

"The Killers of Men, that's right. And this is the
man who constructed a second terra-cotta army as a
monument to his ego, and nobody has ever *seen* it. Can
you imagine what those figures must be like? Wouldn't
you want us to be the first in the world to see them, to
bring them to light?"

Gabriel hefted an original hardcover first edition
of *Space, Time & Earthly Gods* by Ambrose and
Cordelia Hunt, first published in 1982, the year their
daughter Lucy had been born. "Take a closer look at
Appendix III—the one where they listed what they
thought were the greatest undiscovered treasures of
the modern world."

The Hunt Foundation's foundation (as it were)
was the success enjoyed by Gabriel and Michael's
parents through a series of improbably popular
books that conjoined history, religion, linguistics
and anthropology for the modern reader. Ambrose

and Cordelia Hunt were hailed as the new Will and Ariel Durant, and at the time of their mysterious disappearance (to this day, even Michael was hesitant to say "death"), their fame had spread worldwide.

Gabriel gestured with the book; did not open it. "It's right there at big number four, before the Bermuda Triangle pirate shipwrecks and after the 'lost pyramid' scroll that supposedly explains the destiny of the world. It doesn't say what it is, exactly, but it talks about 'the legacy of Kangxi Shih-k'ai.' Check Dad's journal library and you'll find a lead he recorded, right outside Shanghai. It's one of the last entries before they vanished."

During the Mediterranean leg of a Millennium-themed speaking tour at the end of 1999, Ambrose and Cordelia Hunt were among the passenger contingent of the *Polar Monarch*, a luxuriously appointed cruise ship of Norwegian registry. The ship disappeared from sea radar for three days, then reappeared near Gibraltar without a living soul on board. Three crew members were found in the wheelhouse with their throats slit. Subsequently, bodies and stores began to wash ashore, but a dozen or so passengers were never recovered in any form—including Ambrose and Cordelia Hunt.

"You're not making this up, are you?" said Michael.

"Kangxi Shih-k'ai was on mom and dad's Most Wanted list. They were on the verge of something and they knew it; they just never had the time to pursue it. Now, I'm not saying there's a connection to Michelle Quantrill and this Russian who wants to run China… but it's enough to make me think there really is something there in China for us to find. It's time, Michael. We should have gone after this years ago."

"Time for you to ruin my reputation on the lecture circuit, you mean," Michael said sourly.

"Come on, no one will pay attention to the lectures themselves," said Gabriel. "You know how it goes in China—they'll want to wine and dine us and tour us around to demonstrate their cultural diversity and goodwill. And I'll be perfectly charming, I promise."

Michael put a hand to his forehead and massaged the deep furrows that had appeared there. "This is sounding worse and worse," he said. Then, as he usually did, he diplomatically tabled the topic. "Let me think about it."

Which was all the approval Gabriel needed.

IT WAS STILL STARTLING FOR MITCH TO SEE uniformed police and soldiers carrying automatic weapons in an airport, even in a foreign country.

The Customs official was unreadable: Round head, military crop, unblinking eyes, a knife scar on one side of his mouth. "Remove glasses," he said to Mitch, speaking in fractured English.

They examined each other. The official spot-checked the entry form boxes on *Criminal convictions* and *Contagious diseases*. Mitch had the feeling she had been processed and found lacking, no doubt an impression the uniforms cultivated deliberately.

He did not stamp Mitch's passport. "Stand in blue area, please."

Mitch was directed to a gauntlet of interview cubicles, where a burly Chinese soldier eviscerated her carry-on bag. She was directed to strip down to her underwear and was scanned with a multiband detector. Then into a scanning booth, to insure no contraband was up her ass or down her throat. Only then did a uniformed female supervisor show up, a black Eurasian who gave Mitch the once-over with disdain. It was designed to be as humiliating and intimidating as possible.

The soldier handed a business card to the supervisor. She squinted first at it, then at Mitch. "Your work is in computers," she said in flawlessly mellow Oxford English.

"Yes," said Mitch, trying to find her shirt in the tangle of clothing on the table.

"You are a consultant for Zongchang, Ltd." Nothing the humorless supervisor said was a question. It was rhetorical prodding, bald statements of facts intended to provoke a confirmation or denial.

"Yes."

"That is a good job for a foreigner to have."

"Yes it is."

About an hour later, Mitch finally made it to the overburdened taxicab queue. If one arrived at the city's more modern Pudong Airport, one had the option of taking the MagLev train the thirty kilometers or so into downtown. Mitch had flown into Hongqiao International, and as an outsider unfamiliar with the grid, was stuck with cabbing it. She knew that if the meter crested more than 200 *renminbi* she would have to have words with the *"helpfull, clean, professional, English-spakeing Driver"*—as a sign on the inside of the door informed her.

Most commercial cabs in China are compact cars with a plexi-shield folded around the driver's seat only, giving the pilots an odd, bottled aspect and muffling nearly everything they say.

"Is biggest of all large bridges," the driver told her as they chugged across the modernist swath of Nanpu Bridge. "Most excellent photo opportunity!"

"We *are* going to downtown Shanghai, right?" said Mitch.

The driver nodded enthusiastically. "Three times! In 1997!"

It was all right. She could already see the spire of the Oriental Pearl TV Tower on the Bund.

Outside the Dongfeng Hotel, the scene was a casserole of Grand Central Station rush hour mixed with Casablanca; a huge and bustling open-air marketplace full of hucksters, eccentrics, exotics and bums. Even the poorest citizen was proud of his suit jacket; in fact, there was a thriving sub-industry whereby designer labels could be sewn onto the sleeve of virtually any garment. The visible labels (usually on the left cuff) were a weird sort of status symbol, whether you were riding a bike or stepping out of a limousine. The sheer crush of human bodies was fantastic: thousands of people, hundreds of bicycles (ten abreast and moving fast on each side of Zhongshan Road), citizens hustling about in a floral rainbow of ponchos, pushcart cages of live food. Mitch saw one intrepid cyclist precariously transporting enough strapped-on TV sets to fill a 4x4.

A liveried doorman took her shoulder bag at the entrance to the Dongfeng.

The rooms at the Dongfeng featured card-access slots on the doors but still used old-fashioned keys. Mitch slumped on a double bed, trying not to let all her energy leak out, wondering where the surveillance camera might be hidden. They certainly were omnipresent in every other part of the hotel, particularly the elevators, which seemed to have two per car. She thought about this as she undressed, thought about the bored government functionary charged with watching this particular room's feed. Probably just made his day, she thought as she pulled a black dress out of her bag and slipped it on over her head.

Downstairs, a very polite but very confused concierge tried to help her get where she needed to go.

Mitch tapped Valerie's business card. "This? Here? Zongchang? Yes?"

The concierge seemed conflicted; apparently there was more than one destination called Zongchang. "A taxi can take you from hotel if you really wish to go," he said, implying that perhaps she did *not* want to go.

"I have an appointment with Mr. Kuan-Ku Tak Cheung," she said.

"Oh. I see." He scribbled a square note to be handed off to the next cabbie. "This is the Zongchang you seek."

"SHE'S LOST HER MIND," LUCY SAID.

Gabriel and Lucy sat in the war zone that had once been Valerie Quantrill's apartment.

"Near as I can figure, she took all the cards," said Lucy. "The business stuff, the photo ID, the credit cards. She left the keys so I'm guessing she wasn't planning to come back."

Gabriel still had a clear mental image of Valerie Quantrill's photo ID. The sisters had looked close enough to one another for Mitch to pass the quick scrutiny she'd get at an airport counter, especially if she'd done something to make her hair match. "A last-minute ticket to Shanghai's not cheap... but if Mitch maxed out the credit cards she could've swung it. And if she got a style cut or a wig..."

"She could pass for Valerie," Lucy said. "Fly on her passport. It's soon enough, maybe nobody knows Valerie is dead yet."

"The people who killed Valerie know."

"Goddamn it," Lucy said. "Why'd she pull something like this?"

"She's your friend. Don't ask me."

"Gabriel, if I'm not on a plane in four hours, I'll have the police forces of two countries after me!"

"So get on a plane," Gabriel said.

"*Someone's* got to help Mitch," Lucy said.

Gabriel Hunt picked up a little snow globe from the floor. Something belonging to Valerie. Little Statue of Liberty, swirling fake snow. Big heart, for NYC.

Lucy cleared her throat. "Will you do it?" she asked.

"Like I've ever been able to say no to you," Gabriel said.

4

IT WAS THE FIRST TIME MITCH HAD WORN A DRESS IN over six years, and the last time had been at a funeral. She felt askew in her rakish feminine attire, but it was necessary if she wanted to blend.

Zongchang Ltd. had tentacles all over urban Shanghai, and the destination to which her cabbie took her turned out to be a casino.

A floating casino.

A floating casino housed inside a converted aircraft carrier anchored in the harbor. The word "Zongchang" was painted on its side in four-foot-high red letters, English and Chinese both.

Inside a buoy-marked perimeter, scuba-capable security staff patrolled from one-man speed skiffs featuring gun mounts.

Loudspeakers advised potential trespassers to stay clear of the boat zone.

At the dock, more security men assisted patrons

onto custom mini-ferries that ran to and from the ship's ornate gangplank. They were dressed in no-nonsense, upscale eveningwear, rather like Mitch was.

Except Mitch was not toting a visible MAC-10 with a huge, priapic SIONICS suppressor stretching the barrel.

The carrier shell had been hollowed out and structurally reinforced to provide for broad, windowed views of the shimmering Bund, with outdoor restaurants on the flight deck. Inside, French staircases curved from level to level. Some bled off toward premium members-only gambling areas.

The main casino floor was anything but Vegas, favoring baccarat and *chemin de fer*, though tables for blackjack, roulette and Texas Hold 'Em were also in view.

At the armored cash windows, the currency of many different countries was being exchanged for the casino's special chips.

Mitch passed through another body scanner at the entry. There was no way she could have come in armed. She thought: *Play it as cool as dry ice. You're not Michelle Quantrill. You're Valerie. You're not dead. You're seeking your employer. You're a guest. Simple. Just ask. Don't panic.*

A tray of drinks was being offered to her before she'd even found her focus on the gambling floor. Mitch hesitated. Chose a martini.

"I'm looking for Mr. Cheung," she said, but the server had already departed.

She tried again with a passing security man who apparently "did not have the English." He arched an eyebrow at her and strode away.

Insane bass-heavy house/trance music thundered at her as she crossed an opaque dance floor of solid glass.

Mitch didn't know it yet, but she had already been made.

QINGZHAO WAI CHIU TOOK NOTE OF THE BLONDE
woman crossing the dance floor. Another lost, clueless
American. Another despised tourist.

Qingzhao looked quite different from her previous
public appearance, when an aerodynamic suit with a
concealed mini-chute had permitted her to disappear
into the blackness of the Huangpu River... instead of
hitting flat water from a 300-meter drop, which would
have been like landing on stone.

Tonight she was dressed to kill, literally and
figuratively. New wig of cascading black curls. Tinted
designer glasses. She had applied makeup so as to
cause light to change the planes of her face. Enough
exposure of thigh and décolletage to ensure she could
steer men. The prostitutes in the casino were tawdry
and obvious. Qingzhao prided herself as a chameleon.

She, too, had entered unarmed.

She, too, sought the man known as Kuan-Ku Tak
Cheung.

Qingzhao found herself a likely security man. A
bald East Indian, super-sized, muscle packed atop
more muscle.

"Ladies toilet?" she said in a high, squeaky voice.

The idol-huge man rolled his eyes, then jerked a
thumb. "That way, gorgeous."

Qingzhao giggled, as though from too much
champagne. In her real life, she almost never laughed
anymore.

The East Indian would not do. She needed somebody
more reckless, younger, a hotshot on staff here.

"Don't mind Dinanath," said a voice behind her.
"He's never polite."

She turned. Bingo. This guy was like a horny raptor with the eyes of a pit viper. He could be steered.

"You're *funny*," she said vacantly. "Listen… I need to find the toilet. I might need a little help getting there without becoming embarrassed."

He offered his arm. "Certainly. My name is Romero."

Qingzhao and Romero navigated across the dance floor, Qingzhao keeping her pace just halting enough to be convincing. By the time they reached the nearest restroom, Romero had already brushed her breasts twice and her ass once, strictly to guide her.

"Wait here, okay?" She gave him a little wave and tottered inside.

What she had been doing while in transit was noting the locations of the security cameras in the nongambling zones. While there was a spy-eye (much more discreet) in the powder room, there were none in the individual toilets, which were set up in Western-style stalls.

Once inside a stall, she levered loose the stainless steel clip-lid of the toilet tank. The plunger works came loose easily enough. She bent the flimsy metal to form a spiked punch she could wrap around one fist.

Then she ventured a shy around-the-corner peek at Romero through the bathroom door. "Hey," she said. "This thing doesn't work." He stepped toward her. She smiled, grabbed his belt buckle, and pulled him along.

The cameras would only see two hard partiers headed for a stall and perhaps a taste of inebriated hanky-panky.

Qingzhao made sure Romero kept his eyes on her smile and other assets as she boxed him into the stall and quickly punched a gushing hole into his neck. One more strategic punch and the man was soundlessly down. She quickly stripped him of an automatic pistol and spare magazine, concealing the gun in the only place her show-offy dress would allow.

Done, armed, and not a drop of blood on her. So far so good.

LONGWEI SZE XIE HAD FEW PEERS OR INTIMATES, BUT nearly everybody called him "Ivory." Even his employer, Kuan-Ku Tak Cheung, used this familiar form. Other times, when matters were more grave, Cheung called him "Long." It had happened once or twice in nearly twenty years.

He was taking a break in the Zongchang's security nest—surrounded by monitors and exchanging monotonous chitchat with a console monkey named Zero—when he saw the blonde American stride across the dance floor. The whites of his eyes went stark with surprise at such naked boldness. He snapped his fingers and Zero backed up the feed in order to print out a photo of the woman, after choosing the best vantage.

Ivory's initial shock had come from seeing what he thought was a woman he knew to be dead, right there, seemingly alive, her body language practically broadcasting the rough retribution she sought for her own demise. Then his rational mind processed the image. *No, it's not her. Close, but no.* He was already on the move.

Ivory had feared something like this. Had prepared for its eventuality.

Cheung was holding forth with some financiers in the craps alcove. This woman would spot him eventually, or locate him indirectly. Then nine kinds of hell would break out—if he didn't get to her first.

He glided up behind her. Took a breath. Spoke calmly.

"Do you wish to enjoy Shanghai, Miss Quantrill?"

Mitch spun, slopping her untouched drink. Sandbagged. "Who the hell are you?"

"My name is Longwei Sze Xie," said the handsome Asian. "Please call me Ivory."

"Do you know Kuan-Ku Tak Cheung?"

Ivory was astonished at her directness. She was processing minor shock, he could tell, yet remained bullishly American.

"Yes," he said.

"I don't suppose you could point him out to me?"

Ivory dipped into his vest pocket, his free hand cautioning her against rash action. He withdrew a packet of airline tickets. "First class back to New York City, with my compliments."

Mitch eyed him suspiciously. "What're *you* supposed to be?"

"I am the greatest friend you have in the world right now, Miss Quantrill."

Past the woman's shoulder, Ivory saw Dinanath, the big bald operative, signaling to him from across the gambling floor. Summoning him.

Ivory clenched his teeth as though mildly pained. "Come with me."

KUAN-KU TAK CHEUNG MADE A HABIT OF KEEPING tabs on his Number One, Ivory, and when he spotted his head of security chatting up a strangely familiar blonde, he snapped his fingers and Dinanath jumped to.

It wasn't quite an arrest, but had more insistence than a mere escort.

Cheung excused himself from the company of his supporters after making sure they had drinks all around. Extra security, all first string except for Romero (who was MIA somewhere), formed an outer ring for privacy as Dinanath, Ivory, and their visitor came over. She was not a beautiful woman, noted Cheung. More... handsome. But there was something compelling about her, something about the hardness in her eyes.

Mitch stared. It was not polite, but she couldn't help herself. Cheung was burly, bristly. Nothing about him seemed Chinese except for the epicanthic folds of his eyelids, and she realized, with a jolt, that the man had probably had surgery to acquire the look. In any event, his eyes were bright blue.

"And, this is...?" said Cheung, not speaking to Mitch, but to Ivory.

"I've come about Valerie Quantrill," said Mitch.

Dinanath was upending her small clutch purse on a vacant table, rummaging.

"Who is Valerie Quantrill?" said Cheung, again to Ivory.

"A woman you left dead in a dumpster in New York," said Mitch, reddening.

Upon hearing this, Dinanath turned to Cheung and shrugged. *It was all we could find. A garbage bin.* As if to say, *so what?*

Cheung looked around to his fellows as though he had missed something, like a punchline. "*And...?*"

"And I want to know what you had to do with it," said Mitch.

Cheung splayed his fingers across his mouth, pondering. "Hmm. All the way from the United States?

Seems like a lot of trouble just to hurl an accusation. Why bother?"

"She was my sister."

Cheung seemed truly at sea. Mitch wondered if he was going to toy with her, string her out, maximize the pain. But what he said was infinitely colder. He again turned to Ivory and said, "What does she want? Money? Then pay her some money."

"I don't want your money," Mitch said through clenched teeth.

He looked at Mitch as though truly seeing her for the first time. "You want an apology?" He shrugged. "Very well—you have my apologies for your loss."

Mitch said, "That's not all. You *know* that's not all."

Cheung had already turned to resume other business, but allowed himself a parting shot: "That's all *you* get, my dear."

Mitch's thumb snapped the martini glass she was holding at its stem. With the base held against her palm, she shucked Dinanath's light grasp and lunged at Cheung's face, putting her shoulder into the thrust.

Ivory was there instantly, his hand arresting her wrist in a vise-grip, as though he had snatched a fly in mid-air. The jagged stem of the glass hovered inches from his own eyes. He had stepped in to shield Cheung with unnatural speed. Stoically, he nerve-pinched the glass from Mitch's hand.

Cheung was grinning—not smiling. The expression was vulpine. "See if you can find another dumpster," he said to Dinanath. "And don't alarm the *dakuan*." Cheung needed the high-rollers to remain unagitated.

* * *

THE BACKWASH OF ADRENALINE IN QINGZHAO'S system was nauseating.

In a vital confluence of dozens of moving people and wavering vantage points, she'd briefly had the perfect shot at Cheung's head—maybe time to get two or three rounds in before general panic ruined the target. And that American bitch had spoiled everything!

Now this… this *amateur* was being escorted to the security nest.

But wait: after a beat, she saw Cheung and his head of security (that son of a bitch, Ivory) headed the same way.

She still might have a chance.

Qingzhao moved across the grand hall as quickly as she could, blending.

"THIS IS REALLY GOOD FOR HEADACHES," SAID THE Chinese security man, who wore Buddy Holly glasses and a goatee, and was apparently named Chino. He was referring to a leather glove on his right hand. The glove had rivets across the knuckles. He punched Mitch a second time in the side of the head. "Got one, yet?"

His first punishing blow had been dealt to the left side of her head, so it was only fair that he rock her back the way she came. For balance.

Mitch lolled in the chair, half-conscious.

Chino automatically became less cocky when Cheung and Ivory entered the security room. Zero kept to his monitors.

"Oh, don't do it *here*," Cheung said, piqued.

Before further debate could ensue there came a businesslike rap on the door. Chino yanked it open prepared to repel all invaders. "What!" he said, full up with brine.

Qingzhao shot him in the head.

Mitch tried to scoot her chair out of the way of Chino's falling corpse and wound up dumping herself backward on the floor. One chair arm cracked violently loose and the bindings securing her fell slack. She freed herself as quickly as she could.

More gunfire. She saw Ivory tackle Cheung and both men disappeared through the slanted observation window in a hailstorm of glass.

Zero huddled in a quivering ball beneath the console where his monitors were disintegrating from bullet hits as Qingzhao tried to track Cheung.

No go.

Qingzhao was holding her hand out to Mitch.

"Come on. We've got to go now."

THE MOMENT CHINO ANSWERED THE DOOR WAS THE same moment that Gabriel Hunt, freshly arrived from America, entered the Zongchang casino ship for the first and only time in his life.

5

GABRIEL HUNT'S FIRST VIEW OF THE ZONGCHANG WAS
impressive—the ship was one of the four Kiev class
warships built for the Soviet Navy in the mid-1970s
and decommissioned in 1995. One was sold to the
Indian Navy for modernization; one was scrapped
and the other two were sold to China as "recreational
pieces." The nonmilitary paint job incorporated a lot of
dead black and silver, in sweeping lines that reminded
Gabriel of formula race cars back in the hero days,
before all the advertising sponsorships.

He wondered if any of the ship's firepower was still
functional.

Gabriel had just gotten his first taste of the vast main
gambling floor when two men came exploding through
a slanted, one-way observation window at the far end.

Flashes of gunfire, from within the chamber.

And a split-second glimpse of the only person in this
place that Gabriel might recognize—Mitch Quantrill,

dolled up as her own sister. Blood on her face.

Gabriel moved as the main floor erupted into chaos.

A Frenchman in the poker pit stood up and stopped a stray round, his busted flush flying into the air like cast-off flower petals. Half the clientele hit the deck while the other half was galvanized into directionless flight. Gabriel shoved one runner aside in time to save his life. The man cursed him in Arabic. The casino's black-suited security men had unlimbered a frightening variety of snubbed full-autos and were handing their disorganization back to the crowd in the form of scattered bullet-sprays at anything and everything that might be an antagonist. Gabriel knew that, in a firefight, those little earphone-buds only worked in the movies, so if the shooters were trying to communicate or coordinate, right now they couldn't hear a damned thing.

The racket was incredible inside what was still essentially a huge metal room. Flat-nosed slugs chuddered up a balustrade and destroyed a fake Grecian urn next to Gabriel's head.

The two acrobats who had made their grand entrance by defenestrating from the security portal were still trying to find their wits and their feet. One man was yelling and pointing. The other was trying to shield his boss.

Forgoing the increasing availability of weapons as a good contingent of assorted bodyguards and security men inadvertently shot each other, Gabriel bypassed his instinctual craving for a firearm (if anything, he would have wanted his Colt, but he'd left that stashed back on the Foundation jet) and made for the vacant security window. Mitch was up there. Alive, dead or compromised—he had no way of knowing except through immediate action.

Slugs tore across the baize at his heels as he hit a *chemin de fer* table at full tilt and vaulted toward the gaping eye of the blown observation port. Its rubberized mount was fanged with shards of glass but Gabriel managed to pull himself up and over.

He found himself in the security nest with a couple of dead guys and one gibbering employee still stashed beneath the console. Equipment was sparking and blowing out all around him as incoming fire destroyed costly electronics the way rock breaks scissors.

Outside the nest door was a secondary corridor more in keeping with the ship's utilitarian naval origins—a lot of cast iron and shatterproof lights.

Thirty yards ahead, Qingzhao and Mitch encountered two security men rushing toward the danger zone. Qingzhao flat-handed one in the face, pile-driving his palate back toward his spine. He collided with his buddy, whose legs Mitch took away in a fast and clumsy sweep-kick. It was enough. The man bonked rivets and decking with his head all the way down. Qingzhao quickly disarmed them and handed off the extra firearm to Mitch.

They had no time for a huddle. No time to exchange numbers. No time to recognize each other as anything but an ally.

"Where to?" said Mitch.

"Out," said Qingzhao.

They untethered a blistering spray of bullets back the way they had come, just as Gabriel Hunt ran into their field of fire.

Gabriel flattened out in a home-run slide. An inch higher, a split second sooner, and he would have caught a bullet in his left nostril.

The women were firing at the gunmen who had

crowded into the passage in Gabriel's wake. Men who were shooting back just as ferociously as the women tried to flee.

Hornet swarms of lead exchanged position above Gabriel as he pulled himself into an opening in the wall—steam piping, cold now, unused in the new incarnation of the aircraft carrier. There would come an eyeblink instant when all shooters had to reload, and that was what Gabriel was waiting for.

The volley ebbed and Gabriel mad-dashed for the next hatchway, knowing from seafaring experience how to grab the upper ledge and swing through without giving himself a skull fracture.

Mitch had spotted him during the exchange. She had even uttered his name—"Gabriel?"—but this had gone unheard in the cannonade. She hesitated. Qingzhao had to drag her along with a snort of frustration.

Her yanked arm erupted with sudden pain and Mitch looked down to see a bullet hole in her left shoulder. Dammit, she'd been hit! *Stupid!*

They were trying to figure out which way to abandon ship when Gabriel came soaring at them from the hatchway in a flying tackle. Expertly catching both women by the neck in the crooks of his arms, Gabriel used his momentum to take them over the observation deck edge and tumbling down into the drink.

THE WATER WAS CLAMMY AND STALE.

Gunners were already shooting at them from the upper deck—automatic swath-fire that sent bullets down into the dark water like deadly snail darters.

Qingzhao had kicked off her heels and was already stroking for the surface, swimming toward one of the patrol boats. Gabriel saw her since she was three feet away. But when they had splashed down, he'd lost his grip on Mitch and had no idea where she was. He tried to see her through the murky water, tried to reach for her, but it was hopeless.

Current was pulling them, still submerged.

"Help!" A voice that blurred as Gabriel surfaced and water decanted from his ears.

It was Qingzhao, ploshing about to attract the attention of one of the security men on a skiff. His face was split in a grin of rough good fortune; here was an enticing female delivered unto him by the sea!

When Qingzhao got a grip on his extended hand, she swung her gun out of the water and shot him.

Modern technology had some advantages, Gabriel conceded. Wet guns could still fire. Modern cartridges had to be submerged for some time to become useless. Otherwise, nobody could ever have a shootout in the rain.

Qingzhao used her leverage to tumble the perforated guard into the water. She quickly took control of the boat, as though this had been her exit strategy all along.

There was still no sign of Mitch, and other boat sentries were catching up in a big hurry.

Gabriel felt a sting at his temple as a bullet passed within millimeters. Enough.

He swung one arm over the side of the skiff and pulled himself in just as Qingzhao floored it. Gabriel was hurled indecorously back against a padded vinyl seat as Qingzhao throttled the boat up full.

"Sit down," she barked over the howl of the engine.

With at least three speed-skiffs behind them, they were ramrodding into a tighter section of the waterway, dodging sampans and houseboats. Qingzhao could not bank fast enough to avoid hitting a *hua-tzu*—one of the smaller, narrower, canoe-like boats used by fishermen. The steel-reinforced ramming prow of the skiff cut the *hua-tzu* in half as Gabriel saw the occupant jack-in-the-box himself skyward in panic.

Their pursuers chopped through in their wake, destroying what was left.

Gabriel felt the sea air cool the sweat on his forehead. The skiff was headed at high speed directly for an elaborate floating restaurant in the middle of the harbor. It was the size of a city block, lit up like a Christmas tree with strung lights, and completely encased in a service latticework of bamboo.

Diners inside enjoying the splendid view of the river were no doubt dismayed by the sudden sight of a speedboat rocketing toward them with no possibility of detour, followed by a contingent of similar boats firing lots and lots of bullets in the direction of the windows.

Qingzhao banked the craft hard, attempting a bootlegger's reverse, but the skiff crashed gratingly into the bamboo superstructure and got hung up with its prow sticking through a shattered window.

Gabriel had a flashpop-image of Qingzhao jamming an extra magazine from the skiff pilot's pistol into her décolletage. Then she was diving into the eatery, the patrons and staff of which had taken some small notice of their cacophonous arrival. Gabriel plunged in after her.

Cheung's men were already coming in the shoreline entrance.

As Gabriel pounded through the swinging double doors of the kitchen, he saw Qingzhao jam the extra magazine of bullets into a flaming brazier.

An instant later, the bullets began exploding.

Cheung's men collided with each other in their haste to find sparse cover and evade what they thought was ambush fire.

Gabriel pushed his way through hanging skinned fowl and fish dangling from cleaning hooks. The cooks were all yelling and taking cover. Steps ahead of him, Qingzhao appropriated a gigantic silver meat cleaver from a bracket on the wall.

Cheung's men would be gathering outside the kitchen door about now, massing an assault.

Gabriel and Qingzhao went out the back, shot glances in every direction. At the southern end of the floating restaurant was a loading spur as crowded as a parking lot with assorted boats that arrived hourly to meet the needs of a business that advertised *fresh-fresh-fresh*. Gabriel took Qingzhao's arm, careful to avoid getting within striking distance of that cleaver, and aimed her in the direction of one particular vessel that had what seemed, from this distance, to be an empty hold. She searched his face for an instant, apparently didn't find whatever signs of incipient betrayal she was looking for, and followed his lead.

THE GUNNERS STOOD DOWN WHEN IVORY CUT through the destruction in the restaurant. He stopped and stood staring out at the water for a moment.

"Did you know who that was?" said Dinanath breathlessly, trundling up behind Ivory.

"My responsibility," said Ivory, more to himself than to his co-worker.

"Stop the traffic and search these boats."

* * *

THE JUNK WAS CAPTAINED BY AN OLD-SCHOOL RIVER rat named Lao, whose grin revealed he had had all his teeth replaced with steel substitutes decades ago. He was the first to be allowed to leave the supply berth at the Floating Feast Superior Restaurant, since all he carried was a hold full of tuna that could not be delayed, for spoilage.

When he put a little distance between himself and the Floating Feast, he saw the tuna piled in his hold begin to move.

Gradually, as though surfacing through a muck of cloudy fish jelly, Gabriel and Qingzhao materialized amidst the odiferous cargo. They had jumped into the belly of the empty hold and Qingzhao had used the cleaver to cut the net holding the fish overhead, burying them summarily.

The smell was… memorable.

Lao extended a courtly hand to help Qingzhao up to the deck first. He jabbered at her in reedy, mutated Mandarin.

"What did he say?" said Gabriel.

"He thanks us for the marvelous new knife," said Qingzhao, indicating the cleaver, which Lao was turning over in his hands like a rare jewel.

His smile matched the metal cutting edge.

Gabriel wanted to say something ironic, tough, and competent. But he raised one hand to his temple instead, where the bullet had stung him earlier and where he now was suddenly conscious of wetness welling. Instead of fish oil or the dank, frigid bilge water of the hold, his fingertips were smeared, he saw, with blood. The last thing he thought before he lost consciousness was: *Well, I guess the whole lecture thing is pretty much blown.*

6

WHEN GABRIEL OPENED HIS EYES, HE WAS STARING at a parked motorcycle.

Which was odd, because he seemed to be indoors.

A series of smells hit his nose—smoke, burning wood, incense, packed dirt, pine-scented air, charred paper, and beneath all that a subtle tang of gasoline, gun oil and engine lubricant.

Most enticing of all was the smell of coffee.

The bike appeared to be a vintage German BMW R-71 from 1938. Four-stroke, 750cc, with a sidecar, just like dozens seen in every World War II movie ever made. This one looked newer, and was more likely one of the painstaking Chinese rebuilds called Changjiangs, very popular with motorcycle clubs in this part of the world.

He heard light rain pattering down into what sounded like a Japanese water garden.

He tried to rise and found he was lying on a raw-hewn wooden pallet and facing a huge rope candle on a rusted bronze stand. The candle was fashioned on the same principle as the gigantic coils of incense Gabriel had seen in assorted Eastern houses of worship. It could burn for hundreds of hours if fed through the windproof receiver judiciously.

Wick-smoke twisted ceilingward and the sudden light of the flame made his head throb. The chamber was roughly circular, the walls formed of ancient cut stone blocks.

There was a dressing on his head. He touched it gingerly. He didn't seem to be bleeding anymore, which was nice. He figured the bullet must've come closer than he'd realized, must have hit him a glancing blow, perhaps scoring a neat groove in his thick skull. He'd made it a while on adrenaline alone, but when that had run out...

He tried to stand up and experienced whirling vertigo. At first he thought it was from his injury but a moment later he realized that the floor of the room actually was slanted, and a moment after that he realized it was necessary to compensate for the incline of the building itself. The effect was disorienting, though he suddenly knew where he was: in one of the leaning pagodas outside Shanghai.

Through a small alcove he caught sight of the temple ruins outside.

He was halfway up a mountainside, inside snaggle-toothed fortifications choked by wild foliage. The leaning pagoda jutted crookedly toward the stars, like Pisa.

Several centuries ago temples like this had served as waystations for travelers as well as locations for worship and ritual. They generally consisted of three sequential courtyards, each with its own shrine. He made his way through an overgrown courtyard to the nearest of the shrine rooms. It was so large Gabriel could see clusters of bird nests near the holes in the domed ceiling. It was mustier in here where the damp had gotten through to the limestone. Vines had claimed the walls.

Gabriel saw Qingzhao toss a packet of ceremonial money into the flames licking up from an iron urn. Greasy smoke corkscrewed into the air.

He cleared his throat and Qingzhao's free hand shot up holding a gun whose barrel looked a foot long. Gabriel tried not to react. Turning her head his way, Qingzhao recognized him and gestured idly toward a small cookstove—pointing with the gun, of course.

"Coffee. All Americans like coffee," she said, her voice having an almost African lilt concealed within it.

She saw him look at the money she was burning. "You wonder why I would burn—"

"For the dead to use in the next world," said Gabriel.

"Don't burn enough, and you're considered cheap. That's the superstition, anyway. How much have you burned?"

"You can never burn enough."

She offered him a tin cup of strong coffee that smelled just the way Nirvana is supposed to.

Gabriel's eyes had adjusted to the sputtering light long enough for him to now make out a mural of a frothing demon on the far wall, obscured by wear and time and the overgrowth of underbrush. He touched the bandage on his head while Qingzhao, apparently, read his mind.

"You are embarrassed," she said. "You are a strong American man, it is your job to save the girl, and here I have saved you instead." She almost smiled. Almost. "I will not tell anyone and thus embarrass you further."

Gabriel was silent for a moment. Then he said, "Why did you bring me with you?"

"I think you and I wish to kill the same man."

"Sorry to say, lady, you've got that wrong. I'm not here to kill anybody."

She stopped what she was doing and regarded him.

"I came here to find someone in trouble who needed help," he said. "She jumped the gun and came here sloppy. Emotions on high-burn, full up with revenge. She didn't even have a plan worthy of the name."

"The blonde woman at the Zongchang."

Gabriel nodded. "Now *she* did want to kill the same man you do—she believed Cheung murdered her sister in New York City, or had her murdered."

"I sensed we had a connection," Qingzhao said quietly.

"Wanting to kill Cheung? I think you've probably got that in common with quite a few people."

"No. Something deeper. This woman wished to avenge her sister, who has been murdered." She tossed some more money into the fire. "Cheung murdered me, as well."

IN A HIGH-SECURITY CHAMBER WITH WALLS OF pumice situated atop the Peace Hotel, Cheung conducted his own rituals in the incense-choked, church-like ambience.

Seated behind an artful, almost ephemeral desktop of hewn onyx, Cheung was working with a leather rollup of antique carving tools, delicately carving a detailed cherrywood casket about ten inches long.

Past the altar-like desk, past the bank of flat-screen monitors, several of his operatives worked damage control by phone, but none would proffer information or news, good or bad, until Cheung addressed them directly.

Finally, Cheung looked up and lit a long, poisonous-looking cigarette.

"Mr. Fleetwood," he said.

Fleetwood, a rangy Anglo wearing octagonal glasses wired around his completely shaved head, terminated the call on his headset.

"How much will last night cost us?" said Cheung, meaning the free-for-all at the Zongchang, including janitorial services.

"Ten days to reopen at a cost of $2.6 million New Pacific dollars. That's the repair versus the lost income."

"They're robbing us because they think we're desperate," Cheung said. He picked up a hardwood abacus and started clicking the beads on the device's lower deck, bottom-to-top, right-to-left, carrying totals to the upper deck, where each bead represented five times more value. It was the simplest base-ten counting system in the world.

"Get everything right. Tell them they have twenty days to reopen. Give them one point one. More time, but less loss."

"What about General Zhang's military loan?" said Fleetwood. "What about the interest the police owe us?"

Cheung waved this away because Longwei Sze Xie had entered.

"Ivory," Cheung said. "My Immortal. Tell me true things."

After a formal bow, Ivory exhibited several printouts salvaged from the surveillance cameras at the casino ship.

"The Nameless One," he said, unnecessarily. "Same as at the Oriental Pearl Tower. And here, again. And again."

"Is she a ghost?"

"No," said Ivory.

"Tell me," said Cheung, his voice succoring. "Is she a genuine threat, or is she just crazy and lucky?" The implication that Ivory's job hung in the balance was clear.

"She will be no threat. I will see to it."

Cheung rose and—very uncharacteristically—laid an avuncular hand on Ivory's shoulder. He rarely touched any of his employees.

"Longwei Sze Xie," he said, using respect language, "I shall need you close by at all times. You help enable my... mad little schemes, and I shall always be grateful. There is one small errand to which I would like you to attend."

"Name it and it is done," said Ivory.

He whispered into Ivory's ear.

"Sir, Nairobi's finally calling back on line two," Fleetwood announced.

"I'll take it," said Cheung, who picked up his phone and began speaking in perfect Kenyan dialect. Ivory had already vanished from the room.

QINGZHAO WAS PUNCHING HOLES IN A SHEET OF TIN with a mallet and chisel. Each time she smacked the metal the perforation made a *pank!* sound that echoed inside the shrine room.

"Was she a soldier, this woman?" she asked.

"Yes," said Gabriel. "A U.S. Air Force pilot."

"Then she knew about soldiers in battle. They die."

"Her sister was no soldier. She was a database engineer at the American office of a Chinese corporation."

"Cheung's?"

Gabriel nodded.

"Cheung is a warrior. Anyone who works for him has to be prepared for the worst."

"Bet they don't tell employees that before they take the job."

Qingzhao shrugged this away.

"What's your connection to Cheung?" Gabriel asked. "Were you an employee, too? Before you were… what did you say, murdered?"

She flared with anger: "You have no right to show disdain. Have *you* fought and killed another man? Ever been wounded in battle?"

In his nearly two-score years on the planet Gabriel had been shot six times and stabbed or cut with edged weapons over a hundred.

"Lady, trust me, I've been wounded plenty," he said.

"Lady," Qingzhao repeated as though testing a new word and finding it inadequate.

Qingzhao inverted the holed metal so the sharp lipped edges of the punctures were facing her. Then she punched the metal with her bare fist.

Gabriel winced.

Qingzhao pounded the metal like a boxer, then turned to a basket of lemons at the base of the shrine. She squeezed one freehanded until it burst, and worked the juice into both bleeding hands. Gabriel knew the pain must be incredible, but Qingzhao's expression did not change.

"Toughens the skin," she said, as though that was answer enough. It ended their conversation.

Some lady, Gabriel thought.

* * *

AT THE ARCHWAY TO THE PAGODA, THERE HAD ONCE
been a gate guarded by immense stone lions of marble.
Now there remained only weathered pedestals and
severed stone paws, one holding a child, the other, a
globe of the world.

Gabriel stood between them watching the setting
sun, trying to frame an argument. Mitch Quantrill
was lost; swallowed by the Huangpu with a bullet in
her. The odds that she had survived were low. Lucy
would be distraught when she found out. And furious
with him. Still—was it his responsibility to pick up her
doomed mission? Would that make things right?

No.

Then there was this woman, with the motorcycle
and the tough skin and the story about having
been murdered. All right, chalk some of it up to the
language barrier, but still, she seemed mildly crazy.
And whatever mission she was on seemed fraught
with who knew what sort of damage in her past. If she
wanted to go after Cheung, was that his problem?

No.

It would be the easiest thing in the world to make
his way back to the city. By Gabriel's reckoning they
were perhaps fifty miles into the mountains along the
Yangtze River. He could jet back to the States. Michael
could reschedule the lecture tour, make apologies
for Gabriel's mysterious absence. And all this would
become a bad bit of history. It made sense.

So why did he feel no desire to do it?

Gabriel tried to kid himself that he was still recovering
from the bullet skid to the temple, but he knew better.
Maybe he was attracted to Qingzhao; was that it?

He was still trying to work out the answer to that
one when she appeared silently beside him.

"Don't let them see you."

Gabriel's senses instantly hit high alert. "Who?"

"The soldiers."

His body tensed, automatically crouching down and scanning the grounds for cover. "*What* soldiers?" he said.

"My army," said Qingzhao. "The Killers of Men."

THE PAIR OF TOSA DOGS WERE SCHOOLED aggressors, each nearly 200 pounds. Also known as Japanese Fighting Mastiffs or "Sumo Dogs," their jaws could render nearly 600 pounds of crush pressure, and this brindle pair stood 25 inches at the shoulder. Highly prized as fighters, this type of dog had been banned in the UK, Ireland, New Zealand and Australia. As a breed they were alert, agile, and quick to respond with unbelievable reserves of stamina, which meant that gladiatorial training amplified all their most dangerous traits.

Dinanath had overseen the training of this pair. Neither dog had a name. Right now, Ivory was holding the remote fob keyed to their electronic discipline collars.

In his other hand he held the gleaming meat cleaver he had just confiscated from Lao, the fisherman.

Aboard his sampan, Lao was busy pleading for his life in Mandarin.

"It appears," Ivory said, "that Qingzhao Wai Chiu had not one ally, but two."

"This is getting out of hand," said Dinanath.

Ivory sighed and nodded. He was tired of trying to maintain a standard of honor that was increasingly irrelevant.

He keyed the fob and the Tosa dogs tore into the terrified Lao. His screams disappeared down chomping gullets, and Ivory rendered the man the small mercy of shooting him in the head before it was all over.

GABRIEL GAZED WITH BREATHLESS DISBELIEF AT ONE of the full-sized terra-cotta warriors inside the shrine room Qingzhao had led him to.

There were four in all, half-buried in deep dirt trenches, broken and weathered like long-vandalized tombstones. Two vacant slots suggested two figures had already been removed.

But that was not the most awe-inspiring thing in the shrine room.

Suffocated by vines and tree roots at the far end of the chamber, clotted with decades of dried mud and impacted dust, was a large bronze statue of a Chinese grotesque, pointing one bony sculpted finger toward the center of the room. Underlit by torchlight it was positively ghoulish, a nightmare vision, an evil god. The scaling and tarnish on the bronze made the looming grotesque appear to be leprous.

"Is this supposed to be Kangxi Shih-k'ai?" asked Gabriel. "The Favored Son of China? He looks like Nosferatu."

The reference was lost on Qingzhao. "I do not know. I only know of Kangxi Shih-k'ai's history because of Cheung's obsession with him. Whether this statue depicts him, I cannot say. But the phrase 'Killers of Men' struck me as appropriate for the others. My soldiers here help my cause." She pointed out one of the terra-cotta figures, missing an arm. "He was a bowman."

"Now he doesn't have a bow or an arm to draw it

with," said Gabriel, marveling at the possibilities. "His face is almost gone."

"They all had weapons of bronze, a long time ago. They did not need shields, nor helmets. Cunning and ferocity were their protection."

Was she referring to the men who'd been the models for these figures or the figures themselves? Gabriel wasn't sure.

"You found them here? Out in the open? Or did you excavate them yourself?"

"They were buried," she said. "I dug them out."

"How did you find them?" She didn't answer. "How did you know they were here?"

"I knew." It was all she said.

"Does Cheung know they're here?"

She shook her head. "I found them; he does not know."

"And were there more? More figures?" She shook her head. "Not necessarily in this room," Gabriel said. "Maybe one of the other shrine rooms, or... is there a way *into* this mountain? A path to the inside?"

"You mean like a secret chamber?" She seemed amused. "No. I have seen all the caves and passageways this mountain has to offer. I was hoping to find more of the Killers of Men myself; I would certainly have use for them. These are all that there are."

Gabriel began scraping debris off the base of the huge bronze statue against the far wall. Maybe she was right that she'd found everything there was to find. But maybe she wasn't. A half-mad assassin using one of the leaning pagodas as a hideout would not search the way Gabriel Hunt could search.

"How do you use the warriors?" he asked as he continued to work his way around the sculpture's base.

"Tonight I will take the bowman to a friend at the Night Market," said Qingzhao. "Perhaps if you come you will find out what you wish to know. I would welcome your help."

She very pointedly did not remind him that he was in her debt.

What the hell, thought Gabriel. He could give China one more day.

7

TRASH FIRES CHOKED THE STREET WITH MILKY smoke. The pedicab in which Gabriel and Qingzhao rode, with their inanimate charge wedged between them, threaded its way through the riot of human shapes that constituted the night life beyond the favored, protected realm of the Bund. Here were thousands of vendors, prostitutes, thieves, *huanquiande* bartering for money, DVD hucksters, homeopathic herbal medicine men, pirate electronics dealers, clothiers, all blurring past. Open petrol and propane tanks warned in English *NO NAKED LIGHT*, meaning fire.

They stopped at the Beggar's Arch, which was a long stone tunnel like a Roman aqueduct, its shadows lined on both sides by castoffs and derelicts. According to beggar etiquette, the seated and squatting men kept their eyes down and their cups (or cupped hands) up as Gabriel and Qingzhao passed, carrying the canvas-wrapped statue of the bowman carefully between them.

They emerged into one of Shanghai's many night markets, a tightly packed maze of tents reminiscent of an American swap meet or flea market, interspersed with solo hustlers and other racketeers working out of the shells of now-useless automobiles. Gabriel saw several more people burning ceremonial cash at drumfires, and a man putting trained birds through their paces inside an entire corridor of bird-sellers.

"It's like Mardi Gras," Gabriel said.

"More dangerous," said Qingzhao.

"You've never drunk a Hurricane, I bet."

Qingzhao ignored the remark. Wit, charm, or humor were not her coinage.

Presently they emerged into a large open area completely engirded in stonemasonry, with drains in the floor. It could have been a covered outdoor patio or a deceptively big space between buildings with a canopy overhead. It reminded Gabriel a bit of an abandoned food court. There was a scatter of tables and chairs. At one, a wizened, skeletal man ceaselessly folded squares of paper into origami shapes and dropped them into an iron pot. Across from him, an equally ancient woman sat surrounded by disassembled cellphones, probing them with tiny jeweler's tools. They were both clad in simple Maoist tunics and the woman smiled at Gabriel as they passed. Every other tooth was missing.

Qingzhao spoke briefly to the old man in a dialect Gabriel could not place.

"Who are we talking to here?" Gabriel asked.

"Sentries."

"Sentries," said Gabriel.

Now the old man was grinning, too. Apparently he

had scored all the woman's missing teeth.

Qingzhao whispered a monosyllable, and the next thing Gabriel knew, two guns were pointed right at his head.

THE OLD FOLKS WERE STILL SMILING AT HIM.

A big, booming, basso laugh rebounded from the rock walls.

The entryway to the next chamber in the maze filled up with a large black man, six-six easy in flat slippers, with a calm Buddha face and vaguely Asian eyes below a close-cropped crewcut.

"Your expression!" The big man thundered with mirth. "Priceless!" He took a moment to settle. "Forgive me."

The oldsters stowed their firepower and resumed their innocuous activities, the woman still smiling sweetly at Gabriel.

"I know what *you* want, I'm sure of it!" The big man embraced Qingzhao. Even more surprisingly, Qingzhao allowed this.

"And I know what *you* want," she said before the breath could be squeezed out of her.

The big man stuck out a hand the size of a catcher's mitt toward Gabriel. *"Ni chi le ma?"* It was a common greeting for a stranger—*have you eaten?*—testifying to the centrality of food in most Asian culture. Gabriel shook the proffered hand in the Western fashion. A more traditional Chinese handshake would have consisted of the men interlocking their fingers and waving them up and down a few times; but today this was done mostly by the very elderly or the very etiquette-conscious.

"Tuan, at your service," boomed the big man, "and the service of our little snapdragon, here."

Like some grandiose, benevolent street pasha, Tuan escorted Qingzhao and Gabriel through the heart of his domain, which rose in tiers from the cobblestoned street into a labyrinth of subdivisions and alcoves overpopulated with mercantile bustle. Over here, you could get your head massaged, cheap. Over there, your ears swabbed out. It was indoor-yet-outdoor; the grandest treehouse of all.

Besides Beggar's Arch, three other tunnels fed into the amphitheater. At one end was a traditional Chinese tea house accessed by a zig-zaggy footbridge over a turbid flow of water.

"Four people are in charge of the Bund, now," said Qingzhao as they trailed Tuan, their fragile burden held between them.

"Like gang turf?" said Gabriel.

"More akin to social castes."

"Classes."

"Tuan runs street level. All you can see."

"It is my privilege," chimed the big man leading them. "An entrepreneur named Hellweg has a lock on municipal services such as power, water. You may have noticed his petroleum tower—the Fire in the Sky. He's some sort of European; Danish, or Scandanavian at any rate.

"Our local army of mercenary police is owned by Lo Pei Zhang, who was once a military general. The soldiers are all ex-Red Army."

"And the fourth is Cheung?" said Gabriel.

"Yes. Qingzhao's former employer," said Tuan, and Gabriel realized it was the first time he'd heard the woman's name. "I believe he made his millions in currency speculation. His *first* millions."

Gabriel fired a glance back at Qingzhao. "So you *were* an employee of his."

"Mr. Cheung arrived in our fair land just as Communism was gasping its last," Tuan rattled on. "The CCC is the new land of opportunity, but it is all quite subsurface now. That's why Occidentals fear it so much, I think."

"And you," said Gabriel to Qingzhao, "used to work for this guy? The one you've been trying to—"

Her hand was on his forearm, extended across the body of the bowman between them. "Yes." Her eyes added: *Not now. Not in front of Tuan. Please.*

This was one raincheck Gabriel was going to follow up on.

Next to a booth whose sign proclaimed CHANGE YOUR I.D., Tuan pointed out an ammo hawker with half a face, masked as though by a giant eyepatch. Most of the man's fingers were missing or truncated.

"Do not purchase ammunition from that man," Tuan said. "Unreliable. Misfires."

"The man or the ammunition?" asked Gabriel.

"Both."

Tuan led them into another cubbyhole with signage halfway-hidden from the commonweal: SU-LIN GUN MERCHANT. It stank of gunpowder and gun oil, and was a cramped warren of firepower old and new. Su-Lin was a gnomish woman with a calm Easter Island gaze; she weighed maybe 75 pounds. Tuan bent from his enormous height to grace her cheek with a kiss.

"You must use the keyboard," said Qingzhao. Two laptops were set up collaborator-style on a small counter, with Su-Lin perched behind one as though ready to commence a game of Battleship. "This translates. First you type the proper greeting."

They set down the bowman and Qingzhao typed: *Your Pig Mother Eats Night Soil*, which transposed to Chinese characters on Su-Lin's screen.

Su-Lin typed back: *I Love You Too.*

Gabriel's attention meanwhile had been arrested by a very special gun hanging from a clip on the back wall. His eye coded it as a close cousin to his faithful Colt Peacemaker, which he still wished he had strapped to his hip. That one was out of reach. This wasn't.

"You have seen something you like?" said Tuan.

It was a large Colt revolver—age-burnished, true, but Gabriel recognized it as the treasure it was. "If this is what I think it is…"

Tuan lifted it off the wall and handed it to him. The gun sprang open cleanly at his touch. There wasn't a spot of rust on it anywhere.

"This," Gabriel said, as if he were introducing an old friend to a new one, "looks like an old Navy Colt, .36 caliber—from when they first started converting cap-and-ball 'percussion pistols' to the more newfangled revolver. They called them 'wheelguns.'" He glanced back at Su-Lin. "How much do you think she might take for it?"

"That depends on whether you *like* it," Tuan goaded.

"I like it very much," said Gabriel. "Anyone who knows about guns would."

"Then it is yours," Tuan said. "For your trouble. With my compliments."

"Why?"

"You are a guest. Qingzhao said you helped to save her life. That is a favor bestowed upon me as well. Please allow me to repay this debt in a way that pleases you."

Gabriel nodded his thanks. He was always ill at ease accepting gifts, because you never knew what obligations might accompany them. But he wasn't about to turn down this one. He had a feeling he might need a good gun very soon.

THE PLACE TUAN CALLED HIS PLEASURE GARDEN featured a cabaret stage—empty just now—and about a million varieties of flowering plant life nourished by misting nozzles and artificial sunlight, here in the middle of a city of stone.

The newly unwrapped terra-cotta warrior—Qingzhao's bowman—watched silently as they ate from a table carved from a monkey-puzzle tree, laden with about forty dishes of food.

Tuan held up a goblet of absinthe for a toast.

"To my newest soldier," he said.

The licorice-flavored drink went down hard and sizzled with an afterbite of burned sugar.

Apparently, Qingzhao bartered the terra-cotta warriors with Tuan for supplies and intelligence. The figures she had discovered near the idol in the shrine room had great value, even as damaged as they were. The two empty slots Gabriel had noticed were remnants of earlier deals between Qingzhao and Tuan; their collaboration had been ongoing for the better part of a year.

"Barter being the best form of trade?" asked Gabriel.

Tuan nodded.

Gabriel surveyed the table. "My apologies, but this seems like an awful lot of food for three people."

"I am showing off," Tuan smiled. "Forgive me."

"It will feed others when we are done," said Qingzhao. "Tuan is responsible for filling many bellies."

"So," Gabriel said, returning to the subject of the clay warriors, "value for value. Like the black market in religious ikons in Russia."

"Not quite," said Tuan. "The Russian way provided an interesting lesson on the subject of smuggled antiquities, because so many of their black- and gray-market religious ikons were forgeries. Of course, one of my business interests is a thriving popular outlet for *replica* warriors. We've copied most of the basic templates from the warriors found in the Xian pits and the army of Emperor Qin. We do custom paintjobs. We even have a service whereby your own features can be worked onto the terra-cotta warrior replica of your choice. My artisans use photographs of the subject. You'd be surprised at how many people want a recreation for their garden or foyer. How many people actually collect them."

"At a couple grand a pop, no doubt," said Gabriel. It was no different to him than some spinster collecting plates from the Franklin Mint. "But the replica market provides cover for moving the real warriors to private collectors who can't show them because it would be illegal to possess them."

"They pay for that privilege," said Tuan. "The funny thing is, the replica company actually started turning a profit last year. And most people cannot even discern authenticity, which has allowed the market in art forgeries to thrive the way it has."

It was true. Forgers had become so painstaking at their craft that the difference between a fake masterpiece (which hung in galleries and toured worldwide to the acclaim of millions) and the genuine article (which hung in someone's expensive, climate–controlled cellar and was available for viewing only by an elite few) had been reduced almost to nil. As far as the world was concerned, the fake was real. The real paintings only increased in value every time a subterranean auction was held, and sometimes the aficionados tried to screw each other. Michael had told him that half the Impressionists in the last Getty exhibition were bogus, but no one wanted to say so. What was the point in starting *that* blaze of controversy unless the whereabouts of the real ones were known?

The epidemic had gotten so dire that within the last five years, even the Mona Lisa had come under serious doubt. Which might explain her goofy, cryptic smile at last. *I'm a fake, boys.*

Tuan pushed back his seat. "My honored guest," he said. "Permit me the ill manner of a private conversation with Qi."

"Qi?" said Gabriel.

"My diminutive for our delectable little fighter. You have no doubt already felt the strange attraction she exerts."

She lowered her gaze.

"No doubt," Gabriel said.

He handed Gabriel a puzzle box of closely worked unlacquered cedar. "We have a few small affairs of business to transact that are not for all ears to hear."

Gabriel accepted the box with mild interest. It called to mind nothing so much as the Rubik's Cube he'd held just days before in Michael's office.

"We'll be nearby," Tuan said. "While we're gone, perhaps you will find this interesting to examine. What most people call a Chinese puzzle box, the kind one buys in the so-called 'Chinatowns' of various cities, is actually a Japanese configuration. Historically this has disallowed inquiry into something uniquely Chinese—a different configuration and puzzle strategy, now overwhelmed by the more common Japanese variants. This one is authentic. Its purpose is not to test skill at solving a mere puzzle…"

"But to test the mettle of the solver," Gabriel said, feeling a tiny surge of dread: of all the ways Tuan might have chosen to test him…!

Tuan and Qingzhao repaired to a curtained alcove to speak in hushed whispers while Gabriel considered the box in his hands.

He wanted to set it aside and perhaps wander near enough to the curtain to eavesdrop on the conversation, but he suspected that neither would be advisable. His host had been cordial so far—but he was clearly a dangerous man and not one to anger.

Gabriel reluctantly focused on the box in his hands. Classic puzzle boxes, he remembered, always featured sliding panels. But no part of this one appeared to slide in any direction. Thinking back to the Rubik's Cube that had so confounded him in New York, Gabriel began exerting mild stress on different parts of the box and sure enough, a triangular corner came free on a little interior hinge, now hanging out like a wing and spoiling the box's symmetry. After a one-eighty revolve, it settled back into its appointed corner upside-down, completing an ideogram that had previously been bisected. He recognized the ideogram: it translated roughly into "as above, so below." Accordingly, Gabriel twisted free the corner that was diagonally opposite—a corner that had not budged before. It flipped out and settled back with mild pressure, and Gabriel felt something *click* definitively inside the box.

Ah. Now we're getting somewhere.

The top of the box, he found, felt loose, as if it would slide if he pressed it. He did, and realized that the entire top half of the box could be eased away from the bottom half, turned like a knob and reseated. Each repositioning completed a Chinese character previously obscured or lost within the filigree of design.

The top half of the box displaced a quarter of its own length. Gabriel realized that if the bulky section could fold over, the box would retain its original size and shape. The engineering seemed impossible, but sure enough—*click*.

Now panels revealed themselves in the conventional manner. The wrinkle of an authentic Chinese box would be that some of the panels would be tricks, traps, or dead ends. These enigmas were dependent on the user's preconceptions of how such things might or might not work.

He pressed on one panel—

"A word of advice, my dear new friend," said Tuan, returning.

Gabriel was embarrassed not to have heard his approach. He'd been more wrapped up in solving the puzzle than he'd realized. He put the box down unfinished, hearing somewhere, in the back of his head, Michael's voice chastising him. *You give up on things too easily.*

"Qi has told me of your adventures and difficulties," said Tuan. "I would say you should not expect to leave China, if that is your thought. You are on Cheung's map now. The caution you take should be threefold.

Really, if it was safety you sought, you should not have even dared to come back into the city at all."

"Mind reader," said Gabriel.

THEY LEFT TUAN IN HIS DEN AND RETURNED, painstakingly to where they'd first met him. The old couple was gone.

Gabriel wanted to ask Qingzhao what she'd gotten in exchange for the priceless terra-cotta warrior this time, but he was prepared to wait to grill her—about this and her relationship with Cheung—till they were alone, far from prying ears and eyes.

Coming in and out of central Shanghai could be like stepping into a time machine. Barely outside the city limits, the terrain and people seemed to come from far in the past. Gabriel had once seen the backlots of Shanghai Film Studio, where an entire small city had been constructed for the purposes of shooting movies. During Gabriel's visit, the street had been dressed as 1933 Shanghai right down to the fake billboard for *King Kong*, in service of an epic called *Temptress Moon*; on the adjacent lot, you found yourself on the same city street, 200 years earlier. Driving through the streets of the city proper could feel a lot like that, antiquity and modernity rubbing shoulders block by crowded block.

It was easy for Gabriel to close his eyes—once again in a pedicab with Qingzhao—and imagine he was some European interloper from ages ago, racing along the cobblestones toward a meeting with Kangxi Shih-k'ai or one of his lieutenants.

The illusion was enhanced a moment later when he heard a pair of gunshots and, looking up, saw twin holes punched in the canvas flap next to his head. He had a fleeting sense of high-velocity projectiles passing inches from his face and then two more holes appeared in the flap next to Qi.

Somebody was shooting at them.

8

GABRIEL REACHED FORWARD TO PULL THE PEDICAB driver out of the line of fire.

The man was already dead, holed through the neck and chest.

The pedicab came to a lurching halt, pitching forward, crashing into a gent on a bicycle and sending him cartwheeling into the air.

Gabriel and Qi dived out and flattened in opposite directions, hugging cobblestones slicked with night mist.

Rolling on his back, Gabriel groped for his newly acquired Colt, still wrapped in cheesecloth and now sitting in the middle of the street as citizens, heedless to the silenced gunfire, crowded around and stumbled over him.

Then he had to claw the big .45 cartridges from his pocket. Conventional wisdom with guns like this held that one should load five shells and leave the hammer down on an empty chamber, since the gun had nothing that could remotely be interpreted as a safety. Gabriel always—*always*—loaded six.

Qi had already whipped out a sleek automatic from a spine scabbard and was seeking targets.

Several gunners in black, with hoods, materialized out of the throng to rake the pedicab with machine-gun fire. It vaporized into toothpicks and floating chaff as Gabriel rolled, sighted prone, and discharged his new gun for the first time. It kicked hard and roared like a cannon, a curling gout of fire licking from the muzzle. One of the gunners arched into the air and fell—a high center hit—knocking down several people who were stampeding at the sound and sight of gunfire.

Gabriel lifted the shattered wheel of the pedicab and with one mighty swing dislocated the jaw of a second shooter who'd run towards him. Almost instantly two more thugs focused their attention on the *guilo* and Gabriel found himself in an unwilling three-way.

He kicked out at one guy grabbing him, heard the picket crack of a blown kneecap, and swung the man into his nearest neighbor. Gabriel had dropped his gun; he retrieved it now and put a round into the chest of one attacker.

Where were the police when you wanted them? A show of force by some of China's ubiquitous uniformed keepers of order might have put an end to this melee. But the police were no more anxious to rush headlong into a situation that might get them killed than anyone else would be, a guilty reality that could cost you your existence if somebody abruptly opened fire on your pedicab.

As he took down another attacker with a slash of his gun hand across the man's face only to see two more pop up in his place, Gabriel wondered: how many shooters were he and Qi worth?

In the words of a famous bank robber: *all of them.*

Gabriel rather indecorously shoved a woman laden with wicker baskets aside as he thumb-cocked the hammer of the Colt one-handed and blew a round into an assailant who surely would have shredded the woman for a chance to nail Gabriel. The big lead slug spanged off the attacker's AK-47, destroying the breech and rendering the gun useless except as a club. It also took away two of the attacker's fingers, putting him out of the fight.

Bullet Number Four reaped a lucky hit, passing through one gunner and into the guy behind him. They would probably live, too, but they dropped their weapons and fell down, and that was all that mattered to Gabriel at the moment.

Gabriel looked around furiously, finally catching sight of Qi as she discarded her now-empty weapon and took on a barreling adversary by imploding a wire birdcage over his head and then delivering an expert pointed-toe kick to a nerve bundle near the man's groin that put him down, spasming. Qi swiftly took charge of her victim's pistol.

Gabriel reversed-out to a kneeling position and fanned his last two shots, blossoming two bright glurts of blood across the chest of another black-clad man seconds away from doing the same to him.

Gabriel leaped to his feet and barreled toward Qi, taking advantage of an instant's lull. If there were a second wave coming, it was stalled long enough for Gabriel to locate Qi and turn an ambush into hot pursuit.

"Come on!" he yelled, grabbing her hand and almost spoiling her aim as she plugged a masked gunner.

"No, this way!" she yelled back. Gabriel accepted

the change of direction; she'd know the streets here better than he would.

Two blocks away, Gabriel and Qi folded into the shadows of a wet bricked alleyway. "Lose your jacket," she said, quickly stripping off her top and revealing a black lace brassiere with a thick backstrap. She mussed his hair, ripped the bandage from his head. "I'm a prostitute, you're a client, we're both drunk."

With his jacket discarded on the ground, the spent Colt was conspicuous in his hand; he had no place to hide it. He reluctantly plunged it into a nearby vendor's basket at the alley's far end. As they moved out of the shadows, Gabriel could not help a mournful backward glance at his forsaken hogleg. Its weight in his hand had been comforting and familiar. But it had done its job. It had saved his life.

Threading her arm around his waist, Gabriel led Qi back out into the seething crowds on the street. She bumped one hip into him and forced him to misstep. She was like a warm, skittish animal in his grasp. She laughed and chewed on his neck. Two gunmen were walking right toward them when she grabbed a fistful of his hair and spun him into a devouring full-on kiss, working his mouth hungrily as though she really meant it.

The gunmen split and walked around them, scanning the shadows past them in a desperate attempt to spot their prey.

Gabriel half expected Qi to turn and go after the men from behind and he raised one hand to stop her, but she whispered, "No," as if reading his mind. "We must get back to the motorcycle."

Gabriel's lips were still tingling. She tasted like mangoes and rare spice. Night-blooming jasmine. "The motorcycle," he agreed.

* * *

"DON'T YOU DARE GET AN ERECTION, OR I'LL HAVE TO shoot you."

They were immersed to the collarbones inside a large cauldron of steaming water, which they had bucketed over from a wood fire inside the second of the leaning pagoda's shrine rooms. Pressed herbs floated on the cloudy surface. Qi had insisted Gabriel join her—for purely therapeutic reasons, she explained, after she had applied antibiotic ointment to his head wound and to a new gouge, raw and red, that he'd acquired on the side of his neck.

As she'd climbed in across from him, Gabriel had noticed that Qi had a tattoo of some Chinese character on one hipbone. Oddly ridged with skin, as though to mask a wound. He did not ask about it.

She closed her eyes. After the action of the day the heat was penetrating to the bone, making them both dopey.

"You may ask me now," she said, not opening her eyes.

"I'm not an interrogator," said Gabriel, squeezing water between his palms. "But I would like to know."

"My father used to bathe me. One day, I remember, he took very special care to make me presentable."

"Special day?"

"Mmm. The day he sold me."

Gabriel's eyes narrowed. "Sold you?"

"At the Night Market. Where we just were, today. And *he* bought me."

"Cheung?"

Qi opened her eyes, gazing at him, frank, stark, unashamed. Her eyes were like black volcanic glass in the flickering light. "It fed the rest of my brothers and sisters. This is *not* America, Mr. Hunt."

Gabriel already knew that centuries of entrenched Chinese dogma and cultural preference held that female children were "undesirable." The modern one-child-per-couple mandate had only made the situation worse. In the past, female children were abandoned; today they could be aborted if an ultrasound revealed a female child in utero—a practice some called "gendercide."

It also stacked the census deck to the point where Chinese men had begun to outnumber women by a significant degree. Far from making unmarried women more desirable, women had come to be treated even *less* humanely… and the world's second oldest profession—bond slavery—had come into a new underworld vogue. The border between China and North Korea was commonly called a "wife market," as thousands of female Korean refugees from economic privation flooded forth to find Chinese husbands. They were destined to be sold in the bars and karaoke clubs of the Chinese mafia, if they weren't scooped up first by the predatory "women hunters" who preyed on the exploding market. Few men were willing to say they had bought a wife, but that didn't mean they weren't willing to buy one. They knew they were getting someone pliable, hard-working and submissive. And from the women's point of view, better that than starving to death in North Korea, watching your family die around you. A Korean woman cost between 240 and 1,700 Euro (about $300-$2,500 American dollars, depending on exchange rates) in a country where the per capita rural income was little more than a hundred bucks a year. Korean customs officers were routinely greased to the tune of $80 per person to cross the border. The bought women were then provided with the birth stats and name of a dead Chinese (for an additional fee), prompting an upsurge in identity traffic among China's legitimate dead.

Needless to say, beauty, age, physical condition, virginity and health were all factored into a woman's price. Qingzhao would not have been brought to market as a mere baby factory or working wife. She was young, attractive, robust, and healthy, and even more importantly, *not Korean*, and so had been brokered to the extreme high-end of the human traffic sector—the highest bidders, the shielded and protected elite who gathered at only the most clandestine rendezvous.

"My tag was here." She pointed to her left earlobe. A triangle of piercings there. Gabriel had assumed it was for jewelry.

"And this." Standing, she indicated the tattoo Gabriel had glimpsed on her hip, distorted with scar tissue. "Cheung put it there. I tried to cut it off once. It didn't hurt." She poked the area. "Now it has no feeling—none at all."

She dismissed the topic with a haughty sniff and sat down again. The last thing she wanted was pity. "In time, I became Cheung's administratrix of protection. Head of security."

"You were his bodyguard? Like that guy I saw take Cheung through a plate glass window at the casino?"

"Not like him. No simple employee could ever gain *that* much of Cheung's confidence. No woman, either." She pulled her knees to her chin in an aerobic stretch.

"Who is he?"

"Longwei Sze Xie. His given name means 'dragon greatness.' He is commonly called 'Ivory.' No one knows why."

"How did you leave Cheung's... employ?"

"Cheung and Ivory became convinced that I would serve as an adequate sacrifice for a bad business decision."

"Michelle Quantrill was in the same kind of situation," said Gabriel. "She was falsely implicated, too. When Cheung killed her sister, he left Michelle to take the heat. I got her out of jail and told her to stay put, but she assumed her sister's identity to come here and..." Gabriel trailed off. "Well you know the rest. It didn't work out."

"And why did you come?"

"To talk her out of what she was trying to do."

"Why?"

"Because I knew something bad would happen to her, like what *did* happen to her. I think she knew it, too. I just don't think she cared."

"She came as a ghost, then," Qi said contemplatively. "She was already dead. I knew we were linked when I first saw her. I just *knew.*"

They sat regarding each other for a silent moment. The connections between people are not reducible to hard statistics, Gabriel knew. Sometimes attraction was a thing of looks and moments, half-drawn breaths and secret approval. Intuitive, as when things denied logic yet felt correct. He resisted the urge to lean forward, to taste the spice again.

"I betrayed no one," Qi said, "regardless of what they claimed. And I survived their attempts to destroy me. Twice now I have tried to take him, and twice I have failed. Once in the Pearl Tower. Once at the Zongchang casino. I failed the second time because your friend was in my line of fire—on a similar mission, though I did not know it."

"And you think you owe yourself another stab?"

Gabriel could not quite bring himself to say, *Let it go; get past it.* Qi would just ignore him if he did. "He's not just going to forget your face. He'll see you coming."

"I want nothing less," she said quietly.

"Then you'll die, same as Michelle did."

"As long as he dies first."

Gabriel had encountered fatalism before, and zealotry, and devotion to a cause; but rarely held with this combination of unquestioning conviction and yet so little emotion.

"I know when the children will next be sold at the Night Market," she said. "Cheung will be there. From high places, the rich bid on the poor. I can kill him there. But I cannot do it alone. Think on this for a night. Do not answer now. I am going to sleep."

With a complete absence of shame or self-consciousness, Qi rose from the cauldron naked, stepped over its iron side, and walked away, leaving a trail of wetness on the ground. Her body was lean and hard, muscular, pantherish. Before she'd turned, Gabriel had seen there was another ungainly X of scar tissue beneath her left breast, where some other possessive malefactor had tried to brand her, or take something away from her. Gabriel watched her until she was out of sight, engulfed by the night.

After a moment sitting alone in the cooling water, Gabriel rose dripping and got his gear, because there was work to do before sunrise.

IT TOOK THE BETTER PART OF TWO HOURS FOR Gabriel to clean, hack, and chip away the main debris around the base of the giant bronze statue presumed to be warlord Kangxi Shih-k'ai, in the second shrine room.

He had to work by fire and lantern-light, with brushes
and chisels, the way the old-school guys had before
the intrusion of modern conveniences like floodlights.
Had workmen built this cumbersome thing inside the
shrine? Had they built it somewhere else and hauled
it here, and if so… how? It was impossible to calculate
the sheer tonnage of the idol, but it would take an
earth-mover to budge it.

It had to be constructed of sections, Gabriel
concluded. Components. Which meant seams. He had
thought of this angle of attack while puzzling over the
cunningly engineered box back at Tuan's. The base of
the idol was a crude rectangular metal slab, not nearly
as detailed as the rest of the statue. It was aesthetically
offensive. Why? Nothing about the composition of an
idol like this was an accident.

Here, on one face of the pedestal, were ideograms.
Spackled with the "alpha decay" common to
archeological bronze, the writing was invisible
until Gabriel was able to sculpt out the calcareous
accretions. Perhaps here were instructions, clues,
leads; unfortunately, the language variant was one
Gabriel did not recognize. And on the other faces of
the pedestal—nothing. No marks at all.

The dry environment of the room and mountainside
had helped retard corrosion, but nothing could stop
the process. Using an improvised potter's cut-off tool
he fabricated from a nail and a paintbrush handle,
Gabriel was able to scrape the patina of ages from a
small seam about two inches down from the top of
the base. Following it, he was able to describe a small,
rough rectangle about a foot high. It did not appear
to want to travel anywhere laterally, so Gabriel struck
it with a hammer. The metal made a loud clang like a

muffled bell, but Qi did not come running.

Decay and flakes of oxidized metal sifted floorward. Gabriel hit it again.

The rectangle had sunk into the pedestal about an eighth of an inch. Maybe the pedestal was hollow. Rough acoustics indicated it might be.

Bang, again. And again.

Whatever this little component did, it had not done it for nearly a century, and it resisted easy cooperation. But every time Gabriel struck it, it retreated into the base a bit further until it was sunk nearly half a foot...

...revealing a small inset on the right-hand side, like the dado joint on a drawer. Gabriel could just curl his fingers around it. It was meant to be pulled out, like a lever.

Using all of his strength and most of his weight, Gabriel was able to budge it about half an inch. He then lost another half-hour devising a rudimentary block-and-tackle system to loop around the exposed end and leverage it.

He had to have more than one warm body on this line. He took a break to wash down some caffeine pills he found in one of Qi's bags with a draught of strong (though cold) coffee, and went to seek his mysterious partner.

He found her asleep on a pallet on the third level of the pagoda, still naked though tightly bound up inside the punctured sheet of tin, which she'd wrapped around her torso and secured with wet leather thongs that constricted as they dried. It was like a penitent's scourging corset and looked intensely painful, but Qi seemed sound asleep.

Then Gabriel caught the flickering residual tang in the air and realized that among the other provisions

Tuan had supplied Qi, besides food, weapons and equipment, there had been a dose of opium. The long pipe was still at her side like a snoozing demon lover.

9

THE WORKINGS OF THE PEDESTAL PROVED MORE frustrating to operate than a public telephone in Beijing.

The hidden lever freed itself by degrees, measured in Gabriel's sweat. At full cock it released a panel on the far side of the iron base. The panel was heavier than the door in a Swiss bank vault and meant to be slid horizontally backward into a recess in the wall that was clotted with decades—perhaps more than a century—of mulch, roots, and earth. Gabriel spent the better part of an hour scraping dirt before he realized the sheer weight of the door would prevent him from moving it; it wasn't as though it was on ball bearings or a hydraulic arm or something.

He hit upon using Qi's motorcycle as a conscripted assistant, since Qi was definitely out of the action.

The revving four-stroke engine raised a hellacious chainsaw racket and the spinning high-treads kicked back a tsunami of dust from the floor. In the lantern light it looked as though the shrine room was on fire. Russet clouds rolled and settled on everything, including Gabriel, who had begun to look a bit like a terra-cotta warrior himself.

The iron panel, nearly a foot thick, was gradually inched backward until there was a gap into which Gabriel could shove a lantern. He saw the boundaries of a twelve-by-twelve cobwebbed room—beneath the base of the statue—and the edge of a stoneworked archway that indicated the passage went deeper.

After more revving and straining, the space became big enough for Gabriel to wriggle through. He was parched from his exertions, though he had already drunk at least two quarts of water, and his shoulders pulsated with fatigue. He grabbed some road flares from Qi's stores along with a flashlight and an extra lantern. He'd figured he'd need all the light he could get.

The interior directly beneath the statue's base, sheeted in iron, was disappointingly vacant. It bore the musty mothball smell of old, dead air.

Past the archway was another room lined with wooden shelves, many of which had dried out, become porous, and collapsed over time. Arrayed upon the shelves that remained were hundreds of miniature warriors, each about nine inches in height and made of fired porcelain. Many of them had been unceremoniously dumped by time and the crumbling shelves; they lay in shards on the floor, which also appeared to be metal, judging by how his footsteps rang against it whenever they weren't squashing something underfoot. He was within what amounted to a big iron box, Gabriel concluded, one that could only be accessed via the statue's base—metal above, below, and except for the archway he'd entered through and another on the far wall, all around, so no one could dig their way in.

Gabriel recalled Emperor Qin's city-sized necropolis, which had been constructed in relative secrecy and then hidden away underground. Logistically speaking, it would have been much more difficult for Favored Son Kangxi Shih-k'ai to pull off such a feat at the beginning of the twentieth century, when labor was more dear and secrecy harder to come by. Perhaps he had rendered his vaunting self-tribute only in miniature, except for the handful of life-size guardians Qi had found in the room outside. Enough niches spun off from this chamber to suggest there might be several thousand doll-soldiers here.

Was this Kangxi Shih-k'ai's grand joke on history?

Was *this* the great prize Cheung sought?

From what Mitch Quantrill had told Gabriel, the would-be warlord thought he was going to claim his putative ancestor's skeleton—which the great man would've been hard-pressed to have inserted into something the size of an action figure.

Gabriel popped a flare and dropped it on the floor. That was when he first saw that the metal surface he was standing on was writhing with worms and salamanders. He examined a nightcrawler under his flashlight. It looked like some sort of troglobitic millipede with a nasty oval mouth. Some were as much as a foot long.

That meant…

Then he noticed the heavily ammoniac, compost stench wafting toward him from the far archway. Opening the portal had caused a tiny bit of air movement, and the flow was eye-watering.

That also meant…

...that there had to be another way in.

Quickly he drew a small automatic pistol—also procured from Qi's stores—and advanced behind his upheld light toward the second archway.

Stone stairs wound down into blackness. The stench was already a physical thing as oppressive as wrapping your head in piece of rotting cloth.

The stairs were long disused, crumbling, slicked with a gray organic fluid that glistened with phosphorescent mold spores. It was like walking on treacherous ice, the kind that could upend you and send you sprawling.

He was traversing downward at about a thirty-degree angle. He could hear trickling water now. He had to duck; the headroom was low.

The stairs broadened into a tiny pavilion with carved rails, all of it indistinguishable beneath caked, stinking muck.

Twin terra-cotta sentries stood mute guard over the pavilion with long-corroded weapons of bronze that had rotted away to stubs and flakes. The standing soldiers appeared to have been dunked in cake batter and left to decay for a century. Their features were not apparent. They were clotted and blob-like, runny pseudo-human monstrosities, more manlike in size and general outline than in any internal detail.

The pavilion faced a grand chamber at least the size of a football field. The distant sound of a small stream or other subterranean waterway was louder here, joining with the other ambient noises and echoing slightly, indicating that this was a *very* big room.

The whole place was a hibernaculum.

The concave dome of the ceiling was wall-to-wall with thousands of nesting bats. He could identify at least three species at this distance—the horseshoe bat, the long-fingered bat, and the roundleaf bat. There were also lizards and annelids and other scavenger-parasites that fed on bat guano, which would be abundant indeed here.

Gabriel stepped forward very cautiously.

To either side of the pavilion he could now make out two large, hinged wooden constructions like catapults or small cranes. A shaft held an ironbound basket the size of a bale of hay aloft over a reservoir which Gabriel presumed had once been filled with water, long-since evaporated.

And below, massed on the floor of the huge chamber, standing in a foot-deep tar-pit of urine and guano, was Kangxi Shih-k'ai's army of life-sized figures.

Then Gabriel heard Qi calling out to him from above, as loudly as she could, and thousands of bats took wing, flying straight for him.

10

GABRIEL SMASHED THE ONLY FUEL LANTERN HE HAD to make a pool of fire near the archway during his hasty retreat, but the bats' sonar had unerringly informed them of a new way out of the cave. Some of them sported a wingspan of two feet or more.

From Qi's point of view it was as though Gabriel was propelled out of the base of the idol by an unbroken thunderhead of swarming bats.

They were not vampires or the dreadnaught-sized killers of the Amazon, but this many airborne teeth and claws could make life terribly inconvenient, especially if the horde was hungry.

Gabriel struck Qi like a linebacker, sprawling them both onto the floor, shielding her face and burying his own into her shoulder in a duck-and-cover as the black beehive madness of the bats filled the shrine room. Eventually they would peter out and find their way into the night. They were just bats. But Gabriel did not know if Qi harbored any phobias or other reactive behaviors that might complicate their survival right now.

When the first wave ebbed, they worked together to seal the sliding iron portal. With two pairs of shoulders and thighs heaving and amped up on adrenaline, they no longer required the motorcycle to move the door.

Stragglers winged wildly about the upper reaches of the room. Gabriel looked as though he had lost a paintball fight, and this time Qi's reaction could not be dammed back. She found his appearance hilarious.

"Very funny," said Gabriel.

"I suppose you'll be wanting to use the bath again?" she said.

"Briefly," he said.

"Bats are good luck all over Asia."

"But not all over my head." Gabriel made his way to the other shrine, stripping off his shirt as he went.

"My mother used to tell me," Qi said, following, "if a bat lands on your head, you should hope the cricket sees rain coming because the bat won't get off your head until it hears thunder."

He ducked his head under the now cool water, ran his fingers through his hair. He finally came up for air again.

Qi was still beset with mirth over Gabriel's condition. It buoyed him to see that Qi *could* laugh.

He described for her what he'd found in the giant chamber below the statue.

"It's almost worth telling Cheung," Qi said. "The thought of him rooting like a pig through tons and tons of dung, looking for his precious skeleton. On his knees. Slowly being driven mad by the smell."

"Except that he'd send lackeys to do the digging while he watched from a safe distance," Gabriel said.

"Yes, and then shoot them when they finished." Qi

wasn't laughing anymore. "I want to see this room for myself."

"Then why'd I bother getting cleaned up?" Gabriel said. But the truth was, he wanted to see it again, too. His explorer glands were firing hotly already, reinvigorating him; he could feel the gnawing need to *find out* burning in his brain afresh. Was one of the figures Kangxi Shih-k'ai? If so, which one? You'd think a man with an ego like that would put himself at the head of his army, leading it—but in the quick glance he'd gotten, there hadn't seemed to be such a 'leader' figure. And to find any one figure hidden among the lot of them, one would have to spend hours digging through calcified strata of crap.

"Let's go," he said. "Before the lucky wildlife returns."

GABRIEL'S SECOND DESCENT YIELDED THREE BITS OF information.

One: that the bats obviously had some other way in and out of the mountainside, some path yet undiscovered, since a good portion of them had returned by the time he and Qi went down, and more filtered in every minute. Qi and Gabriel moved slowly and quietly, to avoid triggering another mad onrush.

Two: that the catapult/crane devices were some ancient form of automated defense against intrusion into the chamber, though fortunately they had long since rotted into inutility. Peering at them more closely, Gabriel saw they were still loaded up with fist-sized iron spheres protruding with spikes on all sides. He lifted one, hefted it briefly, and dropped it back into place, then wiped his hand on the seat of his pants. He wouldn't have wanted to see even one of those flying his way, never mind the hundred or so piled up here.

And three: that Kangxi Shih-k'ai's lost terra-cotta army... wasn't.

"These aren't statues," Gabriel whispered, after examining one from close up. "They're bodies. Skeletons now, but bodies when they were planted here." He pointed at the metal shaft sticking up from the ground and continuing into the seat of the figure's rotting armor. "He dressed them up in battle gear and rammed them upright onto spiked poles. I'm guessing they were alive at the time."

Qi's expression darkened at the revelation.

"I can't imagine even the most devoted warrior army submitting to that sort of death," Gabriel said. "He must have conscripted a special group of victims for the purpose."

"Peasants," she muttered. "Slaves."

"I thought it was just hyperbole when they called Kangxi Shih-k'ai the 'Vlad of China,'" Gabriel said. "But this... There must be more than a thousand people here, all murdered at his hand. And for what? To provide him with... human mannequins for this display?"

They made their way carefully back up to the shrine and forced the doorway shut.

"So these are not the Killers of Men we have found," said Qi. "They are not the members of his army." She took a mouthful of water from a dipper and spat it out on the ground. Gabriel understood the impulse.

"Well, there's no way to know, but I doubt it," Gabriel said. "More likely they're people his army rounded up as a sort of mass sacrifice when Kangxi Shih-k'ai died."

Qi bowed her head. She spoke quietly. "One of the

reasons this area has been abandoned as far back as anyone can remember was a belief that the area was full of ghosts. People said it was haunted by spirits in pain. My mother said people were telling stories like that when she was a girl."

"That would have been, what, in the sixties? Back then there might still have been people alive who had been children when the slaughter took place. Maybe even some who'd been adults."

"Maybe even one or two who'd participated in it," said Qi darkly, "and wanted the traces never to be uncovered."

"Maybe."

"In any event," Qi said, "it's been a no man's land for most of the past century. No one comes here. Except ghosts like me."

Her gaze was abstracted into the small fire they'd built.

"Qi," Gabriel said. "I know your priority is Cheung—"

"My *life* is Cheung. My death, too."

"—but there's something bigger here. The world should know about this discovery."

"So let them know. When Cheung and I are dead."

"There's no reason you have to die." Gabriel tried to take her hand, but she harshly jerked it away.

"Share this discovery with me," he said. "Let me get you safely out of China. The Hunt Foundation has influence, and once we reveal this to the world… we can take action against Cheung in other ways. And we can keep you safe."

"Can you? Can you really? Cheung's men came all the way to New York to murder your friend's sister. They would not hesitate to find me, track me like an animal, and kill me like less than an animal." She fixed Gabriel with a hooded gaze. "You're going to say I could change my identity perhaps. Maybe I could get surgery to alter my appearance, the way Cheung did. No. None of it will matter, in the end. You have not accepted the inevitability of this."

"I don't believe in inevitability," said Gabriel.

"It doesn't matter what you believe," Qi said, shaking her head.

Gabriel was not accustomed to feeling impotent. The Foundation, the specialists he knew, the money he could wield. None of it mattered here in a part of China where it might as well have been hundreds of years ago, where a flock of bats had the power to defeat him and a young woman could embrace a suicide mission because she saw her own death as inevitable.

"If you wish to help me," Qi said, "you can. But there is only one way. By coming with me to the Night Market."

"And doing what?"

"You can get close to Cheung. He doesn't know what you look like. I doubt his men do either—at most they have a blurry image from the cameras on the ship, probably not even that."

"You're forgetting they found us after we left the Night Market, when they ambushed us in the pedicab."

"They were following me, not you. You could have been anyone. And no one who got a good look at your face that night lived to tell."

Gabriel thought back to the brutal firefight in the street. It was true enough. "So what, exactly, do you have in mind?"

"We can both return to the Night Market, Gabriel Hunt. I as a vengeful ghost. You—you as a bidder."

"A bidder," Gabriel said.

"A wealthy foreign guest," Qi said, reaching out with one hand to stroke along his cheek, "with a taste for young Chinese flesh. Cheung will probably pour you a drink himself."

11

QUITE ABRUPTLY, GABRIEL FOUND HIMSELF BACK IN the world. Clean clothes, wired cash, at least semi-legitimate to all outward appearance but for the recent scars on his head and neck. Michael Hunt was in the air over the Pacific Ocean, racing to pick up the lecture series where it had so unceremoniously been abandoned. Gabriel had e-mailed him a brief, discreet summary of everything that had happened, using carefully veiled language on the theory—hell, the certainty—that all outbound e-mail sent from the complimentary terminal in a five-star hotel's business center would be read by the authorities. He'd sent another even briefer message to Lucy, at the anonymous e-mail address she'd given him before getting on the plane for Arezzo: *Am still in China, L, but M is gone—I'm sorry*. Her response: *Gone missing or gone dead?* To which he replied, *Don't know which. Doesn't look good.*

She hadn't written back.

Meanwhile, Gabriel prepared for his visit to the Night Market and his meeting with a contact called Red Eagle. Earlier in the day Qi had pulled together an assortment of goods—galvanized steel pails, tensile wire, firecrackers and cherry bombs, several large jute bags of money all in coins. She did not specify their purpose. But she had pointed out several other things to Gabriel as they toured incognito, both their faces hidden behind the popular surgical-style paper masks many pedestrians wore and shaded by widebrimmed hats.

"Nine corners," she had said, indicating the zigzag bridge to the Tea House. "Nine turns, so that evil spirits will become disoriented and cannot pursue you." Gunmen, Gabriel knew, might not be as likely as spirits to get disoriented, but the nine turns could still help break up lines of sight—and of fire.

Qi's combat access to the Night Market was via tunnels beneath the Tea House, part of the old aqueduct system, and she'd showed him the exit she would use tonight. "Tuan has all the best maps," she noted, adding that on auction nights, Cheung would have all the surface entrances and exits heavily fortified.

She had stopped next to a stand whose sign read CRISPY FRIED ANTS—MARINATED SCORPION—TURTLE SHELL GELATIN and ordered a vile-looking beverage from the vendor, a tiny man in an Edwardian suit with the obligatory status-symbol label sewn to his outer left cuff.

"God—what *is* that?" said Gabriel, his throat constricting at the sight of it. The stuff looked like deep red cough syrup with a floating skin of herbs.

"Double Penis," she replied. "Deer and bull. Good for bones, circulation, heart, memory."

"Also is excellent aphrodisiac," said the vendor with a sly wink. He pointed out the source organs, hanging from a drying rack. The deer members looked like rawhide doggie treats two feet long. The bull penis was the size of a Louisville Slugger.

"Drink," Qi said, as though sealing some covenant between them. "It's expensive."

Gabriel downed the viscid brew, keeping his eye on a Tibetan spinning a prayer wheel in the distance. He swallowed twice, then swallowed again. It seemed there was now a smoldering lump of raw lead between his lungs.

Qi had moved on to a small shrine with an urn for burning money. She lit joss sticks, bowed, and offered some bills to the pot.

"Now you," she said, gesturing for Gabriel to do likewise.

"But I don't believe in—"

"You must believe in *something*," she said, eyes flashing.

That had been their afternoon. Now it was night-time.

Showtime.

THE IRON FIST WAS EXACTLY WHAT ITS NAME IMPLIED: an under-the-table combat venue hiding in plain sight, where human beings tried to beat each other to death for money. Gabriel passed through several dining rooms and then a billiard hall before he found the grand stairway for which he was looking. It swept upward into a well appointed—and well guarded—amphitheater from which he could already hear the flat, meaty sounds of flesh battering flesh, lubricated by blood.

But no crowd noise. No jeers or cheers or frantic yelling.

Gabriel was admitted through a curtained foyer. The central focus of the room was the fighting pit, an oval thirty feet across at its widest point, girdled by a chain-link barrier. Two gigantic urban predators, steroidal nightmares, sought to terminate each other in the pit. They were collared together by eight feet of chain. Each wore a spidery leather mask and a studded bludgeoning glove on one fist.

The room was opaque with cigarette smoke and crowded with bettors wall-to-wall, standing room only. They stood in total silence, like the spectators at a chess match. They wagered with nods and winks and raised fingers. Their manner was of banking, not bloodsport.

One of the fighters finally fell like a chopped oak and stayed still. He was dragged out of the ring by his feet. Then the onlookers came unglued, jabbering in fifteen languages, waving money, offering critique.

Two new opponents entered the ring. It was not obvious at first due to their masks and squarish figures, but they were both women.

"New fighters are always cause for excitement," said a voice behind Gabriel. "Their odds are not known."

"Do I know you?" said Gabriel.

The newcomer was a classically handsome Chinese man who looked like an executive or playboy, clad in an expensive tailored silk suit and obviously packing at least one sidearm in a shoulder rig. There was a fine-cut tightness to the material across his back that suggested body armor. His hair and eyes were jet. He smiled at Gabriel like a matinee idol.

"I am Longwei Sze Xie. Please call me Ivory, Mr. Hunt."

This was the part where Gabriel would discover whether any of his hasty fabrications would hold an ounce of water. They shook hands in the Western fashion.

"Do I stick out that obviously?" said Gabriel.

"Forgive me," said Ivory. "Part of my training. I always index newcomers… is 'index' the correct word?"

"I know what you mean."

Ivory pointed to the fighter on the far side of the pit. "That is the fresh fighter. Called Jin Huáng, for our purposes."

"Chinese for 'yellow' or 'golden'?"

"Very good, Mr. Hunt. Of course there are a hundred character variants for 'yellow' in traditional Chinese. Depending on the usage, *jin huáng* could be an expression for mulled rice wine, pornography, an eel, hell, or…"

"Or, if you reverse it to *huáng jin*," said Gabriel, "it refers to the Yellow Turbans peasant uprising at the end of the Later Han Dynasty." Gabriel silently thanked his brother Michael for this tidbit from his lecture notes, hoping he would not be called upon to discuss the matter in any more depth.

"Outstanding!" Ivory clapped his hands together. "Full marks. But then, of course, you are a man who knows his history."

"That's why I'd like to speak with Mr. Cheung."

"Mr. Cheung is available later this evening, and has expressed great interest in what you may be able to tell him about Kangxi Shih-k'ai. You understand his need for a considerable degree of discretion and personal security. After we complete this diversion—and please don't feel rushed in any way, if you are enjoying yourself—I should advise you in advance that I will have to search you, although I'm certain it is quite unnecessary."

O boy, thought Gabriel, *this guy is* really good *at his job.*

Jin Huáng danced into the fight, making her opponent swing the early blows, high, wide and powerful. None connected. She was going to air her opponent out a bit before wrecking and damage. The mob fell into library silence once more.

Gabriel and Ivory were able—and obliged—to whisper. Gabriel noticed the comm button seated in Ivory's right ear.

"I hope I'm not intruding on Mr. Cheung's, ah, other interests," said Gabriel. "I mean, I understand tonight is—"

"Do not speak further of that here," said Ivory. "That is privileged information. But rest assured I understand your meaning. You are an honored visitor here, and all courtesy must be extended."

Spoken by anyone else, it might have been a veiled threat.

"Watch the combatants," said Ivory. "There is no good or evil here. No ring characters or personae. Only a victor."

"The last person standing."

"Precisely."

Jin Huáng dropped low and launched a perfect pivot kick to her attacker's throat, which slammed the other woman down, sucking dirt in hulking gasps.

"Now, take a moment to admire that," said Ivory. "A single blow decides the outcome of the entire contest. It is always one single act. An atomic explosion or the twitch of a fly's wing—it is all the same, in all warfare, in all times. It always comes down to a single act at the correct time."

"That is what makes history," said Gabriel. "It's what makes my job interesting."

"Would you mind if I asked you what happened to your head?"

The scarlet crease from the bullet wound still defaced his temple in a spot impossible to hide or entirely cover with makeup, though he'd applied some in his hotel room. Perhaps the bullet had been fired at him by this very man, Ivory, with whom he was now conversing so pleasantly. The talk was lulling, almost coaxing or coddling, the kind of innocuous byplay that of course was just another form of warfare according to Sun Tzu.

"The Hunt Foundation jet has very small doors," Gabriel said ruefully. "Hatches. No headroom. It looks worse than it is."

"And your intelligence regarding Kangxi Shih-k'ai? What makes that special? Please forgive my natural curiosity."

"I assume you mean apart from the historical record?"

"Yes. Mr. Cheung is an expert on that particular warlord." The implications were clear, including *Don't waste our time* and *If this is a bluff, we'll know.*

"My father's journals," said Gabriel, not exactly lying. "He recorded certain information. Longitudes and latitudes. Parallel evidence. I believe he was on the verge of a breakthrough at the time of his death."

"That is a pity. A great loss."

"Maybe I can salvage some little piece of that loss," said Gabriel. "Maybe help find the Favored Son's tomb at last, with Mr. Cheung's help. It could benefit us both and become a great boon. For my father, not for me."

"Ah, now *that* I understand," said Ivory. "For you, it is personal, a matter of legacy and duty. An emotional involvement beyond statistics and records and treasure."

"Well, treasure wouldn't hurt…"

Ivory permitted himself a small laugh. "Exactly. Come with me. It is time for us to go present you to Red Eagle."

RED EAGLE WAS A FLORID, PASHA-LIKE WOMAN WHO tipped the scale at about 350 pounds. Her surroundings were garishly Japanese but she spoke with an inflection favoring an affect for the American South.

Her chambers opened onto a wide balcony about five stories up inside one of the subway-crush of tall buildings that broke up this area of the Night Market into a series of large atriums. A few other bidding balconies could be seen across the vast open space above the tents and stalls of the vendors below. From such a balcony, a select section of the Night Market could be locked down with no indication whatsoever to the outside world. Below, the Beggar's Arch and other tunneled accessways into this area would soon be sealed off by Cheung's security force.

Which was why Qingzhao had chosen to come in via the sewer.

Red Eagle took a dainty hit from a hookah and offered the pipe to a Mr. Yawuro, an Armani-suited African gangster with a complement of Masai bodyguards. Red Eagle's own guards and functionaries, Gabriel noticed, all seemed to be turbaned Sikhs. Cheung's men were all clad in black-on-black. There were three other bonebreakers in Secret Service wash-and-wear accompanying a boisterous Texan (complete with Stetson) named Carrington. The real problem of any meeting was finding a place to park all the bodyguards, and make sure their pecking order was not ruffled.

"Please try the quail eggs, Mr. Yawuro," said Red Eagle. "They're very special."

Carrington made a face and scanned the room for more whiskey.

Having satisfied Ivory's pat-down, Gabriel was presented.

Carrington squinted at him. "I know you," he said. "You're that explorer guy. You was at the North Pole awhile back."

"South Pole," said Gabriel, who knew Douglas Carrington III was an oil man. Inherited wealth. Global pollution. Third World usury.

"Why, hell, son—you're *famous*," the Texan said broadly, getting the notice of everyone in the room. Gabriel watched a pit-viper expression cross the man's tanned face. "And you're rich, too. But you ain't *this* rich." He spun on Red Eagle. There were questions of privacy and decorum to be dealt with here.

"I may not have as much as you," said Gabriel, "but I figured I could pick up something small." The Texan eyed him unhappily, as though detecting the undercurrent of sarcasm Gabriel was trying so hard to hide.

"He is here for *me*, Mr. Carrington," said Kuan-Ku Tak Cheung, interceding. "Be wise and do not insult my special guest, for he is a man who has at least *earned* his reputation."

Carrington actually blushed, then gruffly apologized and retreated.

Gabriel almost felt like blushing too, when in response to Cheung's endorsement Red Eagle began fussing over him. She giggled like an adolescent and kissed his cheek, leaving a smear of crimson lipstick. He found himself staring at her. There was, he thought, the distinct possibility that she was actually a he.

Gabriel's eye sought the seams of the illusion. Anything was possible here in this polyglot microcosm.

"I am honored to make your acquaintance face-to-face," said Cheung.

Gabriel could not help wondering what that phrasing meant: Was Cheung toying with him? Had he made Gabriel from the security footage from the casino?

"I have read your book," said Cheung with an eager smile.

"Which one?" said Gabriel.

"*Hunt Up and Down in the World*," said Cheung. "Your most incisive chronicle of excavation and underground exploration. Some of it is quite exhilarating. Exciting and improbable, almost like pulp fiction. It speeds the blood."

"I actually didn't write that book," Gabriel said, "in the strictest sense. It's more of an 'as-told-to.' Dahlia Cerras did the hard part, the donkey-work. But of course her name is smaller on the title page than mine."

"And nowhere at all on the cover," Cheung said, clucking gently. "Poetic license, then?"

"I try not to embroider too much."

He thought back on the book's compendium of snake pits, booby traps, torch-bearing locals, gunfights, and wild escapes. Yes, it probably would seem ridiculous… to anyone who had not been there.

"No literary aspirations?" said Cheung, apparently genuinely intrigued, leaving Ivory to keep an eye on the rest of the room.

"My brother Michael is more the author type," said Gabriel. "In that respect he takes after my parents. I'm afraid I'm the roustabout."

Gabriel also watched Ivory, watching Cheung. This man knew his exits, backstops, contingencies and cover plans. But there was something off about his manner. Ivory was a man of secrets, more than simple hired muscle. He seemed to command the bodyguards and thus be ranked higher. Not quite a partner of Cheung's, but not quite an employee, either.

"Our lots tonight include adult men and women," Red Eagle told her guests, clapping briskly to draw everyone's attention. "Psychics, androgynes, jesters, amputees. Ah, Ms. Carlsen."

A tall Scandanavian woman with an elaborate Maori neck tattoo had just joined them. She drew tiny bird-like sips from a cut crystal flute of champagne.

In his peripheral vision Gabriel saw Ivory running check-ins with his sentries. Very pointedly, none of the security men in the room were drinking.

There was no way, Gabriel knew, that Qi could take Cheung from ground level. She had to be lurking in one of the buildings across the way, with a good angle on the proscenium of Red Eagle's balcony.

Her chosen tool was a "slightly used" bolt-action British L115A1, a sniper rifle co-designed by an Olympic gold medalist shooter and chosen by the SAS to use against the Afghans in 2001. It could destroy the engine block of a truck at 1,200 meters. Body armor did not matter to this weapon.

Gabriel wrestled with the role he was about to play. He did not doubt that Cheung was an unsavory sort—but so far all of Cheung's crimes had been hearsay, not verified. *Someone* had killed Mitch's sister and someone had ordered the attack on the pedicab, but there was no way to be certain who. Meanwhile Qi was hardly the most stable person Gabriel had ever met. Her whole touching story (complete with pathos in all the right places) might have been fabricated to recruit him.

But perhaps Qi was right, and perhaps everything she'd told him was so. At least it jibed with what he'd heard from Mitch. That had to count for something.

Though the question of Gabriel's role remained. He was supposed to steer Cheung onto the balcony and into the path of a bullet. But why? If Qi had the capacity to shoot through a bodyguard to nail her target, why was Gabriel needed? As an on-site witness to confirm the kill?

Red Eagle rang a small gong to indicate commencement. Outside, from high above them, counterweighted cages began to lower into view on chains. The sale stock hung in the air before them like Christmas ornaments. In one cage a twelve-year-old girl stood with her hands on the bars and a tri-pronged lot tag stapled to her earlobe. He could have been looking at Qingzhao, fifteen years ago. The girl's eyes were dull with tears and she stood without energy or focus, as if she did not have any real awareness of where she was or what was transpiring.

In another cage, a Caucasian woman in her early twenties, same deal.

In another, an eight-year-old boy, twirling a black sucker in his mouth.

In another, a man with both forearms missing. He was the most active of the lot, scampering from one side of the cage to the other and calling out in a language Gabriel didn't recognize. He wore a fixed, forced smile, apparently trying to court bidder favor.

Mr. Yawuro pointed at the girl and said, "Open for ten thousand."

"Pacific dollars?" Red Eagle asked. The man nodded.

Cheung countered: "Eleven. In platinum."

If Qi was to be trusted, Cheung had the advantage, when bidding, of a man who knows he is giving money only back to himself. He attended these auctions to play the players.

"Mister Yawuro?" Red Eagle prompted.

"Twelve," Yawuro said.

Gabriel took a step forward and Cheung came forward with him. They had cleared the overhang and were now in plain sight. Ivory was already moving toward the balcony, to advise his master to back up.

Though it wasn't his turn to bid again, Yawuro uttered a small sound, like a chest cough. Then he was flung backward as the incoming round blew both of his lungs out through the back of his ribcage. His blood lingered on the air as fine red mist.

A second shot sizzled through the air, spanged off one of the hanging cages, missed Red Eagle's beehive hairdo by two inches and burrowed into the wall, starting a fire. A tracer bullet. *Why was Qi firing tracers?* thought Gabriel as he hit the deck. That would only happen if—

The muzzle of Ivory's big automatic was nestled beneath Gabriel's jaw, and from his prone sprawl Gabriel saw Cheung's other bodyguards all leveling firepower directly at his head.

Quite abruptly, as one of the men swung the butt of his gun at Gabriel's injured temple, Gabriel found himself out of the world again.

12

QINGZHAO COULD NOT BELIEVE SHE HAD MISSED THE shot, and quickly chambered her tracer—her followup round, to track and correct aimed fire.

She'd had Kuan-Ku Tak Cheung dead in her sights on the balcony across from her, with only a ten-degree angle of correction for a downward shot. The picture in the crosshairs told her that Cheung was history. Her trigger pull was a steady, clean, slow squeeze.

But the man standing next to Cheung had died instead.

Which meant that the sights on this ex-Royal Marines rifle had been tampered with.

Her tracer shot strayed to bounce off one of the hanging cages and ignited the wallpaper inside Red Eagle's eyrie. Perhaps it was because Qi, too, had seen the young girl up for sale, so much like herself, once; perhaps it was because Qi had fired with tears welling in her eyes? But no—the tracer proved the weapon's sights to be decalibrated. The scope was supposed to have been zeroed. It obviously had not been. Useless.

Even more useless: the adjustment ticks on the scope had been shaved down, preventing a fast adjustment with a coin edge or anything else.

Cheung was under cover by now. Ivory's response was frighteningly efficient.

She could have chambered the next powerful Magnum round and taken out one of the bodyguards, but there was little point.

Her window of time had spoiled faster than burning paper. Without checking the window again she fired up her pre-set fuses and ran from the room, abandoning the rifle and going hot on her backup pistol—a super-sized Ruger revolver, so as to avoid even the faintest possibility of a jam.

Ten seconds later, cherry bombs, M-80s and firecracker strings began to detonate around the perimeter below. This would give eager bodyguards false gunfire they would waste time trying to track. The final fuse crisped the support rope for her buckets of coins, which tumbled loose and sprayed a metallic rain of money from the sky, all jingling downward to spin and roll across the cobblestones of the Night Market. Everyone below would scramble to collect the coins, which was good for Qi's escape plan. Sentries would be blocked, hazarded, mobbed and traffic-jammed as they tried to fan out from the archways.

From the doorway into the wild free-for-all of the Night Market, it was five swift steps to the bridge to the Tea House. Qi sprinted across, zig-zagging. The propane tanks she had emplaced earlier were still in position. She shot each one with modified tracers like the big hazard-striped rounds she had used at Pearl

Tower. Both tanks combusted and blew spectacularly, punching the air out of the space with twin fireballs and lopping off the first fifteen feet of the bridge, which noisily redistributed itself over the surface of the pond water, blackjacking a few curious fish.

Inside the Tea House was a narrow stairway leading down to a supply room with a trapdoor in the floor. The access led down into the sewer system, where Qi had a small motorboat waiting.

Gabriel was not there to meet her as planned.

She had to leave the area now. She waited a few extra beats anyway.

At the very least, she had seen Cheung crawling on his hands and knees, clothing disheveled, panic on his face.

That would have to do until next time.

AT THE TOP OF THE PEACE HOTEL, CHEUNG COMMANDED an entire floor. From the elevators one walked across his Junfa Hall, a long corridor lined with statues of Chinese warlords and decorated with ostentatious Peking Opera weapons on wall displays. But for the sliding glass doors, all bulletproofed, and the sentries at each end, the hall held the stately ambience of a museum.

Ivory found Cheung in his Temple Room, a chamber enameled in shiny black and hung with silks. Cater-corner to a small shrine was a custom dentist's chair on a hydraulic riser. Mugwort leaves smoldered from a salver next to a sterile work tray.

A technician in a crimson medical tunic was meticulously inserting long acupuncture needles into Cheung's face and scalp.

Cheung indicated his eyebrow. "Here. Deeper."

Dinanath waited in one corner with the behemoth Tosa dogs on stand-down. Cheung ignored them and kept his gaze on Ivory.

Lurking silently in her usual corner was Sister Menga, a white-haired, pink-skinned Taoist soothsayer with the bearing of a lifelong martial arts practitioner. She was one of Cheung's spiritual advisors and seemed to thrive on breathing fog-thick incense smoke.

"Do we know whose base area is the Night Market?" said Cheung, already knowing the answer. Ivory nodded.

Cheung handed Ivory the small carved casket he had been tooling earlier. His expression was benign, yet made hideous by all the needles sticking out of his face.

The Tosa dogs snarled, sensing the gravity of the moment.

Ivory nodded, turned, and departed.

TUAN HAND-FED A TOUCAN FROM HIS TABLE IN THE Pleasure Garden and meditated on the little coffin that had just been delivered to him. He treated himself to an extra goblet of absinthe and waited for Ivory to arrive.

Ivory entered the room with no fanfare.

Tuan spoke first. "Real warlords made no such foolish rules as Cheung demands."

"This was not a personal decision," said Ivory, taking the seat across from the big man.

It was all smoke in any event, Tuan knew. "Real" warlords were rapists and plunderers, thugs and mercenaries risen to glory via massacre, whose idiom was the raid, not the bargaining-table. Once they got legitimized, the rigors of politics almost always unseated them.

Ivory helped himself to the glass that had been put out for him. "Tell me about the rifle," he said.

Tuan chuckled. "You already know about the rifle."

"A very efficient weapon for its intended purpose," said Ivory, who had examined the gun once it had been recovered from the Night Market. "But tampered with so as to be useless for that purpose. Why?"

"To even the odds," said Tuan. "A last-minute change of heart. A perverse notion of fairness in combat." He lifted his big hands to the air. "What does it really matter, now?"

"You supply the rifle," said Ivory. "But you make sure the sights are skewed. You are still trying to play both sides against the middle, Tuan. Unwise, given your position in this scenario. It suggests that you would prepare to align yourself with whichever side emerged victorious. It should be clear to you that Kuan-Ku Tak Cheung is destined to rule New Shanghai. It is an inevitability, not a choice."

"You sure about that?"

"As I said, it is not a choice," returned Ivory. "We cannot abide allies who are less than committed to our purpose. Collaboration with our enemies is more than interference, it is anti-participation."

"I supplied the terra-cotta figures, as requested," said Tuan.

"Yes. Four so far. Four figures of indeterminate origin, which Cheung found to be useless. A stalling tactic."

"By which I take it to mean that Cheung destroyed them? In his search for a skeleton or a skull or a jewel or a key or *anything* that would relate them to the dynasty of the Favored Son?"

Ivory had, in fact, witnessed Cheung knock off the heads, lop off the arms, powder the fragments with the intensity of a junkie searching for a fix. He'd found nothing to assuage him. Each time his reaction had been more terrifying. Cheung needed a breakthrough to the past so badly that he was apt to start killing his own men left and right just to vent his rage.

"Cheung's quest after his heritage is no longer a concern of yours," Ivory said. "Even in that, you have failed him."

Neither Cheung nor Ivory, nor for that matter Tuan, had any idea that the figures brought to the city by Qingzhao had come from *outside* the tomb, that they had been decoys, leftovers. Vague hints as to what lurked further onward, nothing more.

"Further," said Ivory, "you became culpable by dealing directly with the woman formerly known as Qingzhao Wai Chiu, when you know Cheung has designated her as one of the Nameless. The figures were brokered directly through your offices."

"Guilty," said Tuan. "But I did it to further my own interests, while providing a layer of insulation between the statues and Cheung himself. I may play both sides against the middle, as you say, but I never *cheat* anybody."

"You were the conduit to the Nameless One," Ivory insisted. "You should have informed us of this detail directly. Instead, you kept it shadowed. Needless to say, Cheung can no longer trust you with the lower Bund."

"Is that why I received this delightful item?" said Tuan, meaning the little carved casket. "It's quite exquisite. Is it Cheung's own handiwork?"

Ivory nodded gravely.

"Then Cheung is serious about all this," concluded Tuan sadly. "Real warlords," he said, "found no dishonor is surprise attack, or night maneuvers, or bribery, or shifting alliances—these are our tools, the basic armament of deception."

"In theory I agree with you," said Ivory. "History bears you out. But Cheung's intention is to rewrite history. That means new rules—*his* rules. There can be no gray area."

"My friend," Tuan laughed, "all of Shanghai is one gray area." He finished his drink. "I'm not surprised by Cheung's decision," he said with a massive sigh. "I am surprised by his choice. I expected some cat-eyed assassin, skulking about in the shadows. Someone all steel and no heart."

Ivory merely closed his eyes and nodded, respectfully.

"I suppose whistling up my bodyguards would be futile," said Tuan.

"They have all left already," confirmed Ivory.

Tuan spread his vast fingers across the tabletop like two opposing camps; the tents of honor versus betrayal, love versus hate, good versus evil. "Of all people," he said, eyes down, "I hoped it would never be you."

"So did I," said Ivory.

Tuan extended his hand. Ivory accepted it. They clasped firmly.

With his free hand, Ivory drew his automatic and gave Tuan two in the chest and one in the head, to ensure a quick death. He held onto Tuan's hand until the big man's heart stopped forever.

GABRIEL HUNT CONSIDERED THE LIMITS OF HIS CAGE.
The large, low-ceilinged room was like a pet sanctuary or a bondage emporium. A warren of floor-to-ceiling bars, wire cages, food pans, filth and

dicey light. On a medical tray a series of prepared hypodermic needles was lined up like little soldiers.

His companions were the grist of the slave sale, snoring in drugged sleep or sitting in the corners of their cages with eyes full of fog, blinking little, breathing shallowly, zoned out.

This is no way to treat an honored guest, Gabriel thought.

A case-hardened padlock secured his cell; sadly, Gabriel had neglected to pack his secret agent kit. In any event he had been body-searched down to seams and naked skin before being remanded to Red Eagle's custody. He presumed narcotics came next.

He wondered if Qi had gotten out.

Thinking about her, he realized this was how Qi had begun, perhaps in this very room. He might even be tenanting her old cage. This was the place that had set the path for her whole life.

One cage over, Gabriel saw the doll-eyed twelve-year-old, barely cognizant of her surroundings. She hummed softly and twirled her hair as though she had been left too long to simmer in a madhouse.

From his restricted vantage he could see another prisoner who reminded him very much of Qi—a ruined shadow version of her, same age and same general comportment. The woman was sleeping, or feigning sleep to avoid seeing where she was or attracting the attention of her captors.

It is a general rule of the flesh trade that high profit resides in the tarting up of what is, at heart, rather rude raw material. When up for bids in the open air, the girl would look heartbreaking, done up to entice you to save or pervert her. She would be a dazzling, powerful temptress. Between shows, however, they were all cast back into this dungeon to live like animals.

"Gabriel. You are… Gabriel," said a voice.

He looked up, expecting a jailor or tormentor.

That is the fresh fighter. Called Jin Huáng, for our purposes, Ivory had said. *Chinese for 'yellow' or 'golden.'*

"Yellow" for her hair, Gabriel realized, seeing it now for the first time. It had been shorn, military style, to within a quarter-inch of her scalp, as he could observe now that her fighting mask was off. New wounds on her face, from the pit. One eye crusted with blood from a hard hit. The green gaze of her other eye opaque with some cocktail of drugs in her system.

But it was Mitch Quantrill, live in the flesh, back from the dead, incontrovertibly standing there in front of him.

13

IMAGE YOU ARE IN ANOTHER COUNTRY.

One where you cannot speak the indigenous languages, know no one local, are unfamiliar with the grid, and through no fault of your own, stick out like a hangnail on a sore thumb.

You obviously do not belong here.

And it is only a matter of time before some grown-up, some authority figure, strolls in and asks what the hell you think you're doing.

So—what do you do?

Further imagine that after fewer than 24 hours on this alien planet, you have met the person who objectifies your hatred… and failed to kill him.

That during a mad popper-party of shooting, screams and panic, you may have caught a transient glimpse of an old ally from home—a glimpse so fleeting that it might have been a hallucination of wish-fulfillment.

But you cannot pause to debate that information because

you have gained a new benefactor, a sharp Asian woman who knows how to deal with gunfire.

Your brain, playing mind tricks on you, gives you another flashpop look at the man you think you know, but already your mind is confusing the new helper with the old helper, and the endorphins are flooding because you are in wild retreat and have just stopped a bullet.

Stupid, careless, getting tagged like that.

None of this matters because in one stuttered, broken-film eyeblink of time, you're face-down in a freezing, fast-flowing river with a bullet in your shoulder.

Now imagine what your last thoughts might be.

Sorry, Val. Sorry, Lucy. Sorry, everybody. I could not save anyone, or change a single bad thing. I have disappointed every person with whom I have ever come in contact.

But strong hands fish you from the black maw of the water, telling you no one should die so ignominiously just for the sake of being dead. And your dying mind agrees that this, in fact, is a reasonable point of view.

So—what do you do?

You try to answer the question your rescuer has posed to you.

Where is Qingzhao Wai Chiu?

You say: Dead, I think. I'm not certain.

The rescuer says: Are you certain of anything? Then he says: It is true that if I had needed to kill you, you would be dead. My offer still stands. I can show you a way out. No police. No adversaries.

But first there is the tiny matter of digging his own bullet out of your shoulder.

This is accomplished in an apartment... somewhere... an identity-less box, a clean and well-lighted place, as Hemingway might have said. A window offers a choice view of Shanghai nightlife, far below.

You find yourself naked in an old-fashioned bucket shower, an anomaly in this modern place. You remember a water dipper. Stitches. Candlelight. A bowl of noodles. You're disconnected, but ravenous. Ninety percent of your identity seems to have astral-projected out of your body and gone somewhere else, and you have a quick thought about the pharmaceutical painkillers that are probably coursing through your system along with the soup.

Then you forget the thought.

There is a saying in China, Noodle Man tells you. "The heat of anger burns only the angry."

Great, you think. Did you read that on a fortune cookie?

The fortune cookie was invented in America, Noodle Man tells you with a total lack of irony.

Ivory, you remember. This person is called Ivory. He even introduced himself to you, back at the casino.

I need to express my sympathy, Ivory tells you. For your sister. Is it your intention to avenge her death?

Dumb question.

I did not participate, Ivory tells you. Romero, Chino, some of the others used her very badly. Cheung ordered it. I am far from innocent. It saddens me still.

Spare me, you think. This man Ivory consorts with Valerie's murderers.

Unless he is lying about his own negligence or blameworthiness.

You feel you have begun something, Ivory tells you. A process in which you are trapped, and you feel a misguided urge to see it through to some end. The end can only be catastrophic for you. Do you see that?

Your brain tries to frame a counter-argument but your thoughts are leaking out, wino-bagged in a sieve. Some drug in your blood is definitely messing with you. Would you leave China now, if you had the chance? Ivory asks you.

So—what do you do?

It becomes very important for you to say the word NO. Aloud. Repeatedly.

Shanghai can be a very dangerous place. You are not sure if Ivory says this, or if you just think it. Fifty-fifty.

The drugs keep your brain drunk but your reflexes vital and threat-responsive, you discover later. Most likely, the prescription changed.

You are given an attacker and your entire personality reverts to instinct.

You are given a mask so you may be hidden in plain sight.

You fight through a waterlogged gray curtain, as though puppeteering a bloodless simulacrum in one of the violent games children so love to entertain themselves with back home, sitting lazily in front of the television. But there is no laziness to it here, nor even very much sitting. Just violence.

And in a way you accomplish what you came halfway across the planet to do. You kill. You prevail.

That is what you do. It is who you are, now.

The food, the drugs deftly separate you from a world that had little use for you, back there in behind-time. It is not such a bad life, fulfilling in its primal imperatives. Fight. Survive. Eat. Sleep. Fight again.

You see a man in a cage, less fortunate than you. You are in control of your little universe. The man in the cage has no control. Perhaps you will face this Other in the fighting pit.

But a minuscule ember of memory remains. You recognize this person.

His name is Gabriel. You were introduced to him once.

"MITCH!" SAID GABRIEL, BUM-RUSHING HIS OWN bars. "Michelle! You're alive!"

"I won," she said, as though that were an answer.

She regarded him oddly. Off-center. Head cocked. Sparse recognition in her green eyes. Yet she had remembered his name.

"Who pulled you out of the river?" Of the dozen questions Gabriel could have asked, this one floated to the surface first.

"Some man," she said.

"Don't you remember? We were at the casino. You were shot. We all went into the river together."

"The dream," she said. "The dream of being someone else."

"It's not a dream—look, Mitch, they *did* something to you. Shot you up with drugs or lobotomized you or... I don't know."

"Mitch," she repeated.

Gabriel watched her worry the name in her head. It was a slim hope, a doomed chance for her real self to flicker alight.

"I am Jin Huáng," she said. "I have fought five. I have won five." She showed him the Iron Fist, still strapped to her hand.

"No, you're not! You're—"

"When your time comes," she added curtly, "I'll win against you."

14

"JIN HUÁNG, THIS IS YOUR REST PERIOD," SAID IVORY.

Mitch hung her head and shuffled away.

"Await me," Ivory said to her back. She stopped walking. Then started up again.

"You've drugged her into some kind of... robot," Gabriel said from the cage.

"A preparation from Mr. Cheung's resident mystic," said Ivory. "It subverts the will."

"I'll say."

Ivory unpocketed a pack of cigarettes and offered one to Gabriel.

"No thanks," said Gabriel. "I never got to finish my drink."

"We of course had your identity the moment you entered the Zongchang casino," said Ivory matter-of-factly, not even looking at Gabriel. "I suspected some connection between you and this woman. The cameras confirmed it when you took them both into the river."

"Well, good for you," said Gabriel. "I gather this is the part where I'm just supposed to listen to your brilliant strategy and not ask you why the hell you have me locked up in a cage."

"Unfortunately for you, you have been tricked into consort with the Nameless One," said Ivory. "Mr. Cheung is very protective of his interests, and disapproves of those who would oppose him for shallow and misguided reasons."

"You mean like because he murdered your newest fighter's sister in New York?"

"Ah. That is the link, then." Ivory rubbed his forefinger against his lips, a nervous gesture. "And you sought to redress this injustice?"

"Mitch did," Gabriel said. "All *I* wanted to do was get her out of here. That's the honest truth." He hoped he sounded sincere. "This is not our country. Your fight's not our fight."

Ivory pondered a moment, then said, "Let me tell you a story."

"I don't see how I can stop you."

"Let us say that this story is about an imaginary person named Valerie Quantrill. Who worked quite expertly in the transfer of digital data. Let us imagine that Mr. Cheung's company hired her to bring everything in the organization online for access via the latest state-of-the-art equipment. Broadband literacy is essential to a man who aspires to take an entire country to a new horizon."

"But he didn't count on his imaginary data transfer czar being broadband-literate herself," said Gabriel. "And stumbling on things he didn't want her to know."

"There was no stumbling, Mr. Hunt. It was deliberate, premeditated, and malign. She hacked firewalls, she stole passwords. All deliberate. She deliberately gained access to data that was damaging to us. We foresaw blackmail, threats, sealed envelopes in secret drops. But Mr. Cheung was not enraged—he was pleased. He saw this initiative as a valuable skill. He seeks to encourage people to their best potential—that is why so many in China take him seriously."

"He's a madman who participates in slave auctions," said Gabriel.

"You persist in Western linear thinking," said Ivory. "But I believe you to be an intelligent and perceptive man. Think of the small crime with yield for the greatest good."

"Every madman in history has justified his madness that way. Look at Hitler."

"Yes, yes, Hitler." Ivory glared at him. "Are you quite through?"

"Not quite," said Gabriel. "But I'm the one in the cage. I'm through if you say I'm through."

"Let us say that instead of chastising Valerie Quantrill, Mr. Cheung offered her a new and expanded role in his grand plan—one that would potentially have made her very wealthy, and free to move about the world as she pleased. And let us say further that she came to the meeting in New York to turn him down. That would have been an entirely honorable decision, you understand—but a bad choice. Mr. Cheung would have perceived her disinclination as a threat to use what she knew."

"You mean he lost his temper and killed her. Hypothetically speaking."

Ivory pressed his lips together and looked at the floor for a moment. He released a sigh, as though venting psychic decay.

"If this happened," he said, "I assure you it was not with my approval."

"You didn't prevent it," said Gabriel.

"Perhaps a Westerner cannot understand. It is not my place to prevent Mr. Cheung from doing what he wishes. I am bound by my fealty to him."

"Fealty?" Gabriel shot back. "Ivory, he's not even really Chinese!"

"I know. I have accepted this."

"Look—you're *better* than this guy. You saw Mitch come to kill him and you saved his life, but you saved *her* life, too. Only now you're letting your sense of obligation hamstring you."

"I saved her out of regret for her sister's fate," Ivory said. "Were I a disloyal man, I would not have informed Mr. Cheung. Instead I proposed an alternate course, and he approved."

"And if he hadn't? If he'd told you to kill her? What would you have done?"

"I would have killed her," Ivory said, but he said it quietly, in a voice of utter commitment but also some sadness.

There was a deep conflict aboil just under Ivory's bulletproof surface. Gabriel had sensed it the first time they had met.

"You're *attracted* to her," Gabriel realized. "More than that, you've got the obligation of her sister hanging around your neck. Putting her in a human cockfight may not seem merciful, but it beats killing her—at least she has the chance to defend herself. Cheung is happy. And you get to control her. You're her steward. Her trainer. Her keeper. Her man."

Ivory shook his head forcefully, but not without a little sweat on his face.

"Beats buying yourself a wife—you didn't even have to pay anything," said Gabriel, gripping the bars. "You're the guy who jams her with drugs, I'll bet, and I'll bet you do it in the most loving way. You take care of her after the fights, don't you? Backrubs and front-rubs, all that. And this'll go on until she dies, or maybe until you get tired of her, till your aching conscience quiets down. Then what? Do you throw her away, the way Cheung discarded Qi?"

Here at last was a charge Ivory could answer and he leapt at it. "The Nameless One failed Cheung. I corrected that oversight."

"You *corrected*… you tried to kill her!"

"I *trained* her," shot Ivory. "She was the best of our candidates! And at the critical moment, she failed. Her failure permitted Mr. Cheung to be wounded, something that is not allowable, and I—"

"You nothing," Gabriel overrode. "You turned your back and Cheung threw her to the same pack of thugs and murderers that killed Valerie, assuming he didn't participate himself. Only Qi somehow survived to come after you. Yes, you—not just Cheung, don't fool yourself, she wants you, too. She wants to kill Cheung, but *you*… you she wants to humiliate. And what greater dishonor than to kill Cheung right under your umbrella of protection?"

Ivory's stilted quiet was an indictment in itself. At last he said, "Her story will end very soon. Tuan betrayed her. He betrayed us, too, of course, but that is no more than one should anticipate from denizens of the Night Market."

"And what happens to Tuan?" said Gabriel.

"Tuan's story is already over."

"I see. Did you kill him yourself?"

"It was my honor, and Tuan knew that."

"Your honor," Gabriel said. "You make it sound so very noble. Never mind the dirty, grubby politics of it—the fact that it also conveniently eliminates one of the three other power-bosses on the Bund. Who's left that isn't under your control yet? Hellweg, the water-and-power guy, right? And the fellow who runs the police; I forget his name."

"Zhang," said Ivory. "You are right—to win Zhang to our cause would be to put the entire army at our disposal."

"Why not just kill him the way you killed Tuan?"

"Zhang has not betrayed Mr. Cheung. He will be offered a deal, as Mr. Hellweg will be."

Gabriel almost wished Ivory weren't being so open in discussing his plans—it surely meant he was confident Gabriel would never leave the cage alive.

"Listen, Ivory," Gabriel said, figuring he might as well confront it head-on, "you and I can work out a deal, too."

"I am sorry for your unfortunate confinement," Ivory said, "but no. If I were to let you go, I would have to answer to Mr. Cheung. As I would if I allowed Qingzhao to continue living. There are no options."

"There are always options," Gabriel said. "And if I find one before you do, you may regret not making a deal with me."

"You speak very bravely for a man in a cage, Mr. Hunt."

"I'm not being brave," said Gabriel, "just telling you the truth. I have something Mr. Cheung wants very badly. How long do you think he'll keep me in this cage?"

Gabriel caught the fleeting expression of uncertainty that ghosted across Ivory's face at this news. But he had no time to appreciate it, because while he was watching Ivory someone slipped up from behind and jammed a spike full of joy juice into Gabriel's shoulder.

15

MITCH'S DEFEATED OPPONENT FROM THE IRON FIST
bout that Gabriel had witnessed turned out to be a lot
more important than anyone reckoned.

The woman's name was Garima Bhatia; in her native
Indian dialect "Garima" meant "prowess, strength and
honor." That she had been tough and competent did
not matter. That she had lost money for some bettors
did not matter. That she had been defeated by Mitch
did not matter.

What mattered was that Garima Bhatia had died
soon after the match from a brain aneurysm.

What mattered more was that Garima had been
Mads Hellweg's fighter, bonded and branded.

Mads Hellweg, the underground lord of New
Shanghai's water and power, had long distrusted
Kuan-Ku Tak Cheung, and had significant reservations
about the fixing of matches at the Iron Fist. For the
purposes of inside intelligence, Hellweg had emplaced

most of the Sikh guards used by Red Eagle, having obtained these men through the same channels and business interests in India he had used to procure Garima. But over the prior months the pipeline had broken down and his Sikh spies were being kept out of the information loop. Garima's defeat had come at an inopportune time, never mind her death, and Hellweg was now in dutch with the local Triad Shylocks.

Normally, Hellweg would have requested that Cheung use his influence to take some of the creditor heat off. Except he knew that Cheung was brimming over with his own plans and needed to curry favor with the selfsame Tong bosses to get what he wanted. Hellweg's request was doomed to go into channels and never come out.

Plus, Cheung was visibly becoming increasingly erratic. Assassins were trying to kill him in public. He had taken to soliciting the counsel of an astrologer. And he had fallen into the habit of murdering rivals at the least disagreement or split-hair detail. Hellweg had begun to suspect his uneasy relationship with Cheung was going to blossom into a less-than-equal partnership.

Fortunately, Hellweg had other allies. Quietly marshalling their forces against the Tongs in China were the members of the Japanese *yakuza*. Though nominally subject to a cross-cultural cease-fire, they were just waiting for the right excuse to commence full-scale gang warfare in the streets of Shanghai. Hellweg had maintained a back-door deal with some of the *oyibuns* of the 30,000-strong Kobayashi Clan just in case it ever proved necessary.

And this, he thought, could be the moment. If he deactivated the Iron Fist using yakuza mercenaries, Cheung would blame the Japanese and drag the Tongs in for reprisal. Both sides would suffer glorious losses, including the Triad loansharks trying to bleed Hellweg, and Hellweg himself would skate blame-free.

Then, when the tumult died down, he could debut his own fighting pit, one strictly under his control.

Best of all, if Cheung didn't suspect his involvement, he might even come to Hellweg for support, might ask him to help architect the retaliation against this bold, slap-in-the-face attack by Japan. This moment would bond them as equals in a way nothing else had to date...

Hellweg made the call on his ultra-secure landline.

THE WARNING ON THE SARCOPHAGUS WAS CLEAR. Basically, anybody who opened the tomb was to be cursed, blah-blah, the usual rot.

Gabriel tilted back his pith helmet and mopped his head with a kerchief once white, now gone to oily yellow. Weeks of digging to find a burial chain-of-title regarding a Second Dynastic Period ruler named either Kaires or Seth-Peribsen; scholars disagreed. What Gabriel had found instead was more intriguing—an overlooked intermediate ruler, sort of a vice-president, name unknown, signified only by a unique, untranslatable hieroglyph—a bit like the Artist Formerly Known as Prince, but without all the platinum albums.

According to the glyphs, Mr. Unknown's guardian was supposed to be a kind of Frankensteinian version of a mummy assembled from the parts of all his best soldiers and consigned to an eternity of guard duty in the afterlife.

The sarcophagus creaked on hidden stone hinges—

Pause.

Gabriel snorted water and surfaced, having miscalculated his depth and evacuated the mouthpiece for his air tanks. Frequently the current stirred up the basal muck of this part of the Amazonas, and until it settled it was impossible to see anything underwater. The evidence was thin at best for the missing link between human and fish, and Gabriel was about to give it up for the day when something grabbed his leg while he was treading water—

Pause.

The arctic air in the middle of the Greenland ice cap was so cold that it could shatter a plastic bag, or solidify water thrown from a cup before it hit the ground. To his left, a hundred miles of featureless ice. Ditto for all other directions, save up, where hung nothing but blistering, cloudless sky. Beneath his boots, more ice, ten thousand feet of it, straight down. He was so far inland that there were no birds, for there was nothing here for them to eat. The air would crystallize his lungs if he inhaled it quickly enough. All blinding white, like the end of everything... until he plummeted through a thin scab of crust masking the treacherous layer of blown snow, and crashed into a cavern network that had last been open to the sky sometime during the Industrial Revolution. Even now, glacial drift was narrowing the rift, threatening to seal him in forever—

Pause.

The man-shaped creature, evil and desert-dry, had him by the throat. Gabriel could smell the mold—

The river throwback, an obscenely large mutation of the Paleozoic coelacanth, was in the process of swallowing his leg—

He looked up and saw the sun blotted out while he froze to death in the harsh Greenland icefall—

The narrative nature of dreams denies the concept of build, or the slow accumulation of facts necessary for deductive logic or extrapolation. As soon as your mind thinks of the eventuality, you flash-forward to the heat of it without the benefit of intermediate orts and bits of drama, as in a cinematic jump cut. The velocity of the dream-narrative can relentlessly shove your mind toward wakefulness, which is why many sleepers awaken before they "die" in the dream state.

Gabriel punched and flailed, battling the homicidal monster, kicking at the killer fish, fighting the cold and grinding ice floe. He fought for his life. He fought to breathe. He fought not to die.

And the damned dream would not allow him to wake up.

CHEUNG WAS BUSY CARVING ANOTHER WOODEN CASKET.

Ivory's gaze found it but didn't linger there; he searched Cheung's eyes for illumination.

Sister Menga splashed animal entrails into a bronze bowl. Without looking up she spoke in a monotone: "Victory over an enemy. The exposure of a traitor. All as prophesized."

"Tuan was premature," said Ivory respectfully.

"Nonsense," said Cheung. "I should have killed him a year ago, for the information I did not know he was concealing. Why did *you* not bring that information to me?"

"I only suspected," said Ivory. "I did not know."

"Well, then, now that you *know* that the Nameless One shot Red Eagle's salon to kindling... now that you *know* I was humiliated when that creature Carrington spilled his drink on me and, even worse, when Yawuro got some of his blood on my clothing... now that you *know* all that, Longwei Sze Xie, tell me: when are you going to emerge from whatever dreamstate has clouded your reason and return to be useful to me, other than as a shield?"

"For whom is the casket?" said Ivory.

Cheung snorted. "This is for our friend and fellow Quad Leader, Mr. Hellweg."

"What has Hellweg done?"

"It's not what he's done. It's what he plans on doing. Again, Longwei Sze Xie, your intelligence is tardy. Don't make me turn my scrutiny on you."

Cheung never gave people the benefit of the doubt, and the fact that he was doing so now made Ivory feel a twinge of fear—the kind of reflex horror one feels in the presence of a rabid animal, of some threat that cannot be dealt with rationally.

"Hellweg is as Tuan was," explained Cheung cryptically.

"If you take Hellweg out, the Tong Leaders may object."

"They won't," said Cheung. "I have purchased Hellweg's debts to them and made them good. Let him make his pathetic gesture of protest. Let him discover for himself what true impotence feels like. Then we discard him."

"How?"

Cheung smiled. "I shall resolve Hellweg's difficulties at the funeral."

"Tuan's service?"

"Yes. At the same time I shall find out about General Zhang's fidelity."

Ivory refrained from asking how. Cheung would just tell him again to permit him his "mad little schemes."

"Your path is clear," he said to Ivory. "You know what you must do. I have been patient with you, but the American woman you are babysitting at the Iron Fist has clouded your judgment. It happens to all of us, and it is better that we recognize it has happened to you, and move onward, because we have larger plans. Today you will kill the American woman. Then you will use the information we gained from Tuan's interview to kill the Nameless One. And we shall become whole once more. Sister Menga has prophesied it. Do not beg my forgiveness. It is not needed."

"I will do my duty," said Ivory.

Dinanath hurried into the Temple Room, breathless, neglecting to ask pardon because what he had to say was urgent. "Sirs," he said, sweat standing out on the bald dome of his head. "There's shooting at Red Eagle's."

"Who?" snapped Cheung, his eyes coming up to full flame.

"Apparently... ninjas," said Dinanath.

GABRIEL WOKE UP WITH HIS OWN BLOOD CRUSTING one eyelid half-shut and blocking the hearing in his left ear. His body felt pummeled and tender, as though someone had borrowed it, had a really swell party, and then returned it without dry-cleaning it. His wrists and knees throbbed with pain. He had bruises all over—some severe, with broken skin.

He was still in his cage at the Iron Fist.

He had suffered a dream; a dream of combat against multiple enemies, each defying description. Was that what the mystery drug did to Mitch, he wondered—

make her think she was battling something else entirely when she was in the fighting pit? Geared up and heroic, still soldiering for her country perhaps?

Gabriel would've loved to analyze the stuff in the syringes, almost more than he presently wanted a sauna, a first-aid kit, and a good night's sleep.

He went to work cleaning off his eye, and as he did, two of Red Eagle's Sikhs swept through the cage room. Rather than doing any of the things he might have expected—feeding, watering, or doping up the prisoners, for instance—they went along the line methodically releasing cage latches and unhinging padlocks. In almost no time at all, the doors had all been opened so that everyone could escape to freedom... if they had enough presence of mind to do so.

Gabriel considered briefly the possibility that this might be another hallucination, or some sort of trick, but he rejected it. Something was going down. The Sikhs were gone as fast as they had appeared. Gabriel could not know that they had received a five-minute heads-up from their stealth employer, Mr. Mads Hellweg.

Then came the sounds of panic, violence, and gunfire. Sporadic at first. Growing nearer.

Gabriel kicked out of the cage, his muscles protesting. He grabbed and two of the syringes from the tray and pocketed them. Nothing else at hand even remotely adaptable as a weapon.

Several of the captives—the lot-tagged "merchandise"—were staying put in their cages like sheep.

"Move it!" Gabriel yelled, banging on the bars and wire mesh as he faded along a corridor of cells. "Get out! Get out now!"

But they didn't, and only steps behind him, black

figures entered the holding area, swathed in hoods, bearing automatic handguns with stretch magazines. He heard their racing footsteps, the ratchet of magazines being slammed home, the chatter as they hosed anything questionable with gunfire. Glancing back, Gabriel saw several prisoners—young women, kids—shredded in their cells. They didn't even cry out. He turned and kept going.

He couldn't save everybody. He knew he'd be lucky if he could save himself. His skin was on too loose and felt feverishly hot, making his reflexes and reaction time unreliable. The only other person he could think about was Mitch, and that only because of his promise to Lucy, because she was counting on him. So: get his ass, and hers, out. Save who he could on the way. It was the best he could do.

The cage run was a narrow grid of rows and sections, floodlit from above. Gabriel stalled between two rows in a section which held mostly lot-tagged young men, their eyes drug-dusted, the aluminum bands stapled to their ears. He ducked out of sight just as one boy stumbled from his confinement in time to block a three-bullet salvo from a gunman wielding a pistol that cycled quicker than you can blink.

Gabriel held fast and watched the shadows pass on the floor. They were sweeping the room by section, like a SWAT team following a playbook.

He fished up one of the syringes from his pocket, silently counted to three, and struck, stepping out in a wide pivot, jacking his strength from the elbow and burying the needle into the neck of a slender, lizardy man in black whose face was obscured by a classic *sanjaku-tenugui* wrap. A jetstream of carotid scarlet scribbled a high arc across the air and the man gobbled, clutching, already falling. Gabriel wrested away his pistol as he dropped. It was a Beretta nine modified for auto-fire or three-shot bursts, a nasty little puff adder of a gun.

Instead of engaging, Gabriel stayed ahead of the advancing force, moving into the next of the warren of rooms.

Mitch occupied a cell about seven-by-seven, with a futon pad and a privy hole—the block's Grade A accommodations, in other words. She was wearing a one-piece zippered fatigue jumper and laceless tennis shoes. She sat with her ankles crossed on the pad, staring dead ahead at nothing and feeling her shaved skull with one hand as though trying to identify something in the dark.

"You're not… him," she said when Gabriel entered.

He leapt forward and clamped his free hand over her mouth. "It's Gabriel. *Gabriel.* Remember?"

"Gbrl?" she mumbled against his palm.

He tried to find her eyes. They were still there where they were supposed to be but somewhere else at the same time, distant and dilated and opalescent. He risked giving her a hard crack across the face, open-handed. Her eyes swam into focus briefly and met his, then slipped away. He slapped her again. This time her eyes locked and before he could give her a third crack her hand shot up to lock onto his throat.

"That's it," he croaked, reddening.

"Gabriel?" she said. Her voice sounded confused, disoriented.

"Yep." He freed her grip before his Adam's apple imploded. "Come on, Mitch. We've got to get out of here before—"

A burst of gunfire, from not very far away.

"Who's shooting at us?" she said.

"Time for that later," Gabriel said as he levered her to her feet and thought to himself: *You optimist, you.*

16

IVORY SURVEYED THE DAMAGE. ACCORDING TO WHAT
Dinanath could glean under mild duress from one
incapacitated Sikh, Hellweg had ordered all his spies
to bail out just prior to the assault. The Sikhs had
attempted to liberate all the auction stock and caged
fighters to add to the confusion. About twenty of these
latter were dead now, sprawled on the floors, shot in
their cages, incidental casualties of a sweep-and-clear
by the trigger-happy intruders. If it moved, they had
fired at it, and sometimes if it hadn't.

Those who were not salvaged or recovered, Ivory
knew, would start going into convulsions in about
two days.

Dinanath put the bore of a .357 Magnum to the
Sikh's head and spared the man the chagrin of having
to seek new employment.

From the invading gunmen, Red Eagle had reaped
a bullet in the face for her trouble. She was spread

out awkwardly across a lounging chair in her salon, trailing spilled silk saturated with blood. Her wig was on the other side of the room. She did not appear happy or fulfilled in death.

The lone enemy casualty was not talking. He had suffocated on his own blood, losing the fight to breathe with a hypodermic needle through his windpipe. Ivory found him in a vast, fresh pool of scarlet not far from the cage where Gabriel Hunt had been parked. The intruder's weapon was not to be found.

The woman had also disappeared.

Directly or indirectly, the intervention of Qingzhao Wai Chiu had closed down the Moire Club at the Pearl Tower and disrupted the Zongchang Casino. Then it had compromised the Night Market and now, shut down the Iron Fist. This situation was metastasizing. Cheung was right; Ivory knew what he had to do and each incident that passed without his doing it hurled his loyalty to Cheung further into the shadow of doubt.

The manifestation of Ivory's dilemma—his demon—was Qingzhao, the Nameless One.

The engine of his new uncertainty was Michelle Quantrill.

The unexpected wild card was Gabriel Hunt.

Just kill them, Ivory thought. *Kill them all and be done with it.*

GABRIEL WOULD HAVE DEARLY LOVED TO BLEND INTO the crowd, but it was hopeless and would have been even if he hadn't been dragging Mitch along with him. Gabriel was easily a head taller than any of the Chinese cruising the Bund, and Mitch's buzz-cut blonde pate and green eyes might as well have been a searchlight at a gala premiere. He was carrying the stolen gun and had no good place to conceal it, having been caged in nothing but a soiled T-shirt and trousers; he tried jamming it into a pocket, but enough stuck out to make it no concealment at all. Mitch, meanwhile, was hampered by the laceless sneakers that threatened to fly off each time she increased her speed above a rapid, shuffling walk. Together they looked like a pair of alcoholics who had just spilled out of a bar fight or escaped from a detox facility.

Mitch was slowly coming back into focus. "I don't understand," she said distantly. "It was like a dream—I was back in combat training. I wasn't in a ring waiting for a bell. I was in a desert somewhere, we'd been shot down, and I was trying to keep insurgents from killing me. But it felt absolutely real—more real than the prison. The times when I could see the cell, it felt… it felt like *that* was the dream, because it was the only time I knew I could rest. All the rest of the time, it was combat, non-stop combat."

"I know," said Gabriel, trying to maintain a watchful eye in all directions at once and to keep them moving. "They spiked me with that junk one time and I was in three different places at once, fighting for my life. It's as though the drug uses what you know against you. It produces hallucinations, picks and chooses from your experiences and your imagination to produce a situation of maximum distress."

"I don't see why they bothered," Mitch said. "It's not like the reality of the situation wasn't distressing enough."

"Point," said Gabriel.

As they passed the front lot of a western hotel, he tried to recall whether Michael would have landed in Shanghai yet. It hardly mattered, though; there was no good way to reach out to him. Inquiring through ordinary channels—a hotel, a university, a tourist bureau—would bring the People's Police down on their heads, and the police were controlled by Cheung's partner, General Zhang, formerly of the Red Army school of compassionate understanding. Even exposing themselves on a public street long enough to puzzle out the rat's maze of the Chinese payphone system was a bad idea. No, for now they were on their own and would have to fend for themselves. They needed food, clothing, disguises (sunglasses, a watch cap, *something*), money, transportation, identities on paper, and a way out, a way back to a world where the most agonizing decision they faced involved browsing a selection of tempting desserts.

Gabriel steered Mitch by the elbow toward an enclosed mall area on their right.

"We're going to have to do a little shopping," he said.

GABRIEL HAD NEVER CLASSED HIMSELF AS A CRIMINAL. So much for that comfortable delusion. In the world of the Night Market, everybody was guilty of something.

Right now, Gabriel was guilty of shoplifting.

Of course, in the past few days he had been present at extravagant symphonies of carnage and destruction, playing his little solos where the orchestration required it. But now he had to engineer a grand opera of distraction just to pinch a sweatshirt.

It should have been a simple snatch-and-grab— but the elderly pipe-smoking gentleman who ran the clothing stall had an eye on Gabriel. He checked back repeatedly to see where Gabriel was looking, and each time Gabriel made sure he was looking somewhere else. No point confirming the man's suspicions.

Shortly, the elder got into a spirited haggle with a young American woman, a forceful blonde who fully indulged the elaborate grammar of hand-wringing, waving, coaxing, position-jockeying and street theater necessary to a really satisfying negotiation. It was a thousand bucks worth of production value over a one-dollar item.

Gabriel ducked low, slid two hoodies from the bottom of the rearmost stack beside the counter, and quickly scooted.

His turned one of the hoodies inside-out to hide a blazing Day-Glo logo of some boy band that had been all the rage two years ago. It was an XXL, and with it dangling to his upper thighs at least the gun was covered.

He looked around for Mitch, who, having walked away from the negotiation in a decent simulation of a huff, was now loitering near the restrooms. He saw her chatting up a tall fellow in an expensive sharkskin suit, the sort you'd have to go to Hong Kong to buy. Gabriel raised her hoodie and was about to call to her when he saw her unzip her jumpsuit a few inches and guide the man's hand inside for a sample squeeze.

More crime in the making, and the poor bastard didn't realize it. He watched her lead the man off toward the toilets.

Shouldn't take long for her to roll him, he figured. Gabriel turned to scan the space, keep an eye out for trouble, and found himself face-to-face—well, face-to-chest—with a man a good ten inches taller than him. And stronger: a pair of massive, callused hands gripped Gabriel's neck and hoisted him clear off the ground.

* * *

THE GUY HOLDING GABRIEL LOOKED LIKE A RENEGADE circus strongman, a yard wide at the shoulders, totally hairless but for a drooping Fu Manchu mustache, sumo-sized and well north of six feet tall, with skin-stretching plugs in both earlobes and a grip like a construction crane.

Where had this guy come from? Was he on Ivory's crew or...?

This was not the time to ponder such questions, Gabriel realized. Gabriel's head was struggling to pop away from his body while his neck muscles tried to keep it where it was. The kicks he landed were ineffectual; he was a dangling marionette in the larger man's grasp.

Then the old man from the clothing stall appeared, smoldering pipe in one hand. He commenced hollering in Chinese, jabbing his finger repeatedly at Gabriel and yelling a word that sounded like "queasy," over and over.

As Gabriel's brain started to shut off from lack of oxygen, he realized the man was shouting *qiè zéi*—thief.

The colossus had acres of ridged scar tissue on his bald head. Gabriel could whale on that skull all day and distract him no more than a fly. A small fly. A small, crippled fly.

He reached under the sweatshirt, pulled the gun out of his pants pocket, aimed it outward and downward.

The big man shifted so that he was holding Gabriel with just one hand and swatted the gun away effortlessly with a single swipe of the other. Then he grabbed hold of the purloined sweatshirt Gabriel had on and peeled it off him like a banana skin. He let gravity take over and Gabriel piled up on the wet cobblestones, stunned and insensate, his legs feeling far away.

The man bent down and snatched up the second sweatshirt, which Gabriel had dropped when lifted off his feet. It was filthy. He shook it in Gabriel's face while the old man came near to offer a bit more shouted admonishment. Gabriel let his eyes slide shut and shortly they left, or at least stopped yelling at him. The next voice he heard was Mitch's.

"What are you doing?" she said, one hand under his arm, helping him up. "This after you told *me* not to attract attention."

"Need to work on my Artful Dodging," he muttered. Gabriel saw she'd picked up the gun. Good. At least one of them had done something right. He limped with her away from the glare of the crowd. "How'd you make out with your new boyfriend?" he asked hoarsely.

"Let's just say he didn't have quite the good time he was hoping for. When he wakes up, unties his ankles and pulls up his pants, he'll find his wallet missing." Off Gabriel's expression, she added, "He's not hurt. Just his pride, and he had too much of that to begin with. And we needed the money."

"How much did we get?"

She flashed him a palmful of currency. Not much. Enough.

"All right," said Gabriel. He steered them on. They didn't speak till he stopped short a few minutes later.

"What is it?" Mitch said.

"We're going to need better weapons."

"And...?"

"And I know a place where we can get some."

He pulled her past the half-hidden wooden sign that read SU-LIN GUN MERCHANT.

* * *

YOU WOULD NOT THINK SO FROM WATCHING THE average Hong Kong action movie, but private citizens in China are expressly forbidden to own or sell firearms. The penalties range from several years' imprisonment to a death sentence. This hard line to prevent "gun violence" is maintained by the same government that executed ten thousand lawbreakers in 2008, making China number one in the wonderful world of capital punishment. Preferred method of legal execution: a hollow-point to the head. *Boom*—done, and no one says a word about irony.

"Not to put too fine a point on it," said Gabriel, "but you can also pull the death penalty here for stealing a cultural object. Or killing a panda."

"So *how* is this all legal?" Mitch said, slack-jawed at the diversity of Su-Lin's arsenal.

Gabriel gave her a dour look.

"Never mind," Mitch said.

Capital crime was little deterrent where profit was involved. The temptation here was the same as it was for dirt farmers in the U.S. to move crystal meth. Here, a person could sell a single gun and make three times his or her yearly pay.

Gabriel moved to the dual laptops as tiny Su-Lin grinned in recognition. Repeat customers were highly desirable.

Gabriel typed: YOUR PIG MOTHER EATS NIGHT SOIL.

Mitch read this over his shoulder and gave him a look of confusion crossed with bemusement—but it was cut short by what appeared to be a sudden migraine jolt that caused her to pinch the bridge of her nose and squeeze her eyes shut, wetly.

"You okay?" said Gabriel.

She waved away his concern. "Mm-hm, yeah. It's just a spike—like brain freeze from ice cream, you know?" Gabriel knew—but he didn't think ice cream had anything to do with it.

Su-Lin typed back on her keyboard: I LOVE YOU, TOO.

I NEED A WEAPON, Gabriel typed. He took the ungainly Beretta back from Mitch, passed it across the counter. I CAN TRADE THIS IN.

Su-Lin gamely dug under her counter and came up with the same modified .36 Colt revolver Gabriel had lost after his visit to Tuan with Qingzhao. It was like seeing an old friend. He wondered how many times she'd sold and re-sold the same guns.

IT HAS ALREADY BROUGHT GREAT PROFIT, Su-Lin typed, SO I GIVE SPECIAL PRICE TO YOU.

DONE, Gabriel typed. NOW FOR MY FRIEND?

17

"WE NEED TO GET OUT OF THE MIDDLE OF THIS THING," said Gabriel. "Nobody is going to back down. Everybody is going to get killed."

The leaning pagoda was within view as they crested a jut of rock. Mitch was climbing right behind him, but her attention seemed to be wandering and she had gone from breathing nasally to orally—not a good sign, for someone as fit as she was.

"You're part of it now, too," she said, her breath more ragged than it should have been.

"No, I'm not, and neither are you. We get to Qi's place, I call my brother. I'm pretty sure Qi's got a secure cellphone or can bash one up. Michael calls the embassy and the Marines and we burn our tailfeathers straight out of here."

"You still don't get it, do you?"

He turned and gave her a hand over the next rise. "You're going to tell me that the guy who imprisoned you, drugged you, turned you out to fight for money, the guy who imprisoned *me*, for god's sake, has some kind of hypnotic hold over you that's going to keep you trying to kill phantoms?"

"No," she said. "Stop. Please. I've got to stop." She halted, bent over, hands on her thighs.

Mitch sat down heavily on a knobby outcrop of feldspar.

"It is the drug?" said Gabriel.

"I don't know. Maybe. I can't tell if this is after-effect, or withdrawal, or bad chemistry, or what. But it's starting to hurt so bad I can't keep my eyes open."

"You can't go to sleep," warned Gabriel. "You might not wake up."

She took a deep breath and her vision seemed to clear slightly. "He told me a story," she said. "A parable."

"Ivory?"

"Yes. He asked if I'd ever had a crisis of faith… god, I can't remember what he said. It seemed to make a lot of sense at the time. He was talking about himself, I'm pretty sure, and about Valerie. He said he didn't kill her. But he didn't stop it when he saw it happening."

"That was his crisis of faith," said Gabriel.

"Exactly. His duty versus his honor. Very Chinese."

"I know how this one ends," said Gabriel. "Betrayal. It's who betrays whom I'm having a hard time figuring out."

Meanwhile, Gabriel was suffering his own crisis. He still had a syringe of the Iron Fist happy-hour cocktail in his pocket. He'd grabbed two and only used one on the gunner in the cage room. The other he'd begun thinking he could get to a lab, have them break it down, analyze it. Synthesize countermeasures.

But if what he was seeing in Mitch was the first stage

of withdrawal, he was going to have to use the needle on her. Perhaps diluted. Perhaps in increments. But even so, the sample would soon be gone—and she'd be rendered a null-sum as a team member for the duration.

Part of his mind—the impatient part, the selfish part, the part that had so often kept him alive in tight spots—was asking what, really, did he owe her? Hadn't he picked up that check? Hadn't he been picking them up for Mitch ever since he'd posted her bail back in New York? Hadn't he paid plenty in skin and blood and gunfire; in nightmares and pain?

But his sense of justice was at stake here. That was the other part of his mind, the part that kept getting him into all those tight spots in the first place. He had allowed the undertow to drag him this far because Lucy was relying on him—and because men like Cheung needed taking down. And if Mitch's tragedy was a minuscule one for planet Earth, so what? Move a single grain of sand on a beach, everything in the world is changed. How's that for Zen?

"I'm not so sure Qi won't just shoot us on sight," said Gabriel, considering their range from the pagoda. "If Tuan knew her whereabouts, then Ivory knows, which means Cheung knows. And if she's found out that Tuan's dead, that he betrayed her…"

"…she may be in a mood to shoot anyone that approaches."

"Keep your eyes open," Gabriel said.

"I'll try," Mitch said.

BUT QINGZHAO WAS NOT TO BE FOUND.

They entered the pagoda without incident and searched from room to room without turning her up.

Mitch doubled over with a cramp about the time they entered the third of the shrine rooms.

"God, this feels really... weird," said Mitch, breaking a sudden sweat. Her temperature was skyrocketing.

The puzzle-box base of the idol was securely shut. Qi's bike was gone.

But most of her hair was still here. It lay at the foot of a narrow mirror, hacked off in clumps, apparently with the combat knife lying atop one clump.

The water in the big iron cauldron was room temperature. Gabriel decided to stick Mitch inside to keep her from running too hot. She didn't resist as he undressed her. He helped her up and over the side. She settled in, laid her head back against the rim. Her head jittered against the metal, perspiration beading on her brow.

He had ten cubic centimeters of amber fluid in the needle.

Okay, give her two.

He did not want to waste time or serum on a skin pop that might not take hold, and she was compliant when he tapped up a vein in her forearm. He uncapped the syringe. It was the sort of small, disposable plastic hypodermic found at free clinics all over America. The Iron Fist probably went through these things by the gross.

Very carefully, he allowed about a drop and a half to enter her system.

Her response was instant. The tremor in her head and neck vanished, and she seemed to nod off. Gabriel hurriedly checked her pulse (slow), respiration (shallow), pupil dilation (considerable). Her breathing was barely audible but regular. She wasn't dead.

He checked her again about every two minutes

while he fired up a few torches and managed to get some coffee going on Qi's campstove.

It was the better part of an hour before Mitch cracked her eyes open. Her pupils were huge. Her green irises had subsided to a pale shade similar to algae.

She brought up a handful of water as though it was a rare treasure, and trickled it over her face. Droplets hung from her brow, nose and chin as she watched the water return to the tub in a stream. Her expression was concentrated, one of almost religious intensity. She ignored Gabriel checking her vital signs. Watching the water was paramount right now.

"Are you back?" said Gabriel. "You okay?"

In response she grabbed his wrist, pulled him close. "Where am I? Who are you?"

"I'm Gabriel," he said.

"Who?"

"Lucy's brother." Her face relaxed at the mention of Lucy's name. Her grip did, too. He pulled his arm free. "Lucy," she whispered. "Come here, Lucy."

"Mitch," he said. "Lucy's not here."

"Sure she is," Mitch whispered, her gaze unfocused. "She's right next to you. Why don't you say something, Luce? You mad at me?"

"It's not real, Mitch—it's the crap in the needle. Mitch, are you listening to me?" She'd begun to weep, had raised one arm from the water and was reaching out toward the empty air beside him.

"I can hear your heartbeat, Luce," she murmured. "Come here, baby. Come here. That's it, get in."

"Damn it, Mitch, she's not..." He dropped it. There was no arguing with someone under the influence of a hallucinogen this powerful. At least she wasn't imagining herself at war again. Who knew what she was imagining, exactly, but it seemed to be giving her pleasure. The tears had stopped, and her head was tilted back against the cauldron's edge once more. Her breathing was becoming rapid. Gabriel turned away. Let her have her privacy.

FULL-BLOWN TRADITIONAL CHINESE FUNERALS ARE notoriously ornate, complicated, and lengthy affairs. Some of the more elaborate ones last two years.

In the case of the late Tuan, many of the rites were Westernized in accordance with China's lunging urge toward modernity. But his casket was the traditional three-humped rectangular box, decked head-to-toe with flowers and literally thousands of encomia calligraphed on white paper or cloth. Tuan would be well-honored on New Year's, and on Grave-Sweeping Day.

Presentation of the casket (not sealed until after the wake) was strictly according to *feng-shui*: the head of the deceased facing the inside of his place of residence, white cloth over the entrance, gong on the left side of the doorway. Along with jewelry, red appointments or clothing were forbidden, as red was a color of happiness (exceptions were made if one died eighty or older, but Tuan had been far from this milestone). Inside the casket, Tuan was swathed in finery, a yellow cloth over his face and a blue one over his body. All of his other clothing had been burned, and a pile of ashes on a rattan mat attested to this.

Tuan's send-off was in defiance of the communist imperatives that frowned on lavish funerals. Not only were big funerals seen as superstitious and wasteful, but their sheer level of filigree was in itself an indictment, suggesting that the deceased was a criminal, since only ill-gotten gains could pay for something this fancy. Stacked against this official modern stigma was the common belief that expensive funerals guaranteed peace in the afterlife.

Tuan's would be no simple village funeral. There would come snake dancers and professional wailers, demonstrative mourners, extravagance, fireworks, fury and a party atmosphere lit by a conflagration of burned paper effigies. So what if it implied he'd been a criminal? In his case, everyone knew it was true, and this liberated the planners to spare no expense.

But for now, the private, invitation-only elite entitled to a more privileged remembrance inside the Pleasure Garden were startled by the sight of *two* caskets on the ceremonial bier.

Mads Hellweg and his entourage cast uneasy glances around the area. No sign of Cheung or his number one, Ivory. Their absence was a disappointment to Hellweg. Entrance to this sanctum sanctorum required crawling on hands and knees, kowtowing and offerings. Hellweg had a perverse desire to watch Cheung crawl for something, even if it was only to further his intrigues.

General Zhang's group was present and the stiff-spined ex-military men gave the proper bows and acknowledgement to Hellweg's group. Others present included Cheung's customary cadre of international financiers and a scatter of the best and most influential Tong leaders. All with their bodyguards, of course.

And still, no Cheung. Which suggested deceit, possibly a trap.

No, wait—here was Ivory, acting cordial, even deferential, toward the high rollers in the room.

Then the lid of the casket next to Tuan's opened entirely on its own.

* * *

QINGZHAO WAS SURPRISED LEAST OF ALL, BUT surprised nonetheless. She had expected and anticipated many things, but not this.

When the casket opened, she was standing near Zhang's contingent of police enforcers. She was the only woman present in this boy's club—more nonsense about females not being worthy, here—but so far no one had pegged her as such because she had taken great pains to blend.

She had cut her hair short and combed it straight back. She wore tinted glasses with stainless steel frames to abet the coarsening of her complexion, which she had achieved with makeup. Her brows were bolder, more masculine, and she had expertly stippled her cheeks and chin to provide the illusion of shaved facial hair. She had avoided using a padded suit to keep from making her head look too obviously small in contrast to her frame. The man's suit she wore was black with a black respect band on one sleeve, and plenty of room for the hammerless automatic pistol nestled against her spine.

The secret lords of the New Bund's underworld rarely congregated in one place together, making Tuan's wake and funeral a notable occasion. Most of the important men, from Tong leaders to drug royalty, had come as a measure of respect to Cheung's influence, not Tuan's stature.

And Cheung was not present.

Qi immediately theorized a mass trap; Cheung drowning all rodents at once, slicing through the Gordian knot instead of unraveling it, and clean-slating the entire playing field. It was easy to envision the

Pleasure Garden sealing up and filling with lethal gas.

But no... if trap there was to be, then Ivory wouldn't have shown either. It was highly unlikely that Cheung would sacrifice his right hand man, and here he was as a kind of Cheung manqué, pressing the flesh and making sure everyone was acknowledged, given an equal show of respect.

Unless—

Unless Ivory had finally blown it one too many times, for instance by repeatedly failing to kill Qi.

He surely could have killed her, Qi knew—more than once he'd had the opportunity. She could not chalk her continued survival up to skill on her part or the operation of chance or luck. Ivory's failure to end her life was beginning to seem more willful than inadvertent, a choice even if only an unconscious one and one wrapped up in some other struggle, purely internal, between Ivory's ambition and sense of duty to Cheung on the one hand and, on the other, his sense of honor and duty to himself. Whatever the reason, something had kept him (so far) from completing the preordained arc that ended with Qi's death. Qi was determined not to become similarly handicapped. When she had a clear shot at him, she'd take it. Because ultimately, one of them had to die.

The unexplained second casket opened, then.

Cheung was inside, and sat up. This was his entrance, intended to impress, and he was making the most of it.

The side of the second casket dropped down on hinges so Cheung could dismount the bier.

Qi should have drawn, fired, and fled in that moment. She could not. Even she was momentarily transfixed.

Stunned, rather. As was everyone else in the room

who beheld the spectacle of Cheung's warlord outfit.

Qingzhao stared frankly, her jaw slowly coming undone.

In cut and architecture the costume was essentially military, following the aspirations of conquerors of the early twentieth century, such as a photo Qi had once seen of Manchurian warlord Chang Tso-lin. High, stiff, embroidered collar with pins of rank, Sam Browne belt, tasseled epaulettes, cockades, pips, chevrons and medals with maniacal emphasis on the breast hash and ribbon rack. A sash. Three red stripes on the jodhpurs, also denoting high rank. Riding boots, leather puttees and golden *spurs*, for godsake. For those who care to recall history, it was comparably flamboyant to the outrageous tanker's uniform confabulated by General George S. Patton—yes, the one said to be topped by a gold football helmet. But instead of olive or khaki, Cheung's ensemble was rendered entirely in black silk brocade. The only thing missing was a flag and a plumed helmet.

"Thank you all for coming," Cheung said, straightening his seams and perching one hand on the black leather flap holster belted around his middle. "We gather today to confer honor upon our fallen comrade, Tuan, and to help him toward the afterlife with such ceremony as he merits."

He leveled his gaze at everyone in the room, including Qingzhao.

In his hands was another of the tiny carved caskets.

"And one of you will be accompanying him to the afterlife, right now."

18

GABRIEL RIFLED QI'S FIRST-AID SUPPLIES FOR SALINE with the thought he might be able to play alchemist and whip up a larger batch of the mystery drug from the eight cc's he had remaining in the syringe. Mitch had lapsed into comfortable silence in the big iron tub, much akin to a heroin nod. Without a fresh application of the drug, the slamming headaches and disorientation would soon resurge, and without a medical facility at hand, Gabriel was trying his best to pre-load a stopgap.

All the supplies he and Qi had ferried back from her bartering excursion were still here, indicating that whatever had happened to Qi, she had not yet abandoned her stronghold. But of saline there was none. Gabriel gently set the precious syringe down under a protective protrusion of rock and turned his attention back to the big bronze statue.

He had gathered 200 feet of climbing rope in 50-

foot coils, along with a basic climbing kit—a bandolier of base hooks, rock anchors, carabiners, pitons and spikes; a vertical harness, an array of belay and rappel geegaws, plus a couple of high-impact strap-lamps. Among his other tools and gear were a crate of chemicals in plastic bottles, and a few sticks of dynamite, this last courtesy of Qi's armory.

"How're you doing, Kangxi, old fella?" he said. "Still rotting away inside? Still got bats in your belfry?"

Those bats needed to tell Gabriel how they normally got out of the cave to hunt. He presumed a hole in the ceiling somewhere, fifty or sixty feet above the dung-fouled bowl of the floor.

Only once he'd found this secret could Gabriel put the Killers of Men to work on his behalf.

KUAN-KU TAK CHEUNG SPOKE MULTI-LINGUALLY. Leftovers were handled by interpreters.

"I particularly wish to thank our brothers from Sechen Tong for attending," he said. "It is their work in chemical engineering that will permit us shortly to commence worldwide distribution of our new narcotic, which we have elected to call 'freon' for short. General Zhang's selfless work with the constabulary of the military police and affiliated forces has proven invaluable, and his men have proven to be compassionate and worthy."

Zhang, in the dress uniform of his office, bowed slightly.

"As the West becomes more socialist, so do we inevitably become less communist," continued Cheung. "It is a new century. It is the order of things." He opened his fingers into a butterfly. "Information now flies freely through the very air. This in no way should be perceived as a threat."

Mads Hellweg shuffled foot-to-foot, waiting to be congratulated for his supposedly equal role in the coming new order.

Qi's hand drifted back toward her gun. Was it Cheung's intention to bore them all with a banquet speech?

"I further wish to assure all of our most honored Tong brothers that your Japanese counterparts have been assuaged. I have taken independent action to ensure their noninvolvement. The ruffled feathers are eased."

Hellweg narrowed his gaze. *What?*

Cheung was looking directly at him. "Your plot to disrupt was obvious and doomed," he told Hellweg. Then with the air of someone bestowing a great boon, he handed the little wooden casket to Hellweg.

Ivory saw confusion mar Hellweg's gaze. The man did not understand the meaning.

It became clear as Cheung unholstered the revolver on his belt and fired point-blank, not stopping until all six heavy-powder rounds were snugged deeply into Hellweg's chest. The cacophony of report seemed to stop time itself.

Hellweg staggered backward without a word and fell with his legs in a figure-four. Gunsmoke grayed the air.

Everyone in the room was frozen in tableau, as though posing for a Renaissance painter.

Ivory's crew had all drawn down on Hellweg's bodyguards. Qi, following suit, had pulled her pistol and leveled it at the nearest subject most likely to preserve her disguise.

The uncertainty in the room was thicker than the drifting webs of gunsmoke. Half the other bodyguards had freed their weapons, but nobody dared to aim at Cheung. Ivory had a gun in each hand, pointed at two different men.

Nobody held as much import in that instant as General Zhang, whose hand had flown down to his sidearm. It hovered there, tentative as a hummingbird.

Cheung watched him. "If I have done wrong, General, then it is your duty to kill me right now."

Zhang sought out Cheung's eyes. Their communion was massive. He slowly withdrew his hand from his holster. Cheung smiled.

"You see? The General is with us."

Ivory had to admire the sheer bravery on display, no matter how foolhardy it might have been. Cheung was showing the assembly the sort of leader he was. This was a public demonstration of his capacity to rule as well as a test of his personal magnetism. If he could swing Zhang, then he could swing the Tongs, and the traditionalists, too, especially since he had just coldly blown down another invading outsider. He'd still need to verify his true Chinese identity in the bloodline of older warlords, of course; there would be no winning over the hardcore without that. But today's events would go a long way toward silencing his critics.

Hellweg's bodyguards were left dangling. Most of them were not aiming at anyone. They were gawping at their dead boss, now full of holes and slowly cooling on the cobblestoned floor. To a man, they were all hired Chinese muscle.

"We welcome you," Cheung told them. "You were misguided, but now your minds have been set free. Ivory will see to your employment needs."

Hellweg's men took their cue and departed en masse with nervous shows of respect.

Call it charisma or call it power, Cheung ruled the room. His aspirations were not delusional, thought Ivory. This man could really do it, and he had just proven it.

It was that unmitigated show of power that had caused Qi to hesitate, just at the microsecond she should have been blowing Cheung's brains all over the tapestry.

Now Ivory's grip closed on her forearm from behind. His other hand already had her gun.

"You're coming with me," he said.

As though he had known all along it was her, Cheung gave a little nod and motioned his partners back to business.

GABRIEL FIRED A ROUND FROM THE NAVY COLT INTO the blackness of the cavern, and the bats all freaked out, taking wing.

He ducked down among the dung-encrusted impalement victims, these skeletal Killers of Men, to observe. He wore a hat borrowed from Qi's stores and the rainfall of batshit, both dislodged and fresh, descending from on high spattered on its crown and brim. He tracked their nightwing pattern with a hand-held million-candlepower spotlight.

There.

There, in the back curvature of the ceiling about sixty feet from the cave floor, was a geological rupture that resembled a scowling stone mouth. The bats were piling through it in a centrifugal pattern that indicated it was fairly large. Apparently it led to a switchback to the surface, presumably S-shaped, since that would account for the fact that it admitted no light to the cavern in daytime.

Gabriel roughed out the distance and calculated as best he could the location of the rift on the outside of the mountain. It would have to be on the eastern slope—the steepest and most overgrown side, from what he had seen.

The vent was funnel-shaped, with the wide end inside the cavern. He headed toward its opening, lugging his climbing gear behind him. It should be possible to arrange a mechanism that would lift him toward the opening…

Gabriel had no way of knowing that, as he worked out this problem in engineering, back in the city the Hellweg Tower—sometimes called the Tower of Flame—was already burning for real, a five-alarmer that froze traffic for miles and caused firefighters from four districts to be called in as reinforcements.

He knew nothing about this. He concentrated instead on the work he was doing. Even when it was done, he still had some repairs he wanted to make. So he needed to work hard and work fast and not be distracted.

So he shut out all thoughts and got to work. Only one thought made it past the barrier he'd erected, and it was a thought about Qi: Where the hell was she?

THE MONASTERY HAD STOOD SINCE A.D. 247 ON THE outskirts of Shanghai with the presence of centuries crushed upon centuries, witness to the rise and fall of monarchs and tyrants. Like Longhua Temple it was configured in a time-honored seven-hall structure. Bald monks in yellow robes glided phantom-like through halls appointed with intimidating idols while huge coils of incense smoldered like mutant beehives, rendering the air particulate and opiate.

Ivory had held Qi at gunpoint for more than an hour, all the way from Tuan's funeral to this place, and she liked to think the stress fatigue of staying alert for her every twitch and gesture was beginning to tire him. They held fast in the First Hall while Ivory conferred with a man in monk's robes.

"You bought off Buddhist monks?" said Qi.

"Pan Xiao is not a monk," said Ivory.

Only then did Qi notice the baffled gun muzzle, barely visible, winking in and out of view beneath Pan Xiao's robes as he moved. Some automatic equalizer on a shoulder sling, positioned for rapid deployment.

"Please," Ivory said, indicating Qi should precede him along the corridor. He had to stay ready to shoot her at the first sign of misbehavior or trouble.

He directed her by lantern-light down narrow wooden stairs. They were about two floors beneath street level.

A warren of disused corridors led to a now-dormant fermentation room and abandoned wine cellar. After a few more twists and turns they came to what appeared to be a vault door, anomalous in its stainless-steel frame against the ancient stonework of the wall.

Qi anticipated some sort of dungeon, cell or holding area. When Ivory key-coded the door and opened it, she was frankly startled.

Ivory had brought modernity to this modest series of rooms in the form of electric lights, motion sensors, a security system and several computer monitors arranged on an old rolltop desk. Fish paddled about in a backlit 50-gallon aquarium and a small bonsai tree thrived under an expensive multi-band growth light. The furnishings were all handworked wood, apparently antiques.

Sure this was some kind of trick, Qi said, "Your apartment is in the city."

"My apartment is not my home," said Ivory. "It is necessary for appearances. No one knows of this place."

"Not even Cheung?"

Ivory pursed his lips slightly. He closed the big iron door, then showed Qi he was standing down with the gun. He would not wield a weapon in here, and he was trusting her to listen to whatever he had to say. This was implicit when he stated, "I could have let Cheung have you back at the funeral."

Then, maddeningly, he began to make tea as though it was the most natural thing in the world, even turning his back on her once or twice.

"Have you ever suffered a crisis of faith?" he said.

"Not religious," Qi said, slowly taking a seat in an armless, hardback "drawer chair."

"That's exactly what Michelle Quantrill told me when I asked her the same question. You two have much in common."

"I never saw her before the Zongchang casino," said Qi.

"Nevertheless."

"Why am I here?" Qi asked. "Why didn't you do your duty and kill me when you had the chance?"

"Because I am finding out that some things transcend duty," said Ivory. "Or at least some duties transcend others." He waved this rather significant confession away. "Your holy war is to kill Cheung. Yet despite multiple opportunities, you have not. My conclusion is that you are more interested in discrediting me through attrition. To avenge your status as a Nameless One."

"Perhaps I'm just a lousy shot," she said. They both knew it was not true.

"You were dealt with unfairly. Michelle Quantrill's sister was dealt with unfairly. It is the way of things in Cheung's vision of the world. But while I might be your adversary, I am not your enemy."

"That sounds terrific," said Qi. "But what does it mean?"

"You have heard the parable of the warrior of great honor," said Ivory, serving them both tea in small hammered cups that were both exquisite and comfortably weighty. "He was obligated to a cruel and uncouth master. He discovered such honor as his can be a trap, a snare that tightens the more you struggle against it. The more he tried to serve his master honorably, the more obligated he became, and the more implicated in cruelty himself."

"You have already betrayed Cheung by sparing me. He will not forgive this."

"He might not," acknowledged Ivory. "But I need to see you and this other woman clear of Shanghai. Then my obligations will be ended, and Cheung can take such measures as he will."

"You are wrong," said Qi, "that we two are the only ones you have wronged. You have involved this man Gabriel Hunt as well. The stain of your crisis of honor is spreading like a disease."

"You are correct. If I kill you now, my obligation to Cheung is served, but I have dishonored myself. If I do not kill you, if I let you go free, you have sworn to slaughter the man to whom I owe loyalty. There can be no honor in that. Is there any solution?"

He took a sip of tea as though it was the last one of his life, then handed Qi his pistol.

"I leave the dilemma in your hands."
Ivory resumed his seat. And waited.

19

MICHAEL HUNT WAS MET AT THE AIRPORT BY AN
official car which conducted him into the city, and
the waiting representatives of the Shanghai Cultural
Alliance. Much bowing, many cocktails, even more
handshakes as a modest summit was initiated, and
Michael suffered it all graciously. As Gabriel often
pointed out to him, pressing the flesh took time and
patience—a patience that Michael had cultivated while
his brother was gallivanting around the globe.

His brother, from whom he had not had word in
days. Who was presumably somewhere in greater
Shanghai; who had, by all best guesses based on
personal experience, gotten swept up in yet another
sideroad that rendered him incommunicado. It was
Gabriel's rowdy way. If anything were truly amiss,
Michael would have seen a red flag, a flare, a message
in a bottle, something. Meanwhile his duty was to make
nice with the academics Gabriel had jilted at the start

of his trip and tell them the things they wished to hear.

Michael's schedule awaited him in his suite, printed out and laid against the stacked pillows on the king-sized bed. He was staying in a hotel off the Bund that had apparently been an embassy at some past time. Looking over the printout, Michael saw there were the usual tours of monasteries and museums, as well as a brace of receptions, the first of which was—oh, look at that—in exactly 45 minutes, at some location he could not have found with a map, a native guide, and a GPS device. He was in the hands of his handlers and had no choice but to trust himself to them.

Showered, shaved, plucked, dressed and polished, he presented himself at the appointed time (thanking all the valets and doormen in Mandarin) and found himself whisked to a phantasmagoric skyscraper-top discotheque one entered by walking through the enormous resin-cast jaws of a Tyrannosaurus Rex skull.

The throb of the music was physically assaultive, the bass notes reverberating in his diaphragm. Strangers shouted greetings he could not hear, and the best response he could manage was to smile, nod, and allow himself to be swept along through the strobing neon, the dry-ice fog, the mirrored surfaces that multiplied several hundred jam-packed revelers into thousands. Everyone was smoking, drinking, and whipping themselves into an aerobic frenzy.

Michael winced inwardly, but on the surface showed nothing but serenity, calm, earnest goodwill. Patience.

His stewards guided Michael to one of many private VIP rooms fanning out from the central club floor. These exclusive chambers were lozenge shaped—like railroad flats—and padded with a sort of silver lamé tuck-and-roll on the walls that made them look like high-class cells in some A-list lunatic asylum. Table pods sprouted from the floor like mushrooms. And when the door thunked shut, the music vanished to a mere background thrum.

Michael snuck his cheat sheet out of his pocket, glanced at it. This event involved city fathers and local politicos who wished to have a posed snapshot with the head of the Hunt Foundation. It was the next best thing to a grant, and seen by some of them as a likely (perhaps necessary) prelude to same. As they filtered into the VIP room one by one, he shook hands and accepted proferred drinks, which he then mostly set down on the table behind him, untouched.

Eventually the line of people waiting to meet him had dwindled to just a single, singular individual, a willowy black masterpiece that exceeded six-two in heels. She took his arm like a lover and urged him out of the room. He glanced at one of the handlers who'd been steering him around all afternoon, and the man nodded. Michael allowed himself to be led by this amazon—whose name, he gathered, was Shukuma—toward a table in the back.

A burly cosmopolite rose to greet him, an unusual-looking Chinese with stark blue eyes.

"Mister Michael Hunt," Shukuma said, "may I present Mister Kuan-Ku Tak Cheung."

"This is both a great pleasure and a deep honor," said Cheung. They shook hands briskly in the Western style. "Please join us."

EVERY FIBER OF QI'S COMBAT MIND SCREAMED *KILL him now.*

Ivory sat before her with an infuriating smile of

calm, awaiting a bullet to his head.

She could tell by the weight of the sleek Glock in her grasp that the gun was loaded. This was no trick. Ivory had mentally infected her with indecision. All his buttery-smooth talk of conflicted obligations. But above all, perhaps without intending to, he had reminded her that he, Ivory, was not her target. All of her life's work of despair and foxed chances now offered her an unclear choice.

"You wish for me to kill you?" she said. "Or is it that you wish for me to kill Cheung and free you from the burden of your conflicted duty?"

Ivory shrugged.

She raised the gun, then gave him the barrel in a sweeping backhand to the temple. A tiny grunt eased from him. Bright blood appeared as his eyeballs swiveled up and went opaque. He slumped from his seat, one leg hung up, his foot jutting out. It was undignified.

She took one small moment to arrange him on the floor of his sanctuary. Then she checked the Glock for loads and made for the door.

MITCH WAS FRESHLY DRESSED AND RUNNING HER hands all over herself, as though someone had slid her into a new and confusingly alien body, inside-out. She seemed mildly embarrassed when Gabriel returned to the shrine room.

She peered at him, trying to suss out her recent past. "Did I...?" she said. Her tone was diminished and uncharacteristically modest. "Did we...?"

"No," Gabriel said.

"You undressed me."

"I had to. You were burning up. It's that stuff they stuck you with."

"But I distinctly remember…" Her eyes went a little glassy. "…at least I *think* I remember… being, uh, extremely turned on."

"That part is true," said Gabriel.

"But we—you and I—we didn't…?"

"No."

"Good," she said. "Thank you. Not that you aren't a good-looking man—"

"Understood," Gabriel said. "I saw you and Lucy together, back home."

At the mention of her name, a buried memory seemed to surface, and with it a deep crimson blush. "Your sister is a very special person."

"No doubt," Gabriel said. "Now, if you're through needlessly feeling embarrassed, I'd like to tell you about what I—"

Gabriel stopped speaking when he realized she wasn't looking at him any longer, that she was looking past him, over his shoulder, at a figure behind his back.

Gabriel sucked in a hasty breath and turned. Qingzhao was standing at the far end of the chamber with her arms folded.

SAFE. GABRIEL AND HIS TWO CHARGES WERE ARMED, safe, and reasonably whole.

"Let me get this straight," said Mitch. "Now you don't *want* to leave?"

"Of course I do," said Gabriel. "But not with unfinished business, and I have business with Cheung. Mitch, you were abducted, drugged, pressed into a kind of slavery, shot at. Hell, forget 'at,' you were shot. I was, too," he said, fingering the healed scar where the bullet had creased his temple. "And it'll keep happening unless Cheung is dealt with. To us, to other people, to the whole country—the man needs to be stopped."

"Very revolutionary of you," said Qi. She was stripping and cleaning a gun. "Very inspiring. Except it is easier to say this than to do it. Believe me, I have tried and I know. You forget that we are all fugitives now, and Zhang's police force is looking for us."

"But we have the one thing Cheung wants," Gabriel said.

The women looked at each other, puzzled.

"This place," he continued. "We know the location of Kangxi Shih-k'ai's Killers of Men."

"That is true," said Qi cautiously, "but only to a point. The army we found is not of terra cotta and there is no sign Kangxi Shih-k'ai's remains are there. Surely the warlord did not have himself impaled on a spike. So, impressive as the display may be, it is not what Cheung seeks."

"That bothered me, too," said Gabriel. "I didn't see anything in the cave that would serve Cheung's purpose. So I looked at the statue again."

He led them to the second shrine room and to the back wall where the giant statue reposed in horrible, shadowy splendor.

"Look at the eye sockets," said Gabriel. "You see how they're angled? And there's a slight rim—as though they're settings."

"Settings? For what?" Mitch said. "You mean like a jewel? It would have to be huge."

Gabriel thought back to an expedition that had taken him to the Kalahari Desert. There had been a statue there with jewels for eyes that made even this behemoth look tiny. "I've seen larger," he said.

"Something like this?" Qi said. She climbed down into one of the deep trenches in the dirt from which she'd exhumed the terra-cotta figures she'd traded to Tuan for supplies. She crouched down, vanishing from view for a moment, then emerged holding an object nestled in decades-old newspaper. "I found this on the ground by the idol when I first came here."

It was a dusty, faceted red sphere, like a cut-glass Christmas ornament.

"It fits in the socket," she said. "I tried inserting it. But nothing happens when you put it in."

"Was there another one?"

"There was, at one point," Qi said. "By the time I got here, there was only one that was whole, and pieces of another, shattered on the ground. Fragments. Would you like me to get them?"

"No, that's okay," Gabriel said, turning the faceted sphere in his hands. It was not a gem—it was glass, worth about as much as a chandelier at a discount house. But he'd been around enough giant, ancient statues over the years to know it surely had a function. "Give me a hand here, Mitch, would you?"

Gabriel handed the eye to Mitch and scaled the idol, climbing up to its shoulder. Mitch passed the sphere up to him once he had. It fit equally well into either eye socket on the giant, glowering statue.

"Give me some light," Gabriel said. She turned a flashlight on, pointed it up at him.

After brushing away the accretions of ages with his sleeve, he could see a fine, almost microscopic line of ideograms around the rim of each eye socket.

He called down a description of what he saw. "You think you could you read them?" he asked Qi. "Give us even a rough idea what it says?"

Up went Qingzhao.

"No," she said as she perched in the crook of the statue's arm. "They look like they're upside-down or backward, or both—they make no sense."

"Mitch," Gabriel called, "shine that light up toward the eye. No, the big light." He was referring to the dual-xenon job he had used in the cave, the million-candlepower one.

Nothing. Part of the ceiling turned red as the light reflected, but that was about it.

"Pass it up here," Gabriel said.

Qi descended to the lap of the idol, took the heavy lamp from Mitch and passed it up.

"The glass is faceted," Gabriel said. "In fact—" he shifted the lamp into position "—it looks like it's ground to a very fine tolerance, like optical glass."

"Like a lens?" said Mitch from below.

"You got it."

He held the lamp dead-center on the crimson eye and turned it on.

The tiny glyphs sprang into hard relief in a wide arc on the opposite wall of the chamber, each about a foot high. Optical graffiti.

"They still do not make any sense," said Qi, after straining to read them.

"That's because it's only half the information," said Gabriel, dislodging the crystal and mounting it in the other socket. Sure enough—a second set of characters appeared on the far wall, like a bi-pack cipher. "If we had both eyes and lit them at the same time, the projected images would merge on the wall and you could read them."

"So what do we do?" said Mitch from below.

A low, almost subaural hum had become present in the chamber.

"We start writing down those characters," said Gabriel, *"exactly* the way they appear."

The hum became a louder sound, a kind of chuddering bass note.

"What is that?" said Qi. "Did we start up some kind of machine?"

"No," said Mitch. "It's outside, damn it."

"What is it?" said Qi.

Before Mitch could answer, the sound became loud enough for them all to recognize it.

A chopper, incoming.

20

OUTSIDE, CROUCHED AMONG THE ROCKS, MITCH spotted the helicopter through binoculars, coming in soft about a hundred yards from the pagoda, the blades on powerful Ribinsk turboshafts spinning a silver halo above the craft.

"It's a Kamov," she said. "The kind the Russians nicknamed the Orca. Jesus, there could be twenty guys in there."

Gabriel grabbed Qi's upper arm. "Could you have been tagged somehow? Followed?"

Surprise and incomprehension sparked within her dark gaze. "No, I…"

Then brutal logic slapped her. "The Glock," she said with disgust.

"What Glock?" said Mitch.

Qi snorted, angry at her own lack of vigilance. "Why would he have a Glock? Ivory prefers fully automatic pistols—that is why he has that Russian monstrosity.

He would not have a Glock around unless it was disposable." She drove a fist into her own hand. "Damn it. He handed it to me. He knew I'd take it. *Stupid!*"

"He misdirected you," said Gabriel. "Could have happened to any of us."

"He gave me the chance to shoot him with it!"

"Well, obviously he was confident you wouldn't take him up on it." The location of the leaning pagoda had just ceased to be a bargaining chip. They had been made, blown, outfoxed.

"Load everything," said Qi. She was obviously envisioning some kind of glorious standoff that would get them all killed.

"Wait," said Gabriel. "Let's see if they're soldiers, Red Police guys, or Cheung's men."

"I see the bald guy from the casino," said Mitch, still glassing the slope, where the men from the chopper were now climbing, hunched over in a protective crouch.

"That is Dinanath," said Qi. "Number Two, after Ivory." She ducked into her armory and came up with a Nightforce-sighted LMT rifle, already zeroing in.

"Wait!" said Gabriel. "No shooting! We can still—"

Qi fired without hesitation just as Gabriel shot out a hand, bumping her aim off true. The 5.56 round spanged off a tree branch, severing it two feet from Dinanath's head.

Cheung's crew answered.

The rocks all around began to flint and chip with bullet hits, half of them silenced. The other half of the shooters didn't care if they were heard, time-delay gunshots bouncing around the hillside and trapping them in a weird Doppler cone of weapons fire. Mitch, gunless, had hit the dirt, and Gabriel was trying not to get nailed by flying frags of rock.

He took the binoculars from Mitch, peered through them. At least eighteen men were coming at them up a hillside with excellent cover.

Qi could pick some of them off one by one, pacing her fire, but there were too many. She could never bag them all.

Gabriel held her in abeyance until the first salvo wrapped.

"Don't," he cautioned her. "We have something they want. We still have the upper hand. Cheung's not even with them. Let me handle them."

Disappointment flashed in Qi's eyes.

"There will be no more shooting, Mr. Hunt," came Dinanath's voice over a bullhorn. "We have your brother Michael. You will cease fire and stand down now."

"BOTH OF YOU, GO NOW," GABRIEL SAID TO QI AND MITCH.

"What are you going to do?" said Qi, still bitter at being cheated of deaths she felt were owed her.

"They want the Killers of Men, let's give 'em what they want," Gabriel said. "If they have Michael we have to dispense with all this pawn-pushing and get right to the royalty."

"Chess," Mitch said in response to Qi's blank expression.

"You have a plan?" said Qi.

"Don't worry about it," Gabriel said. "Just worry about getting away. If either of you stay, you'll both wind up in cages. At best—that's if they don't just kill you on the spot. Go. *Now.* Take the back path down the hill."

Both women were staring at him stubbornly. What the hell did he have to do, point a gun at them?

"We can set up in the shrine rooms," said Qi. "Each of us with a rifle, and kill them as they—"

Gabriel overrode her. "No. Don't you see? That won't save Michael—and it won't kill Cheung. Please: go."

Bad trouble would have them cross-haired in moments. A tidal wave of downside was coursing up the hill toward them.

"Get out of here," Gabriel said. "Seriously. Leave them to me."

"You're giving up," Mitch said vacantly. She winced at a sudden spike of pain in her forehead. The last dose of the drug he'd given her had obviously almost worn off. It was why she was as lucid as she was—but it also meant she was just minutes away from suffering serious withdrawal.

He held her face and snapped his fingers to focus her. "I'm going to surrender to them, yes—but no way am I giving up. You have to trust me. I haven't lost my mind. I do have a plan. But if you two don't get out of sight, pronto, none of it'll work—understand?"

"No," she said—but Qi took her by the arm and began pulling Mitch away.

Mitch wrested free and grabbed Gabriel's jacket, turning him around, holding his torso between her hands, staring directly into his eyes.

"You be careful, goddamn it, or I'll come back and kick your ass," she said. "Lucy'd never forgive me if I got you killed."

He nodded and she let go. Qi led her back into the pagoda, toward the rear archway.

"Dinanath!" Gabriel shouted. "Hold your fire! I'm coming down!"

Gabriel left the Colt behind one of the stone lions as he walked into the open, hands raised, to meet his captors.

* * *

"I THINK YOU ARE LYING," SAID DINANATH AS HE circled Gabriel…

…who was lying on the ground of the shrine room, trussed up with rope. Before they'd tied him up, Cheung's thugs had gotten in some good punches, but when Gabriel hadn't either resisted or spilled any useful information, their hearts went out of the procedure rather quickly.

Gabriel quickly used his tongue to take inventory of his teeth. One wobbler; all still present in his mouth. His right eye was threatening to swell shut and his internals felt kicked down a stairwell—but this was all (he reminded himself) a necessary part of the plan.

"Don't believe me then," Gabriel said, his voice a little slurred. "Ignore what I say. That's your privilege. But if it later turns out I was telling the truth, Cheung will have your liver and heart for breakfast."

Dinanath wished Ivory were here to offer counsel. Hell, he wished Ivory were still in Cheung's favor at all, rather than precariously teetering on the edge of a particularly fatal variety of disfavor. Perhaps victory today would enable Ivory to return from disgrace— he had, after all, provided the tin can for the dog's tail and thus allowed them to discover the location of Qingzhao's hideout. Perhaps Dinanath himself would be able to offer testimony that would restore Cheung's faith in Ivory, whom he counted as a good colleague, if not a friend.

But that would be sometime down the line, at best; in the meantime, Dinanath was on his own and had to figure out what to do about this American and his claims.

"Put it another way," said Gabriel. "All you have to

do is check it out. I'll show you myself."

"A trap," said Dinanath. "You would lead us into an ambush."

"Why? So I can knock off or incapacitate a few of your men? When Cheung still has my brother? That would be crazy. I'm offering a trade because I have something Cheung wants and he has something I want."

The other men on Dinanath's squad were starting to debate among themselves. Gabriel had uttered the magic words, in English and Chinese both: *Favored Son, Kangxi Shih-k'ai, Killers of Men.* Looking from man to man around him, he knew each of them had to be weighing how he might put the knowledge Gabriel was offering to use to advance his position with Cheung—maybe even to claim the ten million dollar reward, if they could turn up the big guy's bones.

They had carried Gabriel into the room with the idol, deposited him roughly at its base. It glowered down at them (eyeless now; Gabriel had dislodged the red crystal and stowed it back in the trench before they raced out to spot the helicopter); the statue's tarnished metal surface shone dully in the firelight and the strobe-sweep of the high-powered lamps each man carried as part of a basic assault kit. They were dressed for night-fighting, black-on-black.

"If you think it's a trap," Gabriel said, "just make me walk in first. You can walk me in at gunpoint. Or I'll go in alone. Whatever you say—unless you're not the man in charge and I should speak to someone else who can actually get things done."

Anger flared in Dinanath's sculpted face, so much like the idol itself—rough-hewn, broad-planed, admitting of no subtlety. This was, Gabriel had decided, a man who would not want his authority challenged. Third in line in Cheung's pecking order, his rank made him answerable here. He had been granted this responsibility. He would want neither to lose face nor gain demotion.

Dinanath squatted beside Gabriel and cracked him in the mouth again just to reassert his superiority.

Gabriel spat a small gob of blood onto the ground. "If I'm telling the truth," he said, "you get to bring the Killers of Men back to Cheung and Cheung will be all smiles. That's what I want for my brother. If I'm lying, you can kill me then just as easily as now."

"You do not dictate terms for Kuan-Ku Tak Cheung," Dinanath said, making sure the men heard him proclaim the chain of command.

"Then let me talk to Ivory," Gabriel said.

Dinanath let a tiny snort escape him. "Longwei Sze Xie is dangerously close to becoming a Nameless One."

"Fine. Then it's up to you. Untie me now and let me open it my way—or you can figure out the secret of the idol for yourself," said Gabriel.

"*You* will tell us." Dinanath reconsidered his inflection. "You *will* tell us."

"I'll tell you nothing. You can knock me around all you want, if you try hard enough you can kill me, but believe me, you won't make me talk that way. Better men than you have tried it, and it's never worked." Gabriel prayed his sincere, self-confident tone was convincing them; he hoped like hell they wouldn't test his claim, just to see. "Meanwhile," he said, "how long do you have? Cheung's a man who wants answers *now*. He won't give you days or weeks to figure this out for yourselves. But I can show you. I'm unarmed, for god's sake. You have nearly twenty men."

"The two women," said Dinanath. "They are

armed. Perhaps they are the ambush."

"The women are gone. They ran away. I don't know where they are and that's the truth. Anyway, do you really think two women can pick off twenty armed men? If they could, wouldn't we just have done that when you were coming up the hill? What you're saying makes no sense." Gabriel shook his head. "I'm offering you a good deal."

"How *American*," Dinanath sneered. "A *deal*." He pressed his gun to Gabriel's forehead. To one of his men he said, curtly, "Untie him." Gabriel felt someone go to work on the knots at his wrists. They sprang free a moment later.

"Very well," Dinanath said. "I will trust you—but only so far." He let Gabriel get up on his knees, and then unsteadily stand. "You will instruct us now as to what needs to be done."

"I'll show you. Keep all the guns on me you want."

Dinanath's cellphone trilled then, echoing in the chamber.

"That'll be Daddy," Gabriel said. "Better answer it."

"*Silence!*" Dinanath dealt another backhand to Gabriel's face.

Gabriel felt his jaw swing and heard his neck tendons pop. His dentist was going to be overjoyed if he ever got out of this alive.

Dinanath stepped away for a hushed cellphone conference out of earshot. As he spoke, Dinanath's body seemed to shrink in on itself, diminishing. Awkwardly he returned and held the cellphone to Gabriel's ear.

"Mr. Hunt?" came Cheung's voice. The man might have been excited or he might have been furious, but you couldn't tell—he sounded as calm as still water.

"My man has sketched the situation for me. If you would be so kind as to lend my group the benefit of your expertise, your trained eye, I would be greatly in your debt, and I am certain your brother would find any possible discovery to be of immeasurable value both to me and to your Foundation. Find me the Killers of Men and all debts are paid in full."

"All debts?" Gabriel said, trying to match Cheung cool for cool. He had to work his mouth back into speaking form first. "How about the women?"

"You can have them if you like. I leave that to your judgment. I would only ask that they leave the country and never return. Do you agree?"

"Yes," Gabriel said. "But your man here is eager to pound the crap out of me some more, maybe shoot me, instead of getting you what you want."

"You have found the vault and know the way in," Cheung said. "If I leave it to them, they shall still be loitering around there at this time next month. Prove your worthiness, Mr. Hunt, and rest assured that if anyone harms you further, it will be his final act on earth."

It was pretty clear who Cheung was talking about.

"That sounds good," Gabriel said, "but you're not here. I don't see how you can ensure my safety from wherever you are."

"You'll have to take that risk, Mr. Hunt."

Gabriel raised his voice. "What if there's treasure in the vault—gold, precious stones, old money? Shouldn't you be here to ensure none of it goes astray?"

"Not necessary," Cheung said. "My men have discipline. Anyway, I have another pestersome matter I must deal with first."

Ivory, Gabriel figured.

"You also want to be far away in case anything goes wrong," said Gabriel.

"We understand each other, Mr. Hunt."

"All right," Gabriel said. "We'll play it your way." He heard the call terminate. It would have been good if Cheung had agreed to come immediately, but it didn't matter much that he hadn't. Cheung would not be able to stay away for long, not when it càme out that Gabriel was, in fact, telling the truth. Even if the Killers of Men were not precisely what Cheung had expected—he'd want to see them for himself.

Meanwhile, Cheung's men here in the shrine room, had very clearly heard the words *gold, precious stones, old money*. Already he could see the men whispering, plotting how they might re-team to doublecross one another.

It looked hopeless. It was perfect.

"I CAN'T SEE THE SHRINE ROOM FROM HERE," SAID Mitch, giving up on the binoculars. Her hands were shaking badly and her head was hurting. "We have to go back."

"No, we have to go forward," said Qi. "It is as Gabriel said—we must take the head of the serpent. That is the thing I lost sight of."

They worked their way down the rock escarpment, closer to the reassuring cover of trees and brush, in darkness, undetected.

"Cheung really wants those skeletons you found, dung and all?"

"Yes. Although how Gabriel means to use them, I have no idea."

"You don't think he's just stepping up so we can get away?" Mitch kept glancing back, second-guessing.

"No. That would be foolhardy." Qi's eyes were like flint chips in the dark.

"Maybe just self-sacrificing," said Mitch.

"Illogical," returned Qi. "That is why I believe he has another plan. He may be a reckless man, but he is not a foolish one. If it were only his life at risk, maybe—but with Cheung holding his brother, I have to conclude his choice was tactical."

"Well," Mitch conceded, "I haven't heard any shooting yet."

They could see the helicopter in the clearing below them to the west, on a flat mesa just big enough to provide a landing zone. Mitch got a better look at it through the nightscope on the rifle Qi had thrust into her hands. She tried her damndest to hold it steady as she squinted to see through it.

The Kamov was a Russian special ops aircraft about a decade old, comparable to the Bell 430 or the Sikorsky S-76, Mitch knew. The four-bladed coaxial rotor was still now. Many iterations of the Kamov were manufactured in Russia for foreign sale; knowing Cheung's present orbits, this one had probably come into his hands via India. It was painted combat green over black and—interestingly—featured no registry numbers.

The pilot still had his helmet on, and his buddy was holding at port arms an M4 with a stretch magazine. Both were smoking. The M4 was less accurate at distance fire than the M16 it largely replaced; still, you wouldn't want to be within 150 meters of a 30-round spray... and Mitch and Qi were already well within the bubble.

Qi tugged Mitch's sleeve. "Can you fly that thing?"

"Depends who you ask," Mitch said. "The U.S. Air Force has some doubts."

Qi's face fell.

"But they're wrong," Mitch said. She started down the final slope.

21

RIGHT ON CUE, A WAYWARD BAT FLITTERED OUT OF the crack on the right side of the idol once Gabriel had worked the hidden lever. Its timing could not have been better. Dinanath's men watched it wheel crazily around the upper curve of the shrine room until it found a roost.

"Hold it," said Gabriel, raising a hand. Dinanath turned to his crew and everyone froze. "See that bat? There could be more inside. We don't know how large the chamber actually is. We have to be quiet and cautious."

Fully half Dinanath's force was conscripted to muscle the foot-thick iron panel, which yielded by degrees. Gabriel raised a hand and pointed at the small chalk mark he had made at about the midpoint of the panel's arc—when the opening was slightly wider than a man.

"Stop," he said. "We must not open this all the way."

"Countermeasures?" said Dinanath.

"Yes—remember your history. Traps in tombs. We

must be silent and very careful. Do you smell that? More bats inside. The footing will be treacherous. Excess noise will disturb the bats. Have you ever done this sort of thing before?"

"No," said Dinanath, uncertain whether his rank was being usurped.

Gabriel picked up a flashlight. "Mask these like so. Focused beams, not wide light." He was halfway through the doorway when Dinanath yanked him back, bodily.

"You could have a weapon just inside the door," the big man explained calmly.

"How could I...?" Gabriel raised his hands in conciliation. "Okay. You're the boss."

Dinanath directed two men to precede Gabriel. They self-consciously stayed as quiet as mute cats in a library, whispering back a description of the hundreds of miniature warrior figures they saw inside.

The information grapevined through the rest of the men and Gabriel could witness its effect. They were eager, hoping for treasure and measuring the capacity of their own pockets for same.

Dinanath posted two gunners at the base of the idol. Two more at the mouth of the shrine room. Two more on perimeter, outside. Their check-ins were leapfrogged so that the first sign of trouble would bring a radio alert to the unit on Dinanath's belt.

"Now you," said Dinanath, directing Gabriel to step through.

The men inside were already picking up the small soldiers, examining them for traces of precious metals or jewels. The men behind Gabriel were eager to start nosing around on their own. Dinanath squeezed through behind Gabriel.

"Cover pattern," he hissed to his subordinates. "Keep sight of the man in front of you!"

Men were filing in behind them, grouping, oozing the point of the expedition through the second chamber and toward the head of the stone stairway. They had begun to notice the abundance of creepy-crawly lifeforms among which they were standing, and Gabriel turned back to shush them. "They're not poisonous," he whispered. "Just move through them swiftly." Several of the men nodded. The more he asserted himself as knowledgeable and a leader, the more they would look past Dinanath to him for guidance when things went wrong.

This was Gabriel's third foray into the realm of the Favored Son's Killers of Men. His first exploration had released the bats. His second had revealed to him the ways in and out of the massive vault. Before he'd left the second time, he'd also observed the mechanics of the giant, pendulum-like iron baskets bracketing the stairway that led down from the stone arch. He had set to work on them, using the tools and climbing gear he had to restore the ancient mechanisms' original function. And then he'd paced off the distance from the entryway to the spot below the funnel that wound its way to the outside. Keeping himself precisely oriented as to distance and direction, he could now move to that exact location even in the dark.

Standing at the head of the dung-befouled stairway, Gabriel reached back to tug Dinanath forward by the sleeve. "The Killers of Men," he whispered, shining his masked flashlight forward into the void.

Dinanath's mouth dropped open at the sight. His men crowded in behind him, eager to see for themselves.

Gabriel gave Dinanath a hard shove. The big man

lost his balance against the thick oilslick of guano on the floor. Then Gabriel dived onto the right-hand balustrade and slid down into darkness as everybody started shooting.

QI AND MITCH HEARD A SOUND LIKE TWO CONGESTED little barks. Squirrel coughs in the darkness. The helicopter pilot and his buddy dropped, tumbling lifeless out of the open cockpit doors, their cigarettes still smoldering.

"What the hell—" Mitch said.

Qi signaled her to keep quiet. Neither of them had seen even a muzzle flash.

Qi spoke with her eyes. *Don't move. Not a sound.*

Five minutes later, still frozen and silent, they still hadn't seen anything to explain what had happened. All they could see was the two dead guys by the chopper growing deader.

"Let's take the bird," Mitch whispered, impatient.

"No—too obvious. We would be exposed. We wait."

"I don't know if I can," Mitch said, feeling her condition worsening.

"You must," Qi said.

In the hunter's-hide silence that descended around them, they could finally hear the sounds of gunfire coming from deep within the mountainside.

THE IRON PLATES OF THE FLOOR INSIDE THE ENTRY rooms were pressure-sensitive, Gabriel knew. His investigation showed that the ordeal of sliding open the large iron door at the base of the idol had a secondary purpose, which was to cock the mechanism for the long-dormant catapults. The weight of a single man could not trip it, but the weight of many would cause the floor to shift exactly one quarter of an inch. It was similar to the bed on a truck scale. And its purpose...

Gabriel surfed to the floor of the main chamber in a sludgy mudslide of decay, guano, and worse.

Outside, the counterbalanced door slid back into position and locked, crushing one of Dinanath's men who was half-in, half-out. Six men had been posted as sentries outside the idol. That left Gabriel with twelve inside, plus Dinanath.

As everybody unslung their hardware and started shooting, the thousands of bats in the cave awakened and began flying in every direction.

Thin flashlight beams swung wildly about the room, each extending three or four feet into the darkness before petering out. Muzzle flashes lit up the darkness as well, providing confusing snapshot contrasts of shadows and light, strobing in all directions, not aiding sight but blinding everybody.

The shooting ceased in a wave as Cheung's men furiously swatted at the bats swarming over their heads. Then another wave of shooting came, mostly wild, aimed toward the ceiling.

The floor mechanism—thanks to Gabriel's repair—was now able to do its intended job. Counterbalances clicked and cog-wheeled belaying gears swung the ironbound baskets, hurling their deadly projectiles in the direction of Dinanath's desperate men. Gabriel heard two dozen impacts, some of metal into walls or floor, but many into flesh.

Dinanath was still trying to find his footing, having fallen halfway down the dung-slick stairs as everybody went berserk. The pistol in his hand was lost to a quicksand of liquid waste as though it had disappeared through pie crust.

A wheeling bat smacked him in the face and knocked him down again.

Gabriel shut his eyes and sprinted. *Five running steps, left, touch helmet of skeleton with raised sword on right-hand side, turn ninety degrees and haul ass straight out for twenty steps.*

He kept his eyes shut, depending on his rehearsal in the dark to guide him according to touchpoints. Five more steps.

"LET'S JUST GET THE HELL OUT OF HERE," MITCH whispered. "Please. I can get that helicopter in the air in minutes from a cold start. Whoever shot the pilot can't be out there any longer. Let me do it."

They could hear the thunderous sounds of gunfire below, muffled by layers of rock. "You would just leave Gabriel in there?" said Qi.

"If Gabriel's in the middle of that, he doesn't have a hope in hell. But we still do. We've got to get back to the city. Save his brother from Cheung."

"Is that how you do it?" said Qi. "Exchange one goal for another? Your sister for his brother? Me for someone else?"

"Well, what do *you* think we should do?"

Qi thought for a moment. "I have confidence in Gabriel. I believe he had a plan. But," she said, letting her eyes slide shut, "you are right. Our object must be Cheung."

With one final glance back toward the pagoda, she came out from behind the cover that had shielded them and began to run toward the chopper.

* * *

IN THE HARSH AND UNEVEN ILLUMINATION PROVIDED
by a dozen flashlights, many of which had fallen and
were now casting their beams crazily into the darkness,
Gabriel could see a flurry of still-circling bats and the
bodies of dead men both ancient and new.

Two thirds of Dinanath's crew seemed to be down.
The spiked metal siege balls had killed a few and
bloodied several more—and the bats could smell the
fresh blood. The rest were struggling to regain their
footing and orientation, or firing madly, their bullets
pinholing the muddy air. Panic shots bounced off the
cavern ceiling or ricocheted off moist stone. Scabs
of encrusted dung jumped away from the impaled
corpses in their warrior drag. Near Gabriel, a warrior's
head—a featureless blunt point beneath waxy layers
of droppings—was vaporized like a kicked anthill by
a stray 9mm slug.

Gabriel caught a glimpse of Dinanath. He was
furiously emptying his magazine in what he must have
thought was Gabriel's direction, but he might as well
have been shooting blind. One of his men, trying to claw
a wriggling bat off his face, hit Dinanath from behind
and the big Indian went down to hands and knees.

Falling bats pelted them like black hailstones.
Other bats flew directly into the walls and dropped,
unconscious or dead. The rest of the flock made for the
funnel vent.

Primal fears took over. Terror of the dark, which
their guns could not push back. Terror of the bats,
which their guns could not track. Terror of more sharp
killing objects, perhaps a second salvo of ancient metal
death. Claustrophobia. Group panic, as men retreated

to the sliding iron doorway only to find it cinched shut on the still-spasming arm of one of their comrades.

Dinanath was ground face-first into the sucking black mire by the panicked trampling of his own men.

Gabriel threaded himself into the vertical harness he'd left waiting the last time he'd been here, anticipating the possibility of a return under less than sanguine circumstances. He grabbed a short-handled dagger out of the scabbard at the waist of the nearest impaled skeleton, used it to saw through the anchor rope, and hauled himself toward the ceiling on his three-to-one pulley setup, which towed him at about fifteen feet per second.

Careening bats swept by him as he reached the cavern ceiling and began to corkscrew his way through the funnel. His ascent was designed to leave no dangling rope behind.

Gabriel had left himself a weapon on the eastern slope the first time he'd made this ascent, one of Qi's LMT shortie rifles. He grabbed it now, before quickly scrambling down to the nearest of the shrine rooms.

But when he reached the room, there was no one to shoot. The sentries posted outside the idol were all face-down in pools of their own blood, snipped off by throat hits.

Gabriel hustled past two more deceased guards to the other shrine room, where he dived into the iron tub to wash away some of the foul, clotted wastes clinging to him.

When he rose, dripping, he saw a man walking toward him from the shrine room's entrance… a man with a gun in his hand, and the gun was pointed at Gabriel.

"Hello, Mr. Hunt," said Ivory.

22

WHILE THE ENGINES WERE SPINNING UP, MITCH
noticed the helicopter was not outfitted with any
exterior firepower. Kamovs were workhorses
adaptable to a number of applications, including air
ambulance and search-and-rescue over land or water,
but they were originally developed by the Russians
as antitank choppers. Not this one. Fully stocked
with armament, the machine could chew up and
spit out a Cobra gunship, but this one was fangless,
with not a gun or bomb in sight. At least its defensive
features were still in place: the energy-absorbing seats,
the beefed up landing struts, the non-fragmenting
fuselage. The rotor blades were made of a composite
material that could withstand a hit by a 23mm
projectile and keep functioning.

"This thing is a taxi," Mitch said as the rotors
reached takeoff speed. "Stripped down for fast
insertion and extraction."

"Good," Qi said. "We should try some fast extraction now."

Running from their abandoned cover to the chopper, both Qi and Mitch had scanned the area for any sign— any glint of metal in the distance, any sound—that might portend imminent gunfire, but they'd reached the vehicle and the two dead bodies before it without attracting anyone's attention. The two men had been neatly shot—but by whom? They'd put the question to one side much as they did the bodies themselves, then climbed up into the cockpit and began preparations to leave. As Mitch worked the controls, desperately forcing her hands to remain as steady as she could get them, Qi held their small arsenal of guns at the ready and watched for trouble.

But none had surfaced, and now, after readjusting her seat several times and getting the feel of the throttle, Mitch was able to float their craft into the night air. They hovered at about ten feet while she triple-checked her board. Then she seemed confident enough to loft them into the sky.

The helo accident for which Mitch had been cashiered out had occurred during a soft landing on an aircraft carrier, strictly a milk run. She was an Air Force loan-out for Naval pilot trainees, occupying the Number Two slot on the MH-60S Knighthawk when wind shear and a rolling carrier made tacking on the landing platform more difficult than her superior, the pilot, had been prepared for. They counter-rolled as the ship surged upward on the tide, and the rotor blades snapped off like popsicle sticks against the deck, gravely wounding two runway rats and scratching one chopper at a cost of about $28 million. No time was wasted in assigning a scapegoat, especially since it would boil down to a Navy versus Air Force beef.

But Mitch could jockey these beasts. She knew it, and the brass knew it too, even if they'd never admit it. She'd longed for a gunship and the chance to deploy its devastating firepower in combat, just once. This might have been that chance, but Kuan-Ku Tak Cheung, wily devil that he was, had provided no bang-bang aboard this eggbeater.

They had their rifles, and the guns taken off the dead pilot and his companion. Mitch had spotted a few racked grenades. And they had the helo.

"This puts us into the center of things," said Qi.

"Meaning?" Mitch concentrated on the rudder, which was a little slushy-feeling. She wiped sweat off her forehead.

"Cheung's helipad directly accesses his headquarters. No infiltration, no disguises. No strategy. All that is left to us is the lightning raid."

"You mean barge in, guns blazing, and hope for the best?" Mitch sucked air between her teeth. "Sorry, but that sounds a lot like your other plans, based as they were on the idea of a one-way mission. I'm no kamikaze."

"We have the Killers of Men as a bargaining chip. Cheung may hate us. He may want us dead on sight. But he is not so foolish as to risk this prize."

"So we fly right in like we own the place?"

"Exactly. Without Ivory or Dinanath, Cheung's subordinates will stand down."

"You hope."

Qi almost smiled. "Always. But I also prepare for the worst." She went to work stripping and cleaning the guns.

* * *

IVORY HAD A LAYER OF BANDAGE PADS TAPED TO HIS forehead and his eyes seemed to glitter unnaturally in the dim light of the shrine room, candlefire making them appear too starkly white.

He sat with his lethal OTs-33 held loosely, dangling between his knees as he perched on the canvas-tarped pile of one of Qi's caches.

"You have me at a disadvantage," Gabriel said, even though it was obvious, standing as he was in an elevated metal cauldron.

Ivory said nothing.

"It appears we may have the same enemies now," Gabriel added, waving in the direction of the neighboring shrine room, where Cheung's men lay dead. He pointed at Ivory's gun. "Quite a weapon. Russian, isn't it?"

"It is adequate to my needs."

"Yeah, I heard you weren't too fond of Glocks."

One of Ivory's eyebrows arched. "That, too, served its purpose. Mr. Hunt, is it your intention to waste time with banter? I have never understood that about Americans; their reluctance to address a point directly."

"'Warfare is the tao of deceit,'" said Gabriel, quoting Sun Tzu. He thought he saw Ivory roll his eyes. No doubt sick of Westerners quoting *The Art of War*.

Gabriel considered climbing out, then thought better of it. Any abrupt movement might get him killed.

"These two women," said Ivory without prelude. "Your dedication to them is unusual. My experience of most Westerners is that they are little more than infants incapable of seeing beyond their little personal dramas, attitudes, whims or appetites. What binds you to them?"

"Nothing," said Gabriel. "I used them to help me find the Killers of Men, nothing more."

"Ah, now you are being less than honest. Believe me, I know. I, too, have been less than forthcoming, with Cheung. My covenant was to lead him to this place. Instead I came alone, and found you. And as you have said, we seem to be on the same path, now. But I must understand how you got here."

"All right, I'll be honest," Gabriel said. "I don't want to see either Qi or Mitch hurt. That's what I'm here for. The rest is incidental. There's also my brother—I need to get him free. The quickest and surest way to accomplish these things is to eliminate your boss. I'm sorry, Ivory, but the man is a Grade-A certified lunatic, and I think you know it. If you didn't, I'd be dead already."

"I cannot—"

Gabriel overrode him. "You don't have to. The women are on their own now—they can fend for themselves. And if you return with me to the city and present me to Cheung, I can get my brother back. You were supposed to find this place for Cheung—well, you've found it. By bringing me back to Cheung you will have discharged your duty. Cheung has already offered amnesty if I can reveal the Killers of Men to him; the women go free, my brother and I return to America."

"If you believe Cheung's word."

"I don't, not for a second. But look at what he wants versus what he's got. We have leverage. Frankly, it's what happens to you I'm not so sure of."

"I have earned no mercy in this, no special consideration."

"Except from me," said Gabriel. "I'll help you—if you let me get out of this pot."

He watched this handsome, conflicted Asian work

the variables out in his mind. For whatever it was worth, Ivory had still not pulled the trigger on Gabriel.

Yet.

THEY COULD SEE THE ORIENTAL PEARL TV TOWER coming up fast on the horizon, aglitter with nightlight.

"Spot it for me," said Mitch, meaning the landing platform cantilevered onto the backside of the Peace Hotel. It would be one of the neon-lit vertebrae of the Bund. "I can bank up and over."

"There," said Qi.

The concrete platform was a typical helicopter bullseye, outlined by blue landing lights. Tiny now, far below them as the chopper found its mark.

"Son of a… *bitch*," Mitch grunted as though she'd just taken a bullet.

"What is it?" Qi shouted. In the bounce from the console telltales it was clear that Mitch was drenched in sweat. She was vising the bridge of her nose brutally and drawing air in fast, hyperventilating gasps.

"Goddamn it," she groaned. "Not now, not *now*."

The Kamov jolted drunkenly to port as Mitch tried to correct. Tears blurred her eyes to double-vision.

With a low animal noise, Mitch unwillingly let go of the stick to grab her head. The running sounds, the rotors, were jabbing into the soft tissue of her brain.

The chopper briefly lost float and gyro'ed around like a runaway carousel, slamming Qi into the port door.

Mitch grabbed Qi's hands and posted them on the stick in front of her. "Hold this steady!" she said through gritted teeth. "I can hold the pedals. We've got to try to—"

They were already dropping like a stone. Qi saw

the control dials ratchet alarmingly.

They struggled and together managed to get the copter almost level when a cramp tore through Mitch. It felt as though all her internal organs were being carelessly rearranged by a meatball medic using a rusty saw.

Qi saw the Peace Hotel landing platform whisk past on her left, at a sickening angle. They missed it by fifty yards.

"Hold the stick!" Mitch screamed, her eyes clamping shut. "We're going... going to have to set it down in the street."

It was academic. They were heading for the street anyway, their drop rate making lift unrecoverable.

In the street were thousands of cars, pedestrians, pedicabs, bicycles—all frantically trying to clear a path for what was sure to be a fiery crash.

The Kamov's powerhouses were redlining and worse, starting to hitch and skip.

Mitch fought the craft level and for a precarious moment it seemed like a hard but manageable job of ditching. Then the landing skids rammed like javelins through the front and back windows of a just-abandoned car and tore free, putting the Kamov into a forward roll with no landing gear.

The spinning blades were now front-most, scything like a gigantic lawnmower, snapping off and flip-flopping free as they chewed into pavement, automobiles and screaming people. Cars swerved and collided in the vain hope of not smashing into the upside-down juggernaut now sliding at speed through the congested street.

Despite their harnesses, Mitch and Qi were tumbled and battered like dice in a cage. As the cabin compressed and imploded, jagged plexi showered in on them. The composite armor was good, but not up to the challenge of keeping cabin-forward from crumpling. Sparks rained and scratched spot-welded highlights on their retinas as their safe cocoon clenched into a trash-compacted death trap.

Then the least lucky motorist of all plowed into the chopper from behind.

23

SHUKUMA STRODE FORWARD WITH HER HANDS
clasped behind her. She was not used to addressing
Cheung as his direct subordinate. That was for Ivory,
or Dinanath, neither of whom was here. Romero
and Chino were dead. Tuan and Mads Hellweg had
been eliminated.

Cheung was in his Temple Room, carving another
little casket. Sister Menga was in her incense-clouded
corner between the two Tosa guard dogs, who were
sleeping at her feet like puppies. Her eyes were rolled
back into her head, showing only whites to the world
of mortals.

"Victory over an enemy," Sister Menga mumbled.
"The exposure of traitors. All as prophesized."

"You said that before," countered Cheung. She had
said it in regard to Tuan. "Are you certain your bones and
animal guts are not giving you recycled information?"

"More than one victory," Sister Menga intoned, her

silver eyes coming down to meet Cheung's. "More than one traitor."

"And Longwei Sze Xie is lost to me?" Cheung said. "No. He would go neutral, not virulent. Besides, I would miss him."

The tall black bodyguard knew that, other than Sister Menga's, Cheung rarely accepted counsel from females—more traditional Chinese horse manure, she thought. If the boys on the team could not handle everything falling to pieces, she could prove herself here and now. The lessons of the tenure of the Nameless One were lost on her. Venerable laws, likewise—she thought herself above their teaching, and in doing so made the error that always brings disaster to the prideful.

"The helicopter has returned," she told Cheung. "It is in the middle of the street below, burning."

"Then Dinanath failed," said Cheung. "Let General Zhang handle the rabble."

Shukuma dared to add, "You seem unconcerned."

"The Killers of Men are within my grasp. The disparate threads are all finally twining together. Binding, as Sister Menga foretold, into the pattern of the future."

"And the men that went to the pagoda with Dinanath?"

"Expendable," Cheung said. "Shukuma, you are my new Immortal. You shall assume Ivory's station from this moment forward. If you see the American woman, the Nameless One, Ivory, Dinanath or anyone else other than Mr. Gabriel Hunt, you are to retire them immediately and report to me. If there is fire and chaos in the streets, one or more of them will be coming."

"What about Michael Hunt?" she said.

"Keep him under guard until my dealings with his

brother are concluded. Then you may kill all of them."

"You can depend on me, sir," Shukuma said, happy with her promotion.

The paws of the sleeping Tosa dogs twitched, as though they were dreaming at the feet of Cheung's sorceress. Dreaming of prey, thought Shukuma—human or animal, it didn't matter, we all dream of our prey.

And the first place to check for her prey would be that helicopter in the street outside.

GABRIEL CONDUCTED IVORY DOWN THE MOUNTAIN, and Ivory chauffeured Gabriel into the city. Neither man spoke very much during the trip. Until Gabriel finally said:

"Tell me about the drug."

Ivory inhaled deeply. Gabriel thought the man was preparing to sink into one of his stony silences as though the topic at hand was moot, beneath notice, or beyond discussion. But he surprised Gabriel with his specificity.

"The drug is a hydrochloride distillate of *xipaxidine*," he said, pronouncing it knowledgeably: *zi-PAX-eh-deen.* "It is a true synthetic, refined using the Sturges Method. Do you know it?"

"You're talking about three million dollars of equipment just to start the refining process," said Gabriel.

"Yes. There are nine steps in all to the distillate."

Gabriel recalled the nine jogs in the bridge at the Tea House. "Nine turns, to confuse evil spirits?" he said. It was a recurrent feature in Chinese design.

"Nine stages to seek purity," said Ivory, knowing what Gabriel was referring to. "At each stage the substance is highly unstable, and there is an enormous wastage factor. Also a slender margin for error. Each of these stages additionally requires a great deal of time and constant monitoring."

"What does it attack?"

"The most primary programming of the brain—fight, flight, or mate. In its pure form, the distillate allows for direct suggestion without hypnosis."

"And in its impure form?"

"Each castoff stage has dangers. Psychosis, memory loss, violent self-destructive hallucinations, instantaneous addiction. The only cure for a Phase IV user is death. There is no withdrawal."

"The version you gave me and Mitch?"

"You are in no danger. She had more prolonged exposure. She would require a hospital stay for detoxification—or lacking that, regular dosages indefinitely with periodic increases due to habituation. Interruption causes withdrawal-like symptoms; they are rarely fatal, but they are always severe."

"What happens to all the impure material? Wastage at that level is incredibly expensive."

"Cheung plans to offer it to the world as a new narcotic. His 'freon' is impure Stage VII. He and I have always been in disagreement on this. The pure distillate of xipaxidine has its uses. The impure forms are unspeakably dangerous."

Gabriel's hand searched his pocket for the capped syringe with the remaining eight cc's of the drug he had given to Mitch. But it was gone, probably lost in his escape from the cavern.

Gabriel said, "He plans to sell this stuff? It'll kill people."

Ivory came back at him: "Certainly. But it will also make him rich. And warlords have always disregarded the constraints of conventional morality.

General Liu Xiang had eight concubines all trained to play tennis, so one would be available whenever the mood struck him."

"Cheung may enjoy seeing himself as a warlord," Gabriel said, "but he's really just a two-bit criminal with delusions of grandeur."

"This is your conclusion?"

"It's the only sane conclusion."

"You are suggesting one needs to find a new enemy," said Ivory.

"I'm suggesting that you've already found one," said Gabriel.

Ivory fell silent, his eyes fixed forward. Gabriel thought the man was simply retreating into stoicism again. Then Gabriel's mouth dropped open as he saw what Ivory was staring at: the rolling column of smoke and flames from the crashed helicopter in the street ahead, and the hopeless traffic jam that would keep them from reaching it.

ADRENALINE FLUSHED THROUGH MITCH'S SYSTEM and cleared her circuits long enough for her to register the proper response to the flames melting the synthetic fibers of her pilot harness and licking up her arm. The pain helped focus her.

This was no dream, no drug-induced hallucination.

She and Qi were ensnared upside-down in the imploded cockpit, and everything around them seemed to have become flammable.

Past char-fouled Perspex and wide fractures in the canopy, they could both see elements of General Zhang's police force advancing on them, weapons up. They were coming from all sides, snaking between wrecked automobiles, shoving citizens out of the firing line, and maintaining a textbook group cover pattern.

Qi wrestled her harness as though it were a living thing bent on killing her. When the latches undogged, she was still trapped—one leg bent awkwardly behind a fold of steel, blood caking her dynamic new haircut.

Mitch quickly brought up the nearest available sidearm, a Beretta 9mm with a hi-cap mag, and quickly dispatched twenty shots to pin down the approaching mercenaries with some second thoughts about an easy sweep-and-clear. She chucked the empty gun and sought another.

"Take that rifle and hit the alley, over there," Qi shouted. "I need you to cover me—I've got to get unstuck."

"No. We go together."

"Don't be stupid. We go together, we both get shot. Do what I ask."

Mitch could almost see the logic of it. One blind corner. One escape route not covered by Zhang's police. If she could make it, and then cover Qi, if they could dump weapons and fade into the crowd, they might just walk.

Mitch fielded a few more shots with the LMT rifle she had recovered, although it was awkward to maneuver the weapon inside the crushed cabin. She wished she had a full-auto pistol like Ivory's. The things had originally been designed for use by tank crews who might need to wield gunpower inside a confined space. But once she was out in the open, as Qi suggested, she'd be able to make every cartridge count.

"Go for it," shouted Qi. "Go now. I am right behind you."

Mitch scuttled out. Using the smoke and confusion as cover, she was able to crabwalk to the alleyway Qi had indicated.

Qi was not right behind her. In fact, the incoming cops had gained another ten yards on the ruined chopper. They were going to take Qi, and take her hard, if she did not move her ass doublequick.

Qi's heart surged as she saw Mitch make a break for it. It was correct that Mitch should live. Just as Mitch should not have to know that Qi could feel the ruptured metal biting through her leg all the way to the bone, trapping her in the downed aircraft, making her one with its skeleton as it burned.

Zhang's men crept closer. Qi could see the bores of their weapons, all trained on her, inside.

"Hold your fire," said a voice. "It's the Nameless One."

Shukuma was not in evening wear for this little social event, and so was not packing her unobtrusive .380. She leaned closer to the cabin behind the more awe-inspiring muzzle of a no-frills military .45.

"Cheung will want her," Shukuma told the cops.

"I have a gift for Cheung," said Qi, nearly choking on her own blood. She smiled gruesomely, her teeth outlined in red.

And opened her hands to reveal two grenades, pins already pulled.

The police were already backtracking, diving for cover. Shukuma, however, could not wrest her gaze from the bulkhead tank right behind Qingzhao that was stenciled *NO NAKED LIGHT.*

It was the last thing she saw.

* * *

GABRIEL AND IVORY WERE OUT OF THEIR VEHICLE AND running. The explosion knocked them both to the pavement.

The secondary explosion bathed Mitch's view in white fire, sprawling her backward.

Smoke rolled to make a huge fist in the night sky.

24

IVORY PUSHED UP, GLASS FRAGMENTS IN THE PALMS of both hands, to come face-to-face with General Zhang.

"I have lost men," Zhang said sternly. "What is Cheung doing? Tell me or I shall have to expedite you." He had the backup to prove he was serious.

"The helicopter was stolen by assassins," said Ivory smoothly. "The plot was to kill Cheung in the Peace Hotel."

"Massacre in the streets does not reinforce his position," said Zhang. "The Tong leaders will want an explanation."

This seemed pretty slick, coming from the man who had watched Cheung blow Mads Hellweg into the afterlife right in front of the Tong bigwigs at Tuan's funeral and not said a word against it. Of course, while that had been public violence, too, it had been less public than this.

"Do what you do best, General," Ivory said with

respect. "Order needs to be restored here. Cheung shall answer fully."

Gabriel swore he could see telepathy passing between the two men, and Ivory saying: *I shall fix it.*

"Very well." Zhang turned, pointed, and barked orders to his men. "You say that this assassin—the one who has been trying to kill Cheung—is now neutralized at last?"

A quick check of the steaming wreckage of the chopper, now cordoned off by men with chemical extinguishers, confirmed this. Gabriel saw Ivory's stature warp almost imperceptibly; the cool-as-ice operative's shoulders bowed slightly in sadness.

Qingzhao Wai Chiu had been incinerated. Gabriel felt the regret settle on his shoulders as well.

But there was no sign of Mitch.

"Cheung needs to be told immediately," Ivory said. "And he will not believe it unless it comes from you or me."

"I have duties here," Zhang sniffed with harried-bureaucrat superiority. "It is *your* burden."

Ivory's performance was pretty spectacular, thought Gabriel. But damn it all, the man had not *lied* to Zhang. He had merely found a way to circumvent the truth. And in the bargain, won both himself and Gabriel an armed police escort right up to the entrance of the Peace Hotel.

MITCH FINALLY UNLOCKED HER LIMBS FROM HER frozen fetal position in the alleyway when someone, a stranger, tossed a few coins at her, thinking she was a beggar.

She could not see Gabriel and Ivory palavering with

General Zhang less than fifty yards away. Too much smoke, too many people, confusion squared. Her face was scuffed, scabbed and blackened. Blood on her fatigue jersey.

She snugged her fatigues and retied a wayward bootlace. She had to make it out of this alley and into the Peace Hotel—she had to. And she could, she knew she could find some way in, if only her brain would stop slamming against the walls of her skull.

She slid the syringe from her pocket. Yes, she had deceived Gabriel back at the leaning pagoda when she'd clutched onto him and implored him to watch his ass. She'd meant what she'd said—but it had not been as important as liberating the hypodermic she knew he carried, the syringe that held all the solutions to her distress. She could seek forgiveness later, if they all lived.

She stuck the spike in her arm and gave herself the full remaining eight cc's of the drug, all the while repeating her own instructions to herself. She didn't want to lose her plan to the drug, slip away into sleep or waking dreams of unrelated combat. Somehow she needed to hold onto enough mental control to steer herself even when—

The hit when the drug took effect was similar to a great orgasm, the kind you still remember years later, yet contoured with vitamins and excellent speed, like an energy drink made with plutonium.

A deep breath, and her vision seemed to clear, though it was almost too clear at the edges, realer than real. She would have to concentrate, focus.

She moved directly to a Zhang soldier on the sidewalk who was shouting directives to an apparently deaf gentleman who wanted to argue that he could not extricate his big tricycle from the grille of a wrecked car because it was augured into a phone pole. When the soldier made to strike the man with the butt of his rifle, Mitch grabbed the gun barrel and yanked the soldier off balance. As he turned, Mitch shot a fist into his exposed throat. The weapon came free in her hands as the man went down bug-eyed and crimson-faced, unable to draw air. She gave a quick thumbs-up to the citizen, who looked horrified rather than properly grateful. No matter. She appropriated the Zhang man's helmet and moved on down the street.

The gun settled comfortably into her grasp. With the helmet and weapon, she could pass for another uniformed solider, if no one looked too closely in the midst of all the commotion.

And while Gabriel and Ivory were still occupied with Qi's few remaining molecules and the contentions of General Zhang, Mitch made straight for the Peace Hotel.

"ZHANG AND THE TONG LEADERS WILL EXPECT treachery," murmured Sister Menga, not looking up from her steaming chalice of entrails.

"We shall be allies," said Cheung, making the knot in his necktie hard as a walnut. He was clad in his conventional businesswear, augmented by the sort of veneered body armor Ivory had favored.

"You are children in a nursery, squabbling over toys," said Sister Menga. Each of her pronunciations seemed to issue from the haze of incense smoke just before her. "You carve coffins and hope events turn in your favor. You are losing your grasp, but not the strength of your grip."

"And *you* are starting to sound like a fortune cookie," said Cheung. "Why not feel my skull and tell me the future? I might as well burn Hell Money or seek the favor of paper gods." He spun on his advisor. "Ivory is lost to me. *Guanxi* is lost. That is what it takes to achieve what I want, and I do not shrink from it."

One of the Tosa dogs rose from Sister Menga's nest and padded out into the Junfa Hall. The other followed soon after. Since Dinanath was gone and Shukuma was occupied, stewardship of the dogs would currently be the purview of a man named Yu Peng, who had come to be in Cheung's service from the Gedar Township of the area formerly called the Tibet Autonomous Region after the devastating earthquake there in 2006. Another Ivory recruit.

Cheung wondered how many of Ivory's recruits might turn, how many remain loyal.

The dogs' barking echoed through the museum ambience of the hall. They, too, were impatient for action.

Yu Peng would calm them down.

The other man in the hall was a Brazilian, newly hired by Cheung to salvage his skills from a murder rap in Sao Paulo. His name was... was...

Cheung hated the imprecision in his own mind. Romero? Chino? No, they were dead. Ayala, that was it. Dagoberto Ayala.

The Russian soul of Anatoly Dragunov, smoldering inside the shell of the persona he presented as Kuan-Ku Tak Cheung, resented his inability to enforce brutal fixes to essential, simple problems. In Shanghai the protocols were about ritual first, then political gain. This was frustrating. He understood peace through dominance and reflected that his plays were all logical and effective. Pawn for pawn, he reigned among ruthless men. Gabriel Hunt had come to China for a reason, and that reason had nothing to do with Valerie Quantrill's unfortunate but necessary murder, or with her deranged militant sister. All these events were threads of a tapestry of challenges and rebuttals which Sister Menga had foretold in her cloaked fashion, but which Cheung had also seen in terms of his own destiny. Gabriel Hunt was here because now was the time for Cheung to discover the Killers of Men. Gabriel Hunt's brother was here because a bargaining chip was needed in reserve. If this revelation required the betrayal of Ivory—Cheung's Immortal—then so be it. He had sacrificed his Number Ones before and would probably be required to do so again. Right now, he had no one in mind to sacrifice. While he had carved another little casket, he remained uncertain to whom it should be assigned.

According to a transmission from one of Zhang's lieutenants, the wrecked helicopter in the middle of Zhongshan Road contained none of the nearly twenty men sent with Dinanath to investigate the homing beacon with which the Nameless One, Qingzhao, had been kindly belled by Ivory. This spoke as evidence in Ivory's favor. Yet Qingzhao had no pilot skills. There was a fatal gap in information and hence, treachery was afoot everywhere today.

The soldier had reported back—not Shukuma. Another failure.

Dinanath had not reported back from the leaning pagoda.

His men, his men—were they all cowards or corpses?

Cheung was going to have to demonstrate once again that his leadership was unequalled. True generals, true leaders were unafraid to walk point.

The radiant sense of confidence with which he stood and strode forth was obliterated by the abrupt sound of a single gunshot, a hollow bang largely absorbed by all the fabric hanging in Cheung's Temple Room. Cheung's flesh contracted in a full-body flinch.

Sister Menga fell face-forward into her dish of guts, the coals from her brazier scattering to pit the fireproof carpeting with acrid contrails of smoke. The seer had failed to foresee the bullet that would pierce her skull right where her third eye ought to have been.

Foretell the future? The future was only told when you made it yourself, thought Cheung as he turned to face Michelle Quantrill one final time.

25

THE HAIRY EYEBALL. THAT IS WHAT THE BLACK-SUITED
Cheung men were giving Gabriel. They had been
vaguely alerted, but few specifics had trickled
down the chain of command this far, to the ground-
level enforcers. They were strictly guns, muscle,
hired hands.

Further, they eyeballed every Zhang soldier who
saw fit to trespass upon the Peace Hotel as though
personally affronted their limited authority was being
usurped by the emergency brewing out in the street.

They were tetchy and trigger-happy; itching for
conflict.

"You are going to have to be my prisoner," Ivory
told Gabriel. He drew his trusty OTs-33, his thumb
automatically switching the gun to three-shot-burst mode.

For him to grab Gabriel's arm would be too
aggressive, thus alerting the sentries. For them to
casually stroll in without a declared hierarchy—

Cheung operative plus prisoner—would be too casual. Ivory opted for polite formality: the captive or suspect proceeds one pace ahead, to the left. Normally this was a submissive, almost servile position for the man behind, but the guards would understand that Ivory was keeping a ready weapon trained on Gabriel's kidneys. Under normal circumstances, a jacket would be draped over the weapon in deference to public view. These circumstances were not normal— weapons were abundant thanks to the panic from the chopper crash—hence Ivory's gun would be visible, reinforcing the idea of a general alert. The guards would see the gun and the prisoner and never think this was any sort of deception. This was business, expediently out in the open, and so Ivory would be taken at face value since his disfavor in Cheung's eyes was still not widely known.

The two men bracketing the brass doors to the Peace Hotel were named Bennings and Jintao. Acquisitions, Ivory knew, from a recent canvass of Cheung security candidates based on such employment advantages as blackmail leverage, capacity for violence and general criminal records.

"For Cheung," Ivory said, indicating Gabriel. "Dinanath was sent to retrieve this top-priority guest. He failed and I have assumed personal responsibility for the delivery. Check with Constantine on the fifth floor if you must, but this is most urgent."

Gabriel did his best to look captured and cowed.

Bennings, a rangy Australian, was the guy giving Gabriel the once-over, twice. "Does this have anything to do with that balls-up?" he said, pointing to the wreck of the helicopter and the attendant madness.

"With what?" Ivory said, not even looking back.

Gabriel had to admire the ice-cold resolve of this guy.

Jintao had removed his sunglasses, silently exposing his eyes to his superior, and Ivory gave the man his own stern gaze in response. Jintao averted his gaze first.

"Is there a problem?" said Ivory.

"No problem," said Bennings, waving them inside.

They crossed the lobby in silence. The Old Jazz Bar of the Peace Hotel featured a large easeled placard that boasted *Real Shanghai Style Jazz Nightly!*

"I helped Jintao's children get into their present school," said Ivory finally, when they were out of earshot. "There are many like him in Cheung's employ—decent men who do this work from fiscal necessity. It would have been a pity to kill him."

"Would you have?"

"If it had been necessary," Ivory said. "I am glad it was not."

Cheung's floor was privately keyed, but Ivory still had the magnetic card that permitted direct elevator access.

"Wouldn't Cheung have deactivated your card if he didn't trust you?" said Gabriel once they had begun their ascent.

"Cheung does not wish to admit to himself the inevitability of my betrayal," said Ivory. "I believe that he expects me to return, in fact, of my own accord."

"So he left the door open for you," Gabriel said. "He's hoping you'll come back."

"I have come back, Mr. Hunt. And I have brought him the prize he seeks."

Gabriel was contemplating Ivory's gun, which had not lowered. "Please tell me... that I'm not worth a trap *this* elaborate."

Ivory's eyes indicated the ceiling, and the surveillance camera there.

"You are worth every effort, Mr. Hunt," he said. "Maximum effort."

The doors parted to admit them to the Junfa Hall.

Gabriel stepped out but was halted by Ivory, who merely said, "Hold."

He pointed.

The two Tosa dogs were strewn all over the hallway in a welter of blood. Over there, between two of the warlord statues that lined the corridor, were the protruding feet of at least one deactivated sentry.

A single shot of rifle fire resounded so crisply through the hall that you could hear the ejected brass sing. Gabriel and Ivory hot-footed it to the alcove that lead to Cheung's Temple Room.

Which is where they found Sister Menga with her brains painting the wall, and an insane-looking Mitch holding down on Cheung himself at point blank range.

GETTING PAST THE DOOR GUARDS HAD BEEN EASY. All Mitch had to do was wait for a pair of Zhang soldiers to make for the Peace Hotel doors on some mission, perhaps to set up a triage center or summon medical backup. She blended through in their wake and made sure she was not noticed once she broke away from them. The soldiers were barely aware that they had even been tailed.

The captured helmet over her shaved head covered up a multitude of giveaways.

Getting to the top of the hotel had been tougher. Scaling the exterior wall was not an option. She might fall, be spotted, or get shot. While she felt the drive and had the strength, more nimbleness than she possessed would be required for her to navigate slight brick interstices and dicey, crumbling handholds all the way up. One slip, one misplaced boot-tip, and her life and mission would end in a big wet splattered puddle. Like they'd told her in jump school, *It ain't the fall that kills you, it's the sudden stop.*

Qingzhao had warned her about guards and security elevators. Mitch was going to have to concoct a plan on the fly, and not hesitate lest she betray her own unauthorized presence. She quickly found the utility stairs and took them two at a time, as though she knew where she was going.

On the fourth floor she found a lone Cheung man patrolling the hallway. She hustled toward him with the urgent affect of a messenger, snapped a sharp salute, and hit him in the forehead with the butt of her borrowed carbine. The man's eyes crossed as he fell. She stripped him of a Beretta nine and a fighting knife the length of a bayonet. In a jacket sheath she found a silencer for the handgun that was nearly a foot long. Serious business.

She jabbed the blade into the rubber seal of the nearby elevator and levered the doors about eighteen inches apart—far enough to see cables reeling past. The car squeaked to a stop at the floor below. It was near enough for her to snake into the shaft, spider downward, and put her boots on the roof as softly as a moth lighting on a lampshade.

Mitch flattened out. It would not do to get hamstrung in a big cog or fail to see the metal girder-brace at the top of the shaft if it happened to rush at her suddenly in the near-darkness here. There were no Western numerals spray-painted on the cement stanchions, only Chinese characters. But she knew where she needed to be: the top floor.

Eventually somebody would need to go all the way up.

She ejected the Beretta's clip and verified the pistol was full up, with one in the pipe. She screwed on the hefty silencer and snugged the gun into her waistline, ruefully thinking it would take a week to draw out in combat. She slid the knife into her boot.

Her heartbeat was redlining. She could hear the thumps and clunks of the building's own metabolism— it, too, had a heartbeat. A fine, clean sweat had broken all over Mitch's body. She was an invading virus.

Another elevator car husked past on her left.

Then the car she was on was climbing, climbing. At the apex of the shaft was a short service ladder, which led to a bolted vent. Mitch used the bayonet again. The vent led to a grate, and the grate emptied her into the Junfa Hall.

The Junfa Hall was crowded, but not with the living. Warlords lined the corridor of honor, stolid in their cast metal and forged expressions. Mitch peeked around a life-sized bronze of Zhang Zongchang, also remembered as Marshal Chang Tsung-ch'ang, who died in 1928. Perhaps Cheung had named his floating casino after this man.

Two Cheung men in the corridor, pacing like expectant fathers, sticking more or less to the row of statues, one on each side, their pace so metronomic that they always crossed in the center of the room. One Chinese, one western, Latin American, perhaps. The Chinese man looked like the boss hog, so Mitch took him first, at the end of his circuit.

When he turned, she yanked him backward by the

strap on his shortie M4 rifle, chopped his throat to shut him up, and buried the bayonet in his solar plexus. Thrust, twist, withdraw. He fell into her grasp behind a Wu Dynasty bronze.

"Hey, Penga," said the man from the opposite end of the corridor, realizing his partner had vanished. Yu Peng, when alive, had wrongly assumed that Dagoberto Ayala's nickname for him was a friendly diminutive—like "Bobby" for "Robert"—but in truth, it was closer to a dirty pejorative. Ayala detested anybody higher than him on the command chain.

Ayala keyed open the bulletproof glass doors. If kept open, the doors allowed the Tosa dogs to run back and forth—endlessly—between the Junfa Hall and the Temple Room, as if the retarded mutts could not decide whose butt to sniff more, Cheung's or Peng's.

"*Podido*," Ayala griped. "You go to the can, at least tell me—"

Mitch took him. Thrust, twist, withdraw.

But the Tosa dogs in the adjacent room had already whiffed Yu Peng's freshly-liberated blood, and came charging in like assault tanks. Mitch heard their claws scrabbling on the slate tile of the corridor and had no idea how to close the glass doors.

She caught the first headlong animal with her forearm, feeling the crushing jaws closing to snap her bones as she buried the bayonet to the hilt in the huge beast's chest. It rolled—and her with it—but hung on. She put five shots from the silenced Beretta into the second one, which at least slowed it down, but also seemed to piss it off.

She jammed the pistol under the dog's chin and blew the crown of its head off, swearing she could feel the slug pass right by her own arm. By then the other one had a grab on her leg at the bootline. She had to fire without hitting her foot, and abruptly realized there was blood everywhere. Her own, in part, plus a generous geyser from the first dog. Its demon pal finally relaxed its chomp after Mitch emptied her mag into it. She felt the teeth slowly withdraw from her leg as the bite went slack, but that caused even more blood to course out.

The xipaxidine would roadblock the pain, though only for a time. Her leg felt malfunctional but just now she could still stand on it.

Valerie would have been horrified. Her sister had transmogrified into a butchering monster who even killed animals. Poor doggies.

Yeah, thought Mitch, *say that when you see your own limbs hanging out of their mouths, little sis.*

Her vision zoned out for an instant, then snapped back into focus. The edges glistened now, as if she were seeing through a glaze of ice crystals.

She collected her rifle and moved for the glass doors, wondering how many more mad dogs she would have to put down before she was done.

26

KUAN-KU TAK CHEUNG WAS LAUGHING. HE LOVED THE
theatrical. Exaggerated gestures. Glandular suspense.
Cheap thrills.

He and Mitch were pointing guns at each other.
Ivory was pointing a gun at the back of Mitch's head.
And Gabriel Hunt was pointing a gun at Ivory.

Alliances were more fluid than they seemed.

"Laugh at me, you bastard, and I'll blow your
tongue through the back of your head," said Mitch,
holding steady with the Chinese carbine. She could
do it, too, with this gun—maybe twice before gravity
dropped the man. Upon entering the Temple Room,
Mitch's first sight was Sister Menga raising a hand
against her. The seer's ornate fingernails caught
the light and suggested a weapon. Mitch was aboil
with endorphins and the drug coursing through
her, and her body reacted without the time-delay
of premeditation. She had automatically put Sister

Menga down because her eyes had seen a threat. Her eyes had lied. But so what?

In response to Sister Menga's moist demise, Cheung had whipped out a Czech CZ-52 pistol, two pounds of gorgeously machined steel filling his enormous hands.

Their stand-off was about five seconds old when Gabriel and Ivory brought up the rear.

Ivory put his pistol, still set on three-shot-burst, within four feet of the curve of Mitch's occipital.

Gabriel's hands familiarized themselves with Dagoberto Ayala's M4, which he'd scooped up on the run from the Junfa Hall. Cocked, locked, ready to rock. He did not think Ivory would actually shoot Mitch, but he had to draw on *somebody*, and Cheung was already staring down the bore of Mitch's rifle. Tension ran molten-hot through the room, thickening the air. Hell, sheer trigger reflex would kill them all if somebody sneezed.

That was when that son of a bitch Cheung started laughing.

"You impress me," Cheung told her. "You have accomplished the unthinkable. You got under Ivory's skin. You have truly earned my awe."

"Mitch," Gabriel said softly. "Don't take him. Not yet. He's got my brother."

"He already got my sister."

"I could use someone like you," Cheung told Mitch, "as my new head of security." His gaze indicted Ivory, but Ivory did not waver.

"Lower the weapon, Jin Huáng," Ivory said. It was not a request.

Gabriel saw Mitch *almost* comply.

"No." She refocused on Cheung. "Valerie Quantrill."

"Who?" said Cheung.

"*My sister.* You should think more about the people you murder."

"And how many have you murdered?" said Cheung, almost avuncular. "Killed in the name of your just cause? You should thank me. I determine what people like you become."

"Don't listen, Mitch," said Gabriel.

"You may avenge your sister's death," said Cheung, "but it will cost you your own life."

Cheung smiled like a cobra and lowered his own weapon.

Gabriel's hand touched Ivory's back, but he spoke to both Ivory and Mitch: "I need him alive."

Tears were rolling from Mitch's eyes but she fought to preserve her zeroed aim.

"Cheung—let them out of the building and I will take you to the Killers of Men. I alone know the burial secrets of the Favored Son. The men you sent to the site have fallen to those secrets. I will guide you and you may do with me what you will... but you will guarantee the release of my brother."

"That, I believe, was our agreement," said Cheung.

Ivory put a hand on Mitch's shoulder, turned her slowly. "Please," he said. His eyes were entreating. He backed her toward the glass doors, her gun gone wayward.

"I can't just leave—" she began.

"You *must*," said Ivory. "Trust me."

Gabriel let his muzzle drift in their direction. "Get her out of here or I'll shoot you both myself," he said, not taking his eyes off Cheung.

Mitch was still trying to process what had gone wrong, and the drug inside her was not helping. Soon enough the spikes, the flares, the knifing headaches would resume, and Gabriel knew that Ivory knew that, too.

"It seems that our moment is over before it has properly begun," said Cheung as he watched them exit. "Too bad. For just a second, there…" He sighed. "It would have been magnificent."

"WE'LL NEVER MAKE IT OUT OF THE BUILDING ALIVE," said Ivory as they hustled past the bloody remains in the hallway.

"What?" said Mitch. "I thought Cheung—"

"Cheung has a casket already carved," Ivory said, overriding her. "I saw it in the Temple Room. It is for one of us. Or all three of us. How did you get into the building?"

Mitch recapped. While admirable, her ingress route would not serve their escape.

"I watched Cheung shoot down Mads Hellweg," said Ivory. "It was one of the most decisive, cold-blooded things I have yet seen. And Cheung did not particularly *care* about Hellweg. He will have something much worse planned for us."

"We can always hit them frontally," said Mitch, rechecking the loads in her purloined M4. "Go out the front door."

"Not and survive—there are still too many of them."

"Then let's go up. Helipad's on the roof, right?"

"Yes…" Ivory's eyes showed doubt.

"And the chopper is toast, so nobody will be in a big hurry to go to the helipad… right?"

"True."

"So let's hit it, partner. Before my damned headache comes back."

He searched her expression for signs of xipaxidine fatigue. When she finally ran out of gas, she'd drop like a clipped puppet. And with no more drug to dose her with…

Together they found the access stairs that led from the Junfa Hall to the helipad. Four Cheung men were in charge of the perimeter.

"Do you know them?" Mitch said.

"I recruited two of them." Ivory peered through mesh glass to enumerate his potential allies. He indicated a willow-tall fellow in wraparound tinted glasses that seemed to be in charge of the other three patrollers. "Parkman Ng. Kam Ng's brother; took his brother's place when Kam was killed in a yakuza counterattack two years ago. Very loyal. And Kong—" he pointed to a broad-shouldered, hairless man "—he might be sympathetic, too. The other two, I just know their names. Güyük and Breedlove. Breedlove is British."

"So take the white guy and the short-round-fat guy first?" said Mitch.

Ivory stared at her, remembering that Americans were not famous for their tact. But he nodded.

They came through the push-barred door to the helipad brisk and businesslike, Ivory in the lead.

Guns came up to meet them. Mitch dropped to a solid kneeling position and did the smart thing—she patched the two men carrying rifles, which would be more accurate in a firefight. Breedlove the Brit folded and fell with multiple hits, followed by Güyük. By then, Parkman Ng had spun like a dancer and popped a wadcutter that sang past Ivory's right ear. Return fire was instinctual, and Ivory's weapon was on full-auto cycle. Red punctures jump-stitched up Parkman's long torso and he collapsed onto his face. Mitch could see the unhappiness in Ivory's eyes as his recruit fell.

Ivory raked the autofire toward the last man standing, the one he'd called Kong. But Mitch saw Ivory do an amazing thing—he pulled his weapon up out of the firing line *while* it was firing, before his finger left the trigger. The errant shots flocked away to make someone else's life miserable.

Because though Kong had reacted professionally, cross-drawing and sighting, he had jerked his own pistol up into neutral when he recognized Ivory.

"Ivory!" Kong yelled. "Parkman said Cheung's orders were to kill you. What's going on?"

Ivory kept his weapon dead-on as he approached Kong.

"I cannot believe it," Kong sputtered. "I will not believe it! Not of you. Many of us have heard the rumors, the news you were to become a Nameless One. I say that if Cheung decides you are a Nameless One, then I am a Nameless One as well." He was as frantic as anyone might be, presented with the prospect of killing a friend. "Longwei, please, tell me, what is the truth?"

Kong actually placed his weapon on the deck, stepped away from it.

"For the things you have just said," Ivory said softly, "for disloyalty to our master, the penalty is death. You understand that, Kwong Leung Kong Ngan?"

"Yes," Kong said, lowering his gaze. "The penalty is death."

"Under normal circumstances," said Ivory, drawing even closer.

Fearing the most intimate of killings, Kong kept staring at the concrete and said, "What…?"

"Under Cheung's rule the penalty is death," said

Ivory. "But Cheung's covenant is false. Were I to kill anyone for such a violation, I should first kill myself. You understand the gravity of what I say."

"I—I do?" stammered Kong. He regained some of his composure. "I mean, I do." Leery of the American woman with the weapon in the background, he leaned closer to Cheung, as there were some things so toxic and important that women should never hear them. "We heard Dinanath was gone. That you were turned. All our information is unreliable. Tell me, please— what is happening?"

"The foundations of Cheung's New Bund are collapsing as we speak," said Ivory.

"Can it be?" Kong said. "At long last…"

"My friend," said Ivory. "I need an Immortal, and you shall do quite nicely. You say there are others of like disposition."

"Yes. Jintao. Yu Peng. Hsiang Yun-Fa."

"Stop. Do not betray them until you see with your own eyes the evidence of my intent." There was no use in telling Kong that Yu Peng was already dead. "But gather them close. If I survive, they will be needed. If I do not survive, you must—you *must*—go for yourselves, is that understood?"

Kong directed them to a secure ladder that put them onto a disused fire escape, then headed in the other direction to round up his men.

"I've never seen anything like that before," said Mitch as they descended along a rear face of the building to street level.

"I have never done anything like that before," said Ivory. "But I suspected that Kong might be with me in spirit. I gambled on that."

"You should think about it, you know? Taking

Cheung's place. You could undo a lot of damage."

Ivory pressed his lips together until they were white and bloodless. One never said such bald things out loud. Putting such words into the air was unwise.

Instead he said, "Hurry. Just because we regain the streets, it is no guarantee of our safety."

"Where're we going?" said Mitch.

"I have to take you to meet a monk."

27

KUAN-KU TAK CHEUNG STARED DOURLY AT THE DEAD man's arm sticking out of the base of the giant bronze idol in the shrine room. His expression seemed to say: *Hmm, he almost made it.*

Gabriel was the focus of two aimed guns, in the hands of the pair of Cheung men who had accompanied them in an armored limousine to the leaning pagoda. Short-handed, Cheung had snatched them off guard duty in front of the Peace Hotel and both men, smelling imminent promotion and favor in the boss' eyes, were eager to comply.

They seemed just as eager to fill Gabriel up with bullets.

"A booby trap," said Gabriel. "As I warned you."

"It certainly seems that the obvious way in is not *the* way in," said Cheung.

"My brother. What assurance do I have you will release him?"

"You have no assurance, Mr. Hunt. Once my needs are seen to, then I shall consider the disposition of your brother."

"Then you are not a man of your word," said Gabriel.

"And you are not naïve," said Cheung. "It is your duty to acknowledge who holds the power in our brief relationship. You have cost me immeasurable time and resources. Your help inside this tomb could compensate for all that, but in the meantime you are at my command."

The two Cheung men glanced at each other.

"I was you, mate," said the taller Cheung man in an Australian accent, "I'd answer direct questions as asked, and otherwise keep my big yap shut."

"But you're not me," said Gabriel. "Too ugly and stupid, cowboy."

The guard bristled but kept his place.

"Now, Mr. Hunt," Cheung said. "As you say in New York: time's wasting."

Under the gaze of the guards, Gabriel climbed down into the trench and brought up the big, faceted orb of crimson glass.

"There were two at some point," he told Cheung. "Now there is only this one. Watch."

As Cheung and his bodyguards looked on, Gabriel climbed the bronze idol and mounted the jewel in the socket. Under direct lamplight, they all saw the arc of backward ideograms projected on the far wall.

"Now, if we move it to the other socket…"

Gabriel had a good grip on the jewel and hated to let it go. The thing was at least a century old and surely unique. But survival called for sacrifice. He made a show of carelessness and let an expression of not entirely false horror emerge on his face as he allowed the orb to slip from his fingers. It shattered into a million crushed-ice fragments on the floor.

"What have you done?" demanded Cheung, growing red in the face, but when he looked up again he was staring into a pistol in Gabriel's hand. There'd been more in the trench than just the jewel.

The Australian leveled his .45 automatic at Gabriel, but Gabriel said, "Don't move or your boss gets it."

"Shoot him," said Cheung, regaining his composure. "Just not fatally. We still have need of him."

A pair of gunshots erupted—but not from the Australian's gun and not from Gabriel's. The blasts came from the other guard's M4. The Australian, Bennings, clenched tight with hits and fell down dead.

Cheung quickly raised his own pistol and blew the other man apart at the seams with three perfect shots.

"Poor Jintao," said Cheung. "I was hoping Ivory had not gotten to him." He prodded Jintao's corpse with the toe of one boot. "You see, Mr. Hunt? Betrayal at every turn." He waved his gun in Gabriel's direction. "Come down off that statue, please. And throw the gun away. You will not shoot me, not when I hold your brother's life in my hand. Let us stop wasting each other's time, shall we?"

Slowly, reluctantly, Gabriel tossed his gun and began to descend.

"TELL ME HOW MY SISTER DIED," SAID MITCH. SHE was having difficulty keeping focus. The headaches were starting to belabor her skull again.

Pan Xiao had conducted them to Ivory's safe haven deep within the monastery. From supplies he had on hand, both herbal and medical, Ivory had prepared an injection that would help Mitch cycle down from the effects of the xipaxidine.

"You will feel weak," he said. "The effect is compensatory. This is a buffer, it is not a cure. Your body will have to cure itself. But while that happens, this will at least keep you from hurting yourself or suffering too severely."

"Thank you," she said, shivering.

Ivory lowered his gaze. "Do you trust me?" he said.

She extended her arm to him to accept the waiting needle.

"Your sister Valerie was a very strong person," Ivory began as he swabbed alcohol over her skin. She felt the prick as the needle went in. "As you may have guessed, Cheung is tied into banks all over the world. Stocks, securities, laundered money, much of it from illicit business enterprises. Big money, high security. Valerie gained intimate knowledge of this information stream. But Cheung is not the only man with such connections—all men at his level of wealth and power have similar secrets, and Cheung asked your sister to tap into their information streams on his behalf. To engage in industrial espionage. He wanted details on his enemies' activities, their resources. Valerie had learned so much so quickly about him; Cheung simply tried to turn this talent to more useful ends."

"And she balked," said Mitch, beginning to drift, her eyes growing large and dark. "She found the line she would not cross."

"But here is the unusual part," said Ivory, his voice low. "Cheung wanted to convince her so badly that he flew to the United States himself. He exposed himself to capture, to great physical danger, even possible assassination, hoping that his gesture would impress your sister. Valerie showed no appreciation. It wasn't just that she said no—that he might have accepted. But she didn't respect the gesture."

It's a face thing, Valerie had told her jokingly before heading off to the late-night in-person meeting. *It's all very Chinese.*

"Cheung told Valerie he thought she was extremely talented. He wanted to leave the door open for a possible future reconciliation. Valerie said no. She would be happy to return any file Cheung requested, sign any release, pay back the salary she had received, but her decision was final."

Ivory also remembered how Cheung's gaze had gone flat, reptilian and metallic, as he merely answered Valerie by saying, "A pity."

"I asked you how she died," Mitch said again, half-asleep.

"It was… unpleasant."

"That's not what I asked you."

Ivory called up strength. "He struck her, one time. Not too brutally. I think she expected that to be the end of it. But then he gave her to his men, instructed them to ruin her. There were five. One to hold each arm, one for each leg, and the fifth to… to defile her. They switched off the fifth spot, each man took a turn. She was unconscious before long. They brought her to with water, waited till they knew she could feel it, then continued. It went on for more than an hour. And then they cut her throat."

"You stood by and watched this," Mitch mumbled. "You did nothing."

"My responsibility was Cheung's security," Ivory

said in a voice redolent with shame. "I did my job. And they did theirs."

Mitch tried to lift her head but it seemed to weigh a million pounds. "And you have suffered ever since," she said softly.

"Yes," Ivory said.

"And then you saved me, when you could have let me die."

"Yes," Ivory said.

Mitch felt herself slipping out of consciousness, felt oblivion creeping up on her. "I forgive you," she murmured. "Valerie forgives you."

She was swept away, as on a gently rocking boat, to the sound of Ivory's tears.

28

"THE VENT IS CORKSCREW-SHAPED, WITH A switchback," said Gabriel when they had reached the rockfall that disguised ingress to the cavern. The climbing had been steep, and Cheung had made Gabriel go first, knowing of his physical abilities and desirous of keeping his gun.

"The Killers of Men are inside?" said Cheung.

"Just inside. I can show them to you."

"And this climbing equipment?" Cheung indicated the gear still scattered around the vent.

"Turned out to be unnecessary," said Gabriel.

"This is an interesting conundrum, Mr. Hunt. If I let you precede me, you might enact some futile ambush. If I go first, you could conceivably slam the door on me."

"Maybe you shouldn't have shot your other bodyguard," said Gabriel.

Cheung steamed briefly. "Pah! Bodyguards are no more than physical extensions of my command.

Without my authority, no power exists in the first place, do you understand? Kangxi Shih-k'ai, the Favored Son, was unafraid to lead his men into battle. No warlord fears to put himself at risk above all. That is why I do not fear you."

Gabriel said nothing. He knew his brother's life was dependent on making Cheung believe that whatever happened next was Cheung's own decision.

"Snap these tight, so I can see them," said Cheung, tossing Gabriel a pair of manacles retrieved from some inner pocket of his jacket.

"The funnel is difficult to negotiate."

"You will cuff yourself and hold the lamp as we both proceed." The ever-present gun terminated further debate.

Gabriel dropped the loose climbing gear back into the pile. Why hadn't he thought to leave himself an extra gun here as well? He cinched the cuffs onto his wrists. Cheung checked them, tightened each to make sure Gabriel was secured. Then they went into the hole.

With his hands locked together by four links of tempered steel, Gabriel was reduced to the motility of a snake, his own lamp blinding him as Cheung squirmed through close behind. The rock jags made even a lucky kick impossible.

Several strands of climbing rope were threaded through the passage, like bright blood vessels.

"What are these for?" demanded Cheung.

"I was going to haul out some of the artifacts," said Gabriel. "There wasn't time."

"Yes—robbing the graves of other cultures is a pastime of yours, isn't it? And what is that *smell*?"

"There are bats in the cave."

"And my men?"

"I doubt any survived." Gabriel had to fold up, then extend himself to scoot along, clearing the way for Cheung to follow, never forgetting the pistol pointed at him from behind. The way widened slightly as they proceeded toward the wide end of the funnel. "Kangxi Shih-k'ai rigged the entryway with a series of traps. Once the idol locked shut, there was no way in or out."

"Except this way."

"Yes—see for yourself."

Gabriel expected Cheung's lust to get the better of him as he approached his goal, and sure enough, Cheung was wriggling past him now like an eager child. But there was no room to move. No leeway for a blow or a chokehold. Gabriel felt the gun against him as Cheung passed.

Cheung swept his light across the blunt heads of the Killers of Men far below, his heart pounding, his breath short with astonishment.

"There must be… thousands of them," he said in awe. Then he levered his fist right into Gabriel's throat. "You didn't say anything about there being a drop! You climbed out!"

"I thought that was obvious," Gabriel said, chocking his boots against the nearest outcrop of rock.

"Damn you! It must be twenty meters to the floor!"

"I know," said Gabriel.

In another two seconds, Cheung would be angrily backtracking to get all the mountaineering gear. Which made this the time to act. Gabriel lunged to his knees, swung his chained hands over Cheung's head, pushed off like an Olympic swimmer, and launched them both into the black sky below.

* * *

TOGETHER, CHEUNG AND GABRIEL FELL FROM THE ceiling of the cavern for half a heartbeat, plunging into the void. Their lights and Cheung's gun toppled away.

Then the carabiner locked around Gabriel's belt cinched hard enough to compress several of Gabriel's internal organs into a space rather too small to hold them all.

He had clipped it on before cuffing his hands during his dalliance over the equipment. The lifeline ran anonymously among the other ropes depending down the funnel. Now it convulsed to guitar-string tightness against the anchor pitons in the rock outside, which groaned with the impact and load, but held.

Leaving Gabriel swinging in darkness, nine feet below the vent, with his arms coiled around Cheung's collar. It was the stiff, reinforced collar that saved Cheung's life, since had the chain of the manacles been around his bare throat, he'd have been hanged for sure.

They heard the lights smash against the rocks below; two, maybe three entire seconds after they had dropped.

Gabriel could hardly even see the man below him desperately trying to fight gravity. His arms reached down into an absolute absence of light.

In credit to his nerve, Cheung did not holler or panic. He did not kick his legs. He hung on with grim determination and focused hatred, trying to crawl up Gabriel's arms. Choice was out of the question. Gabriel could not drop or hold, and all Cheung could do was try to maintain his grip against the beckoning fall as they pendulumed in a slow, lazy arc in the damp darkness. Every movement weighed Cheung's collar more heavily against the cuff chain... which burden threatened to unsocket Gabriel's already fatigued arms.

Disturbed bats were beginning to flit around them.

Daredevils, safe crackers, heart surgeons and crazy psychiatrists call it "supertime"—the moment that elongates under stress. It seemed that they dangled on the tether for an hour, when in fact it was mere seconds.

Every dram of oxygen was vital to both men; for Gabriel, head-down, to keep the blood vessels in his face from exploding, and for Cheung, lathered with terror-sweat, choking on his own knuckles while trying to hang onto the cuff chain that was cinching his hard collar into the flesh of his throat.

"Where..." Gabriel managed to choke out, "is... Michael?"

The body below him twisted in his grasp, but didn't reply.

"*Where*? I'll... save your... life if you... tell me."

Cheung barked out a laugh.

Then, chinning himself with an iron grip on Gabriel's forearms, Cheung lifted his throat out of the constricting embrace of the chain. "I'll order him killed," he spat in a single breath, his face inches from Gabriel's, "while you hang here for eternity." Then with a monumental effort he shifted one of his hands to grip Gabriel's belt. He began hauling himself upwards along Gabriel's body with a fierce, almost incomprehensible strength.

"He's in the Peace Hotel," Cheung taunted. "Eighth floor, west side, last room. And what good does this knowledge do you Mr. Hunt? What can you do with it now?"

"This," Gabriel said, and bending one knee, kicked Cheung hard in the face.

For a moment, Gabriel continued to feel Cheung's weight pulling him down like a lead apron; then just the scrabbling of the man's fingertips against his chest; then nothing, a burden lifted, and seconds later he heard a wet crunch followed by a long, keening wail. All was darkness—but in his mind's eye he saw Cheung far below, impaled on one of Kangxi Shih-k'ai's spikes, the previously impaled skeleton crushed to dust beneath him by the impact of his fall. Here was a Killer of Men indeed to add to the ancient warlord's collection.

Gabriel felt no satisfaction or fulfillment—merely relief that he could draw air again. His vision was spotting and his sense of direction was shot. He tried to pull himself up by the rope, but made little progress; he had no more strength in his arms.

The bats continued flitting around him; he could not have said for how long.

The next thing Gabriel knew, he was being pulled out of the hole on the line that had nearly garroted him at the waist.

Strong hands brushed debris away. Sat him down. Gave him a blessed sip of water.

"You have shown Kuan-Ku Tak Cheung the Killers of Men?" said Ivory.

"Yes," said Gabriel, finding his voice.

"Then your business here is concluded?"

"You mean, in China?"

"No. This mountaintop."

"For now," said Gabriel.

"You must permit me to give you a lift back to the city."

A moan drifted up from the funnel vent, amplified by the cave acoustics, muffled by the mountain.

"Did you hear that?" said Gabriel.

Ivory nodded. "The history of the Killers of Men is well known. This entire area is full of ghosts, and sometimes the ghosts speak to those who will listen. Come."

Gabriel and Ivory picked their way carefully down the mountain.

Behind them, the moaning from the cave became louder, more insistent, interspersed by hysterical laughter, and finally devolving into a long, drawn-out scream. But there was no one there to hear it.

29

THE JAZZ BAND AT THE PEACE HOTEL WAS ACTUALLY quite good. All the musicians looked to be over sixty, and the saxophonist seemed to be channeling Coleman Hawkins directly when he blazed out the solo to "Body and Soul."

Gabriel caught Ivory tapping his foot more than once to the music.

"I still don't understand how I could have been duped so thoroughly," complained Michael Hunt. "It never occurred to me I was a captive. I just assumed, you know—gunfire in the street, my floor on lockdown, no cellphone service…"

"You blamed China," Mitch said. "I made the same mistake, I suppose. In my own way."

The barman in the lounge had talked Gabriel into sampling a drink that was essentially vodka on the rocks with most of a lemon squeezed into it. Gabriel considered the beverage moodily. It was good but somehow the celebratory atmosphere seemed askew.

"It turns out the coordinates in our parents' notes were about five miles off," said Michael. "They were amazingly close to discovering the Killers of Men."

"The official discovery now must be handled with utmost delicacy," said Ivory. "I agree with your brother, Gabriel—he should finish the lecture series as planned and in that context he can provide a clue that our own scholars may follow to deduce the location. Let it be done that way. Credit will accrue to our cultural historians and you will not be blamed for the damage discovered at the site."

"And what of Cheung?" said Gabriel. "Or should I say Dragunov."

"That was also not his real name," said Ivory. "It is just the identity he used in the Soviet Union. I believe he was born in Ukraine, and from what few facts I learned over the years, it is entirely possible that his birth mother really was Chinese." His voice had a tinge of sadness to it. "We met in the midst of a gun battle, you know. It was a long time ago. He was a bad man even then—a drug smuggler. But not yet an insane one."

Mitch shifted uncomfortably at the mere mention of drugs. She wasn't drinking, just nursing a tall glass of seltzer. The purge program for xipaxidine worked on her by Pan Xiao, the monk-who-was-not-a-monk, had been effective but fluidly gruesome, and her insides were still fragile.

"What about the big payoff?" she said quietly. "The gold statue, or the treasure, or whatever it was that was supposed to be there?"

Gabriel and Michael looked at each other with an air of conspiracy.

"What?"

"We went back," Gabriel said, keeping his voice low. "After putting in a call to the Foundation and having a truckload of gels and gems and lenses overnighted. We tried them all in the statue's eyes, various combinations. Eventually got an arrangement that mimicked the jewels and allowed the ideograms to converge on the far wall."

"And what did they say?"

"It took a while to translate and some of it is still obscure," Michael said, "but—"

"But it boiled down to 'Dig here,'" Gabriel interrupted. "Kangxi Shih-k'ai's burial place is behind about a foot of rock directly across from the idol—the idol's looking right at him."

"The ideograms describe his tomb," Michael said. "His body was apparently installed inside a hollow jade carving of a warrior. It is described as weighing five hundred pounds."

"Five hundred pounds of jade?" Mitch said this a little too loudly and some heads turned their way.

Michael waited till the eavesdroppers had returned to enjoying the music. "Yes. And supposedly his body was completely outfitted in gold. Gold armor, gold clothing, gold weapons. Please don't shout."

Mitch restrained herself. "And this will all now be discovered by the Chinese government."

"It is their treasure," Michael said. "Their history."

"And what of Cheung?" Gabriel asked again.

"He perished, sadly, in his sleep," Ivory said. "It seems to have happened the night of the unfortunate helicopter crash in the street outside this hotel. It may have been a heart attack, perhaps brought on by the shock. He has already been cremated, in keeping with his instructions."

"And who's going to take his place on the Bund?" Gabriel said.

Ivory lowered his gaze in modesty. "There are enough of us. Enough loyalists to repair the New Bund without the incursion of gangsterism."

"Will Zhang give you trouble?"

"General Zhang is content to run the People's Police," said Ivory.

"You won't have an easy time of it," said Gabriel. "Cheung left quite a mess behind him."

Ivory nodded in agreement. "Yes, but... I have excellent advisors."

When he said this, Mitch took Ivory's hand.

"I'm staying," she said.

Gabriel and Michael exchanged their second glance of the evening, less conspiratorial this time than incredulous.

"You're staying?" Gabriel said.

"What have I got to return to? My sister was my only family. She's dead. The Air Force doesn't want me back. I have as much to offer here as anywhere."

"What about—" He'd been about to mention Lucy's name, but realized that doing so in front of Michael would be opening a can of worms; in front of Ivory, too.

But Mitch knew what he'd held back from saying. "I'll see her again," she said. "When the time is right."

"Who?" Michael said. "That nurse from Khartoum?"

"Yes," Gabriel said. "The nurse from Khartoum."

The four of them drank their drinks, and the music played on.

"What about you, Gabriel?" Michael said finally. "Would you like to come with me on the lecture circuit or would you prefer to go home?"

Gabriel was sunk in thought. He'd spent the past day trying to make amends and lay ghosts. He'd sought out the little old lady in charge of the Su-Lin Gun Merchant shop and crossed her palm with enough money to fund her retirement in the country and out of the firearms trade. On her little translating screen she had typed: I THANK YOU AND TUAN THANKS YOUR GRACE.

It had made him feel better, briefly.

"What about me?" Gabriel repeated. "I was thinking I might take a trip someplace quiet."

Which is how Gabriel Hunt found himself winging back to America all by his lonesome on the Hunt Foundation jet, his trusty Colt revolver never drawn nor used, his collection now enriched by the Colt .36 wheelgun from Su-Lin's. He stared out the window and composed in his head the e-mail he'd send to his sister when he landed, the one in which he'd explain to Lucy what Mitch had decided to do and why. It wouldn't make any sense to her if he started there, at the end of the story. He'd have to tell her the whole lengthy and unimaginable tall tale of what she had started.

If they'd been children still, she'd have sat at his side and soaked it in wide-eyed, believing every word. But childhood was far behind them, and now he imagined she'd parse every word cynically. Assuming the message even reached her—assuming she hadn't skipped house arrest, fled to another country, and abandoned her last anonymous e-mail address for a new one he didn't know.

But he would try. She deserved to know the story.

There was just one part Gabriel would leave out; one memory that was his alone, not for sharing.

The taste of Qingzhao Wai Chiu's lips on his own, during the only time they had ever kissed, there in the life-threatening panic of the Night Market, the two of them trapped in their own transient bubble of supertime, the scant seconds that became days where they were briefly in love. The taste and smell of mangoes and rare spice, of night-blooming jasmine.

ABOUT THE AUTHOR

David J. Schow is the author of nine novels—including the Bram Stoker Award-nominated novella *Pamela's Get*—and many short story collections and screenplays. His film credits include *The Crow* and *The Texas Chainsaw Massacre: The Beginning* and his story "Red Light" won the 1987 World Fantasy Award for Best Short Fiction.

Read on for an extract from the next

GABRIEL HUNT ADVENTURE

HUNT THROUGH NAPOLEON'S WEB

1

GABRIEL HUNT'S GRIP ON HIS PICKAXE WAS SLIPPING.

He had been in worse scrapes before; it's just that he didn't particularly relish the thought of dying while caving for fun and practice. That would be an embarrassment. When it was truly his time to check out, Gabriel would much rather have his obituary say that he'd been eaten alive by an angry tiger or felled by gunshots from enemy assailants. Or old age. That wouldn't be so bad.

But to fall into a gaping pit because he had slipped on bat guano? *Preposterous!*

Gabriel called down to his friend and caving partner, "How you hanging, Manny?"

Horizontal and belly-down, Manuel Rodriguez dangled in mid-air on the end of the static nylon rope, fifteen feet below Gabriel's legs. His only hope for survival was Gabriel's grip on the pickaxe.

"Is that a joke, *amigo*?" Manny shouted. He was

trying to keep the terror out of his voice but wasn't doing a very good job.

It had happened quite innocently. Every two or three years, Gabriel made an excursion to one of various caves around the country so that he could hone his skills. His travels sometimes required that he perform a bit of spelunking—an outdated term, but Gabriel liked the sound of the word. It had a certain romance to it.

Dangling within an inch of one's life over a dark abyss, though, didn't have any romance to it at all.

Manny lived in New Mexico near Carlsbad Caverns National Park. Besides the exceptional landmark that was open to the public to tour on a daily basis, there were several other caverns in the park that were available only to experienced cavers. All it took to access them were a small fee and a license. Gabriel had done it many times, very often with Manny, a fifty-eight-year-old former ranger at the park and an expert spelunker.

They had been in one of the more "challenging" (as Manny had described it) caves for a little more than three hours when Gabriel and Manny—secured to each other by a fifteen-foot-long buddy rope—sat down to rest on a ledge above a black pit that supposedly led to a chamber of noteworthy formations. The hole was ninety-six feet to the bottom. They had come equipped with all the right gear. They each wore the necessary helmets, grubby clothing, knee and elbow pads, sturdy boots. Both men carried plenty of light sources and extra batteries, as well as water, snacks, trash bags, empty bottles in which to urinate, and a first aid kit. For the vertical descent, Manny had brought along an assortment of tools such as carabiners, rope, waist and chest harnesses, Petzl stops, rappel racks, handled ascenders, pitons, chocks, hammers, and a couple of pickaxes. The goal, however, was to accomplish the journey without damaging the cave at all. Hammering pitons into the rock face was to be avoided if possible. It was best to use non-invasive tools such as Spring-Loaded Camming Devices that wedged into already-existing cracks or in between stone protrusions. "Leave nothing but footprints" was the motto amongst serious cavers.

Gabriel had finished eating a power bar, coiled a long section of rope around his shoulder and back, and stood on the ledge to locate a convenient spot to install a chock or SLCD for what was called an SRT—Single Rope Technique—descent into the hole. The plan was that Manny would follow him, staying tethered to him throughout the excursion. But when Gabriel had stooped to examine a possible position, his boot slipped on something wet and slick. He slammed hard into the ledge, face down, and continued to slide across the slimy ridge until his body was falling through space. He must have plummeted twenty feet or so before he realized that he had pulled Manny off the ledge as well. Another dozen feet shot past before Gabriel swung the pickaxe that was, miraculously, still in his right hand. He chopped the rock face in front of him as hard as he could—and broke his fall. Hanging on to the axe's handle was another thing altogether. It had a ridged rubber grip and a lip at the bottom against which the side of his right hand collided painfully—but it was enough to enable him to hold on. He gripped the axe handle as tightly as he could with both hands, but already he could feel the strain in his fingers and arms. Making matters worse, his palms were moist from the sudden shock. And when Manny reached the end of the tether with a violent jerk, Gabriel really did damn near lose his grasp.

Then Gabriel was presented with the ultimate insult—he smelled the stuff he had slid across. It was all over the front of his pants and shirt.

Bat turd.

Gabriel winced, remembering a cave full of bats he'd found himself in half a year earlier in China. The smell was the same all over the world.

"This is the last time I go caving with you!" Manny called. His added weight dangling at the end of the line was slowly pulling Gabriel's shoulders from their sockets. "I'm a fool for letting you talk me into this again!"

Gabriel resorted to an old ploy—bravado could cover up genuine terror every time. "Come on, Manny," he yelled down, "you know you have to stay on top of the game. Sharpen your skills every now and then."

"I'm nearly sixty years old. I don't have anything left to sharpen."

Gabriel attempted to flex his arms and pull himself up, but with the extra load hanging below him it was impossible.

"What the hell do we do now?"

"Relax, Manny. I've got it under control."

In fact, Gabriel had no idea how to get out the predicament they were in. The rock face sloped inward in front of him, so there was no foothold within reach. The more serious problem was that he had only two hands, and they were busy holding on to the pickaxe for dear life.

After a few seconds of silence, Manny asked, "Anytime you want to start letting me know how you've got it under control is okay by me."

"Your light's still working, isn't it?"

Manny had a light affixed to his helmet. As he twisted slowly on the end of the line, the beam traced the pit's circumference.

"It's the only part of me that isn't failing," Manny answered. "My bowels are gonna be the next to go."

"Hold on, Manny. Take a look around you. Is there a ledge you'd be able to stand on if you could get to it?"

During his next 360-degree turn, Manny replied, "Yeah. Over on the other side. Behind you. But I can't reach it."

"All right. Let's see if we can get a little swing going, okay?"

"We need music for that, *amigo.*"

Sweat poured off Gabriel's forehead beneath his helmet, ran over his brows, and stung his eyes. Another problem on the rapidly expanding list.

"Shut up, Manny, and see if you can swing over to the ledge. Slow and easy. I'll try and get you started with my legs."

Gabriel managed to grip the taut tether with the insteps of his boots. He then strained to wiggle the rope enough to send some movement down to his partner. At the same time, Manny flapped his arms and legs as if he were trying to fly—anything to propel himself back and forth in the air.

"You look real graceful," Gabriel said through his teeth. It was becoming much more difficult to hold on.

"Not half as graceful as we're going to look when we're flat as tortillas on the bottom of the cave." Gabriel was glad that Manny was keeping his sense of humor. A good sign. But as his friend attempted the circus feat, the pickaxe started to squeak. As if it were about to come out of the rock. Gabriel needed to lessen the weight on his body in a big way. The sooner Manny got over to the ledge, the better.

He tugged on the rope with his legs some more and felt his partner's momentum increase a little. Manny was now a human pendulum, swaying feet first toward the target ledge, back and forth at a 20-degree angle... which soon increased to 30 degrees... and finally to 35 degrees. And then Manny's boot touched the edge of the stone outcropping.

"Almost there, Gabriel!"

The pickaxe creaked again.

Manny swung back to the ledge and came close enough to push off from it with his legs. The maneuver gave him more speed and force—but it also placed much more strain on Gabriel's wrists and the pickaxe. The metal lip at the bottom of the handle was deeply embedded in the flesh of Gabriel's hands. Then the axe slipped a few millimeters with a painful wrenching sound.

"One more push and I think I can make it!" Manny announced.

Gabriel was unable to speak. He simply closed his eyes and willed his partner over to the other side of the pit.

Anytime, Manny, anytime...

Manny returned to the ledge and pushed off hard. He swayed so far to Gabriel's side of the hole that he was able to touch the wall there. Then, on the way back to the ledge, he hurtled himself up and over—and fell onto the ledge with a *smack*.

"I made it!" Manny rolled and came to a sitting position. He panted for a few seconds and said, "Pardon me while I say a few Hail Marys."

The subtracted weight relieved the pressure on Gabriel's arms. He was now able to concentrate on the next problem at hand—saving himself. Manny was on the opposite side of the cave from where Gabriel hung and a couple of yards lower. The two men were connected by a fifteen-foot tether. Gabriel could simply let go, fall, and hope that Manny was able to pull him up to his ledge. But then they'd be stuck there. Most of the ascending equipment was back at the top, on Bat Guano Ridge.

No, wait.

He had some tools in his pack and in his trouser pockets. A few pitons. A couple of ascenders. A rappel rack.

Gabriel thought that if he could place an anchor in the rock face, he just might be able to attach his rope and a carabiner. He could then use the assembly to raise himself a few feet. Then he'd have to plant another… and another… all the way to the top. If he ran out, he could pull out one of the lower ones and re-use it. The trip would be slow going and painfully tedious… but it could be done.

Now if he could just grow another arm or two…

"So now what?" Manny called. His voice echoed in the well. "Dying from the fall would've been better than starving to death here."

"Don't be a pessimist, Manny," Gabriel growled. "I'll get us out of here. Trust me."

He took a deep breath. What he was about to do required concentration.

Gabriel squeezed the axe handle harder with his right hand… and let go with his left. Hanging by only one arm, he reached back with his free hand and dug into his pack. His fingers found one of the pouches—he hoped it was the correct one—and wormed them into it. He felt something cold, hard, and metallic. A piton! The angle was awkward, but he managed to grasp it. The next step was to pull it out of the pouch without... *dropping it...*

The piton fell into the darkness below.

He and Manny heard the clang when it hit bottom.

Gabriel rarely cursed, but he did so—loudly.

Let's try that again...

Still clinging to the handle with a very sore right hand, Gabriel reached back to the pack a second time. He dug into the pouch and took hold of another piton. This time he made sure he had it firmly in hand before removing it.

His right shoulder and upper arm were killing him. The strain was becoming unbearable.

To hell with not damaging the rock.

With the piton in his left hand, he eyed the rock face in front of him. A small crack ran diagonally across the limestone. Aiming as best as he could, Gabriel jabbed the piton's point into the crack. The first attempt only chipped some of the stone away. The second try created a small hole. With the third stab, the piton stuck.

Gabriel grabbed the axe handle with his left hand to relieve some of the tension on his right arm. Then, with his weakened but now free arm, he reached for the small hammer that hung on the right side of his belt. He succeeded in pulling it out of its sheath... but since the piton was to the left of his body, he now had to switch it to his other hand. He'd never be able to hammer it with his right hand.

Only one thing to do, and Gabriel knew he had only one shot to do it. There would be no second attempt.

Okay, the left hand is holding the axe. The right hand has the hammer. Let's do it...Ready?...One... two... THREE!

Gabriel tossed the hammer into the air and

grabbed the axe handle with his right hand while simultaneously releasing the handle with his left. The hammer had reached the top of its arc while he was making the exchange and was now plunging downward. Gabriel's left hand shot out and snatched the hammer out of midair as it fell.

He had to stop and breathe for a moment after that little stunt. Compared to it, hammering the piton into the limestone was easy.

Still using one hand, he unwrapped the rope from his shoulder and stuck an end in his mouth. He gripped it with his teeth, and then dug a carabiner out of a pocket. It was yet another awkward operation to secure the end of the rope to the 'biner with a bowline knot one-handed, but he did it. He then hooked the carabiner into the eye on the exterior end of the piton. The rope was now fixed and safe to use.

Then his cell phone rang.

"What the...?" He looked back at Manny. "You mean to tell me there's actually *service* down here?" Gabriel took hold of the rope with one hand and his legs, let go of the axe handle, and hung there, suspended.

The phone rang again.

"You're not gonna answer that, are you?" Manny asked.

Gabriel hated cell phones the same way he hated most modern technology—but that didn't stop him from feeling compelled to answer the thing when it rang. He fished it out of his trouser pocket and brought it to his ear.

"Hello?"

"Gabriel?"

"Michael?"

Gabriel immediately pictured his younger brother

sitting at his desk back in the luxury of his clean and comfortable New York office. He'd rarely envied his brother his stay-at-home life—but at this moment he came close.

"Are you sitting down?" Michael asked.

Gabriel grimaced. "Not precisely."

"It's Lucy, Gabriel."

The urgency in Michael's voice gave him pause.

Lucy—short for Lucifer—was the youngest sibling in the family. Their imaginative parents had named each child after one of the archangels in the Bible. It didn't seem to matter to them that their daughter would have to bear the ignominy of her moniker for the rest of her life. In an attempt at kindness, her brothers had called her Lucy, but in the years since she'd run away from home at age seventeen, she'd taken to calling herself "Cifer" instead. Pronounced like *cipher*, it made a fine name for the scofflaw computer hacker she'd turned herself into.

"What *about* Lucy?" Gabriel asked.

"Are you sitting down?"

"No, Michael, I'm not sitting down! Just tell me!"

"She's in terrible danger. You need to come back to New York as quickly as you can."

"How is she in danger?"

"It looks... it looks like she's been kidnapped."

He wasn't sure he'd heard Michael correctly. "Say that again?"

"She's been *kidnapped*."

"Are you serious?"

"Yes. And there's a ransom demand."

"How much do they want?"

"They don't want money, Gabriel. They want *you*."

2

GABRIEL TAPPED THE INTERCOM BUTTON OUTSIDE
the Hunt Foundation to announce his arrival,
unlocked the front door, pocketed his key, and
stepped into the foyer. The room was full of artwork,
antiquities displayed in glass cases, and brochures
about the organization for the rare occasions when
some museum curator or endowment representative
might visit the building. The rest of the ground floor
consisted of a dining room and kitchen, a small library
(the larger one was on the second floor), and one of
Michael's offices, where Gabriel was headed.

The brownstone, located on East 55th Street and
York Avenue, overlooked the East River and was
designated as a landmark. Ambrose and Cordelia
Hunt had lived and worked there, raised three children
there, and left it in trust to the Foundation in their wills,
which had been triggered when they'd vanished at
sea at the turn of the millennium. Michael, being the

responsible one in the family, was legally appointed the manager of both the trust and the Foundation. That was perfectly fine with Gabriel. The less he had to deal with paperwork, taxes, endowments, grants, bills, and bureaucracy, the happier he was. He did find it handy to have money—you couldn't mount international expeditions the way he did without it—but he had no interest in the management of the various accounts and funds. Michael was a superb administrator and Gabriel knew such things were better off in his hands.

"There you are," Michael said as his brother stepped through the office door. The room was spacious, containing a pair of antique trestle tables, a gorgeous nineteenth-century mahogany desk, one wall lined floor-to-ceiling with filing cabinets, and two more lined similarly with packed bookshelves. What generally irritated Gabriel was how organized and uncluttered it was. And normally Michael's appearance matched the room's: tidy, neat, unruffled. At thirty-two he was quite the opposite of his older brother. Where Gabriel was six feet tall, broad-shouldered, ropy, and apt to show up with stains from smoke or grease or blood on his clothing, Michael was slight and bookish, wore wire-rimmed spectacles, and was never seen with a strand of his thinning, sandy hair out of place. Except for the thinning hair, he hadn't changed much since he was a boy. Gabriel had spent a fair portion of their childhood protecting Michael from neighborhood bullies, in neighborhoods all over the world, and not one of the encounters had discomposed Michael in the slightest.

But he was discomposed now.

"Talk to me," Gabriel said as he dropped into the chair in front of the desk.

Michael shook his head. "It doesn't look good. I received an e-mail from an anonymous account. I printed it out." Michael handed it across the desk. Gabriel took it.

TO: MICHAEL HUNT—HUNT FOUNDATION

THE ALLIANCE OF THE PHARAOHS INFORMS YOU THAT WE HAVE LUCIFER HUNT. DO NOT CONTACT POLICE. DO NOT CONTACT FBI. YOUR SISTER WILL DIE IF YOU DO. WE REQUIRE THE SERVICES OF GABRIEL HUNT. HE SHALL MEET OUR REPRESENTATIVE ALONE, REPEAT ALONE, IN CAIRO.

The message went on to designate the time and place of a rendezvous three days in the future. At a stall in a public bazaar.

"After nine years, Gabriel!" Michael snatched the paper from Gabriel's hand and waved it in the air. "Nine years we don't hear from her, we don't know if she's alive or dead, and then this."

Actually, Gabriel knew, Michael *had* heard from her a few times—but only over the Internet, under her 'Cifer' pseudonym, which Michael assumed belonged to a thuggish, unsavory male who eked out a living skulking around the alleyways of the online underworld. It was an impression Gabriel had not disabused him of, even after learning the truth himself.

"My god, Gabriel. If they hurt her—"

"Do we know anything about this Alliance of the Pharaohs?" Gabriel asked.

"I spent the last twenty-four hours going through

everything we have on Egypt. There's no mention of the group in any of the books we have, nothing in any of our files. The best I could do was a few hits on the Internet."

"And?"

Michael ran his fingers through his hair anxiously. "In the last two years, there have been two instances of Egyptian artifacts being stolen from major museums. The more recent was from the Louvre, in Paris. The French police attributed the crime to an *'Alliance Pharaonique.'* Another theft occurred in Istanbul a year earlier; Interpol isn't sure they're related, but the items stolen in both cases were from the same period. We're talking *ancient* Egypt—solid gold jewelry supposedly worn by Ramses II in Turkey, a goblet dating from Cleopatra's reign at the Louvre."

"That's all we've got?"

Michael turned his hands palm-up and the furrows on his forehead deepened.

"Great," Gabriel said. "So we know they like Egyptian artifacts, which we might have been able to guess from their name. And we know they were able to find Lucy, despite her best efforts to stay hidden." Gabriel didn't mention that he'd met with Lucy a handful of times over the past few years himself, once in this very building—no reason to make Michael feel worse than he already did. Besides, in each of those cases it had been Lucy who had found Gabriel, not the other way around. "What I don't understand is why they'd kidnap her just to get me to meet with them. Couldn't they just make a phone call? We take appointments, don't we?"

"They're criminals," Michael said. "I mean, if these *are* the same people responsible for those museum thefts. And if you're the sort of person who does that, you're probably perfectly comfortable kidnapping young women and probably don't like to do things through ordinary channels... Gabriel, *what are you doing?*"

Gabriel stopped stretching his arms. He'd been doing it unconsciously. "Sorry. I pulled some muscles yesterday in that cave. It's nothing. Just a little sore."

"I can imagine," Michael said, a censorious note creeping into his voice. "All I can say is thank goodness I was able to reach you down there. If you'd been out of range..."

"I thought I was," Gabriel said.

"Well," Michael said, "when you pay thirty thousand dollars for a cell phone, you do get something for your money."

"Thirty thousand? Really?" Gabriel said. "I'll try not to leave it in a cab."

"Gabriel, what are we going to do?" Michael threw the printout onto the desk, where it slid off onto the floor. He didn't pick it up. "I could never live with myself if they hurt her."

"Lucy's a tough customer," Gabriel said. "She can handle herself. She's probably giving them orders already."

"She's twenty-six years old," Michael said. "These men are killers."

"You didn't say anything about killing," Gabriel said.

"Two guards at the Louvre," Michael said. "One in Turkey." He paused, took a deep breath, let it out. "Decapitated."

There was a beat of silence.

"So I guess I'm going to Cairo," Gabriel said. Michael nodded miserably.

"I'll get her back," Gabriel said.

"She may be dead already," Michael said, his voice dropping to a whisper.

Gabriel picked the sheet of paper up from the floor. "They pulled this stunt because they want something from me," he said. "As long as that's the case, she's alive."

THE DISCOVERERS LEAGUE WAS EMPTY AND QUIET that night.

Gabriel had calmed his brother by taking him to Andrei's place for a bite (Michael had protested that he wasn't hungry, but after his third glass of *divin* he was able to put away a plate of Andrei's *parjoale*). By the time Gabriel had seen Michael home and hopped a taxi to the building on East 70th Street, it was nearly midnight.

Hank, the elderly doorman who'd been with the club seemingly since its founding, greeted Gabriel warmly and handed him a bundle of mail that had collected since the last time Gabriel had been home. Gabriel got into the elevator and took it to the top floor of the building, where he kept a suite of rooms. The League's Board of Directors tolerated Gabriel's presence in the building because of who he was—the Hunt Foundation contributed generously each year—and because some of his higher-profile finds brought the organization the sort of attention that helped with their other fundraising. But their feelings about him were mixed. They'd had to spend a portion of the funds he donated on patching bullet holes in the walls and getting blood out of the upholstery, not to mentioned paying soaring insurance premiums, and some of the more staid directors complained that his exploits attracted less attention than notoriety. This discussion regularly consumed twenty or thirty minutes at the start of every board meeting; as the meeting room was directly below his apartment, Gabriel could sometimes hear the raised voices. But so far, no eviction notice had been slipped under the door, and the bullet holes kept getting repaired.

The two-bedroom suite was a little piece of paradise for Gabriel. Like most New York apartments, the place wasn't large, but it was everything he needed. The master bedroom had a four-poster and a dresser, though barely enough room to walk between the two. The guest bedroom was more of a catchall; it contained a lot of his "stuff," such as traveling gear and clothing. The living room was comfortably compact, dominated by a tiger skin rug (Gabriel had reluctantly been forced to shoot the animal when it had tried to eat him in India). The space had a lone couch, a desk, a few shelves of books. No computer, no television. Gabriel's prized piece of furniture was an antique Baldwin upright grand piano, manufactured in 1924 and as near to mint condition as one could get after nearly ninety years. He took better care of it than he did his own body—his sore arms attested to that.

Michael had arranged things so Gabriel could take the Foundation's private jet the following day. It beat having to deal with commercial airlines, and it also meant Gabriel could bring his Colt .45 pistol in his carry-on without anyone batting an eye. He hated being out of the country without it—so whenever possible he took the jet.

Michael had been delighted to put it at his disposal, but had been surprised when he'd insisted on flying into Nice, France rather than directly to Cairo. "Why there, Gabriel? I'd understand if you wanted to stop in Paris, talk to the people at the Louvre, but—"

"There's an Egyptologist I know," Gabriel had said vaguely, "in Nice."

"Really?" Michael had said. "Who? Bourgogne? But no, he hasn't been at Antipolis since '08…"

"It's no one you know," Gabriel had said.

"An Egyptologist I don't know?"

"Yes, hard to believe isn't it," Gabriel had said, and changed the topic as quickly as he could.

There was no Egyptologist in Nice that Michael Hunt didn't know. Nor was there one Gabriel was going to meet. What there was in Nice was the last address Gabriel knew of for his sister. She'd been under house arrest for a time in Arezzo, Italy, and then somehow the charges wound up being dropped, or anyway that's what she'd claimed in her e-mail. The hasty change of countries was typical, and for all he knew she'd since abandoned the apartment in Nice. But since Nice was the last place he'd known her to be, Nice was the first place he had to go.

Gabriel showered, toweled off, and studied himself in the bathroom mirror. His slightly curly, midnight-black hair was in need of a cut, but that could wait. The various scars and bruises on his well-toned torso told many tales. He even remembered some of them.

Barefoot and bare-chested, Gabriel went to his kitchen, grabbed a bottle of Remy Martin, and poured himself a shot. He then sat on the piano bench and let his fingers roam absently over the keys. After a moment a melody emerged—"In the Still of the Night," one of his favorites. But somehow tonight it didn't fit his mood.

A framed photograph of the three Hunt children sat atop the piano. Gabriel had just turned sixteen when it was taken. That would make Michael ten and Lucy only four years old. She'd been an adorable little girl. Somewhere between four and fourteen, the adorable had faded and all sorts of simmering hostility had taken its place—but somehow never directed at Gabriel. Their parents, Michael, her classmates, her teachers... they'd all come in for their share of Lucy's particular brand of resentment. But Gabriel had always been spared. Maybe, he thought, it's because I wasn't around much.

By the time she'd run away—run away for good, Gabriel corrected himself; there'd been briefer disappearances before—she'd become quite the rebel, outspoken and independent and always looking for something to tear down. If she'd grown up in the sixties, he imagined Lucy would have found her way to Haight-Ashbury or onto Kesey's bus; in the seventies, she'd have been into punk rock. In fact, she *was* into punk rock, or at least the trappings that went with it. She had so many tattoos and piercings now that Gabriel had stopped counting them the last time he'd seen her.

He had to save her.

It was that simple. They'd taken her because of him, and now he had to find a way to get her back.

The first step toward which was to find her, period.

Which was not so simple.

Thinking about Lucy in Nice—or was she now in North Africa?—put him in mind of *Casablanca* and he found himself picking out the melody line of the *Marseillaise.*

Allons enfants de la Patrie
Le jour de gloire est arrivé!
Speaking of rebels.

Come, sons of France: the day of glory has arrived!
Followed by: *To arms, citizens! March!* Music to shed
blood by.

They all were, anthems. Bombs bursting in air,
and all that. Gabriel knew that at one point Napoleon
Bonaparte, when he was Emperor of France, had
banned the *Marseillaise*—but what had he replaced it
with? A cheery tune called *Le Chant du Départ*. Gabriel
picked it out on the keys and sang softly to himself.

La trompette guerrière
A sonné l'heure des combats...

The war trumpet has sounded the hour of battle.

Gabriel pulled the cover shut over the piano keys,
downed his drink, and stood up.

Those bastards who took Lucy probably had an
anthem of their own, some Egyptian version of the
same bloody sentiments. War trumpets, battles,
marching, marching.

Well.

They'd be singing a different tune soon.

**DON'T MISS THE NEXT EXCITING
ADVENTURE OF GABRIEL HUNT!**

THE GABRIEL HUNT ADVENTURES

"A pulp adventure series with classic style and modern sensibilities... Escapism at its best."
Publishers Weekly

From the towers of Manhattan to the jungles of South America, from the sands of the Sahara to the frozen crags of Antarctica, one man finds adventure everywhere he goes: Gabriel Hunt.

Backed by the resources of the $100 million Hunt Foundation and armed with his trusty Colt revolver, Gabriel Hunt has always been ready for anything—but is he prepared for the adventures that lie in wait for him?

HUNT AT THE WELL OF ETERNITY
James Reasoner

The woman carrying the bloodstained flag seemed desperate for help—and the attack that followed convinced Gabriel she had something men would kill for. And that was before he knew about the legendary secret hidden in the rain forest of Guatemala...

HUNT THROUGH THE CRADLE OF FEAR
Charles Ardai

When a secret chamber is discovered inside the Great Sphinx of Egypt, its contents will lead Gabriel to a remote Greek island, to a stone fortress in Sri Lanka... and to a confrontation that could decide the fate of the world!

HUNT AT WORLD'S END
Nicholas Kaufmann

Three jewels, lost for centuries and scattered across the globe, hold the secret to a device of unspeakable power, and only Gabriel Hunt can prevent them from falling into the hands of an ancient Hittite cult—or of a rival bent on world domination…

HUNT BEYOND THE FROZEN FIRE
Christa Faust

Dr. Lawrence Silver vanished while researching a mysterious phenomenon near the South Pole. His beautiful daughter wants to know where and why—and it's up to Gabriel Hunt to find out. But what they'll discover at the heart of nature's most brutal climate could change the world forever…

HUNT THROUGH NAPOLEON'S WEB
(August 2014)
Raymond Benson

Of all the priceless treasures Gabriel Hunt has sought, none means more to him than the one drawing him to the rugged terrain of Corsica and the exotic streets of Marrakesh: his own sister's life. To save her, Hunt will have to challenge the mind of a tyrant two centuries dead—the calculating, ingenious Napoleon Bonaparte…

HARD CASE CRIME
From Mickey Spillane & Max Allan Collins

THE CONSUMMATA
Mickey Spillane & Max Allan Collins

Compared to the $40 million the cops think he stole, $75,000 may not sound like much. But it's all the money in the world to the Cuban exiles who rescued Morgan the Raider. So when it's stolen, Morgan sets out to get it back.

DEAD STREET
Mickey Spillane

For 20 years, former NYPD cop Jack Stang has lived with the memory of his girlfriend's death. But what if she weren't actually dead? Now Jack has a second chance to save the only woman he ever loved—or to lose her for good…

DEADLY BELOVED
Max Allan Collins

Marcy Addwatter killed her husband—there's no question about that. But where the cops might see an open-and-shut case, private eye Michael Tree—*Ms.* Michael Tree—sees a conspiracy. Digging into it could mean digging her own grave… and digging up her own murdered husband's…

SEDUCTION OF THE INNOCENT
Max Allan Collins

Comics are corrupting America's youth. Or so Dr. Werner Frederick would have people believe. When the crusade provokes a murder, Jack Starr—comics syndicate troubleshooter—has no shortage of suspects.

TITANBOOKS.COM

HARD CASE CRIME
From Michael Crichton writing as John Lange

THE VENOM BUSINESS

As an expert handler of venomous snakes—and a smuggler of rare artifacts—Charles Raynaud is accustomed to danger. So the job bodyguarding an old acquaintance about to come into a fortune shouldn't make him break a sweat. But when the attempts on the man's life nearly get Raynaud killed, he's left wondering: is *he* the killers' real target…?

DRUG OF CHOICE

On a top-secret island in the Caribbean, bioengineers have devised a vacation resort like no other, promising the ultimate escape. But when Dr. Roger Clark investigates, he discovers the dark secret of Eden Island and of Advance Biosystems, the shadowy corporation underwriting it…

GRAVE DESCEND

Diver James McGregor is used to exploring sunken ships. But there's something strange about the wreck of the *Grave Descend*. No one aboard tells quite the same story about what happened. Then there's the mysterious cargo they were carrying… If McGregor's not careful, he may find himself in over his head.

BINARY

Political radical John Wright is plotting an act of mass destruction—and federal agent John Graves has him under surveillance. When a shipment of nerve gas gets hijacked, Graves puts the pieces together—but can he stop Wright from unleashing his weapon…?

A TOUCH OF THE EXOTIC

From India to war-torn London to an estate in Essex, Samira's life is one of rootlessness and unpredictability. With her half-Indian heritage, wherever she goes she's seen as 'exotic', never quite fitting in despite her best efforts. To add to her troubles, her beauty attracts attention from men that she's not sure how to handle. But when she falls for handsome RAF pilot Luke, none of her charms seem to work, as it appears his heart is already bestowed elsewhere . . .

DAWN KNOX

A TOUCH
OF THE
EXOTIC

Complete and Unabridged

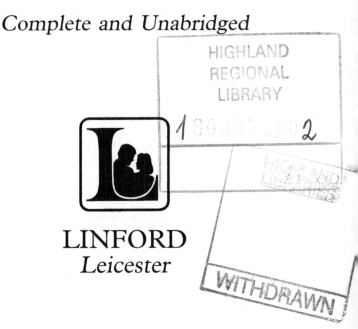

LINFORD
Leicester

First published in Great Britain in 2019

First Linford Edition
published 2019

A catalogue record for this book is available
from the British Library.

ISBN 978–1–4448–4065–0

Published by
F. A. Thorpe (Publishing)
Anstey, Leicestershire

Set by Words & Graphics Ltd.
Anstey, Leicestershire
Printed and bound in Great Britain by
T. J. International Ltd., Padstow, Cornwall

This book is printed on acid-free paper

1

'Samira Stewart! Stop loitering!' Sister Mary Esme spoke with mock severity and smiled at the school girl as she hesitated outside Mother Superior's office. 'Come on, dear, don't keep Sister Mary Benedicta waiting. You know she hates tardiness and procrastination . . . you also know how much she hates your hair when you haven't tied it back,' she added, fishing in her pocket for a piece of string and handing it to Samira. 'I'm sure you're not in trouble, dear, but it would probably help if you didn't look so guilty. Unless of course you *are* guilty of something!'

She smiled at the girl, who was dragging her lustrous black hair off her face into a ponytail and securing it with the string.

'That's the way,' she said, tucking a stray wisp behind Samira's ear and patting her shoulder. 'Now, knock!'

Samira knocked.

At the sound of Mother Superior's voice telling her to enter, she took a deep breath and opened the door.

There was nothing welcoming about Sister Mary Benedicta's office. It was cold and bare; the only item in the room that could be considered even slightly decorative was the simply framed painting of Mary and infant Jesus hanging behind the desk. There were no curtains, cushions or rugs, and the fireplace had not been used for years. Sister Mary Benedicta did not approve of *fripperies* and *fol-de-rols* — terms she used to describe many of the things that people commonly accepted as everyday comfort. Samira hesitated at the door, staring at the two chairs in front of the desk. She'd been sent to the office many times during the last ten years to explain her behaviour, but never before had she seen so much as a stool in front of the desk. Each time she'd been summoned to the study, she'd stood, weight shifting from foot to foot, as she squirmed with embarrassment and shame under the critical eye of Mother Superior while she awaited her punishment. But this time, there were two straight-backed wooden chairs opposite Sister Mary Benedicta.

'Ah, at last! Sit, please, Samira. I'm just finishing your documents.'

All the other schoolgirls had been given a school report and character reference when their parents or guardians had arrived to pick them up from school. Despite there having been no word from Papa, the fact that her papers were being prepared, and the second chair, indicated that he was coming. Samira felt torn. She was excited at the thought of seeing her father again after so long, but unhappy knowing that her time at St. Theresa's Convent was finally over. She'd known this day would come eventually; but if she'd had word from her father announcing his arrival, she'd have had time to get used to the idea of leaving, rather than this very abrupt end to her school career.

She sat down on one of the uncomfortable chairs and watched with trepidation as Mother Superior's nib glided across the paper, leaving spidery black loops in its wake. Samira felt like a pinned butterfly being scrutinised through a magnifying glass — except it wasn't her appearance that was being reviewed and judged, it was every one of her misdemeanours and failures during the previous ten years. If only she'd studied more . . . behaved better . . . tried harder. But it was too late now to influence what Sister Mary Benedicta was writing — the point of no return had been reached. She consoled herself with the thought that if Papa took her home to India, she would not be allowed to work and therefore was unlikely to need either a school report or a character reference; but it merely underlined the uncertainty of her future.

If Papa took her home. Of course he would take her home! He wouldn't want his daughter to remain alone in a country at war. The sadness at realising her schooldays were over was followed by a rush of confusion and guilt. How would Papa feel if, not having seen his daughter for four years and having travelled halfway round the world to fetch her, she told him she wasn't sure she wanted to go back to India with him? Well, of course, he'd be desperately hurt. And who could blame him? But if by some miracle he permitted her to remain in England, would Sister Mary Benedicta allow her to stay and help the nuns?

Samira had hardly been a star pupil, as Papa would no doubt shortly see from her report. Not that she'd been deliberately naughty — far from it; but the first seven years of her life had been spent in India and her memories were full of colour, excitement and mystery. So different from the grey, drab monotony of life in the convent. It had

5

taken the seven-year-old girl some time to adjust. After all, coming from a household where servants were on hand to pamper and play with their master's children, and to carry out their every whim, the austerity of the convent had been a challenge. For a while, it had seemed as though she would never belong in this whispering world of chanting and prayers. Her heart longed for the warmth, noise and exoticism of India; but after ten years in the convent, she now wondered how she would fit into the place of her childhood — especially since her mother had died.

When Samira had arrived at the convent, her memories of India had been frozen in time. Each night in the dormitory, she'd wept silently, consoling herself by reliving scenes from her past when she was still with her younger brother Vikash, Mama and Papa, and Mama's parents, Nana and Nani, on their tea plantation. She recalled the smell of spices hanging in the air, vases of vibrant flowers filling the house with their scent and colour, Cook feeding her delicious sweets . . .

Her childhood had been perfect until she'd been sent to St. Theresa's Convent in the heart of the Kentish countryside and expected to live a life as far removed from anything she'd previously known as if she'd been sent to the moon.

Samira first returned to India six years later, when Mama had become ill. It hadn't occurred to her that anything would have changed, and she was shocked to find that life was very different when viewed through the eyes of a thirteen-year-old. Papa had stayed by Mama's bedside and had sent a trusted family servant to England to collect Samira from school and accompany her home, but by the time they'd reached the tea plantation in north-eastern India, Mama had already died; and as custom decreed, the cremation had taken place the following day. Samira had been distraught at not having been able to see her mother and say goodbye, or attended the funeral. Vikash had been at school in Calcutta, so he'd been at home for their mother's final few days and had kissed her before she passed away.

When Samira finally arrived, Vikash had greeted her coldly and had pompously told her it was better she hadn't been there because she would have found it too upsetting and would probably have disgraced herself and the family by crying. He went on to describe how the illness had apparently changed their mother from the beautiful, slender woman that Samira held in her memory to a wasted figure who looked lost in her parents' enormous bed. Samira had been stunned at the change in her brother as well. At five years old, he had been a loving, gentle boy; but eleven-year-old Vikash was turning into a young man without sympathy or warmth. *Upset?* Of course she would have been upset! Of course she would have cried! She was devastated! But Vikash seemed to be

8

inferring that whereas his sadness was noble, hers was somehow inferior. She noticed that since she'd gone away, Vikash's attitude towards girls and women — his sister included — had altered and now seemed to border on contempt. This change in the boy she remembered carrying on her shoulders and teaching to swim in the river had, along with the pain of losing her mother, increased her isolation. It had caused her to question her place in the family; and for the first time she realised that what she'd previously thought of as home — and yearned for while she'd been at St. Theresa's — now appeared to be foreign and alien. She found the Indian heat oppressive, the colours too bright, and the crowded streets of the city over-whelming after the peace and calm of the convent.

But what had really disturbed her was the angry conversation she'd overheard between Papa and Mama's brother, Uncle Rahul. It had given her nightmares that only subsided once she'd arrived back in England and found sanctuary in the convent. Until she'd left India at the age of seven, she'd never been aware that having an English father and an Indian mother was unusual. Her parents had been so in love, and Mama's parents had accepted Papa and treated him as one of their own. He'd overseen the family's tea plantation, and in his usual modest manner, he'd significantly improved and expanded the business.

Uncle Rahul had not been interested in growing tea, and he'd spent much of his time in Calcutta where he'd married a wealthy heiress. When Mama's parents died, Uncle Rahul was quite happy for Papa to continue managing the family estates and he'd rarely visited — until Mama had died. There was something about Uncle Rahul that made Samira wary. She didn't know why, because he was very polite to her; but the conversation she'd overheard that day confirmed her perceptiveness.

'She's old enough to marry,' Samira heard him tell Papa.

'She's thirteen! I won't allow her to marry yet.'

'You've lived here for years, you know our customs. She's old enough. I've started negotiations with a wealthy family — '

'You've what? How dare you! She's my daughter, and I won't have her married off to someone to suit you or anyone else! She'll choose her own husband . . . when the time's right. And it's not right yet. Nor will it be for many years.'

'If you think I'll stand by and allow her to bring shame on our family like my sister brought shame on ours, you're very mistaken — '

'I think you've said enough, Rahul. Be very careful! Rani and I inherited the plantation from your parents. Now it belongs to me. If they'd been ashamed of our marriage, they would have left everything to you. Perhaps living in a big city has changed your values, but I won't stand for any interference with how I bring up my daughter.'

'Ah, so now I see why you were so keen to send her to England. You wish to find her an English husband. You wish her to lose her Indian heritage.'

'You see nothing, Rahul! I adored my darling Rani and I treasure her daughter's Indian heritage! I sent Samira to England to get a good education, nothing more. And when she's finished at school, then she will decide what she wants to do.'

'Women do not decide — '

'Well, in my house, they do!'

Uncle Rahul had stormed off, and Samira had run outside and hidden amongst the trees by the river, trying to make sense of the overheard conversation. The exchange between the brothers-in-law barely lasted a minute, but it had shaken Samira to the core. Her uncle's words repeated over and over in her mind. How could Mama possibly have brought shame to the family because she'd married Papa? They'd been so in love. And how could Uncle think that Samira would bring shame on her family unless she married someone of his choosing?

Marry?

At thirteen?

It was unbelievable. And yet, she knew that girls did marry young in this part of the world. But she didn't feel she belonged in this society, or that she had to obey its rules. Suddenly, she'd longed to return to England, to the safety and predictability of the convent . . . and yet, she couldn't truly say that she was happy there either; it was merely a refuge.

She simply didn't seem to belong anywhere.

Once back at St. Theresa's, she'd settled into the routine, avoiding thoughts of the future, concentrating on her studies and living in the moment. She still had another year at school before she needed to consider what she was going to do with her life — or so she thought. When war was declared, suddenly everything changed.

'It's like the Great War all over again,' Sister Mary Martha had wailed in an unguarded moment.

'Thank you, Sister,' Mother Superior had remarked sharply. 'We don't need any hysteria in our convent.'

'Sorry, Sister Mary Benedicta,' the nun mumbled; but Samira had seen tears well up in her eyes before she turned away. And it appeared that it hadn't just been Sister Mary Martha who remembered the horrors of the war that had ravaged the world between 1914 and 1918. The older nuns seemed preoccupied, and although they were mainly silent, there was now a cloud of despondency hanging over the convent that was obvious to Samira and her fellow pupils. The younger nuns had succumbed to the gloom; the singing from the chapel seemed to have acquired an added depth of emotion, as if collectively the sisters were taking it upon themselves to plead for the lives and souls of the whole world. Ostensibly, nothing had changed. The nuns' routine carried on in the same way as it had since the order had been established, but the war had somehow penetrated the thick, stone walls of the convent and had swept away their peace.

Eventually, Sister Mary Benedicta, who steadfastly resisted any change the world might try to impose on the order, had given in and had decided that her sisters would be of more use nursing wounded soldiers than educating young girls, and she'd written to all the parents to tell them of her decision. One by one, the girls had left after tearful goodbyes in the dormitories and promises to keep in touch.

As soon as most of them had gone, lessons were discontinued. Samira and the other girls who were waiting for parents to come from far-flung places helped the nuns to carry medical supplies into the convent, clean and tidy the dormitories and make everything ready for the first influx of soldiers. Gradually, parents arrived from glamorous locations such as Hong Kong, Canada, Australia — and took their daughters away, leaving Samira behind. Before the girls had left, they'd talked about going home with varying degrees of enthusiasm, but at least they were clear where their home was. Samira envied them all.

With a flourish, Sister Mary Benedicta signed the final sheet, bringing Samira's thoughts back to the present. She blotted the page and, folding the report and reference, she inserted them into a large envelope and looked expectantly at Samira.

'So, Samira, do you know what the future holds for you?'

'No, Sister Mary Benedicta, but I was wondering if it would be possible to stay . . . '

'No, my child, that will not be possible. Very soon we will have lots of men arriving. This is no place for a young girl. Unless, of course, you intend to join our order.'

'Oh no!' The words were out before

Samira had time to consider. 'I . . . I mean I don't think I'm cut out to be a nun. I . . . I just thought I might help with the nursing.'

'That's not possible, I'm afraid. You are not qualified, and none of my sisters will have time to supervise you. The patients' welfare must come first. And surely, your family will have something planned for you? But a word of advice, Samira: you need to apply a little more thought to your life, think before you speak, and curb that hot-headed wilfulness you so often display — '

A knock at the door interrupted what was likely to become a lecture about Samira's faults.

'Come!' Mother Superior called.

Sister Mary Esme opened the door. 'Mr Stewart here to see you, Sister Mary Benedicta.' She smiled encouragingly at Samira.

'Show him in, please.'

The nun opened the door fully and Samira gasped, her hand flying to her mouth as if to stifle a scream. She knew her father had suffered bouts of malaria in the past, but he'd aged so much she hardly knew him. If it hadn't been for the eyes, she might have passed him in the street without recognising him. His hair was much thinner and very grey, and he'd put on weight, especially round his middle, and he seemed shorter. But his face! It was so familiar and yet so unknown. So *old*.

'Good afternoon, Mr Stewart,' Sister Mary Benedicta said, rising and extending her hand to the visitor. 'May I introduce you to Samira, your granddaughter.'

2

Mr Stewart started the ignition and turned the wipers on to clear the fine drizzle from the windscreen.

'Please wait!' said Samira, peering at the convent doors.

'Have you forgotten something?'

'No, it's just that . . . I hoped Sister Mary Esme . . . '

Gentle and loving Sister Mary Esme had been Samira's favourite. The other nuns were remote and disengaged from everything, as if their bodies were still on earth but their minds were already in heaven. It was Sister Mary Esme alone who'd made certain she'd been at the convent's enormous wooden doors to wave goodbye to each of the girls as they'd left school for the last time, escorted by their parents or guardians. Occasionally, one or two of the other nuns who'd taught the girls had waited at the entrance with her, but it was obvious that bidding farewell to their pupils wasn't the priority that Sister Mary Esme seemed to think it was.

A tear trickled down Samira's cheek. She told herself that all the nuns were busy preparing for the wounded soldiers and that Sister Mary Esme would undoubtedly have been there if she could. Nevertheless, the pain of separation from everything that was familiar was somehow greater without the appearance of her favourite nun at the door to wish her godspeed. It felt as though she'd been forgotten already — and she hadn't even got as far as the convent gates.

Mr Stewart handed her a folded handkerchief and she wiped her eyes. 'Is there anything I can do to make it better?' he asked.

She shook her head and dabbed at her eyes again.

'Is that her?' he asked.

Samira looked up, and through her tears she saw Sister Mary Esme with an apron over her habit and her sleeves rolled to her elbows, waving at the door. She'd obviously been in the middle of something but had taken the time to bid Samira goodbye. Fresh tears came to Samira's eyes, and she rolled down the window, leaned out and waved back. The pain of separation was still there, but at least now she knew she hadn't been forgotten.

'All right to go now?' Mr Stewart asked.

'Yes, thank you . . . ' She'd paused, not sure how to address him. 'Mr Stewart' sounded rather formal. She'd called her maternal grandfather 'Nana' and grandmother 'Nani', much to the amusement of her friends at school, who'd pointed out that in England, 'Nana' was another name for 'grand-mother'. She didn't think this man would want to be 'Nana', and anyway, the name belonged to her Indian grandfather.

Should she call him 'Grandfather'? 'Grandpa'?

He picked up on her hesitance. 'So,' he said jovially, 'I imagine you're wondering what to call me? It must be strange to suddenly meet your grandfather after all these years.'

She nodded.

'Do you have any suggestions?' he asked.

'What would you like me to call you?'

'My daughter Amelia's children call me 'Pop' . . . well, they used to when they were younger . . . I don't see much of them now,' he said sadly.

''Pop' would be fine. And do I have a grandmother?'

'Yes, I'm taking you to see her now.'

'What do you think she'd like to be called?'

'Um . . . oh . . . probably best you ask her,' he said vaguely. 'She can be a bit . . . well . . . a bit particular. Anyway, I expect you'll find that out for yourself soon enough. Now, you're not to worry about your father. He's much better, and the hospital sent him home a few days ago, but it did mean that he didn't know about your school closing. As soon as he found out, he sent me a telegram and asked me to pick you up.'

'But why didn't anyone tell me he was in hospital? Are you sure he's all right now?' Samira bitterly regretted her earlier longing to stay in England. She now knew her place was in India, taking care of Papa.

'Yes, he's absolutely fine. He didn't go into detail about his illness, but he's fully recovered.'

'How soon will I be able to leave?'

'Leave?'

'For India, to see Papa.'

'Oh no, I'm sorry, love, you won't be leaving. Your father was quite insistent about that. He thinks it's too dangerous to travel by ship now we're at war.'

'But if I don't go back to India, where will I go?'

'Well . . . yes . . . your father asked if I would be able to look after you. But my cottage is rather small and . . . well . . . ' He seemed to be struggling for words. 'Anyway, we . . . that is I . . . thought it

23

might be best if you stayed with my niece, Joanna, and her family in Essex. She said she'd love to have you, and you'll be better off in the countryside, rather than with . . . err — what with the war on. Anyway, it'll give you a chance to think about what you want to do with your life; and as soon as the war's over, you can go home or do what you like.'

If it hadn't been for the similarity she'd spotted between Pop's eyes and her father's, she might have started wondering whether he was indeed her grandfather or an imposter. He seemed very vague at times and almost embarrassed at others, as if he was hiding something.

For a few miles, they drove through the Kent countryside in awkward silence, which was finally broken by Pop.

'So, love, why don't you tell me about yourself? We've got loads to catch up on.'

Samira told him about her life in

India on the tea plantation in the lowlands of Assam in the Brahmaputra River Valley. She described the family's white bungalow with its covered verandas. The backdrop of lush vegetation covered in vibrant flowers which filled the house with perfume. And nearby were the fields of tea bushes, where women in colourful saris and large baskets on their backs picked leaves with amazing speed and dexterity. She spoke of St Theresa's Convent, her school friends and the nuns, and made him laugh with her impression of Sister Mary Benedicta denouncing the world's fondness for *fripperies* and *fol-de-rols*. But she didn't tell him how lost she was — how she felt torn between two worlds — because that was the sort of thing that you confided in someone special, and this man who she'd just met was still a stranger, and worse, he was a stranger with a secret whom she couldn't bring herself to trust. He was obviously in touch with Papa, so why hadn't he known about her past? Or perhaps he did and he just wanted to get her to talk and put her at ease.

'Perhaps you'll tell me a little about your life, Pop,' she said, hoping that he'd reveal why he was being so vague.

'Well . . . ' he began, and Samira noted yet more hesitation. 'Well . . . there's not much to tell — nothing to interest you, really. I live in a small village in Sussex called Ribbenthorpe and I own a hardware store in town. All very dull.'

There was so much she wanted to know. Why hadn't he seen Auntie Amelia's children — her cousins — for some time? Why didn't he seem to know much about her and Vikash? She didn't remember her father ever having mentioned him or her grandmother. Perhaps there had been a family row and Pop didn't want to admit it.

Fields and meadows had given way to suburban sprawl and leafy avenues, then to streets of terraced houses with iron railings. Mothers pushed prams along the busy streets, with children of varying sizes hanging on to their skirts, and dogs wandered, dodging between the cars and buses. She was sure Pop had said he was taking her to see her grandmother, but this didn't look like a sleepy Sussex village.

'Where are we?' she asked in alarm.

'We'll be crossing over the river on the Woolwich ferry soon. Look! You can just see the Thames.'

The Thames! They were already in London! Samira was disappointed. Pop seemed to have forgotten that he'd said he was going to take her to see her grandmother. Instead, they were obviously going straight to Essex, to his niece's house. Perhaps he was tired. It had been a long drive and she was almost nodding off. Perhaps she would have an opportunity to meet her grandmother another day.

But once they'd crossed the river, instead of going east towards Essex, Pop turned west, towards central London. Shops and pubs lined the busy streets, jostling for a place between churches and narrow alleys; and as they drove through the increasing traffic, she spotted market stalls, a cinema, several synagogues, countless factories and even a bell foundry. Samira was just about to ask where they were when Pop turned left off the main road.

'Not much further,' he said. 'But before you meet Ivy . . . er, your grandmother, I think I need to explain something. I've been wondering how to break this to you for most of the journey, but there's no easy way to say it . . . and you need an explanation. So I'm just going to come out with it. Please don't be too hard on me. You don't know me yet and I would like that to change, really I would, but things are very complicated. And you may decide you're better off without me in your life.'

He pulled up in Aylward Street and turned the engine off, although he made no attempt to get out of the car.

'It's like this, Samira. Your grand-mother and I don't really get on. We haven't done for years. You'll probably see for yourself that she can be a difficult woman, and probably more so because I didn't have time to let her know we were coming. I haven't lived with Ivy for a long time. I still pay for her to live in our house, but I moved out into a cottage in Sussex. She's never forgiven me, of course . . . and . . . well, I suppose I'd better tell you the whole truth, because if I don't, Ivy probably will. I met someone else in Sussex, and well . . . we live together. Now I know you're probably shocked. I'm not proud of it, and my two children — David, your father, and your Auntie Amelia — were pretty angry with me, which is one of the reasons I don't see much of them — or my grandchildren. And the other reason is that my . . . er lady friend, Edie . . . and I have two children of our own. So, not only have you acquired grandparents today, but you also have two aunties who are only a few years younger than you.' He paused and looked at her pleadingly, 'Please don't judge me too harshly until you've met Ivy. She can be quite a handful, but please don't think I'm trying to shift the blame. Marriage should be for life, and I've broken my marriage vows . . . Say something. Please. Even if it's that you think I'm a disgrace and you're ashamed of me . . . '

The confession had shocked Samira, but it was hard to be emotional about people she hadn't known existed until a few hours ago. She imagined that it must have been much harder for Papa and Auntie Amelia — and of course, for her grandmother.

'Well, we'd best get it over with,' he said with a sigh, misinterpreting her silence for condemnation, 'At least I had a lovely journey getting to know you, before you knew about me. At least I had that.'

She placed her hand on his arm, and when she saw the glimmer of hope in his eyes, she smiled. 'Mama always said that you should never condemn or criticise anyone until you've walked a mile in their shoes.'

He laid his hand on hers and with tears in his eyes, he said, 'Your mama was a very wise woman, and I wish with all my heart that I'd met her.'

There was a tap on the car window, and a stout woman with her hair in rollers covered by a scarf crossed her beefy arms and glared at them.

Pop rolled the window down. 'Good afternoon, Mrs Thomsett. How are you and your family?'

'All fine and dandy, thank you, Mr Stewart. Come to visit Mrs Stewart, 'ave yer?' She bent down to get a better look at Samira and glared at her.

'Yes, I've brought my granddaughter, Samira, to see Ivy — '

'Oh! Granddaughter! I thought she might be yer fancy woman. Oh yes,' she said screwing up her eyes to get a better look at Samira, 'you must be Davy's daughter. I can see you've got a touch of the exotic about you! Welcome, lovey, welcome. Although prepare yerselves. Ivy ain't at 'er best.'

'Is she ever?' Pop asked.

Mrs Thomsett's expression changed, and she looked over her shoulder at number ten, as if she expected someone to be watching. 'No, Mr Stewart, I mean *really* not at 'er best. We had to call Dr Jenkins in yesterday after she had a turn. But I would think 'er granddaughter would be just the tonic she needs.'

'Thank you, Mrs Thomsett. I really appreciate your help.' He tried to slip some money into her hand but she stepped back, refusing to take it.

'Ain't no need,' she said.

'There are bound to be expenses, and it's not fair you should have to pay, Mrs Thomsett. It's so good of you to keep an eye on Ivy. We both know she can be a challenge. Please take this . . . for the children, perhaps.'

'Well, that's very kind of you, Mr Stewart,' she said, taking the pound note and tucking it into the enormous pocket of her apron. 'I've put the key back under the front mat as usual.

Right, I'll leave you to it . . . Cheerio,' she added. She stooped to pick a toddler up from the pavement, settled him on her hip and strode towards two young boys who were circling each other with fists raised. She warned one of them what his mother would do when she found out, then grabbed the other by the ear and marched him back to number twelve.

'Mrs Thomsett has a heart of gold,' said Pop. 'She calls a spade a spade, as you may have noticed, but I like that. At least you know where you stand with her. It's when people talk behind your back that things get unpleasant.' He sighed as if he'd been the subject of a great deal of gossip. 'Well, there's no point putting it off any longer. Come and meet your grandmother.'

3

The commotion had been enough to bring Mrs Thomsett rushing in from next door.

'Ooh, not that lovely china milk jug,' she said, bending to pick up the broken pieces. 'Now, Mrs Stewart, you look like you're getting yourself in a right ol' state. Why don't I put the kettle on and we'll all have a nice cuppa. What d'you say?'

'I'm not drinking anything while that man is in my house,' Ivy yelled, pointing a finger at her husband, who was standing protectively in front of Samira. She'd been dozing in an armchair next to the fire, wrapped in a tartan blanket when Pop had entered; and when she realised who her visitor was, she had picked up the nearest object and hurled it.

'He's got no right to be here!' She

seized her empty cup.

'Now, now, Mrs Stewart,' said Mrs Thomsett as if speaking to a child, 'why don't you put that down. It's part of your best china set. You wouldn't want it broken, would you? Mr Stewart has brought your granddaughter to meet you. What d'you think of that?'

'Granddaughter?' Ivy tried to stand, but the effort seemed to be too much and she sank back into the chair, 'Don't be ridiculous, woman. I don't have any grandchildren.' She pointed at Pop. 'You! Get out! You've got no right creeping in here as if you own the place!'

Ignoring the fact that he did actually own the place, he tried a gentle approach. 'Ivy, I know you're angry with me. You've got every right to be, but there's something you need to know — '

Ivy held up her hand. 'I don't have to listen to anything you say. Now get out. Can't you see the nurse has come to see to me? Get out! And don't come back!'

Silence. Eyes swivelled left and right, searching for the nurse Ivy had referred to.

'Blimey, it's worse than I thought,' whispered Mrs Thomsett. 'I knew she were bad, but I didn't know she were seeing things. Shall I telephone the doctor?'

'I ... I don't know,' said Pop uncertainly.

'Nurse! If you take my advice, you'll move away from that man. He is *not* to be trusted,' she said, looking straight at Samira, who was peeping out, wide-eyed, from behind Pop.

'Blimey, she thinks you're a nurse, lovey,' Mrs Thomsett whispered. 'It must be the school uniform.'

It occurred to Samira that for the first time in her life, she was involved in a situation where the adults had no idea what to do and she was the only one who could offer a solution. She smoothed her navy-blue gymslip with perspiring hands, patted her hair to ensure it was tidy, and stepped forward.

It had been fortunate that Sister Mary Esme had reminded her to tie her long hair back in a ponytail, as she doubted that nurses would be allowed to have their hair loose.

'Mrs Stewart,' she said, offering her hand, 'my name is Samira, and I am very pleased to meet you. Perhaps you would permit me to make you a fresh pot of tea.' She prayed that her grandmother would not require anything more complicated or medical than that.

'At last!' said Ivy. 'Someone with manners! Yes, please, Nurse, I would like some tea. And perhaps you'd be good enough to show *him* out. He's upset me enough for one day.' Her hand shook as she pointed an accusatory finger at Pop.

'Perhaps, Mr Stewart,' Samira said, her eyes pleading with Pop, 'it might be best if you leave. I'll show you out . . . '

Mrs Thomsett followed Pop and Samira into the hall. 'Well, it looks like it's under control, so I'll leave you to it.

You're a good girl,' she said, patting Samira's shoulder.

'I'll go to the post office on the corner and telephone Joanna to find out what time she expects to arrive to pick you up. Will you be all right until I get back?' Pop asked.

'Yes, I think so. I'll just make tea and chat to . . . to my grandmother for a while.'

'I won't come in the house again — it upsets her too much, so I'll send Mrs Thomsett or one of her family in with a message.'

Samira hurried back to Ivy in the kitchen, tucked the blanket around her, and placed the kettle on the range next to the fire.

'Thank you, Nurse. Well, it's certainly good to know Dr Jenkins is so thoughtful, although he didn't mention anything about sending you,' Ivy said. 'But I'm very glad you're here. It's kind of Mrs Thomsett to drop in, but she's such a gossip, and I don't like the whole neighbourhood knowing my business.

Sometimes it's easier to deal with strangers, don't you think?'

Samira busied herself making a fresh pot of tea, answering 'Oh yes' and 'Definitely' where appropriate.

She was beginning to have second thoughts about allowing her grandmother to believe she was a nurse. It seemed deceitful somehow, but at least now Grandmother was calm. And making someone tea and ensuring they were comfortable was hardly dishonest. If only Mrs Thomsett or one of her children or grandchildren would come in to let her know when Joanna would be arriving! Now that Pop had gone, Ivy seemed quite rational, even if she was rather weak, and Samira wondered whether her claim that she didn't have any grandchildren was due to confusion. After all, as far as Samira knew, she had three grandchildren besides herself and Vikash. Auntie Amelia had Hannah, Joseph and Jack. But perhaps what she'd meant was that she never saw them, rather than that she didn't know they existed.

There was a gentle tap at the kitchen door, and when Samira opened it, a small girl held out a note. 'Me gran says I'm to give you this, miss.' Samira thanked her and, unfolding the paper, she read it.

'If you'll excuse me, Mrs Stewart, I won't be a moment.' Samira walked towards the front door.

'Where are you going, Nurse? You won't be long, will you?' Ivy's face had gone white, and she gripped the arms of the chair.

'No, no, I'll be right back.'

'You're not just saying that, are you?' There was panic in the woman's voice.

'No, Mrs Stewart. I'll be a minute, that's all. I promise I'll come back.'

How would her grandmother react when Joanna came to take Samira home?

Pop was waiting on the front door step. 'Oh Samira, love. I've just spoken to Joanna's husband, Ben, on the telephone and he said that her car has broken down in Ilford and he's going to drive there and pick her up, but Joanna won't be able to fetch you today. I'm afraid I'm going to have to find a room in a hotel for you tonight. I'd love to take you home, but I really can't. I know I said there wasn't enough room in our cottage, and that was true, but the real reason is that Edie — my lady friend — has a jealous streak and doesn't like any reminders that I'm married. Well . . . it's just not possible, I'm afraid. I'm so sorry, love, I really am.'

He looked so dejected that Samira felt sorry for him. The women in his life seemed to cause him nothing but problems.

'Nurse! Nurse!' Ivy's voice could be heard rising in panic.

'She doesn't seem to want me to go,' said Samira. 'What shall I do?'

'This is a disaster! I'm sorry, love, I had no idea she was so disorientated. I've never seen her like this before. She's usually prickly, but this is something new. Normally, she's very suspicious of people. She barely tolerates Mrs Thomsett going in the house, but she certainly seems to have taken a shine to you. I'm afraid we're just going to have to leave Ivy to it. It's a shame, but I need to find you somewhere to stay before I can go home.' He checked his watch and frowned. 'Edie will already be at the window waiting for me, so I need to hurry.'

'Nurse! Where are you?' The exasperation and fear could be heard in Ivy's voice.

'Pop, I can't just walk out and leave her! It would be cruel. I told her I'd be back.'

He bit his lower lip. 'I don't think we've got much choice.'

'Unless . . . ' said Samira, almost afraid to voice her suggestion.

'Yes?' he said, his eyes alight with hope.

'Unless I stay with her tonight. Perhaps in the morning, Mrs Thomsett could phone for the doctor to come and he could have a word with her. And then Joanna could take me home tomorrow.'

'Well, that would solve the problem,' he said doubtfully, 'but it's an awful lot to ask of you.'

'It might give me a chance to get to know my grandmother a bit — even if she doesn't seem to know who I am.'

'Ah, about that . . . I'm afraid she may have spoken the truth about not knowing she had grandchildren.'

Samira looked at him, aghast. 'How can it be possible she doesn't know about us?'

'Because our son and daughter severed all ties with her and neither of them told her when the grandchildren were born. It's very sad, but Ivy made their lives miserable. She tried to control them and ended up alienating them both. I thought one day she'd mellow — not towards me of course — but I always hoped that she'd be reconciled with her children. I've tried to persuade them both, but so far they won't hear of it. So I'm pleased that even though she doesn't know you, she'll be able to spend time with you.'

'Nurse!'

Pop brought Samira's suitcase and bag and put them in the hall. He took her hand and kissed it. 'We're still strangers, really, so I won't kiss you on the cheek. But one day, I hope we'll really be granddaughter and grandfather.'

He waved to her as he drove off down the street, several small children running beside him until he reached the corner and was gone.

Samira went back into Ivy's kitchen.

'You came back!'

'Yes, Mrs Stewart, I told you I would.'

'That's what they all say. But sooner or later, everyone leaves,' She shook her head sadly. 'It's just a fact of life.'

4

Samira woke early the next morning, unaccustomed to the sounds in the street outside. The clip-clop of the horse's hoofs as it pulled the milkman's cart along the cobbled road, and the rattle of the glass bottles of milk in metal crates, roused her.

It was still dark when she got out of bed and washed her face in the china bowl that stood on the tallboy in the corner of her bedroom. Despite sleeping in a strange bed, she felt refreshed; and anyway, she was used to rising early in the convent. The previous evening, Ivy had seemed worn out after her angry outburst. She'd refused anything to eat and had announced she wanted to go straight to bed. Samira made her hot cocoa, and Mrs Thomsett had popped in to help her up the stairs to bed. Samira told Ivy she'd be sleeping in the other bedroom and had expected to be called during the night, but Ivy had obviously tired herself out; and other than the occasional bout of snoring, she'd been quiet.

When Mrs Thomsett arrived in the morning with a cheery 'Coo-ee!', Samira had already laid the table and put the kettle on the range.

'I'll 'elp her down the stairs, lovey, and then I'll nip along to the post office and telephone Dr Jenkins. You're a little marvel!' she said, smiling at Samira. 'It's such a shame Mrs Stewart doesn't know who you are, but there were harsh words spoken between her and your Pa. Young Davy were a lovely lad. I were quite upset when he left . . . And then to find he'd gone all the way to *India!*' She spoke as if India was on the outer reaches of the universe. 'But Mrs Stewart would insist on threatening to cut Davy and his sister Amelia off . . . Sometimes, giving a child an ultimatum is the best way to lose them. Look at me, going on as if I'm an expert! I've got so many children and grandchildren, it might be an idea if I gave a few of them an ultimatum and lost a few of them!' She laughed loudly.

The small girl who'd delivered the note the previous day poked her head round the kitchen door. 'Gran, you'd better come quick — Sid and Georgie are fighting again!'

'You tell them I'll 'ave their guts for garters if they haven't made up by the time I find them, Rosie! I'm just going to 'elp Mrs Stewart downstairs. Run along now! When I've finished, you can come to the post office with me.'

Rosie nodded and skipped out.

'What's she doing in here again?' Ivy asked when Mrs Thomsett returned after her phone calls.

'Just seeing if the nurse wants anything, Mrs Stewart. Just being neighbourly.'

'Huh! Snooping, more like!'

'Oh no!' said Samira. 'Mrs Thomsett has been really kind . . . '

'Don't you worry, lovey. I don't take

no notice,' Mrs Thomsett whispered. 'Dr Jenkins will try to call later and check her out, and Joanna will be here just after lunch. So, not much longer. D'you think you can bear it?'

'Oh yes! She's no trouble, really — '

'What are you two whispering about?' Ivy asked.

'Nothing, Mrs Stewart. I'm just telling yer nurse the best place to buy a loaf of bread.' She winked at Samira and added loudly, 'As I said, it's Patterson's Bakery round the corner.'

When Mrs Thomsett had gone, Samira tried to make conversation, but she soon discovered that Ivy would neither talk about Pop nor her children. In desperation, she'd told her grandmother about her childhood in India, and for the first time, Ivy seemed to take an interest.

'I thought there was something foreign about you,' she remarked. 'But you're a pretty thing — and very kind too.' It was as if she considered prettiness and kindness were qualities sufficient enough to make up for the regrettable foreignness. 'In fact,' she added, 'you remind me a bit of my Davy. Not that you look anything like him,' she said quickly. 'He had blond curls when he was young, and such a gentle manner . . . ' She tailed off, her eyes narrowing as if remembering something unpleasant. She took hold of Samira's wrist and spoke urgently, as if passing on vital information.

'Let me give you a word of advice, Nurse. You're only young, so you may not have found this out for yourself yet; but you will, mark my words, you will. People may promise you the world, but in the end, they'll let you down. In the end, everyone leaves. Take every chance you get to be independent. It's not easy for a woman. The law's been against us for so long, not allowing us the vote until recently, not allowing us to be in charge of our own destinies. But the war will change things. You mark my words. Things changed for women after the last war, and they'll change again.

Put by as much as you can, so when you're finally on your own, you'll be all right . . . ' She dabbed her eyes with a handkerchief.

If Samira could have thought of something to say, she wouldn't have been able to voice her feelings because of the lump in her throat. She felt so sorry for this woman — her grand-mother — who seemed to drive away anyone who might care for her and then bear a grudge against them when they left.

A loud rat-a-tat-tat at the door brought them both back to reality, and Samira rose to open it. A smartly dressed young woman with chestnut curls framing a heart-shaped face stood on the doorstep and smiled with relief when she saw Samira.

'I hoped you'd answer the door,' she said, holding out her hand. 'I'm Joanna. Uncle John said Aunt Ivy was being even more difficult than usual, and I know I'm not her favourite person . . . Anyway, I'm so sorry about not

50

picking you up yesterday, but the car conked out on Ilford Broadway. You should have seen the traffic holdup! Anyway, I've got Ben's car today and that seems to be running smoothly, so as soon as you're ready, we'll head back to Essex. If you want to get your things together, I'll go and have a word with Aunt Ivy . . . or more likely, Aunt Ivy will have a few insults to throw at me!'

Samira was drawn to the young woman, who was probably only ten years her senior. She seemed to be full of confidence, and the upturned corners of her mouth gave her face a permanently happy expression.

'Nurse! Who's at the door? What's going on?' shouted Ivy from the kitchen.

Joanna blanched. 'The last time I saw Aunt Ivy, I was only eighteen, and she used to frighten me to death with her sharp tongue. Nine years later, I'm married with two children of my own and I still feel terrified! You deserve a medal for putting up with her last night!'

'Nurse!'

'Right,' said Joanna checking her hat in the hall mirror and taking a deep breath, 'let's get it over with.'

Samira opened the kitchen door.

'Who is it, Nurse?' Ivy asked.

'You've got a visitor, Mrs Stewart.'

'A visitor? I never have visitors. Can't you get rid of them? I don't want to see anyone.'

Before Joanna could step out of the gloom of the hall into the kitchen, the front door opened.

'Coo-ee! Only me. I've brought the doctor.' It was Mrs Thomsett and a thin, bald man with a worried expression who hovered uncertainly in the doorway. He passed his leather briefcase from hand to hand.

'What is this?' shouted Ivy. 'Paddington Station? What are all these people doing in my house? Get out! Nurse, show them all out!'

Dr Jenkins' professionalism took over and he glided past Mrs Thomsett and Joanna in the narrow hall. 'Now, Mrs

Stewart, you really must calm down. Your heart isn't strong, and you need to rest.'

'How can I rest with all these people in my house? Who is that woman in the hall?'

Joanna stepped into the kitchen. 'Aunt Ivy — '

'No!' Ivy screeched, her hands gripping the arms of the chair and her face contorted with rage. 'I told you never to cross my threshold again — '

'Enough!' roared Dr Jenkins. 'Ladies and . . . *you*,' he said to Samira, 'please leave. No one will come in again until I say so. Mrs Stewart needs peace and quiet.'

'Please don't send the nurse away, Doctor,' said Ivy. 'She's been a godsend.'

*   *   *

Dr Jenkins emerged from the house some time later. He explained that he'd given Ivy something to calm her down and that she would probably be sleepy for the rest of the day. He forbade Joanna to go back in the house; and despite his misgivings at passing off a schoolgirl as a nurse, he strongly suggested that Samira stay with Ivy for a few days or possibly weeks until she recovered.

'So, she will recover, then, Doctor?' asked Joanna.

'It's hard to say. Her heart is weak, and any agitation is extremely bad for her.'

'But Samira can't stay here for weeks!' said Joanna. 'Perhaps Uncle John could find a live-in nurse.'

'Well, good luck with that!' said Mrs Thomsett, who was aware that when Dr Jenkins had to call on Ivy, he always knocked at her house supposedly to see how she and her family were, but really in the hope that she would accompany him on his visit.

'Well, we could always try it . . . for a while,' said Samira hesitantly. 'We were getting on really well this morning. And it's not like I have any plans, so it might be the best thing for all of us. With the war on, I could make myself useful and do some voluntary work . . . '

'Are you sure, Samira? It seems like everyone wins except you,' said Joanna.

'Yes, I'm sure. It will give me a chance to get to know the grandmother I never knew.'

5

It was late September, but the breeze was wintry and the heavy clouds raced across the sky, threatening rain. Samira shivered, did up the buttons on her uniform overcoat, and straightened her hat. The night promised to be long, uncomfortable and dangerous. Already this evening, several bombs had dropped on London, but they had exploded far to the west and now there was a red glow in the sky, and smoke in the wind. She'd joined the Women's Voluntary Service a few months before, so she had some idea of what people must be going through and wondered how the fire fighters and members of the other organisations that had been set up to handle wartime disasters were coping.

The Germans had increased their bombing of London, in what the newspapers were calling the Blitz; and because Stepney was so close to the East London Docks, the night-time aerial attacks were ferocious, and Samira and the other WVS members had been increasingly busy, serving refreshments to civilians whose homes had been bombed, as well as to the men and women in the various rescue services.

When Ivy had discovered that Samira was expected to pay for her own WVS uniform, she'd insisted on buying every item of clothing, despite making it very clear that she didn't approve of her being out at night. Samira had been touched at Ivy's generosity, and this evening she was more grateful than ever to be wearing the grey-green tweed overcoat over her WVS suit. Ivy had recovered after her illness, and if she suspected Samira was her granddaughter, she'd never said, although she no longer treated the girl as if she was a nurse — more of a distant family member and live-in carer. And she now called Samira 'Samantha' because in her opinion it sounded 'less foreign' than her given name. Samira had been relieved that she hadn't insisted on the more formal 'Miss Stewart', raising the possibility of a discussion of their shared surname. Ivy, who Samira addressed as 'Mrs Stewart', was still prickly and difficult, but it felt like a relationship was developing between them, even if it was hard to define exactly what the bond was.

'Penny for 'em!' An attractive girl with shoulder-length auburn hair and a dusting of freckles across her nose came round the corner of the tea van and found Samira deep in thought. Kitty Fletcher, also dressed in a WVS uniform, was the unofficial leader of the girls and had taken Samira under her wing when she'd first joined several months before. It had been obvious that there was a world of difference between the Cockney girls and the slim, dark-haired young woman who had been born in India but spent much of her life in a convent.

When Kitty first introduced Samira to the other girls, Mavis, one of the local girls, had asked her if she spoke English, and the others had stared at her with distrust. But with Kitty's determination that her team would work together, she set about finding similarities between the girls and ignoring differences. It had taken a few days, but once the local girls realised that Samira's English was better than theirs and that she was quick to learn and keen to exceed anyone's expectations, they accepted her as one of them.

Mavis had been impressed that Samira was taking driving lessons from Kitty. 'I don't know how you do it,' she said when she'd seen Samira at the wheel. 'I wouldn't dare.' Kitty had been pleased to teach Samira to drive the van — the more skills they shared, the more effective they would be in their war effort.

'Why're you so deep in thought?' Kitty asked.

'Oh, I was just thinking about Mrs

Stewart and hoping that if the siren goes off, she'll go under the stairs. I know she doesn't like it under there.' Samira had been vague about her relationship with Ivy, hinting that she was a distant relative.

'Doesn't your neighbour keep an eye on her?'

'Yes, but she's such a handful, and Mrs Thomsett's got lots of family of her own to gather up and keep safe.'

'You're doing the right thing, you know,' said Kitty. 'You could stay home and look after her, or you could help lots of people who're really in need, with us.'

'Yes, I know. I just feel so sorry for her. She looks so lost when I leave in the evening.'

'Well, let's take your mind off it before the other girls arrive. We've time for a drive round the block, if you'd like.'

But before Samira could get to the driver's seat, the air raid warning siren began to wail, rising and falling' and people spilled out of their houses, clutching blankets, cushions, flasks of tea and bags, heading for the public shelter.

'It's going to be lively tonight,' said Kitty a little later as the *ack-ack* of the anti-aircraft guns cut through the air, and bombs dropped to the east. 'It looks like they're targeting the docks.'

* * *

Many of the fires caused by the incendiary bombs had been extinguished, but there were sufficient flames to light up the dockland area to show the German pilots where to bomb. By the early hours, Samira was exhausted. She'd served tea to the air raid wardens and fire fighters as well as civilians. Many had been evacuated from dangerous buildings and some stood near the WVS van, comforting each other or staring at the piles of rubble that had once been their homes. Many people had been wounded by falling masonry, and Samira and the other girls had helped to dress minor wounds and lead people to safety.

'All right, miss? You look done in,' a young air raid warden said to Samira. 'I don't suppose there's any chance of a cuppa?' he added, smiling cheekily. He took off his tin helmet and wiped his forehead with his sleeve, smudging soot across his face. 'James McGuire,' he said, holding out his hand, 'but everyone calls me Jimmy.'

'Samira Stewart,' she said, shaking his hand. 'And yes, there's every chance of a cuppa!'

But before she could go back to the van, screams ripped through the night, followed by the rumble and crash of a building collapsing. Jimmy joined the other air raid wardens who were running towards the source of the sound, and they were soon lost to sight amongst the smoke and dust.

It was almost light before the bombing had ceased and Kitty was satisfied the van was clean and tidy. The fires were out, although here and there smoke billowed upwards into the grey dawn, and the smell of charred wood filled their nostrils. She thanked the girls and told them to go home and get some rest if they could.

'Ain't that Mary McGuire's younger brother lurkin' over there?' asked Lizzie, pushing her smeared spectacles further up her nose.

'Yeah, that's Jimmy,' said Mavis. ''E lives round the corner to me. It looks like 'e's eyeing up our Sam, don't it, ladies?'

The other girls laughed good-naturedly, and Samira blushed. 'I'm sure he's not,' she muttered, and turned away to hide her flaming cheeks.

As the other girls walked home in ones and twos, Samira set off for Aylward Street alone, and Jimmy fell into step beside her.

'I hope you don't mind me waiting for you, but I wanted to apologise for rushing off like that and I . . . I hoped that perhaps we could still have a cup of tea together . . . later. That is, if you're not too busy. Or you're not seeing . . . anyone else.' He reminded Samira of a puppy with expressive eyes that were begging her not to turn him away.

'Well, I don't know . . . It's just that my . . . aunt . . . isn't very keen on me going out.'

'That's all right,' he said, his face registering first disappointment and then resignation. 'I understand.'

'No,' she said quickly, 'it's not that I don't want to. It's just that I live with my aunt, and she can be a bit . . . well . . . difficult. I don't really like to leave her when I'm on duty with the WVS, so I'm not sure it would be fair to just go out and leave her.'

His face lit up. 'Just a quick cuppa?' His eyes begged her again.

'Well, yes, all right. So long as we're not long. There's a café not far from where I live; perhaps we could go there?'

'We'll go anywhere you like,' he said, his eyes now sparkling.

As he walked her home, he told her about his welding apprenticeship in the London Docks and how he really wanted to join up, but welders were needed at home to mend the ships and for other vital work in the docks. While he chattered about his role as an air raid warden, his job and his family, she was silent — painfully aware of her inexperience with boys. She'd barely seen a male during her time at the convent, let alone held a conversation with one; and since she'd met Kitty and the other girls, who spoke about dances and trips to the cinema with boys, she'd realised how naïve she was.

The closer they got to Aylward Street, the more she was regretting accepting his offer of a cup of tea, because to him, it obviously meant a lot more than a hot drink. It seemed that she'd unwittingly given him the impression that they would be more than just friends, and she was feeling rather overwhelmed. It wasn't that she didn't like him — she did. Or at least she liked the warm glow that washed over her every time he looked at her as if he couldn't believe she was with him. But she was out of her depth, and if she hadn't felt so tired after the long, harrowing night, she might have been able to think clearly and to extricate herself without hurting his feelings. But it was too late now. He took her to Ivy's door, shook hands and told her for the third time that he'd be there for her at seven o'clock sharp.

When she'd gone to her bedroom, she'd peered at her hazy reflection in the old mirror that hung on the wall. There hadn't been many opportunities to see herself while she'd been at St. Theresa's, Sister Mary Benedicta declaring that vanity was a grave sin. What could Jimmy see when he looked at her so intently? His expression had been one of such admiration that she'd been amazed. She pulled the ribbon off her ponytail and shook her silky black hair free to fall over her shoulders. Beneath her straight fringe, enormous eyes stared back at her quizzically. Her skin was a shade or two darker than the other girls she knew, but other than that, she didn't think she looked any different from them — other than for her eyes. At the convent, Sister Mary Benedicta had told her off several times for looking in an insolent manner, but Jimmy had said her eyes were exotic and that he'd never seen anything so beautiful.

At ten to seven, Samira slipped out of the house. She'd told Ivy she was visiting one of her WVS friends; she was afraid Jimmy would knock at the door and Ivy would see him. He was already there at the corner when she quietly closed the front door.

'I couldn't wait to see you,' he said, smiling at her; and she wondered if he had mistaken *her* early arrival for eagerness to see *him*. If only she'd simply told him she couldn't go out to the café with him, she wouldn't be in such a predicament. How was she supposed to behave? What should she say? What should she *not* say? She simply had no idea, and her stomach was so knotted with nerves, she was sure she wouldn't be able to drink a mouthful of tea. He tucked her arm beneath his as they crossed the road, and she fervently hoped he couldn't feel her trembling.

But to her surprise, the time passed really quickly — and even more amazingly, she was enjoying Jimmy's company. He was quick-witted, funny and kind; so easy to be with. She lost track of time, only remembering that she'd told Ivy she'd be home in an hour — which she'd thought would be far too long. His face fell when she said she'd have to go home, but he gallantly leapt to his feet, paid for their teas and helped her into her coat.

'When can I see you again?' he asked as they turned into Aylward Street. 'How about Thursday afternoon?'

She agreed. After all, she'd had a lovely time; but she was acutely aware that in making it so obvious that he liked her, he'd placed her under pressure. She wouldn't deliberately hurt him, but it made the possibility of turning down his invitations much harder.

Ivy had been upset when Samira had told her she'd be going out for a few hours on Thursday afternoon. 'More training?' she said crossly. 'Well, make sure you're back by five.'

Samira had promised she would and had then felt guilty at lying, and cross with herself for agreeing to meet Jimmy. Life would be so simple if she'd simply turned him down, but she knew how dejected he would have been had she done so. And anyway, it was flattering that he was so obviously smitten by her.

She'd asked him not to knock at the door for her, but in case he forgot, she made sure she was waiting for him in the street. Mrs Thomsett was standing in her doorway, arms crossed looking up and down the street.

'Afternoon, lovey. You 'aven't seen my Alfie, 'ave you?'

'No, sorry, Mrs Thomsett; I've only just come out.'

'Oh well, if you see 'im, tell 'im I'll 'ave 'is guts for garters if he don't get his backside home immediately.'

'I will,' said Samira, hoping that Jimmy wouldn't arrive before Mrs Thomsett went back in her house.

'Waiting for yer young man, are you?' Mrs Thomsett was in no hurry to leave her doorstep. 'That Jimmy McGuire is a lovely young man,' she said softly, her eyes warily on Ivy's windows.

'How do you know?' Samira was aghast.

'There ain't much I don't know around these parts, lovey.'

'You won't tell Mrs Stewart, will you?'

Mrs Thomsett tapped the side of her nose. 'Mum's the word. But be careful — she won't like it. I've seen it 'appen afore with Davey and Amelia. 'ere's an idea, lovey — ask 'im to meet you round the corner, rather than risk upsetting her.' She nodded her roller-clad head at Ivy's house. 'And be careful. With this war on, people are living for today and not giving tomorrow much thought. Take my Sally. She's in the family way and her young man's gone off to fight.'

'Oh, Mrs Thomsett!' Samira didn't know what to say.

'I know, I know. Sally's always been wilful. But you — you've got a good 'ead on yer shoulders. So, be careful . . . and if I was you, I'd start walking down the street. Yer young man's just turned the corner.'

★ ★ ★

Despite the unpromising start to the afternoon, Samira thoroughly enjoyed herself. She forgot her guilt at lying to Ivy and the shock at knowing her secret had been discovered by Mrs Thomsett, and therefore probably most of the other women in the street. They regularly gathered on each other's doorsteps gossiping, and it was only because Ivy rarely set foot outside of the house that she hadn't yet heard.

Perhaps it was time to tell her; although Mrs Thomsett had suggested otherwise, warning her simply to conceal the truth. Without understanding what her relationship with Jimmy was, it was hard to work out the boundaries. Perhaps it might be best not to tell Ivy yet.

Yet?

That thought anticipated there was more to come in this friendship with Jimmy. But she felt like she was riding a runaway horse — it was exhilarating but frightening.

'And next Wednesday evening, I'll take you,' he said. 'You'll love it!'

They were sitting on a bench that encircled a huge tree in the small park in Arbour Square, watching the children play on the lawn.

'Sorry?' she said, ashamed that she'd been lost in her own thoughts.

'The dance at the Old Mahogany Bar in Graces Alley. Next Wednesday — '

'*Dance?*' She was horrified. 'Oh no, I couldn't!' The excitement drained from his face. 'What I mean is,' she added gently, 'I don't know how to dance, so there's really no point.'

'You don't need to worry about that! We can go early and I'll show you a few steps. I promise I won't leave your side all night, so you won't be on your own. I'll make sure you enjoy it . . . '

How could she get out of it without hurting his feelings?

'Please . . . ' he said, and she knew that the hope in his eyes would be kindled or extinguished depending on her answer.

'Well . . . '

That was enough for Jimmy. 'I'll pick you up at six, and then we'll go in early and I'll show you a few steps.'

She arrived home before five o'clock so Ivy wouldn't have cause to complain; and while she was spreading margarine on some bread for tea, the air raid siren began to wail. She sighed. An evening, and possibly night, under the stairs with Ivy wasn't a pleasant prospect.

'We could always go to the Thomsetts'

Anderson shelter,' Samira suggested, although she already knew the answer.

'What? Share a night with that family and all their brats? I don't think so!'

'It was really kind of Mrs Thomsett to ask us.'

Ivy sniffed. 'That's as may be. But I'd still rather stay here.'

When the all clear sounded, Samira helped Ivy out of the confined space under the stairs.

'I'm going to bed,' Ivy announced. 'And I don't care how many German aeroplanes come over, I'm not going back in that cupboard tonight!'

While Samira was clearing away in the kitchen, Mrs Thomsett let herself in to the house. 'All okay, lovey?' she asked.

'Yes, thank you. Mrs Stewart's gone to bed with orders not to be disturbed.'

'Well, if you ever get fed up cramming yerselves under the stairs, don't forget yer welcome in our shelter.'

'Thank you Mrs Thomsett . . . '

'Yes, I know, lovey, Mrs Stewart

wouldn't come into our shelter with my brood if the Jerries were here in the house! I know what she thinks of us. But if you ever want to come, yer very welcome.'

'Thank you.'

'Well, out with it!' said Mrs Thomsett. 'You look as happy as a wet Wednesday. Did your young man upset you?'

'No . . . not exactly. But I said I'd go dancing with him next week.'

'And that's a problem because . . . ?'

'I don't really know.'

'Right,' said Mrs Thomsett, 'put the kettle on and we'll see if we can sort out what's worrying you.'

'Well, I'm not exactly worried,' said Samira, pouring tea into Mrs Thomsett's cup. 'I just feel at a bit of a loss. The other girls in the WVS talk about walking out with boys, and they seem to have such fun . . . '

'And you don't have fun with Jimmy?'

'Yes, he's good company. He makes

me laugh, and he really seems to care about me . . . '

'Sounds like he's Mr Perfect! So, what's the problem? 'E's not pressuring you, is 'e?' she asked, suddenly looking serious. 'Only if 'e tried that, I'd 'ave 'is guts fer garters. An' you can tell 'im I said that!'

'No, no, nothing like that. I suppose it's just that I thought it would be different. My parents adored each other — you could tell they were made to be together. And sometimes I see Jimmy look at me in a way that tells me he likes me more than I like him. And then I feel bad and wonder why I don't feel the same way.'

'Ah! I see. Well everyone's different, of course. But sometimes love don't always 'appen neatly. Take my Wilf — I met 'im when I were sixteen. I know it's 'ard to believe it looking at 'im now, but in those days he were so handsome. I was head over heels in love with 'im — along with most of the other girls in my street. But it took 'im several years before 'e came round to my way of thinkin'. Sometimes things just move at different speeds. There's nothin' wrong in that. So, why don't you go to yer dance and just enjoy it?'

'The other thing is, I've never been to a dance before. Jimmy says he'll take me early and teach me a few steps but I . . . I just feel I'm going to make such a fool of myself.'

Mrs Thomsett drank the last of her tea and stood up. 'You'll be fine, lovey. Come round tomorrow and I'll get my son John to show you how to waltz. Yer'll pick it up in no time; and if you haven't got anything to wear, we'll alter something of Sally's. She's about your size — or she was before she got in the family way. She'll 'ave no need of smart frocks for some time yet.'

'I hadn't even thought about what I should wear!' Samira was horrified. 'You see? I don't have a clue!'

'You're just young, that's all, an' I don't s'pose the nuns taught you much dancing! Don't worry about it. We all 'ave to start somewhere.'

'Thank you so much, Mrs Thomsett. I don't know what I'd do without you.'

'Think nothing of it, ducks. We all stick together in this neighbourhood and 'elp each other out when we need to. That's what life's all about.'

★ ★ ★

Jimmy switched his torch on briefly every few yards to light their path through the dark as they walked along Cable Street to the Old Mahogany Bar. There was no moon to guide them through the blackout, and a heavy mist had descended, making the visibility even worse. Since blackout had been introduced, the incidence of road accidents had increased, and he took Samira's hand and held it tightly as they crossed each road, lacing his fingers with hers. He assured her that despite the walk taking longer than he'd anticipated, there would still be time for her to practise a few dance steps. As they entered the Old Mahogany Bar, several friends greeted him, and it wasn't until Samira had taken off her coat that he looked at her for the first time since he'd met her in the dark of Aylward Street. He gasped and his jaw fell open.

'Jimmy? What's wrong?' Her cheeks blazed as he stood rooted to the spot, staring at her.

One of his friends nudged him, 'Don't tell me this wondrous creature's come with you, you great lummox!'

Jimmy suddenly regained his composure and, taking her arm, he said proudly, 'Yes, she came with me. I've never seen anyone as beautiful as you, Samira,' he whispered to her as he took her arm and led her to the empty dance floor.

Relief flooded through her as she realised that far from embarrassing him, she seemed to have got everything right, and the uncertainty she'd experienced earlier that evening drained away.

When Samira had announced she

was on duty that evening, Ivy had believed the lie, and for the first time she'd not complained about being left alone, making Samira feel even more guilty about deceiving her. She'd slipped out of the house in her uniform, but instead of setting off down the road, she'd gone next door to number twelve. The blue dress Mrs Thomsett had altered for her fit beautifully, and Sally had pinned her shiny dark hair up in an elaborate style. They'd told her how wonderful she looked, but she hadn't been able to see much in the small mirror Sally held up for her, and she'd left their house not sure what she looked like. When Jimmy had stared at her, she'd thought his shock was because her appearance was completely inappropriate. But now he was beaming, and she could see how proud he was that his friends were envious of his date.

There had been no need for a lesson with Jimmy before the dance began, because Mrs Thomsett's son John had taught her how to waltz. After a circuit of the hall, her feet began to move automatically to the music without her having to count the beat.

Once the band had tuned their instruments, they struck up their first piece of dance music, and other pairs of dancers joined Jimmy and Samira, gliding and whirling round the hall. When others cut in to take Jimmy's place during the gentleman's excuse-me, he'd glowered from the edge of the dance floor until the opportunity arose to claim Samira again. He made certain that he held her in his arms for the last waltz, taking her hand and leading her away, so there would be no doubt he was the one who would take her home.

The mist had thickened, and their progress back to Aylward Street was slow; but Samira's earlier nervousness about the dance had been replaced with exhilaration, and despite the darkness, she almost felt she could dance home. When the other WVS girls had talked animatedly of the dances they'd been to, her imagination had failed her. But now that she'd experienced the excitement of the rhythm pulsing through her body when she and Jimmy wove between the other couples in the subdued lighting, she understood their enthusiasm.

The blanket of fog felt like a coat of invisibility, and Samira allowed Jimmy to take her to Ivy's door, knowing that they couldn't possibly be seen by any of the neighbours.

'Would you like to go next Wednesday?' Jimmy asked.

'Yes please,' she said, and taking his hand, she raised it above her head and twirled on the spot.

'You're so beautiful, Samira. I could stare into your eyes forever,' he whispered, taking her other hand and pulling her close. 'I can't believe you're my girl.'

For the first time, Samira didn't feel alarmed at his obvious infatuation, although she wasn't sure if it was because she was still caught up in the magic of the evening, or if indeed she was beginning to feel more than just friendship for him. There was no spark as yet, but it might come.

He put his hands on her shoulders and pulled her closer. 'I'd love to kiss you, Samira,' he whispered.

It was enough to break the spell. Samira drew back in alarm. 'No!'

When she thought about it later, she wondered whether, if he'd simply taken her in his arms and kissed her, she might have been swept along with the enchantment of the night. But declaring his wish in advance had given her time to be rational — and fear had suddenly gripped her.

He let go of her and stepped back, horror-stricken. 'I . . . I didn't mean to upset you or . . . ' he said anxiously. 'I'd never do anything to hurt you . . . you know that, don't you?'

'I've got to go,' she said, slipping into the house and closing the door. She stood with her forehead against the door, feeling thoroughly foolish and wondering if Jimmy was still outside.

How could she have been so stupid?

He'd been the perfect gentleman, And she'd rudely and childishly rejected him. If only she'd told him she'd never been kissed before and explained she had no idea what to do, he might have understood. But instead, she'd pushed him away, spoken without thinking and then left him on the doorstep. Stupid, stupid!

When she got to her bedroom, she looked for him through the window, but the fog was impenetrable. After such heartless treatment, it was highly unlikely he'd still be there. Sitting on the bed, she closed her eyes, touched her lips gently with her fingertip, and tried to imagine what it might have been like if he'd simply kissed her. The thought made her feel warm and tingly, and she determined that the next time she saw Jimmy . . . assuming that he ever talked to her again — she would find some way of making it up to him and allowing him to kiss her properly.

6

Samira looked out for Jimmy each evening when she was on duty with the WVS, but despite seeing him in the distance, she hadn't been able to talk to him or to give him the note she'd written explaining that it had been fear that had stopped her kissing him, not distaste, as he may have thought. She realised with shame that she knew very little about him — not even where he lived. He'd been so interested in her, asking questions about her life, and she'd never thought to find out about his. When he had talked about himself, she hadn't listened because she was wondering what to say or do next.

Two weeks after the dance, Samira was on duty. The night was clear and the moon was shining brightly, illuminating the London streets below. The German pilots were taking advantage of the excellent visibility and were fiercely attacking the docks with incendiary devices and bombs, and many fires had taken hold in the warehouses and workshops. The rescue services worked furiously to contain the damage and to extinguish the flames, but it seemed like the Luftwaffe weren't going to go home until they'd flattened the area.

Samira had kept an eye out for Jimmy, and although she thought she caught sight of him with another air raid warden, she wasn't certain, and before she could find out, he was gone. As the hours passed, fires raged, filling the air with the acrid smell of burning and with thick black smoke that stung their eyes. There was no time to think about anything other than helping wherever she could.

The girls were exhausted but determined to remain until they were no longer needed. 'You're doing a great job,' Kitty told them, trying to keep their spirits up, 'Keep at it! The lads are getting everything under control now.

We'll be able to pack up and go home really soon.'

But she'd been wrong. By the time anyone realised the fire had spread to an oil store, it was too late. Within minutes, there was an inferno with flames that licked the sky, and shouts as the roof of a warehouse collapsed with a terrific roar. For a second, everyone stopped in horror, then exhausted men suddenly found the strength and determination to renew their efforts, knowing that such an enormous disaster would probably involve a large number of casualties and if the fire wasn't contained, it would quickly spread.

The German pilots presumably thought they'd caused enough havoc for one night and flew off, leaving the docks ablaze. It was hours before the flames were brought under control and a slight breeze blew the smell of charred wood away, down the river. At first, Samira took no notice when she saw Kitty talking to a group of the girls, until she realised they were staring at her and Mavis was shaking her head sadly. Kitty walked towards her and the other girls stood silently, watching.

'I'm not sure how to say this, Samira, so I'm just going to come out with it, love. Some of the ARP wardens were trying to put the fire out when it blew. Mavis just saw Tom Riley on a stretcher. I'm afraid he's burned badly. But . . . there are three others unaccounted for . . . and no one knows if your Jimmy was one of them. I'm really sorry.' She put her arm around Samira's shoulders. 'He still might turn up, of course,' she added without much conviction. 'Go home, love. Mavis said she'll walk with you . . . ' She petered out, not knowing what else to say.

Samira looked at Kitty, her face expressionless.

'Samira, you understand what I've just told you, don't you?'

'Yes.'

As Mavis put her arm round Samira's shoulders and led her away, she turned to Kitty and mouthed, *She's in shock. I'll look after her.*

The other girls stood together, watching Mavis lead Samira home.

Ivy was waiting at the front door when Mavis delivered Samira home. 'Are you all right, Samantha?' she asked, eyeing Mavis suspiciously. 'Mrs Thomsett told me there's been a terrible accident at the docks. I was so worried.'

Samira was silent.

'She's fine,' said Mavis. 'But her friend is believed to have been . . . ' She mouthed *killed*. 'No one's sure what happened but lots of people are missing and — '

Ivy stepped forward and drew Samira into the house. 'Thank you,' she said to Mavis. 'Thank you for bringing her home. I'll look after her now.'

'Of course,' said Mavis. 'When she's feeling a bit better, please tell her I'm sorry.'

After she'd put Samira to bed, Ivy made a cup of sweet tea and took it upstairs. 'Drink it, dear. It'll help with the shock. Then get some sleep. You look exhausted. Things'll be better when you've rested. You'll see.'

Samira lay in bed, staring at the ceiling.

Missing? What did that mean? Burned? Crushed beneath a pile of masonry? He'd been so full of life with his jokes and playfulness — sometimes more like a boy than a man. But then, he was only eighteen. Her eyes filled with tears, and one spilled out of the corner of her eye. She didn't even know when his birthday was. He'd known about hers, and since she'd turned eighteen just before he'd met her, he'd promised that the following year he'd take her somewhere special on her birthday. The night of the 'kiss that never was' replayed in her mind, and each time, she sighed and fresh tears spilled onto her pillow. Now she'd never know what his kiss would have felt like.

He'd never asked much of her. How difficult would it have been to allow him just one kiss?

She knew from the shadows on the

wall that it was late afternoon. Her eyelids were swollen with the smoke, tiredness and tears, but she couldn't feel them. She felt nothing.

Voices drifted up from the hall, and she realised that it had been the door knocker which had woken her. There was a tap at her door, and Mavis anxiously poked her head round it.

'I've got some news for you, Samira,' she said gently. 'Can I come in?'

Samira nodded.

'I'm not sure if your aunt knows you were stepping out with Jimmy, so I just told her I had news about a friend who's missing, and she assumed it was one of the WVS girls. But Jimmy's family live round the corner to me, and I went to visit his mum earlier. Apparently he was nowhere near the fire. He's not even in London.'

Samira sat up. 'Are you sure?'

'Yes, I'm certain.'

'Where is he, then?'

'He handed in his notice and joined up. There was nothing anyone could do to stop him. He's left for training camp, but Mrs McGuire didn't know where. She was furious he was giving up his apprenticeship, so he went without telling her where he was going. But he left this letter for you. I'm afraid she was so upset he'd gone, she opened it to see if he'd told you where he was going.'

'And did it say?'

Mavis shook her head. 'No. It was very wrong of her to open it, but now she has, she blames you for Jimmy going away. I'm really sorry, Sam, but you must feel better knowing he's still alive . . . don't you?'

Samira nodded and took the letter.

'Well, I'll leave you to read it,' said Mavis, turning to go. 'I'm glad he's all right, although I suppose it depends on where he gets stationed as to how long he remains safe. Anyway, Kitty says to take your time before you come back.'

When Mavis had gone, Samira slowly took the single sheet of paper out of the torn envelope.

My dearest Samira,

I'm sorry to go away without saying goodbye, but I think it's for the best. I suppose you know I've loved you from the first time I ever saw you. But I also know you're much too good for me. Thank you for being kind, but I could see in your eyes you didn't feel the same way. It was foolish of me to hope. Anyway, I'm sorry for upsetting you after the dance, but you were so lovely it took my breath away. I could have stared into your eyes forever, and I guess I got carried away. I hope you can forgive me. I can't bear to be near you and know you'll never be mine, so I'm leaving. By the time you read this, I will be at training camp, possibly even out of the country. I'm looking forward to being a soldier and travelling. I reckon it will make a man of me. Perhaps one day we'll meet again and I'll be the sort of man you might fall for.

With all my love,
Jimmy

Tears slipped through Samira's swollen eyelids as she slowly folded the letter and tucked it back in the envelope. At least he was still alive. She wondered how his mother must feel knowing that he'd thrown away the chance of his apprenticeship and gone away because of her.

Would it have been so hard to love him like he'd loved her? She closed her eyes and tried to bring Jimmy's face to mind, but the harder she searched for him, the fainter his image became. Did that spark that she imagined she needed before she could give her heart really exist? Or had she just ruined her chances of having a kind, loving and sweet man?

7

The aerial bombardment of London intensified during the weeks after the night of the great fire in the docks. Samira didn't like to think of Ivy on her own under the stairs during the nights when she was on duty, and had insisted that she either go to the Underground station overnight or to the Thomsetts' Anderson shelter.

'Do you know how early the queues start before anyone's allowed down the Tube station at four o'clock? Some people are there all day! I'm not standing around for hours just so I can cram myself between some unsavoury people on a train platform! And don't ask me to go next door with that rabble. I'd rather die in my bed.'

But surprisingly, Ivy had taken notice of Samira's fears and had paid Mr Thomsett and two of his sons to build an Anderson shelter in her backyard. Samira wasn't entirely happy with Ivy being on her own anywhere, but despite being damp and cold, at least they could stretch out and sleep if the noise of the bombs allowed — something that was not so easily done under the stairs.

In order to take her mind off Jimmy, Samira had thrown herself into her voluntary work with the WVS. She'd taken over driving the van because Kitty had lacerated both hands when rescuing a child who'd been buried in rubble. As well as serving food and drinks to the rescue servicemen and women, Samira helped evacuate hundreds of young London children, sending them to parts of the country that were less likely to be attacked by the Luftwaffe. Most of the time she was too busy or too tired to think about Jimmy, but occasionally she'd see an ARP warden of similar build and height to him in the distance and it would bring back the evening of the fire when she thought he'd died. She'd heard that he'd been stationed somewhere near the French-Belgian border, but Mavis didn't know more than that; and if she did, she wasn't telling.

Samira had come to the conclusion there was something lacking in her character which meant she couldn't fall in love. Or perhaps she was just too emotionally immature. If she'd had a mother, she would have discussed it with her, but there was no one she trusted enough to ask. She came close to asking Mrs Thomsett once or twice, but embarrassment made her draw back. After all, how could the next door neighbour answer questions about her personality when she herself couldn't? Perhaps one day it would become clear; and in the meantime, she turned down any offers of dates or outings, and concentrated on her WVS duties, and on caring for Ivy.

One morning in June 1944, as she returned to Aylward Street after a particularly busy night, she'd been surprised that Ivy hadn't been in the kitchen waiting for her. The all clear had been given hours ago, and usually Ivy didn't hesitate to leave the damp Anderson shelter and make for the kitchen to put the kettle on. Samira climbed the stairs and hesitated to knock at Ivy's door in case she hadn't bothered to leave her bed when the air raid siren had sounded and she was fast asleep. She tapped gently and opened the door, but Ivy's bed was still made and had obviously not been slept in. Rushing down the stairs, she ran into the backyard and opened the door of the Anderson shelter to find Ivy gasping for breath and clutching her heart. Samira helped her from the shelter and shouted for help as she half-carried Ivy back to the house. Mrs Thomsett came rushing in, followed by several young children, who stood by the kitchen door with wide eyes and open mouths.

'Bertie, run down to the post office and tell Mrs 'Iggins we need Dr Jenkins fer Mrs Stewart! Now! The rest of you, go and get yer Pa.'

The children turned and ran down the hall. Samira wiped the sweat from Ivy's face with a damp cloth, holding her hand and speaking gently to calm her. Her eyes bulged with the effort of drawing sufficient air into her lungs, but she seemed slightly calmer and her breathing started to become less laboured.

Mr Thomsett lifted Ivy and carried her gently up the stairs to her bed, and Samira and Mrs Thomsett had just finished making her comfortable when Dr Jenkins arrived and asked them to leave him with the patient.

'Don't fret so, lovey,' Mrs Thomsett said. 'Dr Jenkins'll soon 'ave 'er as right as rain. Even her colour is better now than when I first saw her. 'Er face was positively grey. She'll be all right. Now, I'll put the kettle on and make us a nice cuppa. I expect she'll be demanding a cup of tea any minute.'

When Dr Jenkins allowed Samira back upstairs with a cup of tea, Ivy was sitting up in bed and her colour had returned, although she still very pale.

Her breathing was normal, and she smiled weakly when she saw Samira.

'Here's a prescription for Mrs Stewart, and I'm insisting she has bed rest while she can. When the sirens go, you'll have to help her down to the shelter and stay with her. I'll call back tomorrow and see how she is. But it's important she remains calm — well, as much as anyone can during this dreadful war. Her heart isn't strong, as you know, but there's no reason why she shouldn't carry on for years, so long as she takes my advice. Well, I'll bid you good day. It seems that half of Stepney has need of me this morning.' He handed Samira the prescription, snapped the clasp of his briefcase shut, and hurried out of the bedroom.

'That was quite a scare you gave me,' said Samira with a smile.

'Thank you for your quick thinking, Samantha. You saved my life.' Ivy craned her neck to see round her. 'Is Mrs Thomsett still here?'

'No, everyone's gone.'

'Are you sure?'

'Yes, I saw them go before I came up to see you. Did you want to speak to her?'

'No! I just wanted to make sure she'd gone. I need to tell you something and I don't want that busybody to know. Now, I want you to open my wardrobe door and look inside on the left. You'll find a hatbox under a few other things. There's a biscuit tin in there. I want you to bring it to me.'

Samira lifted the hatbox out of the wardrobe and placing it on the bed, she pulled off the lid. After taking out four identical black velvet evening bags decorated with jet beads, she could see the two faded bluebirds on the lid of an octagonal biscuit tin. When she lifted it out of the hatbox, it was surprisingly heavy; and at Ivy's instruction, she prised the lid off to reveal rolls of bank notes and an assortment of trinkets.

'Nobody knows about this box, Samantha. Just you and me. It's my insurance, but I may not need it much longer.'

'What do you mean? The doctor said if you rest you'll be fine,' said Samira, aghast.

'He's an old fool. He might be right and he might be wrong, but I need to know you'll take this if he's wrong and anything happens to me. I don't want anyone else to have it. You're a good girl and you deserve good things to happen to you, but what we deserve and what we get are not always the same. You're young and you don't have the experience I have, but take my word for it, in the end you have to look out for yourself. People will come into your life and people will leave, but trust me, they'll let you down and in the end you'll be alone. The only thing you can do is make sure you've got enough to keep yourself. There's money in here for my funeral, but you must keep the rest. Sell the other pieces if you need to . . . ' She picked up a silver-framed photograph of a baby and a pearl brooch. 'I don't suppose they'll bring much, but it all helps. Here's my wedding ring,' she said, holding it up between finger and thumb, 'it's gold, so it'll raise something. But don't tell anyone about this. You can't trust anyone, d'you hear?' She leaned back against the pillows, as if the effort of talking about the tin and its contents had exhausted her.

Samira repacked the tin, then placed it back in the hatbox, which she put in the wardrobe. 'Please don't talk like that. You'll soon be back to normal.'

'Promise you'll do as I ask,' Ivy said weakly.

'Yes, of course. Now please rest. I'm going to go to the chemist to get your medicine. Would you like me to call Mrs Thomsett and ask her to sit with you while I'm gone?'

Ivy shook her head, 'No, I'll just have a sleep while you're out. Perhaps we could have some tea when you get back?'

Samira ran to the chemist shop, waited patiently until the medicine was ready, and then ran back to Aylward

Street. She knocked on Ivy's door but there was no reply, so she quietly let herself in. Ivy was lying as Samira had left her; but her eyes, although open, were unseeing, and her chest, which had previously been rising and falling with the exertion of breathing, was still.

8

The undertaker straightened his top hat, checked the coffin was steady on the pallbearers' shoulders, and turned to lead the procession into the church.

'Are you all right?' Pop asked, taking Samira's arm.

She nodded. 'I've never been to a funeral before . . . '

'It'll be fine, you'll see,' he said, holding open the enormous wooden church door for her.

If Samira hadn't spotted Mrs Thomsett sitting at the back, she'd have thought they were taking her grandmother's coffin into the wrong church. As far as Samira knew, Ivy didn't have any friends while she was alive, so she was amazed to see so many people at the funeral service. She recognised Joanna sitting next to a handsome man — presumably her husband, Ben. Next to her was a vivacious-looking woman who turned and smiled at Pop.

He gasped and waved to her. 'It's Amelia!' he whispered delightedly to Samira. 'She came!'

Pop's daughter, Amelia, was sitting with a man and young girl — presumably her husband and daughter, as the young girl was a miniature version of her mother. Several neighbours from Aylward Street flanked Mrs Thomsett, and tears began to fill Samira's eyes at the thought that people had bothered to show respect to a woman who'd been less than friendly to them when she'd been alive.

On the other side of the aisle, an attractive woman sat alone, watching Pop intently, and Samira knew from a photograph that Pop had shown her that she was his mistress, Edie. In front of her, there was an older man, and Pop stopped to shake hands with him. 'Thanks for coming, Pete,' he whispered. Next to him was a young couple. The woman was smartly dressed in a dark grey suit and matching hat, and from his uniform, Samira could see the man belonged to the Royal Air Force. She didn't know anyone called Pete, and assumed that he and the young couple were friends of Pop's. As she moved further forward, she looked back at the group and realised that the couple were probably her age and bore an uncanny resemblance to each other with their blond hair and good looks.

Samira and Pop slid into the front pew on their own while the coffin was being settled on a plinth, and she half turned to get a better look at the young couple. She'd never seen such a handsome man, and it wasn't until she saw the girl smiling at her that she realised she'd been staring. With glowing cheeks, she turned away and busied herself looking through the hymnbook. The girl appeared to be very sophisticated, and Samira wished she was wearing something more glamorous than one of Ivy's dresses that she'd altered.

This is your grandmother's funeral, not a fashion show, she told herself angrily.

With a large black bible tucked under his arm, Reverend Pettifer walked up the steps into the pulpit. He obviously knew very little about Ivy — not surprisingly, because as far as Samira knew, Ivy had never been a church-goer — but the lack of warmth in his voice made the whole service impersonal.

Perhaps all funerals are like this, Samira thought. She had the impression from some of the WVS girls who'd lost family members that there was a great outpouring of grief at funerals. Glancing around, she didn't see anyone dabbing eyes or looking anything other than dutiful or bored. Samira supposed that wasn't surprising, really. It was enough that people had bothered to come to the funeral of the woman who'd ultimately driven many of them away.

The eulogy was brief, unsentimental and devoid of much detail, but Samira decided that Ivy would probably have approved and been grateful that her life and her death were private matters.

'Amen,' said Reverend Pettifer, bowing his head briefly as he concluded the service. He closed his bible and ran his gaze over the congregation until it reached Edie and then moved to Pop, and his expression hardened. He glared for several seconds, then gathering his robes, he climbed down the steps of the pulpit with his bible under his arm. Signalling to the pallbearers to raise the coffin, he led them into the graveyard for the burial. When Samira thought about it later, she could remember very little about what happened at the graveside other than that everyone had huddled round the hole in the ground, shivering in the unseasonal bitter wind that had threatened to freeze the tears on her cheeks.

Finally, the funeral service was concluded and the mourners walked back to the path out of the churchyard, leaving the gravediggers to fill the deep hole with earth. Reverend Pettifer stopped briefly to speak to Edie, and then clutching his enormous bible to his chest, he strode back to the church without a backward glance. Edie's cheeks had turned crimson, and in an instant, her face changed from attractive to petulant. Pop had been introducing Samira to Amelia and her husband, and hadn't noticed the change in Edie until she marched up to him and took his arm, insisting she have a word with him. Although Samira wasn't trying to eavesdrop, she was standing close enough to hear snatches of heated conversation, which included the words 'vicar' and 'married' and 'widower'.

'Now's not the time, Edie. We'll talk about it later,' Pop said, leading her away; but Samira knew he was angry, and judging by Amelia's expression, so was she.

'What a cheek that woman's got! How my father could put up with her rudeness, I just don't know. He's obviously never had much sense with women,' she said. 'First Mum, who wasn't the easiest person to get on with, and then that *creature*! I know I didn't get on with my mother, but she was worth ten of that spoiled woman! How dare she try to persuade my father to marry her just because the vicar told her off for living in sin! At my mother's funeral too!'

'Very bad form,' said Will, her husband, nodding in agreement.

'What's very bad form?' asked Joanna, who'd caught up with Samira, to introduce her husband, Ben.

'Never mind,' said Amelia, hugging Joanna. 'Let's not worry about Edie. How are you, darling? You're looking wonderful!'

'I'm fine, thanks, Amelia. And I see you've met your niece at last!' She put her arm round Samira's shoulders. 'How are you, love? We've been so worried about you with all the bombing raids on the East End. Thanks for phoning regularly and keeping us updated with your news. I'd have loved to have visited you, but . . . ' She shrugged. 'It would only have upset Aunt Ivy. You must be an angel to have charmed her! Now she's gone, I expect you're feeling a bit lost.'

'Well, I definitely wouldn't describe myself as an angel! It is very strange though. I can't quite believe she's gone. There is one thing that really bothers me — sometimes I had the impression she believed I was simply a carer, paid for by Pop; but occasionally she acted in a way that suggested she knew I was her granddaughter. I just wish I knew the truth.'

'Aunt Ivy was a very secretive person. Perhaps she didn't even want to admit to herself that she knew who you were. But we'll never know. She obviously enjoyed having you with her, whether she knew who you were or not.'

'She was definitely one of a kind,' said Amelia. 'And I think you deserve a medal, Samira! I couldn't have lived in the same house as her. She was impossible! But let's forget past squabbles — I want to know all about you. Come in our car with Will and me back to Aylward Street, and you can tell us all about what my big brother, Davy, has been up to in India.'

Ivy's kitchen was full of people and Samira found herself redundant. Despite the food rationing, there was an enormous spread on the table in Ivy's kitchen, and Mrs Thomsett stood guard, making sure the family had plenty to eat before the neighbours helped themselves — especially the children who were hiding beneath the table. Amelia and Joanna poured and served tea, and Pop had taken a sulking Edie into the backyard to talk in private. Samira felt like a stranger in what she had almost come to consider her home.

'I've finally got you to myself!' It was the sophisticated girl who'd been sitting with the man Pop had greeted as Pete and the young man in the RAF uniform. 'I'm Alexandra Jackson, but my friends call me Lexie, and I know who you are.' She shook hands with Samira. 'It's lovely to meet you! I've heard all about how you looked after Ivy. Of course I never met her, but Granddad has told me a few stories!'

'Granddad?'

'Oh, I'm so silly. You probably have no idea who I am.'

She was interrupted by a cry of 'Ow! Ow!' as Mrs Thomsett dragged two small boys by the backs of their collars away from the table.

'You've 'ad enough! Show some manners and leave some fer yer betters!' She marched the lads to the front door.

'Is there somewhere we could go to talk?' asked Lexie. 'It would be lovely to get to know each other better, especially if we're to be housemates.'

'Housemates?' Samira began to feel foolish. So far, she'd said nothing except echo what Lexie had said.

'Oh no! Me and my big mouth! Joanna hasn't asked you yet, has she? And I think your grandfather probably has more pressing matters on his mind after the vicar lectured his lady friend on the virtues of marriage.'

'Did he?'

'Oh yes, he said that their domestic arrangements were thoroughly sinful and that she now had the chance to redeem herself. But of course, she's got to convince your grandfather first!'

Samira couldn't help liking the girl. Her blonde hair was brushed back off her face in victory rolls; and with her porcelain skin and blue eyes, she reminded Samira of a doll. But when she smiled, she had a mischievous air.

'Let's go to my bedroom and talk,' Samira said. 'That is, if we can get out of this crush.' They squeezed through the crowd in the kitchen and hall and Samira led Lexie upstairs.

'I swear there are more people downstairs than there were in the church,' said Lexie.

Samira laughed. 'Yes, word's obviously got out round there's food on offer.'

'Isn't that rather a liberty?'

'No, not really. Pop knows how kind

the neighbours have been to me. And they would have been good to Ivy too, if she'd let them. Many of them have such large families, they struggled before the war, but now with rationing they're really finding it hard to make ends meet.'

Samira opened the bedroom door for Lexie and motioned for her to sit on the bed. The elegant girl looked completely out of place in her bedroom, and Samira wondered why she'd never noticed the sagging mattress, the threadbare counterpane and the wardrobe with the broken door. Life in St. Theresa's couldn't have been described as luxurious, and she was used to shabbiness; but now with Lexie sitting on her bed, she saw the room through different eyes. She looked down at her plain navy dress, which was reminiscent of a school gymslip, and then at Lexie's dark grey suit and white shirt with a bow at the neck. But more than the clothes, Lexie glowed with confidence. Samira thought she would still have looked marvellous dressed in a sack.

'So,' said Lexie, 'firstly, I ought to tell you how we're related. Joanna's parents, Rose and Tom, are both dead, but Tom was my Granddad Pete's brother, and your granddad is Rose's brother. So we're only related by marriage, but Granddad Pete spent a lot of time with Rose and Tom before Joanna was born and he knew them very well. When he bought a farm in Devon, he saw less of them but always kept in touch.'

Samira suddenly realised she hadn't seen Lexie's grandfather in the house, or her handsome brother.

As if reading her thoughts, Lexie added, 'I hope you don't mind, but Granddad's gone home. He was very nervous about coming up to London with all the bombing, but he wanted to pay his respects at the church. Once he'd done that, he decided he'd go home to Devon tonight rather than stay with Joanna, as planned. Granddad fought in the Great War with Tom, and although they came back, they both had shell shock and never really got over what they'd experienced in northern France. You didn't get a chance to meet my twin, Luke; he's taken Granddad to the station. He'll be back later — I'll introduce you both then.'

'So what's this about us being housemates?'

'Well, that's if you want to be, of course. Joanna is going to suggest you stay with her in Essex. It'll get you out of London and all the air raids. I'm going to stay with her too.'

'That would be wonderful. I was planning on getting a job and renting a room somewhere. Pop asked me if I'd like to carry on living here rent-free, but Edie wants him to either sell it or find tenants. I don't want to be the cause of problems for Pop, and anyway, I'm not sure I want to live here now Ivy's gone.'

'Marvellous! I'll tell Joanna! Come tonight. Luke'll be there too. He's going to be stationed at RAF Hornchurch, but he's got two days' leave.'

Samira's heart beat faster, and she

could suddenly see Luke's face clearly in her imagination — his short hair, the same colour as Lexie's, and the smile that lit up his face. It was all very well having a crush on someone from afar, but she feared she'd make a fool of herself if they were staying in the same house. She had no idea how to behave with men — Jimmy had shown her that — and for some reason she knew she'd have even less idea how to behave with Luke. It would probably be best to wait until he'd gone to Hornchurch — assuming that Joanna asked her to stay, of course. Yes, it would be best to wait for an invitation.

'Will Joanna have enough room for us all?' she asked

'Oh yes, her house is enormous! Ben's parents were wealthy landowners, so don't worry about that.'

⋆   ⋆   ⋆

When all the neighbours had left, Pop told Edie that there were several things

119

he needed to sort out and pack up, so they'd be staying in the house at least overnight. Edie's mother was looking after their daughters, so they had no need to rush home, and he wanted a chance to make sure Samira was happy too. Edie had told Pop she wouldn't stay in Ivy's house overnight under any circumstances, and demanded he take her home; but when Pop told her he intended to stay, and if she didn't like it she could return on the train on her own, she'd been very shocked. He'd looked appealingly at Amelia and Will, who were just about to leave in their motor car; and picking up the silent signal, Amelia had offered to take Edie to the station.

'Thank you, Amelia,' he'd whispered in her ear when he'd kissed her goodbye. 'I owe you.'

Edie had stomped to the car and got in the front passenger seat without checking where Amelia wanted to sit.

'She gets travel sick in the back seat,' said Pop apologetically.

'Dad, you need to stand up to that woman!' said Amelia. 'Honestly! She's so spoiled!'

Pop and Samira waved them off and went back into the kitchen to do the last of the tidying up.

'Let's have a cup of tea, love, and talk about the future,' said Pop, putting the kettle on the stove. 'Are you happy about living with Joanna and Ben?' he asked. 'Because just say the word, and you can stay here. I'll pay for everything — you don't need to worry about that. But I want you to be happy — and safe, of course.'

'Yes, I'd like to go to the country. And now that Ivy's not here, I don't think I want to stay in this house. Joanna said she or Ben would come and fetch me on Thursday at midday, so I've got two days to pack up my things.'

'Remember that Ivy left whatever she had to you in her will, so you won't be penniless.'

'I'm so sorry, Pop. Whatever she had really belongs to you. I feel awful.'

'Don't be silly, love. I forfeited my right to anything that Ivy owns several years ago when I walked out.'

'Pop, there's something I need to show you. Ivy didn't want me to tell anyone, but I'd feel really bad if I kept it to myself.'

Samira went upstairs and returned a few minutes later with Ivy's hatbox, and taking the octagonal biscuit tin out from amongst the black evening bags, she put it on the table in front of Pop.

'Ah! Ivy's tin. I knew she hid money and things in it. I came across it once when she used to hide it in the scullery. If she wanted you to have it, then take it, love. No, don't open it. I don't want to see what's inside. You keep the tin and do what you like with the contents, they're yours.' He patted Samira's hand. 'But you might want to show those evening bags to Joanna when you get to her house; they look like they might have been her mother's. They're just the sort of thing she used to make to sell, and I can't think why Ivy should have so many of them. One I can understand, but not four. Now,' he said and yawned, 'it's been a long day, so I'm going to try to get some sleep before the air raid siren goes off, as I assume it will before morning. If I were you, I'd get some sleep too. I'm going to stay down here on the sofa — I can't bear the thought of spending any time in Ivy's bed. Tomorrow we'll sort the house out and put the word around to try to find some tenants. There are plenty of people who need housing at the moment, so we shouldn't find it hard to rent the house out.'

★   ★   ★

It hadn't taken Samira long to pack her belongings, but she'd spent a lot of time saying goodbye to Kitty and the other WVS girls, and to Mrs Thomsett and the neighbours in the road.

'Look after yerself, Samira,' said Mrs Thomsett. 'And don't forget to come back and visit before yer go off home to foreign parts, if that's what you plan to do. Yer a lovely girl, and Mrs Stewart was lucky to have had you. Yer our little bit of exotic in dull ole Stepney.'

Her cases were in the hall ready to load into Joanna's car, but she wanted to spend a few minutes in her bedroom trying to reconnect with the life she'd known with the grandmother who she'd never had the chance to call 'Gran' or 'Nan' or indeed anything less formal than 'Mrs Stewart'.

She stood with her hands on the window sill, looking down at the children playing in the cobbled street. This would be the last time she'd see this view. Tomorrow she'd wake to . . . what? Fields? A garden? She had no idea. Was this strange ache she was experiencing sorrow at leaving London, or anxiety at an unknown future? It seemed like neither — it was just an emptiness waiting for something meaningful to fill it.

The day after Ivy had died, she'd noticed a small colourful bird perched in a bush in the backyard and had thrown out some lumps of bread for it. When it had seen her, it had flown into the tree and watched until she'd gone back inside; then it had soared down to land on the roof of the Anderson shelter, looking at the scraps. The brilliant plumage stood out against the brown earth, and she realised it was a budgerigar — probably a pet that had escaped during a bombing raid. For some time, it watched the food from the shelter roof, its head swivelling left and right as if it were afraid to take a chance on the crumbs. Samira wished she'd thrown the bread closer to the shelter, but it was too late now. She knew that if she opened the door, the nervous bird would simply fly away hungry. Having been fed all its life, it was probably struggling in the wild. Then, perhaps hunger or rashness drove it to swoop down to the grass and to peck at the bread. Within seconds, two sparrows joined it, jostling each other for a meal, and the budgerigar flew off. Samira stopped herself from shooing the sparrows away — after all, it wasn't their fault the budgie was afraid. Life in a cage hadn't prepared it for survival in the wild.

Samira kept an eye out for the colourful bird, but it had never reappeared, and she assumed it hadn't been able to adapt to a world where it didn't belong. How similar she was to that budgie! She wasn't as obviously different from her neighbours as the budgerigar was from the wild birds. Or perhaps she was. Mrs Thomsett's words came back to her *You're a little bit of exotic in dull old Stepney*. They were meant to be kindly words, she was sure; but despite living in the same street, wearing a WVS uniform and thinking she'd been assimilated into the community, it appeared she was still perceived as being different, as if she didn't really belong. But would she fit in any better at Joanna's? Would she ever find a place to call home?

One of the girls in the street dropped

her skipping rope and pointed excitedly. The other children turned to see what had caught her attention and began to run towards the car that had turned into Aylward Street. Samira sighed, and with one last glance round the empty room, went downstairs. Pop was waiting in the hall next to her bags, ready to carry them out to the car. His face fell when he saw the tears in her eyes.

'Have you changed your mind about going? It's not too late to stay. I'll put the new tenants off. Just say the word.'

'No, no, Pop; it's all right. I'm fine, really. I just don't like goodbyes, that's all.' How could she tell him she was upset because she didn't feel she belonged anywhere? What would be the point of telling him? There was nothing he could do about it.

Pop opened the door — and there on the doorstep, just about to knock, was Luke.

Samira's heart sank. What on earth was she going to say to him? But Joanna seemed very chatty; perhaps she would do most of the talking on the way home. And possibly they would drop Luke off at Hornchurch, so she wouldn't have to endure the whole journey with him to Laindon.

'Joanna sends her apologies, but her son's been up with earache all night and she's waiting for the doctor to call, so I volunteered to come and fetch you.'

'That's really kind,' said Pop. 'Isn't it, Samira?' he added, filling the silence.

'Er, yes, yes, thank you.' Samira bent down to pick up her bags to hide her flaming cheeks.

'Let me,' said Luke, stepping into the hall to get her bags.

Pop opened his arms to hug her. 'Luke seems like a nice young man,' he whispered to her as she clung to him. 'Now keep in touch. Joanna has a telephone, and I'll try to call as often as I can so I know you're all right. I haven't heard from your father recently, have you?'

'No. I've written several times to tell

him I'm going to Joanna's but I haven't had a reply. I've sent several letters to Vikash too.'

'I'm sure they're all right, love. Anyway, it looks like Luke's ready to leave. Don't worry if you've forgotten anything — it'll give me a wonderful excuse to visit you.' He held out a handkerchief to her. 'I always seem to be here when you're upset because you're saying goodbye,' he said with a sigh.

'But at least you're here,' said Samira. She kissed his cheek. 'I would feel worse if I was alone.'

He took her hand to kiss it, but she pulled it away and turned her cheek towards him. 'When you left me here that first day, you said you wouldn't kiss me on the cheek because we were little more than strangers and that one day when we were really grandfather and granddaughter, you would. Can that day be today?'

There were tears in his eyes when he kissed her gently on the cheek.

9

The children ran alongside the car shouting their farewells as it pulled away from the kerb, and one of Mrs Thomsett's grandsons threw a dandelion through the window which landed in Samira's lap. She looked over her shoulder and watched them stop at the corner, waving as the car picked up speed along Jamaica Street and left them behind.

'You obviously made a good impression on the local children,' said Luke with a smile. 'The journey'll take a while — why don't you tell me about your life here? You were the only person who showed the slightest emotion at the funeral, so I assume Ivy meant a great deal to you?'

And then, to her surprise, Samira began to tell him about Ivy, her time at the convent school and her early life in India. He seemed to know exactly the right thing to say to put her at her ease, and by the time she realised how long she'd been talking, they were approaching Romford. How rude he must think her, talking about herself for so long!

'But tell me about you,' she said. 'Lexie told me you live in Devon.'

'We used to. But I don't suppose either of us will ever go back. It's a beautiful place, but our farm's rather remote, and Lex and I felt a bit isolated. It suits our parents though. Granddad moved down there after he came back from the Great War looking for somewhere quiet after the horrors he'd seen in northern France. Mother was about fourteen when they moved there, and luckily she loves the solitude, but for some reason Lexie and I have always looked for something more exciting. I suppose that's why I joined the RAF and trained as a pilot.'

'You're so brave. I'd be scared stiff. I'm too much of a coward to fly in an aeroplane.'

'Flying's something I've longed to do

since I was a young boy. Lex and I used to dream about the places we'd visit in our own private aeroplane. India was one of those countries. It seemed so mysterious and exciting. How lucky you are to have lived there!'

'It just seemed normal when I was there,' she said with a smile, amazed that he was so easy to be with.

'If you don't mind, I'd like to stop off near the airfield at Hornchurch. I've been staying with a friend, and I left some photographs at his house that I promised Joanna I'd show her. It won't take long, and you might see some of the aircraft take off. It's a wonderful sight.'

'Yes, I'd love that.' Her anxiety had drained away with each mile that passed — firstly through streets of town houses and shops, and then gradually country lanes in which she could see farmhouses and cottages. The landscape was similar to the Kentish countryside around St. Theresa's Convent, and it seemed familiar and welcoming. She hadn't felt so carefree and content for a long time. In fact, she couldn't ever remember feeling as happy as she was now watching the countryside glide past with Luke at the wheel, manoeuvring the car as if it was an extension of his body. If he'd announced he wanted to keep driving to John O'Groats, she'd have been thrilled. Glancing at Luke's hand resting on the gear stick, she wondered what it would be like to hold it, to have his long fingers laced with hers.

She observed him out of the corner of her eye, keeping her head facing forward in case he noticed her stare. Her breath caught in her throat — even in profile, he was handsome. She'd been too embarrassed to make eye contact with him when he'd introduced himself at Ivy's house after the funeral, so she hadn't noticed his crystal-blue eyes, but now she watched with fascination as they took in the road ahead and checked the rear-view mirror. As he concentrated on the road and the increasing numbers of pedestrians on the approach to the centre of Hornchurch, she couldn't tear her gaze away from him.

'Can you see the horns up there?' he asked, pointing up at the roof of St. Andrew's Church. 'It's a bull's skull. That's not something you often see on top of a church.'

His words and the movement of his arm jerked her out of her reverie, and she hoped he wouldn't notice the heightened colour of her cheeks.

'Archie's house is a bit further on along the High Road, then off to the left, so it's not far now. Are you hot? I can open the window a bit if you like.'

'No, I'm fine, thanks,' she said, her blush deepening. She pretended to be preoccupied with the dandelion in her lap, and with her head low, she willed the colour in her cheeks to fade.

Luke pulled up outside a large detached house and turned the engine off. 'Would you like to come in?' he asked. 'I won't be a minute, but you might like to stretch your legs.'

Samira was about to accept when she

saw a woman waving from the doorstep of Archie's house. 'Darling!' she shouted, hurrying down the path towards the gate. 'Why didn't you tell me you were coming?'

Luke got out of the car, and the woman flew towards him and wrapped her arms round his neck. They were standing so close to the car window that Samira couldn't see their heads, but their bodies were pressed together and she could see hands with perfectly manicured red nails on the small of Luke's back. He laughed, and reaching behind, he took one of her hands and led her up the path into the house.

Samira let go of the door handle. Luke seemed to have forgotten about her. Well, what had she expected? That he would fall for such a young, inexperienced girl when he obviously had stylish women ready to throw themselves into his arms? She might have left St. Theresa's Convent months ago, but she still had the air of a schoolgirl with her simple dress and shoes and her hair worn long and straight. The woman who'd greeted Luke was probably not much older than herself, but her dusky pink suit was nipped in at the waist, giving her an hourglass figure. The matching hat sat at just the right angle to show off the curls and waves of her blonde hair. Samira had only caught a glimpse of the woman's face, but it was enough for her to notice her lips were bright red, a shade that matched her nail polish. Samira had no doubt the rest of her face was impeccably made up too.

She looked down at the dandelion that she'd cradled carefully in her hands all the way from Stepney. How childish! She was sure *that* woman wouldn't be seen anywhere near a dandelion, unless it was growing in the grass she was walking on. No, she would have colourful orchids or vases full of red roses. Samira opened the car door a fraction and dropped the dandelion flower on to the road. She didn't want any reminders of this car journey that had been so enjoyable and had made her feel special. It had raised her hopes and then dashed them.

Hopes? Hopes of what? she thought bitterly. No one had promised her anything; she'd simply fooled herself.

When she heard the front door open, she stared resolutely at her lap. She didn't want to see the woman again or the kiss that she and Luke would undoubtedly share when he left.

'See you Saturday, darling,' the woman called as Luke climbed into the car. He turned and placed a photograph album on the back seat.

Samira couldn't help but turn to see the woman standing at the gate, blowing kisses, as he started the engine and eased the car away from the kerb.

'That was Vera, Archie's sister. Sorry, I'd have introduced you to her, but it was hard to get a word in edgewise! By the time I realised you weren't behind me, it was too late. But I'm sure you'll meet her again. I'll introduce you properly then.'

The lump in Samira's throat wouldn't allow her to reply, and he looked at her quizzically. 'What happened to your dandelion?' he asked.

She finally managed to say, 'It died. I threw it away.'

10

Luke pointed out some Spitfires taking off from the RAF airfield and related some of his experiences since he'd joined the force. Samira attempted to appear interested, but she couldn't help feeling that it was like being out with an uncle who was trying to entertain her despite wanting to be somewhere else. She knew that wasn't a fair analogy, because he hadn't changed from when they left Stepney; any change that had taken place had been in her. And she had no right to feel let down, because it was obvious there would never be anything between a handsome, charming pilot and . . . and what? What *was* she, exactly? She was no longer at school, but she felt as worldly-wise as a schoolgirl — homeless, rootless, and lacking direction for the future.

Eventually Luke fell silent. Samira

stared out of the windscreen with unseeing eyes; she couldn't bear to look at him now. He had a smear of the ruby-red lipstick that Vera had been wearing on his cheek, and she could now detect a floral fragrance that hadn't been in the car before.

'We've just passed Brentwood. It won't be long now,' he said as they stopped at a T-junction and turned right.

'Thank you.'

She sighed. He must think her so dull. If the journey was now dragging for her, how much more must he be longing to reach Joanna's house in Laindon?

'You know, it's all right to feel upset,' he said.

She looked at him in alarm. 'Upset?' The colour drained from her face. Surely she couldn't be so transparent that he knew what she'd been thinking?

'Yes; it must be hard to uproot and start again after you've lost your grandmother. But you'll love Joanna, I promise. She'll make you feel at home in no time. And I'm sure you'll be good friends with Lexie — she's great fun.'

Samira let out the breath she'd been holding. 'Yes, I suppose so. Thank you,' she said, relieved that he'd misread her silence.

'I hope you don't mind, but I'd like to ask a favour.'

'Yes?' Samira looked at him in surprise. What on earth could she do for him?

'It's Lexie. I love her to bits, but she's rather . . . well . . . headstrong. She acts before she thinks, and I wondered if you'd look out for her while I'm not around. You seem very sensible and level-headed, and I know you'll be a good influence on her . . . if you don't mind, that is . . . '

So that was what he thought of her. 'Sensible and level-headed'. More like 'boring and dull'. Well it could be worse, she thought. At least it wasn't 'silly and childish'.

'Yes, of course,' she said, wondering

what Lexie would think about his request. She looked out across the fields that stretched as far as she could see, longing for the journey to end; but the peace of the countryside was suddenly broken when an air raid siren began to wail.

Luke accelerated, gripping the steering wheel tightly. 'We need to find somewhere to shelter,' he said, leaning forward and taking in the sky at the same time as he concentrated on the road. 'I know it looks pretty quiet here in the country, but it's not called Bomb Alley for nothing. The Germans fly over here and up the Thames corridor to London, and it's not unknown for them to drop any bombs they still have on board on the way home.'

Further ahead, where the lane bent sharply to the right, a collection of roofs could be seen above tall hedges, suggesting the presence of a farm; and further off still, above the roofs, what looked like a swarm of bees was approaching.

'We'll shelter wherever the farmer is,' Luke said, and swung the car up to the house. He groaned when he saw that the door and windows of the farmhouse had been boarded up and the farm obviously deserted. The wheels spun, flinging up dust, as he rapidly reversed the car and drove towards the barn on the other side of the large farmyard. The drone of aeroplanes now could be heard above the roar of the car's motor.

'As soon as I open the doors, run into the barn. I'll drive the car in if there's enough room,' he said; and leaping out of the driver's seat, he ran to the doors and flung them wide open.

'Come on!' he shouted, beckoning to her. But instead of getting out of the car, Samira slid into the driver's seat and, taking off the handbrake, slowly edged the car forward. The interior of the barn was dark, although here and there cracks in the wooden planks of the walls allowed thin shafts of light to penetrate the gloom. Rusty chains hung from the rafters at one end of the building over an ancient tractor, assorted engines and a heap of tools. Samira had no idea how to turn the headlights on, so she eased the car into the darkness slowly, hoping there was nothing in her path until she was clear of the doors; then she stopped and turned off the engine. In the rear-view mirror, she saw Luke look up to check the progress of the enemy planes, then firmly close the door.

'Well, I wasn't expecting that!' he said with admiration as he opened the driver's door and helped her out.

'I learned to drive in the WVS,' she said shyly, aware that he was still holding her hand. When she'd imagined how it might feel several hours ago, she hadn't envisaged they would be sheltering from enemy aeroplanes in the seclusion of a deserted barn. He put his other arm protectively round her shoulders and they stood together, allowing their eyes to become accustomed to the darkness and listening to the throb of the engines as the aeroplanes passed overhead.

'You're shaking,' he said. 'Don't worry; they're heading to London, and I'm sure they won't waste a bomb on an old barn. We're probably only in danger when they're on their way home. We'll be fine.'

How could she tell him she was trembling because he was holding her to him? She knew he didn't belong to her, but was it so wrong to pretend, just for a moment, that they were together?

He pulled her close, wrapped one arm round her shoulders and held her head against his chest, gently stroking her hair.

A rat scampered across the floor and dived under the old tractor, causing a small avalanche of tools, making them jump.

'We might as well make ourselves comfortable; we could be here for a while,' said Luke, letting her go. He found a travel rug on the back seat and, folding it up, he placed it on a large wooden beam. 'I know it's not very comfortable, but if there is an emergency, we'll be able to escape faster from here than we will do if we're sitting in the car.'

The seat was only wide enough for them both if Luke put his arm round her and they squeezed together. 'Tell me about India,' he said, leaning his head against hers.

She knew he was trying to distract her from the drone of the aircraft passing overhead, and she tried to think of something interesting to tell him, but her mind was numb. The scent of something she couldn't identify filled her nostrils — was it sandalwood? It was hard to concentrate with him so close. And the touch of his fingertips as he stroked her hair sent shivers of delight through her body.

Her mind seemed to have divided into two. One tiny part allowed her to tell Luke about her childhood in India, but the rest was given up to the pleasure of the pressure of his body against hers and the touch of his fingertips on her hair and cheek.

The shafts of light that filtered

through the cracks in the walls were much softer than they had been when she and Luke had first arrived, and when the all clear siren began to sound, Samira judged that it was late afternoon. Usually the familiar wail was a welcome relief, but on this occasion it heralded the end of her time with Luke, and she felt a deep sadness.

He stood, and taking her hands, raised her up. 'Well, we survived. Now I suppose we ought to hurry up and get to Joanna's house. Lexie'll be frantic with worry, wondering where we are. I'll open the doors. Will you be able to reverse out?'

She nodded, too disappointed to speak. *How wonderful it would have been to have remained together a while longer*, she thought as she reversed into the farmyard, then slid over to the passenger seat. Luke got in the car, and as she caught sight of the lipstick smear on his cheek, her stomach sank. It had been too dark to see it in the barn and she'd forgotten about it — and about

Vera. While they were sitting together on the tartan rug, Samira hadn't been able to smell the floral fragrance that had clung to him as tightly as Vera had clung to him at Archie's house; but now it filled the car — sweet and sickly.

'You might want to clean your cheek,' she said, offering him a handkerchief. He glanced in the mirror and winced.

'Vera,' he said and wiped the mark away. 'I don't know why she thinks she has to wear all that stuff on her face. She's good-looking enough without it. Anyway, thanks for telling me; and I'll get this washed for you,' he said, tucking the handkerchief in his pocket.

'That's all right. I thought it best you didn't turn up at Joanna's house covered in lipstick. And don't worry about the handkerchief.' She didn't want it back. It was now tainted.

Lexie was waiting at the gates to Priory Hall when they arrived, and she ran towards them. 'Thank goodness you're both all right! I was so worried when the air raid siren went off. I wondered if you'd be in the middle of nowhere and wouldn't find anywhere to shelter. I couldn't bear to lose my baby brother and my new best-friend-to-be!'

'Baby brother! You're only a few minutes older than me!' said Luke. 'Come on, hop in — I'll give you a lift up the drive!'

Joanna opened the door with a small boy in her arms and a girl at her side. 'I'm so glad you're both safe,' she said. 'Come in. Samira, this is Mark.' She turned so they could see the young boy's face, but he buried it in his mother's neck. 'He's still not over his earache,' Joanna whispered. 'He's not usually as quiet as this, is he, Faye?' she asked the girl who was peering up at Samira with undisguised admiration.

'Are you really an Indian princess?' Faye asked.

Samira crouched down. 'Well, I'm half Indian, but I'm sorry to disappoint you — I'm afraid I'm not a princess.'

'But you're beautiful like a princess,' Faye said. 'And your hair's shiny, just

149

like satin. Could you make mine look like that?'

'Your hair is lovely as it is,' said Samira, touching one of the brown curls that had escaped from the clip that restrained the rest of her hair.

'Shall we let Samira settle in before we plague her for hairdressing tips?' said Joanna with a smile. 'I'm going to take this little man back to bed, and then we'll all have dinner. Ben's gone to fetch his mother. She's living in our house at Dunton at the moment, although I have a feeling that she'll soon be moving back in with us. But let's get your things and take you to your room, Samira.'

Lexie took Samira's arm; and with Faye skipping ahead and Luke following with Samira's cases, they went upstairs.

'I hope you don't mind sharing with me,' said Lexie. 'We could have had a bedroom each, but Mrs Richardson — that's Ben's mother, not Joanna — will probably be living here from now on.

She's had several falls recently, and since she lives alone, everyone thinks it's better if she comes here.' She turned to Faye. 'Would you be a love and fetch Samira a clean towel please?'

When the young girl had gone, Lexie continued, 'Not that Ben's mother's happy about it. Apparently she doesn't like Joanna — never has — and I think she's going to be quite a handful.'

'How could anyone not like Joanna?' Samira asked.

'What's that about not liking Joanna?' asked Luke, who'd just appeared at the bedroom door.

'Ben's family are very well-to-do, and when Joanna arrived in Dunton nearly ten years ago, she was almost penniless. Her mother had left her the deeds to a plot on Dunton Plotlands, and Joanna thought there would be a house on it; but when she got here, she found it was just a piece of land — no house, nothing — and she had no money to build one. The neighbours took her in and she got a job at Ben's firm,

Richardson, Bailey and Cole, and
... well, they fell in love. But Mrs
Richardson didn't think Joanna was
good enough for her son — and by all
accounts, she still doesn't.'

Luke cleared his throat, heralding the
return of Faye carrying a pile of towels.

'I didn't know which one to bring, so
I brought them all,' she said, peeping
shyly round the heap.

Samira unpacked, and Lexie helped
her put everything away whilst telling
her about life at Priory Hall.

'Ben's really a solicitor. When his
father died, he became a partner in
Richardson, Bailey and Cole; but now
with the war on, he's using the estate to
grow food. That's why he hasn't been
called up. Not that he wouldn't like to
go. And Joanna's terrified he might yet
join up. But so far, he's managing the
estate with some farm workers and a
few Land Army girls. I've been helping
them. The weather's been lovely and
I'm used to farm work, so I've been
teaching them how to milk cows and

other things. They all come from London, so they haven't much idea about farming. And then, of course, there's the Italians.'

Lexie was lying face down on her bed, resting on her elbows, with knees bent and feet waving in the air. 'Italians?'

'Yes, you know, the men who were living in Britain before the outbreak of war and who've now been interned. We've got half a dozen of them working on the farm.'

Samira looked at Lexie. The tone of her voice had changed when she'd spoken about the Italians. But Lexie's face was turned away, and Samira wondered if she'd just imagined it. Perhaps Lexie didn't like the injustice of men who'd lived in Britain for years being removed from their families and held in camps.

Lexie got off the bed and looked out of the window. 'Do you have any plans while you're here, Samira?' she asked.

'No. I want to do my bit for the war

effort, but I thought I'd wait until I settled in before I decided.'

'Then you must come and work with the Land Girls and me.'

'And the Italians?'

Lexie turned away, but Samira thought she saw her face redden. 'Well, yes, I suppose so,' she said, and then added quickly, 'Anyway, I can see Ben's car coming. Come on, let's go down and help Joanna. I don't suppose Mrs Richardson is going to make this evening easy for her.'

★ ★ ★

Lexie was correct.

'It's like being hauled up before the headmaster knowing you're going to get a caning,' whispered Luke as he stood with Joanna, Lexie and Samira in the hall, waiting to greet Mrs Richardson on her arrival at Priory Hall.

'Shhh!' said Lexie, elbowing him. 'Behave!'

He'd described the mood quite

accurately, thought Samira, who despite never having met Ben's mother, had the sinking feeling she'd experienced whenever she'd waited outside Sister Mary Benedicta's office.

The crunch of the tyres on the drive told them Ben and his mother had arrived, and Joanna closed her eyes, fixed a smile on her face and stepping forward, opened the door.

Samira was surprised to see a tiny birdlike woman leaning heavily on Ben's arm as they slowly climbed the steps into the house. From Lexie's description, she'd imagined someone much larger and more aggressive-looking. It didn't seem like this woman would be able to withstand a puff of wind.

Ben handed his mother over to Joanna and excused himself while he fetched her bags from the car.

'Benjamin!' Mrs Richardson's voice was much stronger than Samira was expecting from her frail appearance. 'Since when have you carried bags about? Send a servant!' She glared at Joanna as if it was her fault that Ben had forgotten his heritage.

'I've been carrying bags about, Mother, since the last servant left,' he said quietly. 'There's a war on. People are no longer fetching and carrying for the elite few; they're sacrificing themselves fighting for our freedom.'

'Really. Then who are these?' she said, waving her arm at Samira, Lexie and Luke.

'Some of Joanna's relatives who've come to stay.'

Mrs Richardson sniffed and looked the three young people up and down. 'And what about the foreigner?' she asked, pointing at Samira. 'Surely she's not staying in the house.'

There was a sharp intake of breath, with eyes swivelling left and right to see who was going to react.

Ben was the first to speak. 'This is Samira, and she's one of Joanna's second cousins. She is very welcome in this house. She is a guest. As are you.

And any guest in my house is treated with respect,' he added.

Mrs Richardson sniffed and peered at Samira. 'A bit on the dark side, but pretty enough, I suppose.' Then turning back to Ben, she added, 'But some of us still know how to maintain standards, Benjamin. I have a servant even though I live in that tiny miserable house.'

'That tiny miserable house that you mention, Mother, was the house I had built on Plotlands, and no one is forcing you to live there. You left this house voluntarily. Joanna and I pay the girl who cooks and cleans for you double the going rate in order to keep her. She's just handed her notice in, as she's now old enough to join up, so you no longer have a servant. They're things of the past for most people now.'

'I see. Well all I can say is, what a sorry state of affairs. Where's my walking stick?' She let go of Joanna's arm and hobbled into the dining room.

Joanna took Ben's arm and squeezed it as he shook his head in dismay and disbelief. *I'm sorry,* he mouthed to Lexie, Luke and Samira.

'Don't worry, it's not your fault,' whispered Luke, and then he said more loudly, 'But I'd like to say she was wrong about one thing. Samira isn't pretty — she's absolutely beautiful.' And linking his arm through Samira's, he led her into the dining room.

'Thank you,' she whispered, knowing that with his quick wit, he'd helped to lighten the situation, even if he didn't mean it.

Surprisingly, the meal wasn't a disaster despite Mrs Richardson's initial behaviour. She obviously realised that it would be far more pleasant for everyone if she were civil, and at the end of the meal she even complimented Joanna's cooking. Luke entertained them with stories about his fellow pilots and their antics, and if he hadn't talked about Archie so much, Samira would have felt completely at ease. But the mention of Archie brought back memories of his sister, Vera, with her confidence and glamorous looks. She glanced at Lexie, taking in her clothes and hairstyle, then looked down at her dress — the same one she'd worn to Ivy's funeral — and determined to ask Lexie to help her. It was all very well blaming rationing for her lack of style, but everyone else seemed to manage. Even Joanna, with two children and an enormous house to run, seemed to find time to look elegant with her chestnut curls caught back off her face and her smart dress.

By the end of the meal, Samira was feeling so shabby that when Ben said he'd help Joanna clear away and suggested Lexie and Luke show her round the garden, she almost made excuses and escaped to her bedroom.

'Come on, Samira — you'll love it,' Luke said. 'The sunset's going to be glorious this evening.'

How could she refuse?

Once they were out of sight of the dining room, Lexie said she was going to the Land Army girls' cottage to discuss the following day's work, and left Samira and Luke at the lake.

'She wasn't so keen on farming when we were in Devon,' said Luke. 'But I suppose she wants to do her bit for the war effort. I can't blame her for that. She tells me you're going to help out on the farm too.'

'Yes, although I've never worked on the land before. When I was young, I used to watch the women in the plantation picking the leaves off the tea bushes; but other than sowing a few seeds in Ivy's backyard — which never came up — that's my entire experience.'

'I'm sure everyone will help you until you know what you're doing. Anyway, you might find your driving skills mean you're in demand to drive the tractor.'

'Yes, I hadn't thought of that. It's funny, but not so long ago, Sister Mary Benedicta asked me what I was going to do when I left school. Driving a tractor wasn't something that crossed my mind.'

160

'Becoming a pilot's always been my dream, but I never really believed it'd come true. And in two days' time, I'll be flying my own plane across the Channel.' He sighed. 'Well, let's not think about tomorrow. Let's watch the sun go down. You never know how many more sunsets you'll ever see,' he said with a laugh, but Samira knew it was bravado.

'Come on,' he said; and taking her hand, he led her up the slope along a narrow path between dense bushes. When they reached the top, the undergrowth gave way to lush grass and the ground fell away steeply.

'This is the best place to see the sunset,' he said; and she wondered how he knew. But she dared not ask who he'd shared the spectacle with before. *Perhaps it was Lexie*, she thought. *Or perhaps it was Vera*, her inner voice whispered.

'Shall we sit down?' he asked. 'I wish I'd thought to bring something to sit on. Here, let's use this.' He started to take his jacket off.

'That's fine, it's quite dry,' she said, and sat down on the grass.

He looked at her for a second, and joined her. 'Most girls would complain about grass stains on their dresses and goodness knows what. But you . . . you're so natural and . . . well, easy to be with.' He put his jacket round her shoulders and held it in place with his arm.

The dilute blue of the sky became tinged with pink and orange, and the underside of the fluffy clouds that drifted above the woods on the horizon glowed yellow. Eventually, the brilliant disc slipped behind the trees, leaving a rosy blush.

Despite Luke's jacket, Samira shivered. But it wasn't simply the chill of the evening breeze, now the sun had set. She'd seen tropical sunsets in India with skies the colour of jewels that made this seem quite insipid. But she'd never been as moved as she felt now, watching this Essex sunset with Luke's arm round her shoulders and the warmth of his body against hers.

The last hint of pink faded in the sky as the blue deepened, and here and there, stars began to flicker.

'We'd better go back.' Luke rose, and extending his hand to help Samira up, he pulled her close and wrapped his arms round her. 'I wish I'd had more time to get to know you,' he said. 'I've only spent one day with you, and yet I feel . . . ' He sighed. 'I can't promise you anything . . . ' He ran his hand through his hair. 'I don't even know if I'll be alive by the end of tomorrow . . . but it would mean so much to me if I knew you'd be here for me . . . '

'Yes,' she whispered. 'When will you be back?'

He gently shook his head and placed a finger on her lips, then he closed his eyes and leaned towards her. She held her breath and waited for his lips to replace his finger.

'Luke! Samira!' It was Lexie.

Luke let go of Samira and stepped

back guiltily. 'We're here,' he called.

Lexie emerged from the bushes, and despite the growing darkness, Samira could see she was frowning.

'Oh there you are,' she said crossly. 'The sun went down ages ago. Don't you think we ought to go back?'

'Lexie?' Luke said gently.

But she'd already turned back into the bushes and was gone.

Luke held out his hand to Samira, and they walked back silently, holding hands until they were within sight of the house. Then Luke let go of her hand.

11

Lexie was in bed when Samira entered their bedroom. She'd left the bedside lamp alight on the chest of drawers between their two beds, but she lay motionless, her face turned to the wall. Samira undressed quietly. It seemed her friendship with Lexie was over before it had even begun. How the day could have finished like this, she had no idea. But she was certain that she couldn't stay in Priory Hall now. Tomorrow she'd look for a way of getting back to India. Ships still sailed from England to other parts of the world; and yes, there might be a threat of being torpedoed by the Germans, but it was a risk she was willing to take.

She'd walk into Laindon in the morning and find out if she could book a ticket on a ship. Papa wouldn't be happy, having told Pop not to let her return; but by the time anyone realised she'd gone, it would be too late to do anything about it. Lexie would be getting up at four o'clock to help with the milking, Luke was returning to the RAF base at Hornchurch, and with Mrs Richardson moving back into the house, Joanna would be very busy, so no one would miss her. It would have been nice to know what she had done to make Lexie so annoyed, though.

She sighed and reached out to turn off the bedside lamp.

'Oh, it's no good, Sam,' said Lexie. 'I can't sleep when I feel guilty.'

'Guilty?'

'I upset you, and I upset Luke, and now I feel dreadful.' She sat up, rested her chin on her knees, and hugged her legs. 'I expect Luke'll be cross with me,' she added. 'But then, I'm very cross with him.'

'You are?'

'Yes and I've got every right to be angry! He promised. But on the other hand, I was in a bad mood because

. . . well . . . that's another story. And of course, that wasn't his fault at all . . . And it certainly wasn't *your* fault! To think you got caught up in all that! What must you think of us?'

'I honestly don't know,' said Samira. 'But I think I must have done something — '

'Darling! You didn't do anything! Trust me! Luke has no idea how devastatingly handsome he is. Back in Devon, most of the girls in the village were in love with him, but he wasn't interested. He broke a string of hearts. Girls just don't seem to be able to resist him. The trouble is, he's not aware of his charms, and he can easily . . . well . . . lead a girl on.'

'But he didn't do anything.'

'No, I know. But he promised me he'd be more careful, especially now he's joined the RAF. And he agreed. He promised! He said he'd have fun but he wouldn't let anything go further than that. Not until the war's over, at any rate.'

'Fun?' The word stabbed at Samira like a knife. Did Lexie believe that Luke had just been having fun with her?

'Well, yes. He's a pilot, not a monk. I know that, and I know those boys face death each time they fly, so they have to have some sort of recreation. But I've told Luke it's not fair to lead anyone on and give the impression he's serious. Now that he's a pilot, his life expectancy's measured in weeks. He knows he's got nothing to offer a girl. He won't even tell anyone when his next leave is, because he thinks it's unlucky.'

Samira remembered him holding his finger to her lips when she'd asked him when he'd be back. So it had all been a bit of fun; a way of amusing himself before he returned to Hornchurch.

'Well I suppose we should be grateful you've hardly had any time to get to know him and I put a stop to things before they had a chance to get serious,' said Lexie. 'I may well have saved you a lot of heartache, Samira. I hope you don't mind me saying, but you don't seem to be very experienced with men.'

'No, I suppose not. But you don't need to worry about me. Luke really isn't my type.'

Lexie looked at her with a quizzical expression. 'Well, if you're sure . . . '

'Oh yes,' said Samira brightly. 'Well, now, perhaps we'd better get some sleep. We've got to be up early tomorrow.' Then before Lexie could see the tears in her eyes, she turned the light out.

'I'm so glad we sorted that out. I couldn't have slept a wink with that on my mind. I'm going to apologise to Luke. I couldn't bear it if he left in the morning before I had a chance to make up. I'd never forgive myself if . . . ' She didn't finish the sentence. Climbing out of bed, she tiptoed to the door. 'I won't be long. I'll try not to wake you when I come back. Night night.'

'Night night.' Samira hoped Lexie hadn't heard her voice break. Hot, bitter tears rolled down her cheeks. It wouldn't matter how much noise Lexie made when she came back; she would not be asleep.

How could she have been so stupid? She'd seen Luke with Vera earlier that day.

Earlier that day? Had it really only been a few hours ago that she'd left Stepney with Luke? So much had happened. Lexie had read her correctly; other than Jimmy, she'd had very little experience with men. And today she'd surpassed herself. She'd been about to fall in love with a man whose sister admitted he was a heartbreaker.

⋆   ⋆   ⋆

Considering the hour, Lexie was remarkably cheerful. She turned the alarm clock off seconds after it rang at four o'clock, as if she'd been waiting for it. Samira, on the other hand, had lain awake for hours, and when she'd finally fallen asleep, her dreams had been filled with Luke. He'd walked away from her and she'd run after him, calling repeatedly, but he didn't stop or turn to look at her. She'd woken from her dreams, feeling exhausted.

'Darling! You look dreadful! Are you feeling all right? Your eyes are all red and puffy. If you're not well, stay in bed.'

'No, I'm fine, thanks.' It wasn't true but a day at home wasn't going to solve her problems. The war would still be raging whether she was moping in bed or not, and the only sensible course of action was to carry on as if she'd never met Luke.

She'd heard him rev his motorbike shortly before Lexie's alarm had rung, and then the crunch of the stones on the drive as he'd roared away.

Lexie lent Samira some overalls and tied her hair up so that it could be easily tucked into her hat. She hummed a tune as she brushed her own hair and arranged it in victory rolls, then dabbed cologne behind her ears. When she noticed Samira look at her with a puzzled expression, she blushed.

'Well,' she said defensively, 'just because we're working on the land doesn't mean we can't be feminine.'

A quick application of powder on her nose and a little lipstick finished her preparations, and she led a weary, gritty-eyed Samira downstairs to breakfast.

Joanna was at the kitchen sink, washing up, as they entered the kitchen. 'Morning,' she said cheerily. 'Help your-selves to breakfast. Ben and Luke have already eaten and left. Oh, by the way, Ben said he'll see you after milking. He seemed to think you knew where to go.'

'Oh yes,' said Lexie cheerfully. 'Is Mark better today?'

'Yes, thanks. Well he slept all night, so I think he's almost back to normal. If Mother-in-law's up to it, I'm hoping she'll play with him today, then Faye and I can get on with the vegetable garden. Are you all right, Samira?' she asked anxiously. 'You're looking a bit pale.'

'Yes, I'm fine, thanks.' Samira tipped

her head down as she concentrated on slicing a loaf.

'As soon as I get a chance, we'll sit down together and have a talk about what you want to do in the future, then we'll see what we can do to make it happen — Herr Adolf Hitler willing, of course!' she said putting her arm round Samira's shoulders. 'But until you've made plans, I'm sure you'll miss everything that was once familiar. It's perfectly all right to feel bit homesick, you know.'

'Thank you.' She was touched by Joanna's thoughtfulness, but she couldn't possibly explain that she wasn't homesick at all. That would have required her to be longing for somewhere she considered home.

'Ready?' Lexie asked as she drained the last of her tea and grabbed one of the slices of bread Samira had cut.

'Anyone would think you loved digging ditches, Lexie!' said Joanna.

'No ditches today. Ben says we're going to cut hay. But we've got to milk the cows first. Are you ready, Sam?'

'Someone's happy,' Joanna said as Lexie left the kitchen humming a tune.

The sun was just beginning to brighten the sky to the east as Samira closed the front door. Lexie was holding two bicycles, and she mounted one and held the other out.

Samira looked at it in horror. She'd never ridden a bicycle before, but felt too foolish to admit it. It couldn't be so hard to ride, could it? She took it by the handlebars and copied Lexie, who'd already begun to pedal down the drive.

Her first attempt ended with her breaking her fall on the lawn, and by the time she'd reached the gates of Priory Hall, she'd tumbled off twice and only managed to keep her feet on the pedals for a few seconds.

'Why didn't you tell me you couldn't ride a bicycle?' Lexie asked when Samira finally caught up with her. She'd given up trying to pedal and was now pushing it along by the handlebars.

'I felt too stupid.'

'Darling! Don't worry! It's not that

hard — look, I can do it, so it can't be difficult! We'll make time today to teach you. But you can't wheel it all the way to the milking shed. If you put one foot on the pedal and hold the handlebars, you can scoot along. It'll be faster.'

Despite deep shadows obscuring ruts and potholes, Samira managed to propel the bike along, gradually finding it easier to balance — although, she admitted to herself, there wasn't far to fall, and it would be very different when she mounted the saddle. But it was faster than walking, and she hadn't lagged too far behind.

'You must be Samira,' said the tallest of the Women's Land Army girls when she and Lexie arrived. 'I understand you're staying with the Richardsons. I'm Cissie, and this is Marge.' She indicated a smaller, plumper girl with mousy hair and freckles. Pointing to a third girl, she said, 'And this is our new Land Army girl, Ruth, who arrived yesterday morning. Ruth, this is Lexie and Samira.'

'Pleased to meet you, ladies,' she said, her accent giving her away as someone who might be more used to afternoon tea in the drawing room than milking cows as the sun was rising.

'She won't last the week,' whispered Marge.

'Shut up and give her a chance,' whispered Cissie, nudging her. Then she added, 'Rightio, girls, let's get cracking.'

★ ★ ★

They'd finished the milking, and were walking back to the Land Girls' cottage to make a cup of tea when it suddenly occurred to Samira how strange it was that Lexie and Ruth had never met. The previous evening, when Luke had taken her to watch the sunset, Lexie had said she was going to see the Land Army girls; and if Ruth had arrived in the morning, then surely she'd have been there when Lexie had arrived.

There could, of course, be many

explanations as to why the two girls had never met. Ruth may have been tired after her journey and might have gone to bed before Lexie's visit. But nothing that had happened that morning during milking suggested that Lexie had seen Cissie or Marge the previous day either.

The girls had been incredulous when Samira had admitted she'd never learned to ride a bicycle, but Lexie pointed out that a convent probably wasn't the best place to acquire skills like that. When they took a short cut across the fields to the cottage where the Land Girls were staying, Samira was relieved. The ground was too uneven to cycle across, and she and Lexie wheeled their bicycles over the ruts.

'Slow down please, ladies; I've got a blister,' said Ruth. Marge rolled her eyes and nudged Cissie, who ignored her.

'A nice strong cuppa will sort that out,' said Cissie, 'And guess what? Mr Richardson dropped by last night. His wife sent over some bacon rashers, so it's bacon sandwiches all round this morning!'

'Have we got time?' asked Lexie, checking her watch.

'Time? There's always time for tea and a bacon sandwich!' said Marge. 'It's all right for you, living up at the big house. I don't suppose you're ever hungry. But we working girls need our food. I haven't had bacon for . . . well, I can't even remember. The last farmer I worked for was so mean, I think he fed his pigs better than his Land Girls.'

'That's shocking,' said Lexie.

'I know! He actually thought he was doing us a favour when he allowed us to dip our bread in the fat his bacon had been cooked in. What an oaf! He wasn't married, and he expected us to cook and clean as well as do the farm work. You'd have thought he'd have been grateful to have us and would've treated us well.'

'I had a similar experience,' said Cissie, 'except my farmer was married and it was his wife who treated us badly. Her two sons are away fighting, and I think she resented us taking their places on the farm. We tried to be sympathetic, but . . . ' She paused and shrugged. 'Still, war affects people in different ways, and I've no idea what it must be like to have two sons in such danger.'

'Well, you're more generous and understanding than me,' said Marge. 'I'd have given her the sharp edge of my tongue!'

'I don't doubt it,' said Cissie.

'I certainly put my farmer in his place before I walked out,' said Marge. 'Mind you, he got his own back. I'd been there six weeks before I gave him a piece of my mind and left, but he refused to pay me a penny.'

'Well, let's be thankful Mr Richardson's a gentleman and so far has treated us well,' said Cissie. 'And Mrs Richardson, of course. And as for those adorable children — such darlings! All the prisoners love them, too.'

'Oh,' said Samira with a smile. 'For a second there, I thought you said 'prisoners'.'

'I did.'

'Prisoners?'

'Yes,' said Cissie. 'We've got about six Germans and four Italians. I would've thought Lexie would have mentioned them.'

Lexie blushed.

'Germans and Italians? Here?' said Samira.

'Oh yes. It's just a small camp up the road, and the inmates help out on Mr Richardson's farm.'

'In fact, as soon as we've had tea, we'll be heading off to the hayfield and they'll be helping us,' said Marge. 'But don't worry,' she added, 'they're all very civilised and friendly. Most of them speak passable English too.'

'So you mean to say we'll be helping the enemy?' Ruth said. 'That's outrageous!'

'No, we won't be helping them at all — they'll be helping us. There's a difference,' said Cissie patiently. 'And just remember, for every enemy POW on British soil, there's likely to be a British POW on enemy soil. If we look after theirs, we can only hope they'll look after ours.'

'Well, I don't know about that!' said Ruth with a sniff. 'I didn't join the Women's Land Army to work alongside the enemy!'

'Just out of interest, what did you join it for?' Marge asked. 'I would've thought you'd be more at home knitting socks from the comfort of an armchair.'

'Well, you'd be wrong,' said Ruth sharply. 'I'm just as capable as you of doing my bit in the fresh air.'

'Let's see if you still feel the same after a day in the hayfield,' said Marge.

'So, which cottage is yours?' asked Samira, trying to change the subject. If she hadn't remarked on the prisoners, the conversation wouldn't have taken such a turn.

Peace-loving Cissie was happy to

answer and steer Ruth and Marge away from an argument. 'We're in the one on the left. Next to us is Bill Grant, or Grunt, as we call him. And then the two next to him are empty — they used to house farmhands, but they've all joined up. Old Grunt's too old to fight, so he's still here helping Mr Richardson, although he's not in favour of having us on the farm.'

The mention of Bill Grant united the girls once more. 'What a terribly rude man!' said Ruth. 'He came out of his cottage when I arrived and waved his stick at me.'

'Did he indeed?' said Marge in a menacing voice. 'Just let me see him do that again, and I'll really let him have it!'

Cissie smiled as she linked arms with the two other Land Army girls and walked up the path to the cottage door. Ruth went upstairs and appeared a few minutes later with a rose-patterned china cup and saucer. 'I prefer my tea in a proper cup,' she said, holding it out to be filled from the large teapot Cissie was holding. Turning bacon slices over in the frying pan at the stove, Marge rolled her eyes but said nothing.

They crowded round the small kitchen table that Ruth insisted on washing down twice, and Marge served up bacon between thick slices of bread.

'Mmm, that was delicious!' said Cissie, wiping her mouth. 'If you're not going to eat that, Lexie, I'll have it,' she said, pointing to Lexie's plate.

'I'm going to take it with me for later,' Lexie said, and blushed.

Samira saw Marge and Cissie exchange worried looks.

Cissie placed her hand on Lexie's shoulder. 'You're heading for trouble, you know,' she said kindly.

'I don't know what you mean!' said Lexie. 'I don't have to eat this now.'

'Have it your own way,' said Cissie.

Samira was desperate to ask what was going on, but fearful of inadvertently starting an argument like she'd almost done before between Ruth and Marge.

She had a feeling that it wouldn't be long before she found out.

Ruth insisted everything was washed up and put away before they left. 'Well, I don't want to come back to a mess, even if you do,' she said.

'Trust me,' said Marge, 'by the time we've dealt with all that hay and got home, you won't care if your precious cup and saucer are dirty or not!'

'So, shall we go?' said Lexie, wrapping her sandwich in a clean handkerchief and putting it in her pocket.

'I thought you were a farm girl,' said Cissie. 'You know we've got to wait till the dew's burned off the hay before we start.'

'I know that,' said Lexie. 'But we've still got to get there.'

'It only takes five minutes across the fields. We'll just be standing around if we go now.'

By the time Ruth had washed up, Cissie decided it was time to leave. Lexie rushed outside, followed by Marge and Ruth. Cissie placed a restraining hand on Samira's arm.

'You're going to have to keep an eye on your friend,' she said.

'Why? What's going on?'

'You'll find out soon enough.'

★ ★ ★

Cissie was right. Samira soon realised why Lexie had been so keen to get to the hayfield. Other small clues that she hadn't noticed or understood before suddenly made sense — the cheerfulness at getting up at four o'clock in the morning, the humming, the perfume, powder and lipstick, and the blushing at the mention of the Italians. And of course, the bacon sandwich that had been carefully saved for later, which Samira saw pass covertly from Lexie's hands to those of one of the men. She knew they were prisoners because each man had a large circular red patch sewn to the front of one trouser leg and on the back of their jacket so they could easily be distinguished from the civilian population. And if there had been any doubt, nearby stood an armed soldier.

Despite the circumstances, everyone seemed remarkably relaxed except Ruth, who stood apart from the others, watching. 'I don't like this,' she whispered to Samira. 'There are ten of them and only four women and one soldier. And they've all got pitchforks. By the time that soldier picks his gun up and gets ready to defend us, we'll all be dead!'

'I don't think it's quite as drastic as that,' said Samira. 'All the prisoners seem very polite, and Cissie and the other girls have worked with them before. If they thought there was a threat, they wouldn't be chatting to them like that, would they? And apparently Joanna will be over later with some food, and she usually brings Faye and Mark. She wouldn't put her children in jeopardy.'

'No, I suppose not. It just seems so contrary to everything I've ever thought. Our men are out in France being killed by men like this, and here we are fraternising.'

'Those men are helping to feed Britain. Would it make our days any happier if we were nasty to them or simply ignored them? I think it's a very civilised way to behave, and if I had a son who was a prisoner abroad, I'd want to know that he was being treated like this.'

'Yes, I can see the sense in that. But I'm not sure I'd be flirting like Lexie is with one of them.'

Samira remained silent. What was Lexie thinking? True, the Italian she was talking to was gorgeous and charming, but even Samira with her lack of experience could see this was not likely to end well for her.

'What a shame one of us couldn't drive the tractor,' said Cissie. 'We could do with all the men working on the ground. It's a waste having one of them in the tractor.'

'I might be able to do it,' said Samira, and then when she saw Cissie's look of disbelief, wished she hadn't. 'I can drive a car,' she added defensively. 'Is it much harder to drive a tractor?'

'No idea, but you could give it a go. What have we got to lose?' Cissie smiled and slapped Samira on the back. 'Well, I'll be blowed! You can't ride a bicycle but you can drive a car!' She was obviously very impressed.

After a brief lesson from the German, Samira mastered the tractor and moved it forward as required so the others could toss the hay into the trailer; and gradually, the field was cleared. By the time Joanna arrived with Faye, much of the hay had been transferred to the barn. One of the prisoners crouched down when he saw Faye and opened his arms wide. She flew into them, and as he picked her up and swung her round, she squealed with delight.

'Poor man,' remarked Joanna as she opened the car boot to get the trestle table. 'He showed me a photo of his little girl, and she looks a lot like Faye. He told me he misses her so much.'

'It seems I was wrong to have judged the prisoners,' Ruth said to Samira. 'If they didn't have accents and large red dots on their uniforms, I don't think I'd know they were foreign. They've worked really hard today, and despite being stuck here, they seem to be polite and good-natured. I'm still not sure it's a good idea to get quite so close to them though,' she added, looking at Lexie.

'Oh, Riccardo, that's such a lot of nonsense!' Lexie said as the handsome Italian bent over her hand as if telling her fortune.

'Si, si, Lexie,' he said. 'Trust me. You will meet a tall, dark, 'andsome stranger.' He pretended to point out the lines on her palm that were foretelling the event, and then raised it to his lips and kissed it.

Samira glanced at Joanna, who was taking jugs of drink and baskets of food out of the car. She was so busy arranging them on a trestle table that she didn't notice Lexie's palm reading. Would Joanna be upset if she knew that Lexie was keen on one of the Italians? Samira began to wonder if it was such a terrible thing. She remembered Mrs Thomsett saying that the war was making people act rashly, doing things they wouldn't have done in peacetime, because life was now so precarious and it seemed sensible to live for the day. Luke had asked her to keep an eye on his sister because he knew she could be reckless, but Lexie just seemed to be having fun. What could she do with a man who spent his days in a field with a group of prisoners and a guard, and his nights locked up?

One of the Germans smiled at her. 'Fräulein, do you know where is the young boy, Mark? I have a gift for him. I myself made it for him.' He took a small carved aeroplane from his pocket and held it out on the palm of his hand.

'He hasn't been very well,' said Samira. 'Shall I take it for him, or would you like to wait until he's better?'

'You will take it please?' he said, and put it in her hand. 'You will tell him Karl made it for him, please?'

Samira assured him she would. She

looked at the skilfully carved plane and thought of Luke. Her stomach lurched when she remembered how much danger he was now facing as a pilot officer. Angry tears came to her eyes. So many deaths, so much misery . . . and yet, people who were supposed to be enemies could get on very well indeed, as shown by the day's events so far.

Karl spotted the tears in her eyes. 'So much sadness in the world,' he said, echoing her thoughts.

* * *

Samira had planned to ask Lexie about Riccardo, but after the dinner table had been cleared, Lexie announced she was tired and went straight to their bedroom. It was probably just as well. Samira was exhausted, too, after their long demanding day and the lack of sleep the previous night. And she didn't want to risk upsetting Lexie. Anyway, she decided, as she climbed into bed, what right did she have to comment? As

Lexie had pointed out only yesterday, she had very little experience with men. So what would she know?

During the following weeks, there was very little free time to consider anything other than rising early, working in the fields and going to bed straight after dinner. Gradually she became accustomed to the long hours and the strenuous work, and had even learned to ride her bicycle. It no longer alarmed her that Lexie made her feelings for the good-looking Riccardo so obvious. It brightened Lexie's day when he was there, so what harm could there be in it?

One morning in early August, however, Samira wondered whether she ought to have talked to Lexie. After all, hadn't she promised Luke she'd look out for his sister?

12

The sun had already risen when she woke, and her eyelids felt swollen and heavy. Had Lexie's alarm failed to go off? It was just after six o'clock — two hours after the alarm should have rung.

'Lexie! Wake up, the alarm didn't go off! We're late!' But there was no reply.

Samira leaped up. Lexie's bed was neatly made as if it hadn't been slept in, but she'd definitely gone to bed at the same time as Samira the previous evening.

She washed and dressed in record time and hurried down to the kitchen, where Joanna, who was eating breakfast with Faye and Mark, looked up in surprise.

'I thought you and Lexie had already left for the day. Is everything all right?'

'Yes, thanks. I think I went back to sleep,' Samira lied.

'I bet Lexie's wondering where you are.'

'Yes, I expect so.' Samira was certainly wondering where Lexie was.

She took a slice of bread and rushed out to fetch her bicycle, planning to ride to the Land Girls' cottage and see if Lexie was there. Her disappearance almost certainly had something to do with Riccardo, but for the last few days, she and Lexie had been cleaning Joanna's house in Dunton Plotlands, so they hadn't seen the Land Girls or the POWs. Ben's mother had finally moved out of the small house and gone to stay with her sister, and Joanna wanted it cleaned, ready for some of Ben's cousins whose house in London had been bombed. Samira had never seen Lexie so miserable.

Could she have crept out really early that morning to try to find Riccardo? And if so, where could they have gone? Samira knew that security wasn't tight in the prisoner of war camp — there was no need. The men weren't going to escape. The distinctive red patches on their clothes ensured they would be easily spotted, and it was unlikely any of them could get to the coast and gain passage on a boat without being challenged. So long as the POWs were well behaved, they had plenty of freedom. Samira suddenly gasped as she realised where Lexie might take Riccardo, if she had indeed gone to find him. The obvious place was Joanna's Plotland house.

The sky was clear, but mist still lingered, clinging to the ground, and Samira shivered despite her jacket. As she rode down the drive, the cool air seemed to clear her bleary brain, and she wondered if she'd jumped to the wrong conclusion. Perhaps it was simply that Lexie had woken early, and not wanting to disturb her, had got ready and gone to help the Land Girls with the milking. Yes, that was surely the explanation.

Samira stopped at the end of the drive. She'd planned to go left and cycle to Joanna's house, but now she turned the handlebars to the right to head towards the Land Girls' cottage. The roar of an engine cut into her thoughts and she hesitated, looking up fearfully in case there was an aeroplane approaching. But the sky was clear, and besides, she could now tell the sound was coming from her right. She paused to let the car, or whatever it was, go first, before she pulled out on to the road. However, it wasn't a car, it was a motorbike; and it didn't pass the drive, it swung in and ground to a halt just behind her.

Her heart beat wildly in her chest when she realised it was Luke. He got off the bike and ran to meet her.

'Where're you off to on your own?' he asked, brushing his windswept fringe off his face. Since she'd last seen him, his hair had grown, his face was thinner, and somehow he seemed older — but of course, after the dangers he faced daily, that wasn't surprising.

'I'm looking for Lexie.' The words

were out before she had a chance to think. Now he'd wonder why she didn't know where his sister was.

'Well, she's not with the Land Girls. I just dropped by their cottage and they said they hadn't seen her for a few days. I hear you've been cleaning up the house in Plotlands.'

She nodded, not sure what to say. How could she tell Luke her suspicions?

'D'you think she might be there?'

'Umm . . . '

'Is there something wrong?'

'Well . . . '

He looked at her for a few seconds with his head to one side. 'Right, let's go and find out,' he said, walking back to the bike. 'Come on, hop on behind me.'

She straddled the bike and wrapped her arms round his middle as he revved the engine, pulled out of the drive and accelerated along the road. The rush of wind took her breath away and she clung to Luke more tightly, laying her cheek against his leather jacket, while the hedgerows sped by so quickly that they were a blur. How enjoyable this ride would have been under other circumstances. But now the dread that they might find Lexie and Riccardo together at Joanna's house filled her mind.

Luke turned off onto the unmade road and slowed down. It was too uneven to go fast, and he wove his way through the furrows and ruts. As they drew up outside Joanna's house in Second Avenue, Samira could see Lexie's bike leaning against the veranda. Luke turned off the engine, and in the silence that ensued, raised voices could be heard coming from the house.

Samira groaned softly. She couldn't hear the words that were being spoken, but she could tell Lexie was pleading and Riccardo was angry.

'There's someone in there with Lexie,' Luke said in surprise. Then, seeing Samira's anxious expression, he asked, 'You know who it is?'

She nodded.

'Well, who is it?'

'Riccardo. I don't know his surname. He's one of the internees — '

Shock registered on his face. 'Please stay here,' he said; and rushing up the path, he climbed the veranda steps and entered the house.

Samira was tempted to run round to the back of the house and peer in through the kitchen window, but she decided to respect Luke's wishes. This was, after all, a family matter. Lexie's screams and the crash of crockery cut through the early morning stillness of Second Avenue, and seconds later, a wild-eyed Riccardo appeared at the door. He looked right and left, then muttering in Italian, he pushed past Samira; and before she could react, he'd climbed onto Luke's motorbike, started the ignition and driven off, bucking and bumping over the uneven road.

Samira ran up the steps and pushed open the door to find Lexie on her knees next to Luke, who was lying motionless on his back surrounded by broken china.

'Sam! Thank goodness you're here! I don't know what to do. Luke's stopped breathing!'

13

Samira's first aid training with the WVS took over, and she knelt by Luke's side and took his pulse. 'He's breathing, but he needs attention. That gash over his eye looks nasty. I'll find something to staunch the flow, but one of us needs to fetch help — and quickly.'

'I'll go. Oh, Sam, thank goodness you're here! This is all my fault!'

'Let's worry about that later,' said Samira gently but firmly. 'At the moment, we need help.'

'Yes, yes, of course. I'll ride like the wind. I promise. Thank you, Sam!' Lexie rushed out of the house to her bike.

Samira found Joanna's first aid box and cleaned all the cuts that she could get to without moving Luke. He was bleeding above one eye, and as she dabbed at it with iodine, he groaned and stirred.

'Lie still,' she said gently. 'Lexie's gone for help. You're going to be fine.'

'Samira?'

'I'm here.'

'I can't see anything.'

'Try to relax. You've had a blow to the head. It might be the result of that. We'll soon have you in hospital. Don't worry.'

'Where's that man? You're not in any danger, are you?'

'No. Don't worry about him, he's gone.' She decided not to add to Luke's worries by telling him about the stolen motorbike. Riccardo would be picked up before long. The large red patches on his leg and back would ensure he was recognised and stopped.

He glanced from side to side, as if searching for something, and she move her face into his field of vision, but he didn't appear to see her. Was the sight loss temporary? How could that be? Ten minutes ago, he'd been steering a smooth path for them on his motorbike down a bumpy road, picking out every dip and mound on a journey she'd wanted to go on forever; and now . . .

She held his hand and whispered a fusion of wishes, thoughts and prayers — anything to try to reassure him, as his eyes sightlessly moved back and forth searching for the light.

★   ★   ★

Samira pedalled through the lane leading to the milking shed. It was earlier than normal because she hadn't been able to sleep, worrying about Luke and Lexie, so she'd finally decided to get up and do something useful. The Land Girls wouldn't be there for some time, but she could at least get ready for the day's milking and try to occupy her mind.

When Ben and Joanna questioned her, she was able to tell them very little, although the fact that Lexie had been there with Riccardo had been damning enough. She didn't mention that Lexie had said she blamed herself for what happened to Luke — they were just words spoken in the heat of the moment, and perhaps Lexie just assumed that if she hadn't been there with Riccardo, the accident wouldn't have happened at all. Samira knew that Ben and Joanna were angry, but neither of them were as critical of Lexie as she was of herself, so there was no point adding fuel to the fire.

Cissie was the first to arrive, and she hugged Samira warmly. 'How's Lexie's brother? How's Lexie? What on earth happened yesterday? We've been able to talk about nothing else!'

Marge and Ruth appeared, both out of breath. 'I wish my legs were as long as yours, Cissie,' said Marge gasping for breath. Then turning to Samira, she added, 'We hoped you'd come. We're desperate for news. Especially about Lexie's brother.'

Samira admitted she didn't know a great deal, but that Lexie had stayed at the hospital overnight and that Luke's eyesight seemed to be improving.

'So Lexie was with Riccardo when

you and Luke arrived?' Ruth asked.

Samira sighed and nodded.

'Well, that's a pretty poor show!' said Ruth crossly.

'I know it wasn't wise,' said Samira. 'But she was head over heels in love with him. Love makes people do foolish things, doesn't it?'

'I'm not talking about Lexie,' Ruth snapped. 'I'm talking about that outrageous Italian prisoner! Fancy leading her on like that! I didn't think any good would come from working alongside the enemy!'

'Oh, get off your high horse, Ruthie,' said Cissie good-naturedly. 'There's a war on. *Carpe diem* — seize the day.'

'Yes, I know what *carpe diem* means, thank you. But if you ask me, too many people are using that as an excuse to act like animals!'

'No one was asking you. Lexie just fell in love. There's no law against it as far as I know.'

'No, but it's not desirable when one party is married.'

There was silence for a few seconds.

Finally, Cissie asked, 'Riccardo's married?'

'Oh yes!' said Ruth heatedly. 'And he has a child.'

'I didn't know! How do *you* know?'

'Karl told me. Apparently Riccardo carries a photo of his family in his pocket. And he said he was desperate to get back to Italy to be with them.'

'You've been getting very snugly with Karl, for someone who doesn't approve of fraternising with the enemy,' said Marge.

'Oh don't be ridiculous! Karl just has a similar taste to me in opera. That's all.'

Samira looked at Ruth in horror. 'So you mean that Riccardo was using Lexie?' she asked.

'It looks like it.'

'Poor, poor Lexie. Her heart will be broken.'

'Don't say it!' Cissie said to Ruth, who had opened her mouth to answer. 'Unless what you've got to say is kind.'

Ruth closed her mouth.

★ ★ ★

Luke stared up at the lights suspended from the ward ceiling. At least he could see them now. The temporary blindness had frightened him, and he was enjoying all the sights that once he would have taken completely for granted. If only he could see things sharply without it appearing that everything he looked at was superimposed by a similar but ghostly shape. His doctor had assured him that in time, the double vision would fade. But for now, he would not be able to fly. What a disaster. Every pilot was needed to defend munitions factories, industry and airfields — not to mention the civilian population, from the Luftwaffe. But there was nothing he could do.

He expected a dressing-down from his squadron leader for becoming unfit for service because of a fight, and he would probably be punished. His only consolation was that he would be convalescing at Priory Hall. His friend,

Archie Cavendish, had suggested that he stay with him; but Luke knew that Archie's sister, Vera, would be there, and she was someone that Luke could only take in small doses. She was confident, loud and . . . well, frankly embarrassing with her over-familiarity. Archie hadn't needed to tell him that Vera had set her sights on him — she'd made it obvious — but he was just as determined that she would never be more than a friend.

It was tempting to spend time in Hornchurch with Archie, who was also unable to fly at the moment, having been shot down several days before. He'd been remarkably lucky, although his windscreen had shattered, resulting in lacerations to his hands; and until they healed, he would be grounded. Other than that, he had escaped unscathed. However, Joanna had invited Luke to Priory Hall, and he had jumped at the chance. He barely dared to admit to himself the real reason, telling Joanna that it would be a good opportunity to spend some time with Lexie. But in unguarded moments, Samira, with her long shiny black hair and her intelligent dark eyes, filled his thoughts.

He had no right to play with Samira's emotions like Riccardo had played with Lexie's. As a pilot, he had very little to offer her except worry and possible heartache if he was shot down. It had been his intention to avoid a meaningful relationship until the war was over, and so far that had been easy because although he knew many girls, no one had really interested him. In fact, he was beginning to wonder whether there was something wrong with him. He was totally in control of his emotions, unlike Archie, who fell in love with a new girl each week.

But it seemed it had been an illusion that he was master of his feelings, because from the first time he'd seen Samira, he hadn't wanted to take his eyes off her. Not surprising, as she was indeed beautiful. He'd assumed that she'd be vacuous and vain, like most of the girls he'd met; but when he'd driven her to Essex, he'd discovered that she was thoughtful, warm and, he admitted to himself, totally bewitching. As much as he would have liked to have been able to switch his feelings off, he stood as much chance of being able to do that as he was to see the lights above his head clearly.

For the next few days, he would have the opportunity to spend time with her, even if he would have to keep his distance. There would be no more shared walks to watch the sunset, and definitely no time spent alone together — he wasn't sure he would be able to hide his feelings for long if she were to look at him the way she had when he'd been about to kiss her before. He closed his eyes and tried to imagine what it would have been like had Lexie not disturbed them.

When he opened his eyes, he could still see twice as many lights above his bed as he knew there were, but he consoled himself with the thought that as long as his vision was playing tricks on him, he would be able to stay at Priory Hall and at least be near Samira.

★ ★ ★

Ben had picked Luke and Lexie up from the hospital once the doctors had discharged Luke, and had brought the dishevelled pair home in the car. Lexie had been at the hospital since Luke had been admitted the day before and had hardly slept, so her clothes were crumpled and her hair was in need of a comb. Luke's face was swollen, cut and bruised — so much so that one eye was almost completely closed, and when she had helped him from the car, he limped to the front door. The welcoming committee greeted them warmly, and Joanna had to warn Faye and Mark not to get too close to Luke in case they hurt him. Joanna hugged Lexie, drawing her into the hall, and restrained the children while Luke entered.

Samira stood back, keeping out of

the way. She'd had to stop her hand flying to cover her mouth in shock when Luke had first got out of the car, and she longed to go to him. But what was the point of that? There was nothing she could do to help him heal faster, and the kisses that she longed to place on his face would do nothing but cause him pain. And of course, she would merely be demonstrating her childishness and inexperience in front of everyone, who would surely know that a young, dashing and devastatingly handsome pilot would not have time for her.

'Isn't it wonderful Luke's back!' said Faye, pulling at Samira's hand. 'Come and say hello!'

'It's probably best to let him rest, darling. He'll be tired and in a bit of pain for a day or two,' Samira said.

Neither Lexie nor Luke appeared for dinner, much to Faye's disappointment. 'But I wanted to hear some stories about flying a plane,' she said.

'Perhaps in a day or so, poppet,' said

Joanna. 'Luke needs time to rest and heal. I can't imagine how he could have sustained such bad injuries from one blow. And the mess at the house was unbelievable. It looked like there'd been a dreadful fight.'

'Well, apparently Riccardo hit him with such force over the head with a stool that he crashed into the dresser,' said Ben. 'You know, we're going to have to be rather understanding with Lexie for a while. She blames herself because when she saw Luke, she screamed, and that was enough to distract him for a second. Riccardo took the opportunity and hit him. Lexie was stunned at the viciousness. I suppose Riccardo felt he'd been cornered. But really, that was no excuse.'

'Well, at least they've got him,' said Joanna. 'Constable Farmer said he got as far as Wickford. And they'll return Luke's motorbike tomorrow. He'll be taken to a more secure prison camp, so we won't see him again. I was dreading the police having to question Lexie about her part in the escape of a POW, but apparently Riccardo told the constable that he'd followed Lexie and that she'd had nothing to do with him escaping. That's probably the only decent thing he's done since he's been here.'

'Well, that's one less thing to worry about, I suppose. You know, it's lucky my mother's gone to stay with her sister for a while,' said Ben. 'She'd have a field day pulling Lexie to bits. I can hear her now calling her 'hussy' and 'harlot'!'

'What's a hussyanharlot?' Faye asked.

'Never you mind,' said Joanna, trying to suppress a smile. 'Just don't say that . . . er word again.'

Samira excused herself as soon as dinner was finished, saying that she wanted to check on Lexie. It was true, and as she hadn't slept well the previous night, she also wanted to go to bed early. Quietly, she tiptoed into the bedroom.

'Don't worry, Sam,' said Lexie, who

was sitting up in bed. 'You don't need to creep about; I'm not asleep. Every time I close my eyes, I see Riccardo with that stool raised above his head a split second before he hit Luke. If only I hadn't screamed, Luke wouldn't have looked towards me, and he might have dodged the blow. There was such anger in Riccardo's eyes. I've never seen him like that before. And that was probably my fault too, because I was trying to make him take me with him.'

'Take you with him? Where did you think you'd be able to go?'

'South America?' She didn't sound very sure.

'But how would you both have got to South America?'

'I don't know, but we'd have worked it out. Two people can't be so much in love and have to live apart.'

'But Riccardo wanted to go to Italy. You couldn't have gone there.'

'I know. That's why I thought it best if we went to South America. Then one day when this dreadful war's over, we could have gone back to Italy. But he just kept saying he needed to get home and one day he'd come back for me. I couldn't bear the thought of being without him.'

Samira sighed. 'Lexie, there's something you need to know about Riccardo — '

'Have they caught him? Is that it?'

'Well, yes, but that wasn't what I need to tell you. I'm so sorry, Lexie, but apparently the reason he was desperate to get back to Italy was because he wanted to be with his wife and child . . . I'm so sorry to be the bearer of bad news.' She slid her arm round Lexie's heaving shoulders and held her tightly as she sobbed.

'He promised me we'd be together one day if I helped him get away from the camp and got him to the coast. How could I have been so stupid?' she said finally when the tears had stopped.

'You weren't to know, Lexie. Love makes fools of everyone from time to time.'

'And after all that, my heart's broken

and Luke's almost blind. Why am I so stupid and headstrong?'

'Lexie, darling, in time, your heart will mend. They always do. And Luke's far from blind. He's just got double vision, and the doctors are satisfied he'll make a full recovery.

'But what if the doctors are wrong?'

'Well, we'll deal with that if it happens. But let's look on the bright side for a moment. While he's in a bedroom along the hall, he isn't in the cockpit of a Spitfire facing goodness knows what. He's safe. Now, why don't you try to sleep? You've had a terrible few days, and you must be exhausted. Things'll look better in the morning.'

'What would I do without you, Sam? You're so wise and good.'

Samira gave her a final hug, undressed and climbed into bed.

Wise?

Hardly. She hadn't seen enough of the world, or of life, to be wise.

And good?

She wasn't sure anyone in the RAF

would commend her for being thankful that one of their pilots was temporarily out of action so that he remained safe.

But with her whole heart and soul, she was glad that for now at least, Luke wasn't in danger.

★ ★ ★

Over the next few days, Luke's cuts healed and the bruises faded, although his vision was still slightly impaired. He played with Faye and Mark, and helped with light chores; but other than at meal times when the family ate together, if Samira entered the room, soon afterward he would make his excuses and leave. If broken-hearted Lexie had noticed, she hadn't said anything; and it appeared to be only Joanna who had detected the tension. She'd taken Luke and Samira aside separately and tried to find out what had led to the strained atmosphere, but both of them denied that there was a problem. She wasn't convinced, but in the absence of any evidence, and given the denials of them both, she began to wonder whether her intuition was at fault.

However, her attention was diverted from Luke and Samira one morning in her Plotland house. Lexie had insisted on cleaning up the mess and paying for all the broken furniture and china, saying it was the least she could do to make amends for her earlier stupidity. Although Joanna told her it wasn't necessary, she thought that it might help Lexie get over the whole incident. Samira had offered to help, but Lexie had insisted it was something that she had to do on her own, and that the Land Girls needed Samira to drive the tractor and help with the harvesting.

Joanna cycled to the house to check on Lexie's progress, and was disturbed to find her sitting on the floor sobbing quietly.

'Lexie, darling, what's wrong?'

It took a while before Lexie could speak. 'Oh, Joanna, I've made such a mess of things. Everything I touch falls to pieces. And I miss Riccardo. Or at least, I miss what I thought I had with him. And I've hurt Luke and let you and Ben down — '

'Shh! You mustn't think like that. You made a mistake, that's all. Come on, let's finish this together and then we'll think of a way of cheering you up.'

'I don't deserve you being nice to me.'

'Hush now and put your energy into tidying up. Ben's cousins are coming on Saturday, so this needs to be ready for them by then.'

When they'd finished, Joanna made them each a cup of tea and suggested they go into the garden and sit in the shade of the apple tree. It reminded her of all the evenings she'd shared with Ben and the Plotland neighbours years ago when they'd gathered in someone's garden during the long summer. Mr Franks had often played his accordion, and there'd been singing and dancing, and food cooked over the fire. It would be wonderful to do something similar to take their minds off the war and to cheer up Lexie.

She decided to arrange a family picnic where they could all enjoy each other's company. Sunday would be the day.

★　★　★

Joanna took Luke aside that evening and told him how she'd found Lexie in tears earlier.

'But I've told her I don't blame her.'

'I know Luke, but she's so unhappy. Perhaps if you had another word with her?'

'Of course. I'll try.'

'I'm going to organise a family picnic for Sunday. Perhaps that'll take her mind off things.'

'That's a wonderful idea — Lexie loves a party. Should I ask Archie? He's great company, and he's met Lexie a few times. They seemed to get on well enough.'

'Do you think that's a good idea? She's only just getting over Riccardo.'

'Oh, don't worry about Archie. He's got a girl for each night of the week, but he and I think along similar lines. Neither of us believe there's any point getting serious — not while the war's on.'

'A girl for each night of the week? I'm not sure that's what Lexie needs right now.'

'Don't worry! Archie won't lead her on. He always makes it clear he's a free spirit. Trust me, he'll cheer her up.'

Free spirit? Joanna thought. How could either of these young men be so sure they could control their emotions? Several years ago, both she and Ben had tried to curb their feelings for each other — and both had failed. But if Luke thought his friend would amuse Lexie, then it might be worth it. And it would give Luke and Samira a chance to spend some time together. Perhaps they would sort out their differences.

* ★ ★

Samira got up early on Saturday morning. She wanted to walk into Laindon before breakfast to post a letter to her father, and pick up a few groceries for Joanna. With her shoes in one hand and her handbag in the other, she crept along the upstairs corridor in her bare feet so that she didn't wake anyone. On the small landing halfway down the stairs, she stopped and opened her bag. She was so engrossed with checking that she had her purse and ration book, she didn't see Luke walking upstairs. She looked up to see who was approaching, and when she saw it was him, she stepped aside to give way. As she moved sideways, her foot slipped and she stumbled forward, dropping her handbag, which bounced down the stairs, spilling its contents. Before she followed the bag, Luke reached out and grabbed her with one arm, steadying her.

They looked at each other in horror

at what might have been.

'Th . . . thank you,' said Samira.

'Are you all right?'

'Yes, I think so.' She peered down the stairs at the bag in the hall below.

'That was close.' He gently pushed her away from the edge of the stairs. 'You're shaking. Are you sure you're all right?'

'I . . . I'm a bit shocked, that's all.'

'You're all right now,' he said, wrapping his arms round her.

She closed her eyes. How safe she felt in his arms, even if she was only inches away from where she'd nearly fallen.

With Luke standing on the step below her, their eyes were on the same level, and he placed his cheek against hers. Samira could feel his breath on her neck, and she suddenly realised that several buttons had popped open and her blouse had slipped when he'd grabbed her, revealing one shoulder. Luke's fingers brushed her skin, slowly tracing a line from her ear, down her neck and across the top of her arm to the edge of her blouse. She shivered with delight as he planted tiny kisses along the invisible line drawn by his finger. Tipping her head back, she closed her eyes and gave herself up to the waves of pleasure that rippled down her body, radiating from where his lips caressed the skin that would normally be covered by her blouse. She hadn't realised she was holding her breath until the back door slammed, shocking them both.

He quickly drew the fabric back in place and fastened the top buttons, then kissed the indentation at the base of her throat.

'It's probably best not to be found like this on the stairs,' he said, smiling at her. 'Can we talk later? I promised Ben I'd go to Romford with him this morning, but as soon as I'm back, can we talk? Please?'

She nodded, unable to speak, unable to catch her breath.

Hurrying downstairs, she retrieved the contents of her handbag, and with a quick look about to ensure they hadn't been seen, she hurried out of the door, the tang of his scent still filling her nostrils and the site of each kiss tingling with the memory.

Luke had been polite and remote since he'd arrived at Priory Hall, so what had changed? she wondered as she walked along the deserted lanes.

Does it matter? A tiny voice in her head whispered. *Perhaps this war will go on for ever and sanity will never be restored. Will you look back and wish you'd grabbed happiness while you could?*

She placed her outstretched hand over her chest as if to hold Luke's kisses on her skin. Nothing had ever made her feel as alive or as valued before, and her senses were still spinning with delicious shock. Ivy's warning about ultimately being alone had been meant to warn her against trusting anyone, but if she never gave anyone a chance, she'd definitely end up alone. Perhaps caution and common sense had no place in this war-torn world. Perhaps it was time to live for the moment.

★   ★   ★

Samira was so desperate to see Luke that she rushed back from Laindon without visiting the Land Girls' cottage. While she waited for him to return, she played with Mark and Faye, keeping them out of the kitchen so that Joanna could prepare for the picnic without interruption.

'Will you wear your hair up tomorrow, like you do when you're working on the farm, Samira?' Faye asked. 'I think it looks better down.'

'Well, I hadn't given it much thought really, darling.'

'Oh, but you must! It's going to be so exciting.'

Samira ran her fingers through the young girl's chestnut curls. 'And how are you going to wear yours?'

'Oh, tied back. Although it never seems to stay in place for long.'

'Perhaps that's because you're always running about.'

'I s'pose so.'

'Why not just leave it like it is?'

'Luke's friend Ernie's coming, and I want to look nice. And Daddy's cousins are coming too.'

'Ernie? Do you mean Archie?'

'Oh yes, that's right. I heard Luke ask Mummy yesterday if it was all right to invite him to the picnic. He said it would cheer Lexie up . . . I still don't understand why she's so upset. And who's Riccardo?'

'Just one of Lexie's friends who had to go away.'

'Oh, I see. Well, it'll be nice if the picnic does make Lexie happy. Luke said Archie's very good company, and apparently he won't lead her on because he's a free spirit. What's a free spirit, Samira?'

'I'm not sure, darling. It probably depends on what people are talking about.'

'Well, all I know is that Luke says he

thinks the same sort of things as Archie. He said they have girls every night of the week and neither of them are going to get serious about it — well, not while the war's on anyway. So Luke must be a free spirit too.'

'Are you sure he said that?'

'What? The free spirit part?'

'No, the part about girls every night of the week?'

'Oh yes. I don't know what he meant, though. I thought they flew every night of the week. D'you think it's another one of the funny things they say in the RAF, like 'Tally ho' when they see an enemy plane and 'Pancake' when they mean they're going to land?'

'Possibly.'

'Are you all right, Samira? Your voice sounds all funny.'

Samira nodded and smiled. It was best that Faye didn't hear her voice break, and most importantly that she didn't see the tears that were threatening to spill down her cheeks.

So, there it was. Evidence that Luke

was taking every opportunity to find happiness. If she couldn't be his special girl, was she prepared to be one amongst others?

14

'Where d'you want me to set up?' Ben asked. 'Under the cherry tree?'

'We're not having a picnic in the garden!' said Joanna, fastening the lid of the picnic hamper. 'We're going to get away from normal life, just for a few hours. We're going somewhere with beautiful views and peaceful woods.'

'Where?'

'One Tree Hill. I did tell you!'

'Ah!' Ben was silent for a few minutes, then catching hold of Joanna's hand, he pulled her close to him and held her tightly. 'We haven't been there for some time,' he whispered.

'I know. This war is getting in the way of everything. But it's the perfect place for Lexie to relax, and I've been a bit worried about Luke and Samira. I think they've had an argument or something. I can't work them out. Every time one of them comes into a room, the other one leaves. And yet, there's no animosity that I can detect — quite the opposite, in fact. There are long, lingering glances when each thinks the other isn't looking. So if they're thrown together, it might give them a chance to iron out whatever differences — or otherwise — they have. Luke only has double vision when he's tired; the rest of the time it's pretty much back to normal. When he sees the doctor next week, he'll be sent straight back to Hornchurch . . . and . . . well, who knows if we'll ever see him again? So this may be the last chance for them to patch up whatever it is that needs patching up. And it might make Samira feel more at home here too.'

'Don't you think she feels at home here?'

'Well . . . yes . . . it's just that she doesn't seem to have anywhere that she can really call home. I know she has family in India, but she rarely talks about where she once lived; and when I ask her, she just says that it was so long ago since she was there that she doesn't remember much. She certainly doesn't talk about it as if she misses it. The only other place she's been for any length of time is the convent, and she never mentions that at all.'

'Well, Jo, if anyone can make Samira feel at home here, it's you.' He kissed the tip of her nose. 'Right, I'd better go and get the car.'

⋆ ⋆ ⋆

Ben parked at One Tree Hill, and everyone climbed out and helped Joanna carry the picnic things further up the hill next to the edge of the woods. Mark and Faye ran off to play with Ben's cousin, John, his wife, Caroline, and three children, who had set up a noisy game of cricket at the bottom of the hill where the ground was level.

'Is your friend coming, Luke?' Joanna asked.

'He said he'd come if the bandages are removed from his hands, but he's always late, so I wouldn't expect him yet.'

'Is that him?' asked Lexie, pointing down the hill at a rapidly approaching car.

'Well, if it is, that'll be the first time I've ever known him be on time for anything!'

Archie pulled up next to Ben's car and leapt out to greet Luke at the same time as the passenger door opened and Vera got out, straightened her hat and smoothed the skirt of her suit with gloved hands.

'Luke, darling!' she said, throwing her arms wide and teetering across the grass on her high-heeled shoes. 'I couldn't wait to see you again. It's been so long, you naughty boy!'

'Who's she?' Joanna whispered.

'That's Archie's sister, Vera,' said Samira.

'How d'you know?' asked Lexie.

'I saw her when Luke brought me

here the first time. We stopped off in Hornchurch at Archie's house, and she was there.'

'Luke's never mentioned her,' said Lexie.

'But it looks like they know each other quite well,' said Joanna.

'Yes, doesn't it?' said Lexie. 'She can't keep her hands off him.' She began to laugh as Luke attempted to keep distance between them and Vera tried to press against him, resulting in them moving sideways. 'If she doesn't stop, they'll end up at the bottom of the hill in the middle of the cricket game!'

'Hey, Luke,' Lexie called, waving her hand, 'I need help with this.' She indicated the picnic basket.

Luke unlinked his arm, and with a brief word of apology, he ran to Lexie.

'Here, just move it to the other side of the rug. I didn't really want a hand but it looked like *you* needed one! What on earth did you invite her for?' Lexie whispered.

There was no opportunity to reply,

because Archie was nearby; and seconds later, despite the high heels, Vera joined them.

★   ★   ★

'Well, at least the children are enjoying themselves with John and Caroline,' said Ben as he helped Joanna carry the empty picnic basket back to the car. 'I know it's not what you planned.'

'Not what I planned? It's a disaster!'

'But Lexie seems happy.'

'I understand Archie is a womaniser. Not only that, but he's a pilot too, and this may be the last time we ever see him. I just wanted to cheer Lexie up. The last thing I wanted was for her to replace one catastrophe with another!'

'But at least she seems happy.'

'Well, yes, I'll grant you that. But poor Samira! She seems so sad and lost. And what about poor Luke having that woman grab him whenever she gets the opportunity?'

'Poor all of us, having to put up with

her loudness! Doesn't she ever shut up?'

'Oh, Ben!'

'Seriously, Jo, she's bruised my eardrums!'

'Stop joking! We need to do something.'

'Well, I can think of a way for Luke and Samira to get a bit of peace and quiet, but it means you and I will have to suffer more trauma to our eardrums.'

'I'm listening.'

'Suggest they go for a walk.'

'That's it? That's your idea? But Vera will just go with them.'

'Not if you suggest they go into the woods and find the well . . . '

'Ah!' said Joanna slowly. 'Yes! Very clever, Mr Richardson. It's definitely worth a go.'

★ ★ ★

Samira glanced at her watch. How much longer?

After they'd finished eating, Archie

had taken Lexie for a drive in his car. John, Caroline and the children were picking blackberries at the bottom of the field; their excited shouts drifting up the hill to Luke, Vera and Samira, who were still sitting on the rug. Joanna and Ben were tidying away the picnic things but seemed to be spending a lot of time packing them in the car boot, then rearranging them.

At least Samira wasn't expected to participate in the conversation. Vera's attention was totally on Luke, her body turned towards him, her face lighting up on the few occasions that he commented on anything she said.

Samira watched the children at the bottom of the hill, working their way along the hedgerow, screaming excitedly when they found a bush heavily laden with fruit. If only she'd gone with them and left Luke and Vera alone. It wasn't too late . . .

Ben and Joanna returned, hand in hand; and to her dismay, Ben suggested they go for a walk and find a well that he and Joanna knew of in the woods.

'It's quite a difficult walk, though,' Ben said, looking at Vera's high-heeled shoes.

'So if you want to stay here, Vera, I'd love you to give me some beauty tips,' said Joanna. 'It's so hard with all the shortages and rationing, but you seem to have found a way of looking lovely.'

'Thank you. That's very kind, but I'm sure I can manage in the woods. I'd be very happy to give you a few of my secrets when I get back, though.'

Vera teetered after Luke and Samira, who'd already disappeared into the undergrowth.

'Luke, wait for me!' Vera called as she hurried after them.

'Don't worry about me, Luke. I can easily go for a walk on my own,' said Samira.

'No! Please wait!' He placed a hand on her arm 'I've been desperate to talk to you, Samira. Where have you been? Please don't leave me alone with that woman.'

239

Suddenly Vera screamed and began to wail. By the time Luke and Samira reached her, she was hobbling along, holding her leg.

'What's the matter, what've you done? Have you twisted your ankle?' Luke asked.

'No!' she said crossly. 'I've torn my stocking on a thorn. Do you know how hard it was to get hold of this pair of stockings? And now I've ruined one of them.'

'Well, Ben did say it was a difficult walk and you might not manage in those shoes . . . ' said Luke.

'I assure you I could climb a mountain in these heels! But no one mentioned thorns. And no one said anything about the wildlife.' She swatted a wasp that was buzzing round her head.

'It's probably attracted by your perfume,' said Luke.

'Well, it can jolly well — ow! It stung me!' She held her hand to her neck and looked at Luke in disbelief. 'It stung me!' she said again, as if she simply couldn't believe that an insect would dare to summon up the nerve to touch her.

'Right,' said Luke, 'I think we'd better get you back to Priory Hall and put some vinegar on that sting.' For the first time since Vera had arrived, the life had come back into his voice.

Luke held the bramble branches back so that Vera wouldn't tear her other stocking or clothes, and helped her back to Ben and Joanna.

'You'll come with me, won't you, Luke?' Vera said when Ben offered to drive her home.

'No need,' said Joanna quickly. 'Look, your brother and Lexie are back. Let's ask him to take you to Priory Hall. Lexie can go with you; she knows where the vinegar is. Luke and Samira can help us clear the rest of our things away and get the children. Then we'll come back in our car.'

'Yes, excellent idea,' said Ben, taking Vera's arm and leading her to Archie's car before she could object.

Archie was less than sympathetic. 'Vinegar? That's an old wives' tale! Come on, old girl, I'll take you home. It's about time we were going.'

Vera turned back to appeal to Luke, but he was already walking uphill to the picnic rug and didn't turn around until Archie hooted, and his car had turned the corner and disappeared.

Lexie waved until he was out of sight. 'Archie's charming,' she said when she caught up with Luke. 'And such a gentleman . . . He's coming here to see me tomorrow too . . . '

'Oh no!' said Luke. 'I'm sorry, but if he brings that woman back tomorrow, I'm going out!'

'Well, if she's that bad, why did you invite her?'

'I didn't. She invited herself.'

'She didn't seem that bad.'

'How would you know? You didn't have to listen to her! And if you take my advice, you'll be very careful with Archie. He's a great chap, but he tends to spend a lot of time with the ladies

— lots of different ladies. I'd hate to see you get hurt again, Lexie. If I'd known he wasn't going to behave, I'd never have invited him. Actually, I wish I hadn't; then that dreadful woman wouldn't have come.'

'Stop being such a crosspatch, Luke! Archie is simply charming — a perfect gentleman. Come on, let's go and get the children. Joanna and Ben have packed up and are ready to go.'

Samira helped Joanna and Ben fold the rug and put it in the car while Lexie and Luke went to fetch John, Caroline and the children. When Luke returned, he was carrying Mark.

'I think he's overdone it a bit; he's almost asleep,' he said, putting the small boy in Ben's arms.

★ ★ ★

The following morning, Luke was in the kitchen when Samira entered. She paused, not sure whether it would be too obvious if she simply turned round and went back upstairs until he'd finished his breakfast.

Lexie was still asleep. Since she was going out with Archie, she'd decided to have a lazy day until she needed to get up and start preparing for her date. Samira had already heard Ben go out, and Joanna was feeding the chickens.

'Samira, I was waiting for you. I wondered if . . . ' He paused as if embarrassed.

'Yes?'

'Well, I wondered if you'd like to come with me to find the well we were going to look for yesterday. Ben said it was okay if you took the day off . . . '

'No, thank you. I don't think so.'

'Please, Samira. If you're angry that I didn't talk to you on Saturday after we . . . well, after you nearly fell down the stairs, Ben and I got held up, and by the time we came home, Joanna said you'd gone to bed.'

'I had a headache.'

'But I was desperate to talk to you. And as for yesterday — I tried to get you on your own. I can't believe Archie brought his sister, and I'm definitely going to have words with him for flirting so outrageously with Lexie.'

'I thought that was how you pilots behaved. A girl for each night of the week . . . '

'Well,' he said slowly, 'it's true that's what some pilots do, but not all. Archie and I agree on one thing — that it's not fair to get attached to anyone special while we're at war. But as for having a different girl each night? That's not for me.'

'It's not?'

'No, it's not,' he said firmly. 'So . . . '

'Yes?'

'I'm going to try to find the well. Please would you come with me?'

'Well . . . yes . . . all right.'

His face lit up. 'I'll see you outside in ten minutes,' he said, and rushed out.

Don't read too much into it, she told herself. *He's simply curious about the well and doesn't want to go on his own.* Why someone should be so interested in a well, she had no idea. But who cared? He'd asked her to go with him, and she intended to enjoy it.

There was no time to change out of her work overalls, as she could hear the motorbike engine revving on the drive; Luke was obviously ready to go. He helped her climb onto the bike behind him, and when he was satisfied she was ready, he roared down the drive and out onto the road.

She remembered the last time they'd driven down these lanes on their way to Plotlands, when she feared finding Lexie with Riccardo. There was dread mixed with the excitement of the ride; but now, exhilaration at the speed of the bike and the closeness of Luke made her breath catch in her throat.

They dismounted and left the bike near where the cars had been parked the previous day, and Luke led her to the gap in the undergrowth where Vera had been stung.

'Do you know where the well is?' Samira asked.

'Not a clue,' he said, laughing. 'So we may be here for some time.' He slipped his hand into hers, their fingers interlacing, and he smiled at her.

The moment was so perfect, she hardly dared breathe.

The slanting rays of the morning sun filtered through the foliage, casting spears of green light on the ground. This was surely an enchanted forest. And he was hers . . . only as long as they remained in this emerald world, of course. Sooner or later they would find the well or they would abandon the search; but just for now, he was hers.

'It's so peaceful here, it's hard to believe there's a war on,' said Luke.

'When do you have to go back to Horn . . . ' She tailed off, angry with herself for forgetting that Lexie had told her he didn't like discussing leave because he thought it unlucky.

He stopped and pulled her to him, encircling her with his arms. 'Too soon,' he said sadly. 'My vision's back to normal now, so as soon as I see the doctor on Wednesday, I'll be recalled. I know I've no right to ask you this, Samira, but I wondered if . . . it's just that I can't stop thinking about you, and I wondered if . . . ' He leaned forward and placed his forehead against hers. 'I know it's a lot to ask . . . I can't promise you anything . . . but I wondered if you'd wait for me?' he whispered.

'Yes. Oh yes.'

A thrill ran through her as he lifted his forehead from hers; and taking her face between his hands, he leaned towards her, his lips touching hers.

Nothing in her wildest dreams had prepared her for the rush of passion that coursed through her body. How right it was that the first person to kiss her should be Luke, and that they should be miles from anyone in the middle of an enchanted wood.

'Here, you're cold,' he said, taking off his leather jacket and placing it tenderly round her shoulders.

She held the lapels and breathed in

the spicy leather smell, not wanting to tell him that she had shivered from pure bliss and not from cold.

'The rest of the world seems so far away. We could be the last two people on earth,' said Luke, raising her hand to his lips. 'And just for the record, there's nobody I'd rather be with.' He paused. 'I promised myself I wouldn't do this — I told myself I'd wait until the end of the war until I looked for someone special. But the truth is, Samira, I wasn't looking for anyone — I just found you. I hardly slept last night thinking about today, wondering if I dared let you know how I feel. I'll be back at the airfield in a day or so. I may not live to see next week, and I longed to feel you in my arms.'

'And I longed to be there, Luke. This war's turned everything upside down. There's no point being cautious and putting things off until later. There may not be a later. I think it's better to spend a few days together — if that's all we're allowed — than never to have shared anything at all. No one knows how long this war will last or what the outcome will be. All we can do is live for the moment.'

He held her to him and she laid her cheek against his shoulder, feeling the beat of his heart. They stood together, holding each other, aware of the impermanence of their world. Luke looked up and stared into the distance. Suddenly, he gasped.

'Look! It's there! We've found it!'

She turned and followed his gaze through a gap in the trees into a small clearing. 'Are you sure? I was expecting something like a wishing well with a small roof and a bucket, not something so big.'

Luke took her hand and led her towards the structure, which sat in the middle of the clearing. Surrounding the well, was a circular building with a roof supported by smooth round pillars, and on top of the roof sat a dome, like an ancient temple.

'No wonder Joanna suggested we

find it,' said Samira. 'Who on earth would believe they'd find something like that in the middle of the woods? Do you know what it's doing here?'

'Joanna said the water's full of minerals, and a few years ago someone was selling it in bottles, but he had to close the well because there was some sort of contamination. She and Ben used to come here for walks. I think it was their special place.'

'D'you think she's lent it to us?'

'I rather think she has,' said Ben pulling Samira close again and kissing her. 'This is the memory I'll take with me the next time my plane's wheels leave the runway . . . until they touch down again. Our temple — our magic wood — and losing myself in your beautiful, exotic eyes.'

15

Joanna put a mug of tea on the table in front of Samira and, placing her hand on the girl's shoulder, she sighed.

What was there to say?

Samira looked up and smiled, but her eyes were brimming, their rims red and swollen with the tears that had already been shed. She strained to hear Luke's motorbike but she knew it had gone. He'd left five minutes ago, and she'd waved until he'd been out of sight; but for several minutes, she still fancied she heard the roar of his engine as he passed through the quiet country lanes on his way to Hornchurch. Now, in the kitchen, all she could hear was the ticking of the clock.

'Why don't you go and lie down, Samira? You look exhausted.'

Samira nodded and sipped the tea. Not because she wanted it, but because

Joanna had been kind enough to make it for her. It had no taste at all, and she wondered if anything would taste, smell or have meaning again until Luke was back.

But Joanna was right; she knew she ought to catch up on some sleep. She'd had very little for two days. After Luke had asked her to wait for him, they'd spent most of the day in the woods. They'd sat on the low wall that separated the well from the surrounding portico, and they'd talked and kissed until they realised with surprise that the shadows were almost equal and opposite to where they'd been when they'd first arrived.

After dinner, they'd walked to the spot where they'd once shared a sunset, ignoring Joanna's delighted wink at Ben when she'd caught sight of them hand in hand. They'd talked more as the sun sank below the horizon, and for some time after, until it was almost too dark to see.

Lexie had been distracted by her date with Archie and had not noticed Luke and Samira's new closeness, or how little time Samira spent in bed that night. How could Samira sleep, knowing that she and Luke had one more day together and then possibly never again? She'd stayed with him in the drawing room until the early hours before returning to her bedroom, and then risen before Lexie, meeting Luke on the landing for an early morning kiss before they crept down the stairs, grabbed some apples and headed out of the house. They'd driven on the motorbike down to the mouth of the River Thames, at Southend-on-Sea, and had strolled along the promenade, watching the tide recede to leave boats stranded on the smooth, shiny mud.

When they returned to Priory Hall, Luke switched the engine off at the gates and wheeled the motorbike up the drive in case they woke anyone. It was well past midnight, and for the rest of their time together, they sat on the enormous leather sofa in the drawing room, holding each other tightly —

sometimes dozing, sometimes kissing. At five o'clock, Luke washed, put on his uniform, kissed Samira one last time, and was gone.

★   ★   ★

When Samira finally went to bed, she didn't think she'd be able to sleep, so was very surprised to wake up and find the afternoon sun shining on her face. She was tempted to turn over, close her swollen eyes again and seek oblivion, but she'd have to get up sometime — she wouldn't be able to stay there until Luke came back.

If he came back.

She'd once wondered if she was incapable of loving, if something was missing from her personality. And now she knew there had been nothing wrong with her at all; she simply hadn't met the right man. But it was scant compensation knowing that the proof she was normal was that she'd fallen in love with a man whose life expectancy was measured in weeks.

Stop wallowing in self-pity, she told herself crossly. Would it have been better never to have met Luke?

I'd rather have loved him for just one day than not to have met him at all, she decided.

Then get up and carry on, her inner voice said.

★ ★ ★

The first thing Lexie and Samira did on arriving home from working on the farm each evening was to check the hall table for post. Samira breathed a sigh of relief when she saw the familiar blue envelopes addressed in Luke's handwriting, and silently gave thanks when Lexie received a letter which made her face light up with pleasure. If anything happened to Luke, it would be Lexie who would hear first, either from Archie or from her parents, and Samira would know instantly if something was wrong.

The spring of 1945 had been

unseasonably dull and grey, and an air of despondency lay over Priory Hall. The war seemed never-ending, with its shortages and relentless struggle. At the beginning of September, the country would have been at war for exactly six years. A few days earlier would be the first anniversary of Luke and Samira finding the well — and each other. She'd only seen him a few times since he'd gone back on active duty — just odd days here and there, although he stayed for three days at Christmas. He'd visited the previous week, but he'd seemed worn out. Perhaps *burnt out* might be a better description. There were the usual tears when he'd left, but Samira felt that something had changed.

Of course he's changed, she told herself fiercely. *He's facing the prospect of an agonising death most days. How could he not have changed from the carefree young man fresh from training to the flying ace he's become?*

But it hadn't affected Archie as badly. 'Bravado,' Lexie had said when

Samira asked her why he seemed to be untouched by the war. 'When you get to know him, he's kind and gentle, and not like the overconfident upper-class idiot he pretends to be!'

Are they all pretending? Samira wondered. Was that how pilots kept going, day after day?

Samira longed to ask Luke, but she knew it would have to wait until she could speak to him face to face, and she had no idea when that might be. She held out very little hope they'd spend their first anniversary together. First anniversary! One whole year of being together, whilst actually spending most of the time apart.

Lexie was in a similar position. Against all odds, and despite their best intentions, Archie and Lexie had fallen in love. They too had seen very little of each other, but after Lexie's earlier liaison with Riccardo, she was reassured by Luke, who reported that Archie's philandering ways were in the past. Samira was pleased at her friend's happiness, and she was also glad that it meant that Lexie could no longer object to Luke falling in love with Samira.

'There's one for you, Sam.' Lexie pointed at the blue envelope with the letter-opener and then sliced open Archie's letter. Samira snatched up the blue envelope, but before she could open it, the telephone rang and Lexie, who was closest to it, answered. It was Archie.

'Hello, darling. I'm so glad you rang — ' She stopped mid-sentence and listened to Archie, her face turning white.

'No!' she whispered. 'Please no! Where is he? Oh, no!'

She let the receiver fall, and Samira could hear Archie's voice coming from the speaker. Grabbing it, she held it to her ear. 'Archie, are you there? What's happened?'

Had time actually slowed down? Or was it that she was trying to fend off the words she'd dreaded for almost a year?

'I'm so sorry, Samira — Luke's been shot down! They've found his plane but . . . but not Luke.'

★ ★ ★

The telephone bell cut through the chatter of the crew room. Immediately, cards, chess pieces and books were dropped; and as the orders to scramble were given, pilots sprinted to their Spitfires, parachutes were strapped on, engines were started, and the aeroplanes taxied for take-off. In minutes, the pilots of 'A' Flight were airborne on their way to patrol the coast near Dover, in an area that had been dubbed Hellfire Corner.

Luke didn't feel well. He'd hardly eaten any of the generous breakfast that had been served to all the pilots who were on readiness. For some reason, swallowing had been difficult; and despite the cold, he was sweating.

I'll be glad of the warmth when I hit the freezing temperatures at twenty thousand feet, he thought. He wondered if he was going down with flu. Perhaps he should have reported sick. But it was too late now; the earth was falling away below. He couldn't let the lads down; and after all, he'd been feeling off colour for a few weeks now. Not sick exactly, just very downhearted. And who could blame him? Despite the bluster and boasting of the other lads, he knew they were all desperately upset. There had been too many losses; too many good men had not come back. And then an audacious German aerial attack last month had resulted in many of the ground crew being shot and killed as well. To say morale was low was an understatement.

Luke checked his instruments.

Would this war go on forever?

The last time he'd seen Samira, Ben's neighbour had visited. Mike Harold had a heart murmur, so he hadn't joined up, and spent the war farming acres of land adjacent to Priory Hall. He seemed to be a nice man, funny and engaging, and he obviously thought a lot of Samira. Luke had watched his eyes follow her when she was in the room. Not that Samira seemed to have noticed, but still . . . she deserved someone who could give her stability and love.

What could *he* give her? Love, that was for sure, but for how long? Might today be the day he didn't return? Each time he took off, the odds against him meeting an accident in the air increased.

The cloud was dense and low, and Luke suddenly realised he'd lost sight of the other planes from 'A' Flight. Suddenly from above, a German Messerschmitt 109 dived at him, firing in short bursts, and Luke banked sharply to the left, turning skilfully so that he quickly had the enemy plane in his sights. He fired, and it exploded, disintegrating as it cartwheeled through the air. Before Luke could turn his plane back on course, another Messerschmitt came from below and behind, firing a hail of bullets at him. Flames began to pour from the nose of his aircraft, and soon he began to choke as the cockpit filled with smoke. Petrol was also leaking over him, and he knew he only had seconds to escape before his clothes ignited.

Turning the aircraft on its back, Luke opened the hood and released his harness, tumbling out of the plane into the freezing air. He spun uncontrollably as he fell, groping wildly for the ripcord and praying that the parachute would deploy. The ground rushed towards him, and he'd almost blacked out when the canopy opened with a violent jerk. Holding on to the lanyards, his last memory was of the wind rushing past him and his flaming aeroplane plunging from the sky towards the green patchwork below.

★　★　★

Samira spotted Archie's car swing through the gates of Priory Hall and accelerate up the drive, the rear of the car fish-tailing as he braked.

She sank down on to her bed. She knew it was wrong, but she couldn't bear to go downstairs to see him. It would be too painful a reminder of what she'd lost. Burned-out pieces of

Luke's plane had been found in a field in Kent, but there had been no sign of his body. At first it was hoped that he'd parachuted to safety, but after five days there had been no word. And as each day passed, Samira's hope had dwindled, until now none remained. She simply felt numb. When she'd first arrived at Priory Hall, she'd shown Joanna the four black velvet bags that had been in Ivy's hatbox, and had been alarmed to see tears course down Joanna's cheeks. She'd picked them up reverently and turned them over and over, caressing them.

'My ma made these. I always knew Aunt Ivy had taken them. She was a hard woman,' Joanna said, shaking her head in disbelief. 'I'm so glad she didn't treat you like she treated everyone else, Samira.'

'She said several times that people come into your life but they always let you down, and in the end everyone ends up alone. Do you believe that?'

'No, Samira, I don't believe that. I

think she was a sad woman who pushed everyone away, so she was lucky to have you there at the end. Not everyone ends up alone. Trust me.'

But Ivy's words now echoed through her mind. Luke hadn't let her down. He would have stayed with her if he could. But in the end, the result was the same — she was alone.

Pulling the pillow over her head to keep out the delighted shrieks that accompanied Archie's arrival, Samira was very surprised when the door burst open and Lexie ran in.

'He's alive!' she shouted. 'Sam! Get up! Luke's alive! Archie says he was found a few days ago. There was an administrative mix-up, but now they know where he is. He's in hospital.'

★ ★ ★

Lexie phoned the hospital in Folkestone and spoke to the ward sister while Joanna, Ben, Mark, Faye, Archie and Samira stood around her, straining to hear the news about Luke.

'What sort of complications?' Lexie asked, and frowned as she listened to the reply. 'So when can we visit him? . . . I see . . . Well, is it all right if I phone back tomorrow for more news? . . . Thank you.' She replaced the receiver on the cradle and looked at all the expectant faces. 'Well, apparently he was badly injured when he landed, and he's broken his arm. He was also hit by shrapnel, but the sister said everything will mend.'

'You mentioned complications,' said Samira. 'What's wrong?'

'She wasn't sure. She said they're doing tests now, but some of the swelling isn't going down and they don't know why.'

'It's probably just the docs being overcautious,' said Archie, putting his arm round Samira's shoulders. 'Don't worry. And as soon as they know what's wrong, we'll all be down to Folkestone like a shot. That's why I came rather than telephoned, because I thought we could all drive down to see him; but obviously we can't today. I've got three days' leave, so perhaps we can go tomorrow, assuming it's okay.'

But the next day, it wasn't okay to visit Luke. When Lexie telephoned Sister Marlowe, she was told that Luke wasn't strong enough to have visitors just yet and that tests were still being carried out. Samira's earlier elation was beginning to turn to despair.

In the end, you'll be alone.

The words cast a shadow on her heart.

★ ★ ★

Lexie had gone to bed several hours earlier with a headache, although now she seemed to be having nightmares. She muttered and mumbled, turning from side to side. Of course, it was hardly surprising that the recent events had broken through into her dreams. Had Samira been able to sleep, she too might have been experiencing nightmares; but she'd been awake for hours, her hands crossed beneath her head, staring up at the ceiling.

Despite the chill in the air, Lexie pushed back the bedcovers, and Samira got out of bed and tiptoed to her. Would it be better to leave her to her nightmares or to waken her? Lexie's teeth were chattering, so Samira pulled the bedclothes over her and smoothed her forehead to try to calm her without waking her up; but when she felt the cold film of sweat, she knew something was wrong.

Lexie opened her eyes. 'Sam,' she croaked, 'I feel dreadful. My head feels like it's going to explode. I don't feel right at all.'

'Shall I wake Joanna?'

Lexie nodded. She was shivering violently now.

Joanna arrived with a thermometer and cupping her hands round Lexie's face, gently pressing her neck. Lexie groaned.

'I think it's mumps,' Joanna said. 'It's similar to what Mark and Faye had a few weeks ago, although they didn't have it as badly as this. I didn't think to ask any of the adults who were here when the children were ill. I assumed everyone had had mumps when they were young. You've had it, haven't you, Samira?'

'Yes, I caught it from my brother years ago.'

'We'd best ask Archie later.'

'And Luke!' said Samira. 'If Lexie hasn't had it, it's likely that Luke hasn't either.'

'Yes. The incubation time's about two weeks, so it's possible. That might explain his unusual swelling. I don't suppose mumps is the obvious diagnosis when a pilot has crashed. I'll ring the hospital to let them know.'

16

Something was wrong.

Luke couldn't work out what it was, but something was definitely wrong.

What was he doing here? He looked from one side of the hospital room to the other, taking in the sister and the doctor who were standing at the end of his bed.

He recalled the jerk of his parachute as it opened, and then he remembered tugging at the lanyards to try to steer it away from the farm buildings below whilst praying that his blazing plane wouldn't cause any damage. And then, just as the realisation came that the wind was blowing him towards a barn, there was blackness.

And now there was light — bright, clinical light; and with relief, he noticed that there was no double vision, such as he'd had the last time he'd been in hospital. He moved slightly, and pain shot through his shoulder and legs, making him gasp. At least, he thought, he'd gasped. He was sure the noise had left his lips, but it certainly hadn't reached his ears. And now the doctor's mouth was moving as if he were speaking to him, but there was no sound.

Luke lay in a silent world of pain.

★ ★ ★

'The patient's progress, Sister?'

'He seems slightly more alert this morning, Doctor. Certainly, he's no longer delirious. The swelling is subsiding, but not as fast as I would have expected. The fracture, contusions and grazing all seem to be healing with no sign of infection.'

'It's fortunate his family told us about the mumps. At least now we know why his swelling's so bad. It's jolly bad luck all the same.'

'Yes, Doctor. I understand he came

into contact with an infected child at the same time as his sister, but she's nearly over it now. In fact, she wants to visit. I told her not come until she's completely better.'

The doctor wrote in his book, and taking his stethoscope, he moved towards Luke. 'And how are we this morning, Pilot Officer Jackson? I'm going to listen to your heart. Just relax. Sister's going to give you something for the pain. Would you like that?'

Luke frowned. 'Doctor, I can't hear you. I can't hear anything at all. What's wrong with me?'

'Don't get agitated,' the doctor said with a reassuring smile. 'It will be all right,' he added slowly.

'Do you think the loss of hearing is a result of his fall?' Sister asked.

'Possibly, although I'm afraid there may be another explanation. Occasionally, deafness is a side-effect of mumps. It's likely to be temporary. But since he's suffering so badly, there's another complication we can't rule out. In very few cases, there's a reduction in fertility. But let's not worry the patient too much. One thing at a time. Let's see how his hearing goes and then do some tests later.'

The doctor placed the chest-piece of the stethoscope over Luke's heart and nodded reassuringly. He smiled and mouthed 'Good' to Luke. 'All normal,' he said to the sister. 'We'll just have to wait and see now.'

As they turned to go, Luke called, 'Sister, please don't let anyone visit. I don't want to see anyone.'

She nodded and smiled. 'I understand,' she said, exaggerating the movements of her mouth so he could lip-read.

* * *

Samira stared at the blue envelope. The postmark showed it came from Folkestone, but the writing wasn't Luke's neat script.

'He's probably asked one of the

nurses to write it for him,' Lexie said. 'He may not be able to write with all his injuries. I wish he'd let us visit . . . Why don't you open it, Sam?'

It was the sensible thing to do. She hadn't heard from him for days, but she had a feeling this letter heralded a change — and one that was going to bring her much unhappiness.

Lexie had phoned the hospital every morning for an update on Luke's progress, and each morning she'd asked when it would be possible to visit him. The sister had repeatedly told her that Luke was too ill, but yesterday a different nurse had taken the call and had let slip that Luke was refusing to have visitors.

'He wouldn't want us standing around looking at him and feeling sorry for him,' she told Samira; but despite her explanation, Lexie had been subdued. Samira had written each day, sometimes twice a day, but this was the first reply she'd received. She sliced the envelope with the letter opener and pulled out the single sheet of paper.

'Sam, what's the matter? What does it say? You've gone completely white!'

Samira handed the letter to Lexie.

'Oh, darling, he doesn't mean it. He loves you. It can't be over!'

'He's discharged himself and asked me not to contact him again. I'd say that pretty much means it's over.'

'Stupid, stubborn man! If he left the hospital yesterday, he'll be in Devon by now. If only we had a telephone at home! I'll ring the post office and get someone to fetch Mummy. She'll talk some sense into him. Or I'll go home and do it myself. Yes, we'll both go . . . '

Samira shook her head. 'I have to respect his wishes, Lexie. I can't make him want me — and neither can you.'

'This is wrong! You both belong together. I'll make him see . . . I'll — '

'Please don't,' said Samira. 'It's over. I just have to find some way of accepting it and moving on.'

★ ★ ★

Moving on, however, proved to be easier than Samira had thought it would be. Not because she didn't think of Luke constantly, or because she loved him any less, but because several weeks later she found herself literally moving on.

Finally, after six long, dreadful years, the war ended. There had been talk about the conclusion of hostilities for some time, but Samira had decided that until peace was declared, she wouldn't believe it.

However, on the eighth of May 1945, the country celebrated VE Day, with street parties and celebrations. Ben suggested everyone go to London to wait outside Buckingham Palace to cheer King George and the royal family, but Samira had stayed home on her own in case Luke travelled from Devon to Essex to celebrate with Archie and the other pilots in his squadron, or indeed with Lexie. Samira knew he wouldn't, of course, but at least she could stay home on her own rather than risk spoiling everyone else's fun. The day she'd longed for had finally arrived, but without Luke it was bittersweet. This was supposed to be their time. The start of life together unhindered by wartime obligations.

The other reason she didn't want to go was because Mike Harold, the next-door neighbour, had asked if he could accompany the party to London. He'd made it clear he was fond of Samira, and she suspected he'd asked to join them because he thought she was going. He was a nice man, but she simply wasn't interested. It was Luke, or no one.

Since VE Day, Mike had become more persistent, inventing excuses to visit Priory Hall and bringing her flowers and small gifts.

'Just tell him you're not interested, Sam,' Lexie said.

'I've tried. But he doesn't listen.'

'Well, if you don't tell him, I will! He's getting on my nerves, hanging round.'

'Lexie! Please don't hurt his feelings.'

Mike had called a few hours earlier to ask if Samira would like to accompany him to Chelmsford for lunch, but Lexie had answered the door and told him Samira was out.

The doorbell rang.

'Oh, honestly! That man is unbelievable! I told him you were going to be out all day. I'm going to sort this out once and for all!' Lexie said, and marched out of their bedroom.

'Lexie! Be kind!'

Samira listened at the door, but she was puzzled when she heard a man's voice in the hall and Lexie telling the visitor she would fetch Samira.

'Who is it?' she asked when Lexie entered the bedroom.

'Come and find out!'

'Lexie! You haven't invited Mike in, have you?'

'Of course not! Come on, your visitor's waiting for you in the drawing room.'

Samira followed Lexie downstairs.

It took Samira a few seconds before she realised that the visitor was her brother, Vikash.

★　★　★

Samira noticed with relief that the disdain with which he'd treated her when they'd been together after their mother had died had gone. Ten years had passed, and she was pleased to see the sulky boy had become a very handsome, engaging man, dressed in an expensive western-style suit. The letters which had passed infrequently between them had been formal and stilted, so it was a surprise to find him so charming.

'What are you doing in England, Vik?'

'I'm on a business trip to London. I don't know if you're aware, but I work with Uncle Rahul now. He's bought a tea plantation, and I've been looking for new business for him now the war's over.'

'Why aren't you helping Papa running our tea plantation?'

279

'Well, I do,' he said. 'But I help Uncle Rahul too. Anyway, Papa is the reason that I've come. He's not well at the moment.'

Samira gasped. 'Why didn't he tell me? Is it serious?'

'No. When I saw him last, he was recovering, but he asked me to come and see you while I was in London and persuade you to return with me. He misses you, Samira. So, will you come?'

'Well, this is all so sudden. When are you leaving?'

'Tomorrow. I sail from Southampton in the morning. And we need to leave here as soon as possible.'

'You sail *tomorrow*?'

'Yes. I know it's short notice . . . '

Lexie looked horrified, her eyes wide with shock. 'What about . . . ?'

Samira knew she was thinking about Luke. But he'd made it clear he wasn't coming back. Perhaps this was the change she needed. There was nothing here for her now. She wasn't sure what was waiting for her in India either, but if Papa was asking for her, then she ought to go.

'I'll pack,' she said.

Lexie followed her upstairs. 'Samira, stop! You can't just leave like that!'

'There's nothing here for me now, Lexie.'

'*I'm* here. And Joanna, Ben and the children love you.'

'But you all have your own lives. You have Archie. Joanna's family have each other and the farm. I'm not sure where I belong. And if Papa is asking for me . . . '

'Yes, of course . . . of course . . . I was just being selfish. But you will write, won't you? And you will come back once you know your father's all right?'

'Of course I'll write,' Samira said, avoiding the other question. 'Lexie, I wonder if you'd be able to do something for me?'

'Anything.'

'Please would you send a telegram to Papa to let him know I'm on my way? If anything happens to him, I'd like him to know I was on my way home.'

'Yes, of course. I'll go into town as soon as you leave.'

* * *

Samira looked out of the rear window until the car turned out of Priory Hall's gates into the lane, and she could no longer see the waving figures at the front door. Faye and Mark had clung to her, crying; and Joanna, Ben and Lexie had hugged her tightly in turn with tears in their eyes. She too had wept, but with Papa asking for her, she had no choice. And Joanna had made it clear that she would always be welcome at Priory Hall.

'Don't worry,' said Vikash, patting her hand, 'as soon as we set sail tomorrow, it'll take your mind off your friends. So, tell me what you've been up to. We've got a lot to catch up on.'

Samira was glad of the distraction. She focused on Vikash's face, and avoided looking beyond him through the car windows to the hedges and cottages that they passed. Not that she needed to see the familiar landmarks to know exactly where they were — she knew every turn and junction, every dip and rise of the road. During her time in Priory Hall, she'd passed through those lanes on her bicycle with Lexie, on foot with the Land Girls, on the tractor with the POWs and of course . . . on a motorbike with Luke.

After a while, with both relief and sadness, she realised the roads were no longer recognisable and that she'd finally left Essex. As she watched the scenery speed past the car, she noticed that periodically the turbaned driver's eyes seemed to follow her in the rear-view mirror. She wondered if he was just keeping a watchful eye out for her and Vikash, like a loyal servant, although there was no softness in his eyes and they seemed to be exclusively on her.

Don't be ridiculous, she told herself. *He's probably one of father's servants who wanted to make sure she got back to India safely.*

But when they arrived in Southampton, Samira learned that the man, who was called Tariq, wasn't one of her father's servants. He worked for Uncle Rahul, and furthermore, her uncle was waiting for her and Vikash, and would accompany them to India on the *Aurora Crown*.

Uncle Rahul had been painstakingly polite when he'd met her and had told her he'd had new clothes and jewellery delivered to her luxury cabin and that she was not to worry about anything because he, Tariq and Vikash were there to make her journey as comfortable as possible. He led them on to the ship, where the chief steward met them and escorted them to their cabins, which proved to be luxurious indeed.

'We will be dining with the captain this evening, Samira, so please dress appropriately and be ready at seven sharp.'

After a long soak in the bath, Samira dressed. The outfits that Uncle Rahul had given her consisted of traditional Indian dress of *shalwar* — baggy trousers which fitted tightly round the ankle, and *kameez* — a long shirt, and a silky scarf. They were colourful and obviously expensive fabrics, but Samira preferred the clothes she was used to, and selected a smart navy-blue dress and matching shoes.

There was a knock at the door at exactly seven o'clock, but when Samira answered it, she found Tariq and not Uncle Rahul as she'd expected. She squirmed with embarrassment as he looked her up and down, frowning.

'Come!' he said, and led the way to the dining room, where Vikash and Uncle Rahul, dressed in robes and turbans, were waiting for her.

When her uncle saw her, he frowned. 'Why are you not dressed appropriately as I instructed? Go and get changed!'

Samira's jaw dropped open. She hadn't been spoken to in such commanding tones since she'd been at school. Vikash took her arm and steered her out of the dining room.

'Uncle Rahul doesn't approve of women wearing western clothes, Samira.'

'But it's up to me what I wear!'

'Yes, yes, of course it is, but he spent a lot of money on those clothes. And he probably wants to show his niece off to the captain. Would it be too much to ask for you to wear them?'

'Well, I suppose not, but I don't think I'm going to feel very comfortable. I'm not used to wearing anything like that.'

Uncle Rahul smiled when she reappeared, and proudly introduced her to Captain Rigby, fussing over her until she was seated at the table — then promptly forgot her. She ate in silence while her uncle chatted to the captain and Vikash talked to a couple from New York. When any of the other guests tried to converse with her, Uncle Rahul took over the conversation and answered for her until she was finally ignored. After dessert, Uncle Rahul summoned Tariq with a click of his fingers and told him to escort Samira back to her cabin.

'Make sure my niece has everything she desires,' he said loudly to Tariq, and the couple from New York looked at him with admiration. They obviously believed he was the perfect uncle.

Vikash topped up his wine glass and avoided her gaze. Had he noticed she'd spent the meal in silence? Perhaps that was what he considered normal. Well, at least when she arrived home, Papa wouldn't treat her like that. His letters, although few and far between, had been warm and loving.

She told Tariq she wanted to stroll along the deck before bed so she could see the shore before they set sail the following morning. He said nothing, but his brows drew together and she knew he wasn't happy. Nevertheless, he followed her closely. *Almost like a bodyguard*, she thought. It would be a relief when she made some friends with whom she could spend time during the long voyage to Bombay and didn't have to rely on Vikash or Uncle. However, the chance of anyone talking to her with the forbidding figure of Tariq at her shoulder was slim. His turban lent him extra inches in height, and the baggy trousers, long shirt and cloak were reminiscent of a wicked vizier from *Tales of the Arabian Nights*. It wasn't beyond the realms of possibility that beneath his cloak lay a sword or dagger. As soon as she was familiar with the ship, she'd insist he didn't accompany her anywhere. After all, she wasn't in any danger, she didn't need a guard, and she certainly wasn't used to having a servant. But she couldn't shake off the feeling that although Tariq seemed to have been assigned to serve her, he was actually watching her.

On arriving at her cabin, Tariq unlocked the door and let her in. She became aware that she hadn't heard his footsteps leave, and a muffled cough told her that he was outside. What was more, he still had her cabin key. She opened the door to ask for it and found him standing in the corridor with his arms crossed.

'Please may I have my key?'

'No need,' he said, staring stonily ahead.

She slammed the door and slid the bolt across. Tomorrow she'd find her uncle and ask him to keep Tariq away from her. She'd lived through six years of war, and she could look out for herself.

There was a tap on the communicating door between her cabin and Vikash's. 'It's me,' he said. 'I wanted to check you're well.'

She opened the door. 'No, Vik, not really,' she said. 'I've been refused my own cabin key by a servant. And the last I heard, he was still outside my room!'

'Yes. Uncle has ordered him to look after you.'

'That's ridiculous! I'm perfectly capable of looking after myself!'

'Well then, consider he's there to serve you.'

'I don't need a servant. I'm used to fending for myself.'

'Well, you'd better get used to it. Your

life's going to be very different from what you're used to.'

'Only while I'm in India . . . and I don't know how long that'll be. From what I've seen of Uncle Rahul, it won't be long!'

'He's fine once you get to know him. He just likes the traditional ways.'

'Perhaps you're right,' she conceded. 'And I must admit I'm looking forward to spending time with Papa.'

'You never know, you might decide to stay for good.'

'I might,' she said. She had the feeling Vikash was steering the conversation.

'When you get there, you might want to stay.'

'It's possible. I haven't decided what I want to do yet.'

'Ah. Well, I suppose I might as well tell you now that Uncle Rahul has suggested a husband for you.'

'What?'

'Yes. Now, don't panic. I know that's not how it's done in England, but before you make a decision one way or the other, let me show you his photo.'

'Is that what this voyage is all about?'

'Of course not!' Vikash said, although his indignation didn't ring true.

'I can't believe you hadn't mentioned this already!'

'It's just a suggestion. You don't have to marry him. But he's very wealthy and you might decide it's a good option. Look.' He took the photo from his wallet and held it out to her.

The prospective bridegroom was sitting in a studio with members of his family around him surrounded by potted palms. In front of him sat two young boys on cushions, and a young girl stood next to his ornate chair, with her hand on his shoulder — presumably they were his siblings. Next to him was his father, a distinguished man with grey moustache and beard.

'What's his name?' she asked.

'Neelam Banerjee. He's one of Uncle Rahul's business associates.'

She guessed he was about thirty years

old, and if it was possible to tell from such a small photograph, he was one of the most handsome men she'd ever seen. Everything about him was perfect: the shape of his face, the intelligent-looking eyes, the thick black hair — everything. Despite the traditional Indian dress, his father's paunch was obvious, but Neelam appeared to be trim and well-proportioned. He was definitely a man who would turn women's heads.

'What d'you think?' Vikash asked.

'Well, he's very handsome, but . . . '

'You'll consider it?' Vikash asked.

'No! I've no wish to marry. And certainly not someone chosen for me by my uncle!'

'But you just said he's handsome.'

'He is, but I want more from a husband than good looks.'

'Well, why don't you meet him when we get home? You might find you like him. You might find you fall for him.'

'No, definitely not.'

Vikram sighed. 'Well, why don't you

keep the photograph? You might change your mind.'

* * *

In the morning Samira rose early, had a bath and was about to dress when she noticed that her suitcase was missing. She'd removed her toiletries and jewellery the previous evening, and the only clothes she'd unpacked had been the navy-blue dress and shoes she'd put on before Uncle Rahul had told her to change. Neither the dress nor the shoes, however, were in the wardrobe where she'd put them, so she had no choice but to wear shalwar and kameez to go to breakfast, and then to go on deck and wave goodbye to England as they set sail.

When she told Vikash her luggage was missing, he suddenly seemed to be uneasy. 'Vik, do you know what happened to my clothes?' she demanded.

'Well, Uncle Rahul doesn't approve of western dress, so I assume he got Tariq to remove them.'

'How dare he!'

'Well, to be fair, Samira, he spent a fortune on silks, satins and jewellery for you to replace your clothes.'

'I don't care! They were mine! You're wearing a western suit. Why is it all right for you, but not for me?'

'Because . . . well, because. That's all. Don't upset him, Samira. Trust me, you'll regret it.'

Vikash was being melodramatic, she was sure. Uncle Rahul was a charismatic man, and her brother was obviously deeply in awe of him. When they arrived home, Papa would allow her to buy whatever clothes she wanted; but in the meantime, it was probably wise to do as Uncle wished. He had, after all, paid for her passage in a luxury cabin and for all the new clothes and jewellery. She ought to be courteous and grateful.

During the next few days, the seas were stormy and mountainous, and Samira kept to her cabin. She felt too ill to worry about Tariq's constant presence outside her door, or his supervision when the steward brought her light meals and cleaned her cabin. At least she hadn't seen Uncle Rahul. Vikash was also sea-sick, and she didn't see much of him either.

One morning, she woke to find the winds had subsided and the sea was once again calm. She decided that she would walk on the deck and get some fresh air. When she opened the cabin door, Tariq was waiting.

'I'm going for a walk — on my own,' she said; but he silently followed her along the corridor. 'I'm quite all right, thank you. There's no need to come with me.'

Tariq ignored her.

It was pleasant to be in the fresh air, but the oppressive presence of the servant began to unnerve her, and she decided to go back to her room and write to Lexie. She'd already written a few letters and had asked the steward to make sure they were posted when they'd docked at Santander, so the letters should now be on their way to

England. The ship would shortly arrive in Gibraltar, and she'd go ashore and post any letters herself. It would probably mean taking Tariq, but at least she'd walk on solid ground again, and it would be lovely to sightsee. Perhaps Vikash would come too.

She returned to her cabin and was happy to leave Tariq outside the door. It didn't matter how many people she smiled at and greeted, everyone seemed intimidated by the servant, and it was unlikely that she'd make any friends on this voyage.

While she'd been on deck, John, her steward, had gone into the cabin to clean, and was in the bathroom when she returned. Whenever Samira had been in her room and John had arrived to clean, Tariq always made certain he supervised; but this time he obviously had no idea the steward was already in the cabin.

''Morning, miss. And where's the big man?' John asked.

'Tariq? Oh, he's outside.'

'Don't you mind him always being there, miss?'

'Yes, I do, but my uncle insists. As soon as I get home, I won't have anything more to do with him. Do you want me to go out again so you can clean?'

'No, don't worry; I haven't got much more to do.'

Samira sat at the desk and got out the writing pad.

'Begging your pardon, miss, but you do realise that those other letters you asked me to post didn't leave the ship?'

'Oh well, never mind. Perhaps you'd give them to me to post in Gibraltar when we dock.'

'No, you don't understand, miss. After you gave me each letter, the big man took them off me. I don't have them anymore.'

Samira was horrified. 'So none of my letters were posted?'

'I don't know. P'raps he didn't trust me with them. He might have disembarked at Santander or Lisbon and posted them, but I don't think he did.'

'Oh no! I promised I'd write and let my friends know I was well.'

'Please don't tell anyone I told you, miss. Your uncle will get me in trouble, and I need this job. If you like, I could arrange to have a telegram sent, then your friends'll know you're all right.'

'That would be wonderful, thank you. I'll write a message. And don't worry, I won't say anything about my letters.'

John finished making her bed and then tapped on the communicating door between Samira's and Vikash's cabins.

'What's up, John?' It was Ted, one of the other stewards who was cleaning Vikash's rooms.

'Let me in, mate. The big bloke's back, and I don't reckon he'll be happy about me being in here on my own with the lady.'

John took the slip of paper from Samira and winked. 'I'll let you know if you get a reply. If the big man's there,

I'll leave a message tucked inside your fresh towels. And chin up! You'll soon be married and won't have to put up with the likes of him anymore.'

'Married? No, I'm definitely not getting married. I'm going home to see my father.'

John looked surprised. 'That's not what your uncle said, miss. I overheard him talking to Captain Rigby. He made it sound like you were engaged.'

'Yeah, that's right,' said Ted. 'The captain told the chief steward you'd be getting married, and before you disembarked in Bombay we'd have to arrange a party for you.'

The two stewards left from Vikash's cabin, and Samira quietly closed the communicating door. When her brother returned, there were many questions she wanted to put to him.

She waited several hours for Vikash to come back, and had almost decided to go and look for him when she heard sounds coming from his room. She'd thought carefully about how she was going to phrase her questions so as to protect John and Ted before she knocked on the shared door.

'If you don't mind, Vik, I'd like to talk to you about the proposed marriage.'

'Of course!' He looked delighted, and she wondered if he assumed she was about to tell him she would agree to it.

'Did you tell Uncle I was considering the marriage?'

'Er, not exactly.'

'But you didn't tell him I'd refused.'

'No, I thought you might like longer to consider it. Just think, you won't have to worry about anything ever again if you marry into the Banerjee family. Uncle wants this. It would be best if you agreed.'

'That's the second time you've said something like that, Vik. Why would it be best? Best for whom?'

'All of us.'

'Why does it concern you?'

'I didn't want to have to worry you with this, Samira. But when Papa was unwell, Uncle took over the running of the plantation, and now our family owes him.'

'How much?'

'Not money, exactly. It's more a debt of gratitude.'

'So you mean Uncle Rahul expects me to marry a man of his choosing because he did what most other people would have done — he helped his sister's family when they were in need?'

'Well, it's not quite like that. He doesn't *expect* you to marry. But it would please him. Is that too much to ask? I mean, what plans do you have for the future anyway?'

Samira was silent. She didn't have any plans at all. No home and no one special. Of course, her friends were wonderful, but they all had lives of their own. And other than them, the only people she had were Papa, Vikash and Uncle Rahul. Perhaps it was time she stopped thinking about what might have been and started concentrating on her family.

'So you'll think about the marriage?' Vikash asked hopefully as she went back into her room.

'Yes, I suppose so.'

17

That night, she dreamed of Luke.

She clung to him while they sped through the country lanes of Laindon on his motorbike, her hair and long silky scarf streaming behind her. When they arrived at One Tree Hill, he helped her off the bike and taking her hands, he drew her into the woods towards the well. The simple dome had acquired a point and now resembled a minaret, and this, like the pillars and walls, was covered in blue and gold mosaics that sparkled and flashed in the dappled sunlight. Luke swung her off her feet and carried her into the temple, her arms clasped tightly round his neck and her face against his shoulder. She could feel the heat of his hands on her back, through the gauzy fabric of her *kameez*. Under the portico, he gently let her feet down and pulled her to him, and she realised that he was no longer wearing his uniform and leather flying jacket — he too was wearing *shalwar* and *kameez*; and as their bodies pressed against each other, it was as though there was no fabric between them at all. He bent and kissed her neck, and as the waves of pleasure rippled through her body, he began to undo the buttons of her *kameez* and slide it off her shoulders.

She opened her eyes and saw that Luke's fair hair was now deepest black, and when he looked up at her, she gasped as she realised she was staring into the dark and mysterious eyes of Neelam Banerjee.

Samira sat up in bed. The shock of her dream had wakened her and she pulled the neck of her nightdress up, remembering how Neelam had peeled her *kameez* down over her shoulders. While her cheeks burned with shame, her body burned with desire.

The rest of the night passed fitfully, and she was afraid of sleeping again for fear of where her dreams would lead her — and with whom. By early morning, she'd made up her mind that she would meet with Neelam. Where was the harm in that? And if she didn't like him, then she simply wouldn't marry him.

She got ready quickly. It was so early that Tariq hadn't yet taken up position outside her room and she ran down the corridor, her sandals slapping on the luxurious carpet. She was grateful that the decks were deserted and the sunrise belonged to her. Far off, she could hear members of the crew talking and the chink of cutlery and china as the dining room was being prepared for breakfast, but no one had any time to lean against the rails and drink in the beauty of the dawn.

When she heard footsteps approaching, she assumed it was Tariq and decided to ignore him.

'Good morning, Miss Stewart. I trust you're enjoying the voyage. We haven't seen much of you at dinner. I hope you didn't suffer too badly during the storms?'

She swung round to find the captain smiling at her. 'Oh, good morning, Captain. I was miles away.'

'Longing to be with your fiancé, I imagine.'

'Well . . . ' She hesitated, not knowing whether to admit she wasn't sure about marrying.

'It's understandable to be nervous, Miss Stewart. Marriage is a big step. I'm very grateful to your uncle for inviting me to the wedding, by the way. It's a great honour.'

Uncle Rahul had already started inviting guests to her wedding? She smiled and hoped it passed for knowledge that he had been asked.

'And . . . ' he added, his eyes sparkling, 'your uncle told me to keep this quiet, but I'm sure you'll be happy to know your honeymoon has been settled.'

'It has?'

'Yes; it would be our great pleasure to

have you and your husband as our guests when we leave Bombay for Australia. We sail a few days after your ceremony, so it'll give you a chance to get to know your new family, and then you'll occupy the bridal suite with no expense spared.'

'Oh, I don't know what to say!'

Samira truly didn't know what to say. So much had been arranged, and she hadn't made up her mind if she even wanted to marry. She was beginning to feel suffocated. If she decided against marrying Neelam, how was she going to get out of it without upsetting people?

'That's very generous of you, Captain; but since I don't really know my husband-to-be, I wonder if his business might not allow him to go on honeymoon. I know he owns several tea plantations . . . '

Captain Rigby looked puzzled. 'I'm sure it'll be fine. Your uncle said he's retired. Apparently his son runs the estates.'

'Oh, I see,' she said, not seeing at all.

Son? Vikash hadn't mentioned anything about a son. So she'd have a stepson?

'Anyway, mum's the word,' the captain said, tapping the side of his nose. 'I do hope you don't think I've spoiled the surprise,' he added, looking crestfallen.

'Oh no, Captain, not at all. You've been marvellous!' She beamed at him and he turned and walked briskly away.

Son? Retired?

She needed to speak to Vikash with all haste.

★ ★ ★

'Well, he's probably been married before. In fact, I think I remember Uncle saying something about him being a widower,' said Vikash. 'Does it bother you that you'll have a stepson if you marry him?'

'Vik! You've missed the point. Look at that man.' She pointed to the handsome young man sitting in the middle of the photograph. 'Does he look old enough to be retired and to have a son who's capable of running his business? He can't be more than thirty.'

Vikash peered at the photo. 'No, I suppose not. Well, perhaps the captain got it wrong. He can't possibly have a son who's old enough to run a business.'

'Exactly! But don't you see, Vik? *He* could,' she said, sliding her finger across to the grey-bearded man on Neelam's right. 'Did Uncle actually say which of the two men is Neelam? Have we just jumped to conclusions?'

'Well . . . '

'There's only one way to find out.'

'No, wait!'

'What for? You can't possibly want me to marry a man who's old enough to be my grandfather!'

'No, but . . . Well, it's just that Uncle Rahul is used to getting his way, and he might be angry.'

'If you won't come with me, I'm going to ask him on my own!' she said angrily, and snatched the photograph away.

Uncle Rahul didn't reply when she knocked at his cabin door, so she returned to her room. Tariq was waiting outside and looked at her in alarm. He'd obviously assumed she was still asleep inside the room and he glowered at her.

'Where's Uncle Rahul?' she asked.

'Busy.'

'Do you know who these people are?' She showed him the photograph.

'Banerjee family.'

'Is this man Neelam?' she asked, pointing at the old man.

He shrugged.

John appeared round the corner with a trolley on which was her breakfast. 'Morning, miss.'

Tariq stepped forward to take the trolley from him, but he ignored the servant and pushed it into Samira's cabin.

'The scrambled eggs are quite delicious today, miss. I'd have brought you fresh towels first, but I thought you'd want the eggs before they get cold.' He gave her a meaningful look, and as he removed the silver dome, he nudged the plate.

'Thank you, John,' she said, looking at Tariq to make sure he didn't suspect anything. 'I'm sure I'm going to enjoy them.'

'I'll be back shortly to pick the tray up.' He glanced at the writing pad on her desk and then back at the plate. 'Just let me know if there's anything you need.' He closed the door firmly as he left.

Samira drew the bolt on the door and lifted the plate. There, neatly folded, was an envelope containing two telegrams.

When she'd read them both, tears filled her eyes and trickled down her cheeks. They were both from Lexie. The first told her that Papa was well and that he had not sent a message to ask her to come home. Furthermore, he advised her not to return to India because he'd discovered Uncle Rahul was going to force her to marry, with or without her consent. He was waiting to hear whether he should travel to England or to Bombay to be there when the ship docked.

The second telegram said that Lexie and Archie would meet Samira when the *Aurora Crown* docked in Marseille and would take her home.

But if she managed to get off the ship in France, Uncle would insist that Tariq accompanied her, so how would she get away?

Her mind whirled. Everything pointed to Vikash and Uncle Rahul trying to force her to marry, and yet there was no real evidence. For any accusation she might make, there could be a rational answer. Uncle Rahul and Vikash might truly believe they were acting in her best interests. Papa had been unwell in the past, so perhaps her brother had persuaded her to go home because he believed that was the best course of action. And it was she who had jumped to conclusions about the prospective bridegroom. As for the clothes, well, it was hardly a crime to lavish silks and satins and expensive jewels on your niece. She hadn't been kept a prisoner in her cabin, even though Tariq had shadowed her everywhere. But both Uncle and Vikash had assured her it was for her safety. It had certainly put people off talking to her, but was that her uncle or her brother's fault?

And yet, there were many things which were puzzling. Her brother's inability to make eye contact when anything concerning her uncle was mentioned was one of them. She'd spent so long away from him while he was growing up that she couldn't be sure, but it seemed that he wasn't completely comfortable with what was happening to her. But if she couldn't trust him, she'd just made a mistake in letting him know that she'd realised the identity of her prospective bridegroom. And even worse, she'd foolishly let Tariq know too.

If her suspicions were correct, then she might find her freedom — such as it was — limited. So how easy would it be to meet Lexie and Archie in Marseille? Seasickness had prevented her leaving the ship when it had docked at Santander and Lisbon. When they'd stopped at Gibraltar, Uncle Rahul strongly suggested that she didn't go ashore, telling her there was absolutely nothing to see, and the torrential rain that lashed the ship when it arrived in port persuaded her to remain onboard. Walking round in the rain with Tariq at her shoulder wasn't appealing. That night as she'd sat at Uncle's table in the dining room, she overheard people talking about the Rock of Gibraltar and the Barbary Apes they'd seen that day, and wished she'd insisted on going ashore. At the time, she'd assumed that coming from India, with its breathtaking scenery and wildlife, Uncle hadn't been impressed by a rocky promontory and a few monkeys, but now she wondered if he'd simply wanted to ensure she didn't communicate with Papa or anyone else. The plan to marry her into the Banerjee family was more likely to be achieved if she were completely isolated and helpless.

A little later, when Uncle Rahul knocked at her door, she knew with certainty that he wasn't acting in her best interests.

'Ah, my dear, I'm afraid I have some bad news for you . . . Nothing for you to worry about; I'm taking care of everything. Apparently there's an out-break of a dreadful stomach virus on board. It's quite an epidemic. So it would be best if you stayed in your cabin and didn't come to the dining room or mix with any of the passengers until it's run its course. Tariq will be on hand if you need anything, and when he's resting, your brother will check on you. I've paid two stewards to prepare your food away from everyone else's, and they alone will bring it to your cabin. Of course, as soon as there is no danger of being infected, you'll be free to wander about the ship again.' He smiled, briefly nodded his head, and turning, he walked down the corridor towards his cabin. Tariq closed her door and turned the key.

So she truly was a prisoner, without friends. Even her stewards were in the pay of her uncle.

At mid-morning, John appeared with his trolley laden with clean laundry.

'Miss,' he said curtly without his usual smile. Tariq stood at the door with arms crossed, watching as John silently changed the sheets and remade the bed, before taking a pile of towels into the bathroom.

'Ted'll be here with your lunch,' he said when he'd finished tidying her room. He pushed the trolley out of the cabin and left without looking at her. When he'd gone, Tariq closed the door and turned the key in the lock. Samira banged on the communicating door between her room and Vikash's, but if her brother was in, he didn't reply.

She stood at the window for some time, staring out at the uninspiring horizon. It was as if an artist had painted a plain blue sky without birds or clouds over an expanse of sea on which nothing bobbed or sailed. The enormity and emptiness of the view echoed the feelings in her heart. How was she going to endure this solitude until they arrived in India? All thoughts of meeting Lexie in Marseille were now completely quashed.

She'd wandered into the bathroom to wash the tears from her face and to brush her hair when she noticed the large pile of towels on the marble top. John usually placed them on the towel rails unless he'd left her a message, in which case, he placed them in a stack on the marble top. She lifted the top towel, hardly daring to believe that she would find anything after John's earlier unfriendliness, but there beneath the top towel was an envelope.

With a glance over her shoulder, she seized it and tore it open to find several banknotes and a letter from John. He wrote that the money was from her uncle, who had pressed it on to him and Ted. They hadn't wanted to keep it, since they had no intention of carrying out his orders; and when Samira got off at Marseille, she would need some money, so she was to hide it until they could get her off the ship.

He went on to say he'd informed the chief steward, who was aware that Samira was now practically a prisoner, and he in turn had notified the captain, who'd been rather sceptical. Captain Rigby hadn't wanted to upset an important passenger such as Uncle Rahul, so it was unlikely that any help would come from that quarter. But if the captain was not convinced that her uncle was doing something unethical, he, Ted and the chief steward were, and they would do everything they could to get her off the ship to meet her friends. He finished by assuring her that there was no outbreak of sickness on the ship and that she should not worry about anything.

For the first time since she'd boarded at Southampton, Samira felt that there was certainty in her life, and the lies and half-truths that had made up her world had been exposed. Nevertheless, the chances of meeting Lexie were slim, especially now the captain knew about Uncle Rahul's scheme — and still supported him.

⋆ ⋆ ⋆

Despite docking in Marseille, Samira's view from the cabin window hadn't changed — just sea and sky, although now there were birds wheeling above and boats slicing through the water. Would the ship leave as it had arrived, without Samira setting eyes on the shore, much less stepping on it?

John had delivered a note hidden under her dinner plate the previous evening, instructing her to be ready to leave in the morning. She'd been up since before dawn and had paced the cabin until John arrived with her breakfast. Tariq let him in and watched while he pushed the trolley towards the table, ignoring Samira. Then with a curt 'Miss,' he left. To her enormous disappointment, there was no note hidden under her breakfast plate.

She ate a small piece of roll and drank some lemon tea, but her stomach was so knotted with fear that she couldn't manage anything else. With eyes downcast, John collected the breakfast things from her room, and after Tariq had locked her door, she heard the china clattering as he wheeled the trolley away down the corridor. Catching sight of herself in the dressing-table mirror, she saw a young woman dressed in bright, baggy satin trousers, long silky tunic and a scarf. How on earth did she expect to slip away unnoticed dressed like this? She'd chosen the darkest *shalwar* and *kameez* in her wardrobe, but even so, she would be more obvious than the POWs on Joanna and Ben's farm who had large red dots sewn on their overalls. She looked down at her jewel-encrusted sandals. How would she be able to run in them?

It was hopeless. She sank onto the stool and stared at her reflection. Her eyes were sunken and shadowed with purple smudges beneath. Luke had once said she had exotic eyes. They were simply sad, resigned eyes now.

18

By his own admission, Frank West wasn't very good at plumbing. Years ago, he'd been apprenticed to a plumber, but by mutual agreement, he'd left and taken up carpentry. After serving his apprenticeship, he'd got a job on the *Aurora Crown*, and he had an excellent reputation. But apparently today, his skills with wood were not required.

'You don't have to do anything, just bash a few pipes and make it look like you're doing something,' said John, handing Frank a large wooden box of plumber's tools.

'You're barmy! Why don't you do it?'

'Because the servant knows us, and it's going to look a bit suspicious if we suddenly turn up and pretend to fix the plumbing.'

'Why me?'

'Because you're a good bloke and me

an' Ted trust you. We'll both be there too, but we need some help. There's a couple of quid in it, courtesy of her uncle,' John added.

'You're on.'

Everyone knew about the beautiful dark-skinned girl with the silent, brooding servant. No one except John and Ted had seen her for days. Her uncle had told the captain she was ill, although when he'd offered to send the ship's doctor, the uncle had declined, saying he was sure she'd be well soon. The captain had confessed to the officers that he was loath to get involved in a family squabble and risk upsetting such a rich passenger. It hadn't taken long for the story to spread to every member of the crew on every part of the ship.

And now, Frank had been recruited to help rescue the girl by tinkering with the plumbing. More specifically, his job was to ensure her brother was out of his cabin for as long as it took to smuggle someone aboard and then to get them both off the ship.

He knocked on Vikash's door, holding his box of tools in front of him to lend credence to his story. 'Good morning, Mr Stewart. I'm sorry to bother you, but I need to carry out some emergency repairs in your bathroom. Apparently the soil pipe is in danger of leaking, and I need to deal with it now. I apologise for any inconvenience.'

'Come in,' said Vikash, scarcely looking at the plumber and his tools. He returned to the desk and sat down.

Frank hesitated. He'd been instructed to make sure the cabin was empty, but Vikash had a large pile of papers in front of him and it looked like it would take some time to deal with them.

Going into the bathroom, Frank turned on all the taps and repeatedly banged the pipes under the sink with his wrench as hard as he dared without actually causing any damage, although he'd been instructed that if it was necessary to flood the bathroom, he should go ahead.

Vikash appeared at the door. 'Are you going to keep that noise up?' he asked crossly.

'Noise?' asked Frank innocently. 'I've only done a few preliminary tests so far, but it's going to get a lot noisier, I'm afraid. And of course with a soil pipe, there could of course be . . . unpleasant, er, smells.'

Vikash rolled his eyes in annoyance, 'In that case, I'm going out. Ensure that someone informs me when I can come back. And please hurry.'

'Yes, of course, sir.' Frank dared not breathe until Vikash had left, then he opened the door and furtively looked down the corridor to check that Tariq was still in position outside Miss Stewart's cabin.

He knocked gently on the communicating door and waited.

Nothing.

He tapped again.

What on earth was going on? John had told him the young woman would be ready.

325

Eventually, she opened the door; and if Frank had any misgivings about this plumbing assignment, he lost them when he saw how wretched she appeared, and then how joy filled her face when she realised he was part of a rescue plan.

'Bring everything you need,' he whispered.

She went back into the cabin and returned with a jewellery box and a toiletry bag.

'Is that all you're taking?'

'Yes. There's nothing else of mine in here.'

Frank allowed her into Vikash's cabin, closed the communicating door softly and locked it.

'Thank you so much,' she said, her eyes full of gratitude. 'What do we do now?'

'I'll unlock the door and we'll wait for Ted to come.'

Seconds later, the steward entered the cabin with his trolley of fresh linen and locked the door behind him. He took Samira's suitcase out from under piles of sheets. 'You might be needing this, Miss Stewart,' he said. 'There appears to have been a mix-up, and your suitcase accidentally ended up in your uncle's cabin.' He winked.

'Oh, thank you!' Samira opened the case and put her jewellery box and toiletry bag inside.

'So far, so good,' said Frank. 'What now?'

'I'm going to take the trolley outside and I'll pretend to sort out the sheets. It'll block the big bloke's view of this end of the corridor, and with any luck, John'll be along in a second or two to cause a distraction. When I signal, you come out and add to the confusion,' he said to Frank. 'You might want your toolbox,' he added.

Ted whistled tunelessly as he wheeled the trolley back out into the corridor, leaving the cabin door slightly ajar.

The rattle of china heralded John's approach, and there was suddenly a crash, an enraged yell and the smash of plates. Ted's hand appeared round the door beckoning, and when Frank rushed into the corridor with his toolbox, he saw Tariq on the floor covered in food scraps and broken plates. Frank rushed forward, and ensuring he was standing on Tariq's robes, he pretended to help him up. John apologised repeatedly and pretended to lift the overturned trolley upright, but actually moved it so that it was blocking the corridor. Tariq shoved John away sending him spinning down the corridor and once again tried to stand, then realising Frank was standing on his robes, Tariq pushed him away and got to his knees amidst the broken crockery. Reaching inside his robes, he withdrew a dagger and lunged at Frank who leaped backwards, narrowly missing the blade.

'Watch out, John! He's got a knife!' Frank yelled; and as Tariq turned to look for John, Frank slammed the wooden toolbox against the side of Tariq's head.

'Good thinking,' said John. 'Quick, while he's stunned, let's drag him into Miss Stewart's cabin and lock him in.'

Frank and John dragged the unconscious figure of Tariq into the room, and making sure he had been relieved of his knife, they locked the door and stood guard outside. Several minutes later, they saw Ted come out of Vikash Stewart's cabin and give the thumbs-up signal. Two women in floral summer dresses slipped out of the cabin and followed Ted away, along the corridor. The women walked swiftly, arm in arm, and the one with bubbly blonde hair that bounced as she walked, was holding Miss Stewart's suitcase. The other was wearing a large summer hat which she held on tightly and which completely hid her hair.

19

Archie was pacing back and forth along the deck while he waited to escort Lexie and Samira off the *Aurora Crown*. He enveloped Samira in a big hug and kissed Lexie briefly on the cheek. 'My brave girl,' he said proudly, and steered them down the gangplank. As they reached the shore, Samira turned to check Uncle Rahul and Vikash weren't following. There was no sign of them, but she was thrilled to see three members of the crew — John, Ted and Frank — leaning over the rails, waving madly. She blew them a kiss and waved back.

A cab was waiting for them, and Archie helped the girls into the back with the suitcase; then climbing into the front, he gave instructions to the driver in perfect French.

Lexie and Samira clung together as the car wove through the crowds around the fish market and sped through the narrow streets of Marseille.

'Darling, I thought we'd never see you again!' said Lexie.

Samira was beyond words. She simply sobbed as Lexie put her arm round her and spoke to her soothingly.

'You're going home, Samira. Don't worry. Joanna and Ben will be waiting to take you back to Priory Hall.'

Finally, Samira felt calm enough to tell Lexie and Archie about her ordeal. 'I can't believe my own brother wanted to marry me off to an old man!'

'Don't be too hard on him, darling. Your father and I have been sending each other lots of telegrams. He's found out that Vikash ran up some gambling debts which your uncle paid. Your father thinks your uncle is taking repayment in the form of cooperation. Once your father pays the debt, Vikash won't be under any obligation, and his behaviour from that time on will be up to him — either he shows loyalty towards his father and sister, or . . . not.'

'It might be an idea to tell Samira the news now,' said Archie. The tone of his voice suggested that the news he was referring to might be important, and it might not be welcomed by Samira.

'Er, yes, I suppose so,' said Lexie. 'Now, darling, I don't want you to panic . . . and I know this isn't going to be quite what you wanted, but . . . In order to get here, we didn't have any choice . . . and it's all going to be right . . . it's just that . . . '

'Lexie, you're frightening me. Please just say it.'

'Right, yes of course. It's just that . . . well, Archie and I are going to get married — '

'But that's wonderful, Lexie! Congratulations! Why on earth did you think I'd panic?' She paused. 'Oh Lexie, if you mean because it didn't work out with Luke and me and you thought I wouldn't be pleased for you, there's no need. That's the first piece of good news I've had for some time.'

'Er, well, no, that's not it exactly. It's

just that we'll be getting married soon and we're planning on moving to France. Archie's thinking of joining an aeronautical engineering company in Toulouse — and that's where we're going now. That means you'll be going back to England alone. I'm really sorry, but there wouldn't be room for all of us anyway.'

'There wouldn't be room?'

'Yes,' Lexie said slowly. 'That's the part you're not going to like. We flew down in Archie's plane. Now, I know you don't like the thought of flying — but really, darling, it's not frightening at all.'

The colour drained from Samira's face. 'Fly? Lexie, I . . . I'm not sure. I . . . '

'It's the fastest way home, darling. Ben and Joanna will be waiting for you at the airfield, and they'll take you straight home and the whole terrible ordeal will be over. But it just needs a bit of courage.'

* ★ ★

Archie carried a limp Samira in his arms to the grey Beechcraft Staggerwing F17D waiting on the airfield, while Lexie followed with her suitcase.

'Are you sure she's all right?' Lexie asked. 'I thought that tablet you gave her was supposed to calm her down, not knock her out.' She took small skips to keep up with long-legged Archie, who was striding across the grass even with Samira in his arms.

'Don't fuss, darling. She's still breathing, and it might be a blessing in disguise. My mother lives on those tablets, so they can't be that strong,' he said over his shoulder.

'Perhaps you should have only given her one. And I'm not sure the brandy helped. I don't think you're supposed to mix medicine and alcohol.'

'I didn't have much choice, darling. She couldn't swallow them, and by the look on her face, they were so revolting I thought she was about to be sick. At least she managed to get them down.'

'Yes, I suppose so. And she's not trembling anymore. D'you think she'll sleep the whole way home?'

'I doubt it. She might sleep as far as Lyon Bron Aerodrome, because that's only about an hour away, but she'll have to get out while they refuel. Then it's about two and a half hours to Essex. I just hope she'll be sleepy enough to get back in the plane for the second leg of the journey. I'm not sure what we'll do if she refuses to get back on board at Lyon.'

'Well, at least she's out of the clutches of her uncle. I suppose we'll just have to worry about that if it happens. What a shame she's so afraid of flying. This all could have worked out so differently. It could have been such an opportunity . . . '

'Darling, you're incorrigible.'

'I know, but I can't give up hope. We're so happy, darling, and I just wish Samira could be. I'm sure if they just talked things over . . . '

Archie managed to manoeuvre the sleeping girl through the small door with the help of the pilot, and strapping her into the seat, he placed her headset on. Then handing the suitcase to the pilot, he shook his hand, slapped him on the shoulder and jumped down from the plane's lower wing.

Lexie blew the pilot a kiss. 'Look after her Luke, or you'll have me to answer to!' she shouted.

★ ★ ★

If only they would let her lie down and sleep. She tried to fight the tiredness, but she was so weak that she barely had the strength to open her eyelids, let alone raise her head off her chest. Every so often, she managed to open her eyes slightly and peer out through narrow slits, but nothing around her made sense. She was sitting upright in a confined space — something like a car but much, much noisier; and a horrible smell filled her nostrils that was similar

336

to petrol but somehow quite different.

But she had to be in a car, because nothing else was logical. How could she be moving at speed over uneven ground otherwise? It was such a bumpy ride, she was reminded of driving a tractor over a rutted field. Suddenly the noise increased, and she knew the car was accelerating because the juddering and bouncing intensified. But just as she was about to make a supreme effort to open her eyes and investigate, the jolting stopped and she felt herself being tilted backwards, her weight pushed towards the back of the chair — it was as if the car had simply lifted off the ground and was facing up to the sky.

It was all too difficult to understand. Perhaps she should sleep a while. When she woke, she'd have more energy and would be able to make sense of whatever was going on. Yes; the more she thought about it, sleep seemed to be the best option.

It might have been minutes later — it

might have been hours, she wasn't sure — but she woke slightly and recognised something was different. The ever-present hum had changed tempo, her ears had popped painfully, and suddenly the car crashed. She gasped, and for a second the shock had jolted her into semi-wakefulness, and she became aware of the countryside moving past her at speed. As the noise increased, she was forced back into her seat, and then the car came to a standstill.

At last she'd be able to sleep.

But no, it wasn't to be. Someone opened the door. She knew because a warm breeze replaced the stuffy air in the car, and somebody was trying to get her out of the seat. If she'd been able, she'd have pushed their hands away and told them to let her be; but even after her sleep, she didn't seem to have regained her strength.

Perhaps something was wrong with her?

And then the nightmare began.

It was Uncle Rahul. He'd found her

and was lifting her out of the car. She could hear men speaking in a foreign language and was aware that she had been passed between several people. Then she was being carried in someone's arms. There was no point screaming — her voice wasn't responding to her brain; and although she managed to make a tiny noise, there was nowhere near the volume that she needed to call someone. Anyway, who would come if she called? If Uncle Rahul was here with his servants speaking in a different language. She must be in India, where the only person she knew was Papa.

All she could do was give up. There was no choice. Uncle Rahul had won, and when she finally woke up, she'd have to do exactly as he wanted. Her head flopped against his shoulder in submission. But rather than her uncle's robes, she was aware that her cheek lay against leather. And rather than the sweet, sickly smell of patchouli that often accompanied her uncle, she could smell something spicy that she recognised. Something that reminded her of Luke.

The nightmare receded, and she realised that it was just one of the normal dreams that filled her nights. Being in Luke's arms. Holding tightly round his neck as he carried her in the woods near their well, her senses filled with him. She closed her eyes and let Luke carry her into the darkness.

* * *

When she woke again, she was in the bedroom she shared with Lexie in Priory Hall. Joanna was sitting next to her bed and she smiled when Samira opened her eyes.

'Hello, sleepy! You've given us quite a turn. How are you feeling now?'

Samira groaned as she moved, and pain flooded her head. 'Better,' she croaked, her mouth so dry her tongue stuck to the roof of her mouth.

Joanna helped her sit up and held a glass of water to her lips. 'Just sips, Samira. A little at a time.' She paused.

'You have Lexie and Archie to blame for this, you know. Fancy giving you medicine that hadn't been prescribed for you! And with alcohol too! I spoke to Lexie on the phone and gave her a piece of my mind. It's no wonder the tablets affected you so badly. She said you'd told her you hadn't eaten much and hadn't been sleeping, so that wouldn't have helped.'

'Don't be cross,' Samira whispered. 'They rescued me. And Lexie was very brave, coming on to the ship to get me.'

'Yes, I suppose so. Now, tell me — ' Her tone of voice changed completely. ' — what do you remember of the flight home?'

'Flight?'

'Ah, I see you don't remember much, then.'

'You mean I was on a plane?'

'Yes, it's Archie's. He bought it a few weeks ago. We thought it would be the fastest way to get you home. Can you remember anything at all about the journey?'

'No, not really. It's all a blur. At the time I thought I was in a car, but everything is starting to make sense now. It's probably just as well I was asleep, because I don't think I'd have been able to get into a plane.'

'So you don't remember being carried off the plane at Lyon or back on after refuelling?'

'No. I thought I was being carried by my uncle, but it was all so unreal, I thought I was dreaming.'

'Do you remember the pilot?'

'No, not at all.' She looked at Joanna's serious expression, and suddenly her heart leapt. 'Was it Luke? Did he bring me home?'

Joanna nodded.

'Where is he?'

Joanna looked at Samira sadly. 'I'm sorry, love, but he's gone back to Devon. He slept here last night but he left first thing this morning.'

Samira sank back on the pillows. Luke hadn't waited until she woke up to see she was all right. He hadn't even bothered to say goodbye. Presumably Archie had asked for a favour, and once Luke had completed his task, he'd gone home. His trip to Marseille had nothing to do with concern for her and all to do with his friendship with Archie.

He had moved on.

And now she must do the same.

★　★　★

Faye brought Samira a plate of toast and insisted on brushing her hair. 'I'll pin it up for you if you like.'

'No, darling, that's fine, thank you. Now why don't you tell me what you've been up to while I've been away?'

'Oh you know, dreary school. Boring stuff. I'd rather hear about you. Mama said your uncle tried to marry you to someone you'd never met. Was he a prince?'

'No, I don't think so. But it wouldn't have mattered what he was. I didn't want to marry him.'

'He might have been very handsome like a prince.'

'He wasn't very handsome at all. If you'd like to see, I still have a photograph of him. It's in my suitcase.'

Faye fetched the photograph. 'He looks handsome to me.'

'Yes, that man is very nice-looking, but he wasn't the one my uncle wanted me to marry.' She pointed to the old man. 'It was this one.'

'No! Samira, he's so old! He's even older than Papa! And nearly as old as Bill Grant, who lives in the cottage next to where Cissie, Marge and Ruth used to live. How could your uncle want you to marry him?'

'Things are different in India, darling. There are different customs. My uncle was trying to ally himself to a very rich family. It would have helped his business.'

'Business? But people marry for love!'

'Well, they do usually, but not always in India.'

'But you're not Indian, Samira! This is your home. You belong here. I hope I never meet your uncle, because I would tell him off, and Mama would tell *me* off for using unladylike language. But I think sometimes there's a need for it, don't you think, Samira?'

'Faye!' It was Joanna at the bedroom door. 'Let's give Samira a chance to eat something and then rest. I think her hair is fine now, love.'

When Samira was alone, she thought about Faye's words. *But you're not Indian, Samira! This is your home. You belong here.*

Well, of course she was Indian — well, half Indian anyway. And her mother's heritage was very precious, but she had spent so many of her formative years in England that she felt more comfortable here. It had taken a cruise with an unscrupulous uncle to show her where she really belonged — and a child to point it out to her. She felt slightly stronger, having made a decision about where her future lay.

★ ★ ★

Not only was Faye instrumental in showing Samira where she would spend her future, but the young girl also gave her an idea about how she would fill her time.

It came about a few days after Samira had arrived home. Faye was staring wistfully out of the kitchen window at the frosty landscape.

'What's the matter, darling?' Samira asked.

'I wanted to ride my pony, but I've got a spelling test at school tomorrow and I keep getting them wrong. I'll never learn them! Stupid spellings! What's the point of spellings? It's preposterous!'

Samira suppressed a smile at Faye's use of 'preposterous', which she was currently using as often as she could. 'Show me those preposterous spellings, darling, and we'll find a way of getting you to remember them. Then you'll be able to ride Rainbow. Let's get some paper.'

Faye groaned. 'It's no good, Samira. I

keep writing the words down, but as soon as I think I've learned them, I find I've forgotten them.'

'We're not going to write them, darling; we're going to draw them.'

Joanna came into the kitchen half an hour later to find them laughing at the stickmen and other drawings that Samira had made to illustrate the spellings.

'See, you won't forget the 'O' in 'people' because there's a face inside that 'O', and she's looking at you and telling you to remember,' said Samira, giving the face in the letter 'O' curls on top of her head.

'Test me, test me, Mama!' said Faye. 'Samira and I've done lots of drawings and made funny pictures of all the words, and now I think I can remember them.'

'That's brilliant, love.' Joanna gave Samira a grateful smile.

'I wish Samira was my teacher. She makes learning stuff so much fun. Not like grumpy old Miss Stephens.'

Teaching! That was something Samira would like to do. She would find out how to train to become a teacher.

That evening, something else happened which was to change the course of her life.

The doorbell rang and Samira answered it, to find Pop standing on the doorstep.

20

'Oh, my dear, how lovely to see you! I can't believe you're back after so long,' said Mrs Thomsett with an enormous smile. 'What a wonderful way to welcome in the New Year! What a shame you couldn't 'ave spent Christmas with us! Still, it's so good to see you!' She cradled a tiny baby in the crook of her left arm and balanced a toddler on her right hip. 'My Sally's latest additions,' she said, nodding at the children. 'Remember she was in the family way when you left? She's got four now. But tell me all about you! Are you going to stay?'

'Yes; Pop's tenants have moved out and I'm going to live here. And guess what? I'm going to study to be a teacher.'

'Well, that's wonderful news. Just wait 'til I tell the neighbours. Those tenants never really fit in. Hoity-toity, they were! Thought they were too good for Aylward Street. I'm glad to see the back o' them and doubly glad to have our bit of exotic back. Now, you must come in and have a cuppa; it's perishing cold out here. My Wilf will be so chuffed to see you, lovey. He always said you was a nice girl — and now look at you! Quite a young lady! And you're going to be a teacher! Well!' She caught sight of one of the neighbours coming down the street. 'Coo-ee! Maud, look who's back! And you'll never guess what! Our Samira's going to be a schoolteacher!'

Samira was shivering before she made it into Mrs Thomsett's house for tea. Several of the neighbours heard Mrs Thomsett shouting and came out to say hello, and the noise of their greetings brought the rest of the residents of Aylward Street out to see what was going on.

Over the next few days, Samira cleaned Pop's house from top to bottom, and in memory of Ivy, she made sure there were vases of flowers in the windows. She cleaned the spare room and made it ready for the arrival of her guest at the weekend. Lexie's wedding would take place in four months' time, on the first of May, and she'd asked Samira and Faye to be her bridesmaids. Mark was to be a pageboy, much to his disgust.

'And Luke?' Samira had asked with dread. 'I expect he's best man?'

Lexie nodded. 'Please say you'll come though, Samira. I'll be devastated, and it'll ruin Faye's day if you don't. She's so looking forward to it.'

Samira sighed. She would go. It would be unkind to refuse and anyway, as she wanted to be at her best friend's wedding. She'd simply keep out of Luke's way. After all, they were both adults — they should be able to be in the same place and be civil towards each other.

'Yes, Lexie, of course I'll be your bridesmaid. I'd be honoured.'

'Darling!' Lexie threw her arms round Samira's neck and hugged her.

'There's something else, though . . . '

Samira guessed from Lexie's tone that it was something she didn't want to hear.

'I'm really sorry, darling, but Luke may bring a . . . friend to the wedding. Mummy said he's been seeing a neighbour — a widow. She lost her husband during the war. She has two children and they may come too.'

It hadn't come as a complete surprise to Samira, but it still felt like something inside her had died.

★　★　★

Samira had put off cleaning the cast-iron range. Pop's tenants hadn't looked after it, and while she dealt with the rest of the house, she'd ignored it; but with Lexie arriving the next day, she decided it was time to do something about it. The two young women had planned to travel into the centre of London to look for fabric for the bride's and bridesmaids' dresses, and since Archie's parents had offered to pay for the whole event, apparently money was no object. Lexie was looking forward to buying the material and lace that were now becoming available after the austerity they'd become accustomed to during the war.

Samira scrubbed at the baked-on food residue and wished she'd thought to tie her hair back before she'd started. She repeatedly wiped wisps off her face and tucked them behind her ears as she leaned forward trying to clean the back of the oven.

There was a knock on the door, and she called 'Come in.' When no one appeared, she called again, 'Come in, the door's open.' Still no one arrived, so with a sigh, she found a tea towel, wiped her hands and went to the front door. A glance in the hall mirror showed her several dirty smudges on her cheeks where she'd pushed hair out of her eyes, and she rubbed at them with the cloth.

'It's open,' she called, expecting to see one of Mrs Thomsett's grandchildren or great-grandchildren waiting. There were indeed children outside her door, but they hadn't knocked. Instead, some were admiring a motorbike that was parked at the kerb, and others were gaping at the man on her doorstep.

'Luke!' Samira gasped, her hand flying to her mouth.

'Stop gawpin' at Samira's guest,' said Mrs Thomsett, who was there so rapidly that she must have been looking through her window and seen the stranger approach number ten. The children made no attempt to move, and neither did Mrs Thomsett, who looked pointedly at Samira, and with theatrical extravagance licked her finger and pretended to wipe her face.

'You'd better come in,' said Samira, standing back to allow Luke into the hall. A quick glance in the mirror showed her what Mrs Thomsett had been trying to warn her — when she'd put her hand to her mouth she'd left behind black smears, and she scrubbed at them vigorously with the tea towel, leaving red marks. She'd imagined that the next time she saw Luke, she'd look glamorous in her bridesmaid outfit — not dirty, with smudges on her face. How dare he just turn up unannounced like that and catch her at her worst! Emotions boiled inside her, anger being the uppermost.

She followed him into the kitchen and motioned for him to sit. 'Tea?' she asked, aware that the way she had asked the question sounded more like a challenge.

'No, thank you, Samira.'

Her stomach constricted as she looked into his eyes. How could they possibly be bluer than she remembered? She wondered if it had been a way of protecting herself during the months after he'd gone. Her memory had diluted the entire essence of him — the paler and more nebulous he became, the easier it was to cope with the loss of him.

She sat opposite him, perched on the edge of the chair, clutching the wooden arms, waiting for him to speak. 'So?' she said finally.

He seemed to be having trouble finding the words. 'Lexie has asked me to talk to you,' he began, and then paused.

'Let me guess. She wants to make sure there won't be any awkward moments at her wedding. Well, there's no need to worry, I shall keep well away from you. I shall smile in photographs when we're put together, but other than that, you don't need to worry about me.'

'No, it wasn't that, Samira. It wasn't that at all . . . '

Her anger dissipated slightly as she saw his disquiet.

'Lexie told me to explain. She said I owed it to you,' he said.

'Ah, that,' said Samira. 'Well, don't bother. It's all quite straightforward. You found you didn't love me and you left. It seems simple to me.'

He shook his head sadly. 'No, it wasn't like that.'

'Well, what was it like then?' she snapped. 'One minute we were talking about our future together, and the next you'd gone. You didn't answer any of my letters.'

He sighed and lowered his head. 'I left you because I couldn't bear to — '

'Oh, just say it, Luke! You don't want me. Be honest! I once thought you were the bravest person in the world, flying those terrifying machines, facing death each day. But now I'm beginning to wonder!'

Luke got to his feet, his face flushed. 'All right, I'll tell you!' he said. He swallowed and looked away from her as if he couldn't quite bring himself to admit it. 'I left you because I couldn't bear to see the pity on your face when you heard it was unlikely I would ever father children.'

'Ch . . . children?' Samira looked at him in disbelief. 'What do you mean? I don't understand! What have children got to do with anything?'

'After I had mumps, there were complications, and the doctors think I may not be able to have children.'

'And that's it?' She stared at him in horror. 'You left me because you couldn't have children?' Her voice rose with incredulity. 'You didn't think to tell me? To ask if I minded? When people love each other, don't they deal with problems together?' She was shouting now, the hurt of him leaving her driving her on. 'Well, it didn't take you long to find someone else, did it? Presumably your new lady knows about this and doesn't mind?' she asked bitterly.

'My new lady?'

'Lexie said you were seeing a neighbour. Oh, no! Of course, it all makes sense now. She already has children!'

'Cathy? Oh, no, Samira, no! Cathy's just a friend, nothing more. I trained with her husband and I know she's struggling financially. I swear there's nothing going on with her. It's you I love. I always have, I always will.'

He was looking at her now, his blue eyes fixed on her face — honest, pleading.

She stared at him.

All those months of pain.

All those unnecessary tears.

She sank back on to her chair, feeling empty.

'So why did you leave?' she asked finally, her voice breaking. He knelt in front of her.

'When we talked about our future, we often mentioned the family we'd one day have. I knew if I told you I couldn't father children, you'd pity me but you wouldn't break it off — you're too kind and caring. Sometime in the future, I thought you'd come to resent me, perhaps even despise me. I couldn't bear that, and I couldn't bear to make you unhappy. I thought if I finished it completely, you'd find someone else and settle down. Ben's neighbour seemed really keen on you. He could have given you a good life. And probably children too.'

'But I didn't want him. And I'm not even bothered about children. I only wanted you.' The lump in her throat wouldn't allow her to finish speaking.

He drew her to him and held her while she sobbed.

★ ★ ★

Mrs Thomsett crept along Samira's hall and quietly let herself out into the street. When she'd heard raised voices, she'd wanted to make sure Samira was all right. You couldn't be too careful these days. Something had been troubling the young woman since she'd been home, and now Mrs Thomsett knew it had been the handsome blond man.

Men! They wanted a bloomin' good shaking, the lot of them! Why didn't they just talk things over like women did? The stupid idiot could have saved himself — and more importantly,

Samira — a lot of heartache. The world was full of children! Most of them seemed to live full or part-time in her house!

Didn't he know about adopting?

Didn't he know about medical treatment?

Didn't he know that Samira was one in a million?

'Stupid man!' she muttered as she went into her house and took up her position by the window. 'If he upsets my Samira again,' she said wagging her finger at a group of toddlers playing on the floor, 'I'll 'ave 'is guts for garters.'

* * *

'You won't want to come shopping for fabric, Luke!'

'I'm not letting you out of my sight — and if that means I have to follow you up and down Oxford Street, that's what I'll do. Lexie won't mind if I come with you both tomorrow. She's been on at me for weeks to come and see you.

She'll be thrilled.'

'Does she know why you left?'

'No; I haven't told anyone.' He looked down as if ashamed. 'I didn't want anyone to know. I didn't even go back for more medical tests.' He placed a finger under her chin and tilted it up. 'Do you want me to go for tests?' he asked, looking deeply into her eyes.

'If *you* want to. As far as I'm concerned, I've got you back; and if children come along one day, I'll be happy, and if not . . . well, I'll be just as happy, because I have you.' She hugged him tightly.

'I can't believe I so nearly lost you. If it wouldn't upstage Lexie and Archie's wedding, I'd marry you now.'

'We could do the next best thing . . . '

'Yes?'

'We could exchange vows in the temple. It wouldn't be legally binding, but we'd know we belonged to each other until after Lexie's wedding, then we could have a quiet ceremony in a church somewhere.'

362

'That sounds wonderful! Is it some sort of Indian custom?'

She smiled at him and shook her head.

★ ★ ★

Early on Sunday morning, Samira climbed onto the back of Luke's bike, and wrapping her arms round him, she held him tightly. The engine roared to life and Luke drove carefully along the cobbled road, turned into Jamaica Street and headed towards Mile End Road. Samira remembered the last time Luke had driven her in Ben's car to Priory Hall and how nervous she'd been, believing he would think her naïve and foolish. She closed her eyes and allowed the wind to whip through her hair, blowing away the pain of the last few months, leaving room for optimism for the future.

The sun was still low in the sky when they reached One Tree Hill. Luke helped her dismount and pulled her to him, holding her face in his hands.

'Are you ready for this, Samira?'

'Yes.' She smiled up at him.

He took her hand and led her into the woods. The last time they'd come, they'd been bathed in a soft green light as the sun's rays penetrated the thick canopy of leaves. Now, however, the trees were bare, and there was a sprinkling of rime over the boughs which sparkled and glittered in the muted sunlight. Covered in frost, the tiny domed temple glistened like a magical fairy palace; and with their breath hanging in the air, Luke enveloped Samira in his arms and kissed her tenderly.

'I'll love and treasure you for as long as you'll have me, Samira.'

'Then you're mine forever,' she said.

We do hope that you have enjoyed reading this large print book.

Did you know that all of our titles are available for purchase?

We publish a wide range of high quality large print books including:
Romances, Mysteries, Classics
General Fiction
Non Fiction and Westerns

Special interest titles available in large print are:
The Little Oxford Dictionary
Music Book, Song Book
Hymn Book, Service Book

Also available from us courtesy of Oxford University Press:
Young Readers' Dictionary
(large print edition)
Young Readers' Thesaurus
(large print edition)

For further information or a free brochure, please contact us at:
Ulverscroft Large Print Books Ltd.,
The Green, Bradgate Road, Anstey,
Leicester, LE7 7FU, England.
Tel: (00 44) 0116 236 4325
Fax: (00 44) 0116 234 0205

WINTER GOLD

Sheila Spencer-Smith

Recovering from a bereavement, Katie Robertson finds an advertisement for a temporary job on the Isles of Scilly that involves looking after a house-bound elderly lady for a few weeks. Hoping to investigate a possible family connection, she eagerly applies. But the woman's grandson, Rory, objects to her presence and believes she's involved with sabotaging the family flower farm. With an unlikely attraction growing between them, can Katie's suspicion of the real culprit be proved correct, and lead to happiness?

AFRICAN ADVENTURE

Irena Nieslony

Amateur sleuth Eve Masters has just married the man of her dreams, David Baker, on the romantic island of Crete. Now they are heading off on their honeymoon to Tanzania. Eve has promised her new husband not to get involved in any more mysteries — but when one of their safari party is murdered, she can't help but get drawn in. It isn't long before she's in the middle of a very dangerous game . . .

COULD IT BE MURDER?

Charlotte McFall

Last year's May Day celebrations ended in tragedy for Gemma with the mysterious death of her Aunt Clara. Having inherited her aunt's run-down cottage in her childhood village of Wythorne, Gemma moves in, hoping to investigate the death, and is drawn to Brad, the local pub owner. But what she finds instead is a dead body, and a basket of poisonous mushrooms that have put her unsuspecting friend in hospital. Can Gemma get to the bottom of things before she and Brad become the next victims?

THE PLOT THICKENS

Chrissie Loveday

The Archway Players are struggling this year to put a Christmas production together in their seaside Cornish town. Adam, a member of the troupe since he was a teenager, is distracted by Gwen, his would-be girlfriend. While Gwen, a health care worker who lives with and cares for her father, doesn't always have the time she needs for the production — or Adam. And when the lead actor is attacked and put in hospital, it looks as if the show might not go on — unless new ideas are found fast.

TAKE A CHANCE ON US

Angela Britnell

In Nashville, Zac Quinn has been a single father to ten-year-old Harper since his wife left years back. Despite his family's urging, he's determined to avoid dating and a social life of his own until Harper is older . . . Rebecca Tregaskas's life in Cornwall is stuck in a rut. So when her American cousin suggests a temporary house-swap to enable both of them to reevaluate their lives, she goes for it. But tragedy haunts Rebecca's past — and when she falls in love with Zac, it rears its head once more . . .